WHEN YOU HEAR A
SNOWFLAKE
FALL

The Gene That Created Religion

WHEN YOU HEAR A
SNOWFLAKE
FALL

Gil M. Pielin and H. Jean Aresto

TATE PUBLISHING
AND ENTERPRISES, LLC

Published by Tate Publishing & Enterprises, LLC
127 E. Trade Center Terrace | Mustang, Oklahoma 73064 USA
1.888.361.9473 | www.tatepublishing.com

Tate Publishing is committed to excellence in the publishing industry. The company reflects the philosophy established by the founders, based on Psalm 68:11,
"The Lord gave the word and great was the company of those who published it."

Book design copyright © 2014 by Tate Publishing, LLC. All rights reserved.
Cover design by Nikolai Purpura
Interior design by Caypeeline Casas

Published in the United States of America
ISBN: 978-1-63185-295-4
1. Fiction / Christian / Futuristic
2. Fiction / Thrillers / Suspense
14.04.08

DEDICATION

To my parents, Ray and Hattie Pielin—
their persistence, integrity and example made me the indi-
vidual I am today. I am grateful for all they did for me
and for their continued prayers for me from above.

To Patrick Aresto, whose dedication to God
and Jesus, have been an inspiration.

ACKNOWLEDGMENTS

Kay Nguyen, Nancy Fretwell, Joyce Hwalliti, Jodi Longo, Diana Steckel, Sue Testa, Christopher Scott, Andrew Jay Koval, Louise Baker, Karen Tate, Janellen Lombardi, Mary Ann Marrone, Beth Colaizzi and my school wife Sharon Volpe. Thanks for reading the preliminary copy and for all your advice and help. God bless you all.

PROLOGUE

THE POPE WAS dead.

There had been no foul play, no suicide, and no murder. He died in his sleep, peacefully, naturally—the death that most men covet.

On December 21, when the aide went to wake him at five o'clock the following morning, he found that Jesus had come for Pope Athanasius during the night. He had suffered a major stroke.

Six days later, on December 27, Athanasius was laid to rest among his predecessors. The Conclave was set to commence on January 9 after the Christmas and New Year's holidays.

This gave Cardinal Cody plenty of time to execute his carefully crafted plan. Soon, he would reap the fruits of his labors.

Meanwhile, on the other side of Rome, in the genetics lab of the Gemelli Hospital, Edger stood up. With a lion-like yawn, he removed his wire-rimmed spectacles and ran his poorly manicured fingers through his disheveled hair. It had been a long and exhausting night, but at last it was finally finished.

The results were perfect.

Now, the time had come for him to execute his carefully crafted plan. Soon, he would reap the fruits of his labors.

CHAOS

Now it came to pass, when men began to multiply on the face of the earth, and daughters were born to them, that *the sons of God* saw the *daughters of men*, that they were beautiful; and they took wives for themselves of all whom they chose. And the *Lord* said, "My Spirit shall not remain in man forever, for he is indeed flesh; yet his days shall be one hundred and twenty years."... *the sons of God* came into the *daughters of men* and they bore children to them.

Genesis 6: 1–4 (KJV)

One theory is that the sons of God are the descendants of Seth, the godly line of Adam while the daughters of men are the descendants of Cain.

Conflict of Adam and Eve with Satan

SPRING 2004

THE MORNING MEETING was *finally* finished. With aggravated grunts, Dr. James McFarland and his colleague, Dr. Bill Schafer, slammed themselves into two factory-made faux wooden chairs set about a freshly bused table at the Café Italiano. They were already ticked that they hadn't been presented with lunch menus. *No tip,* they thought, in concert. For his part, Jim ran the meeting over again in his mind.

"*What's wrong with those people?*" he wondered. *They hadn't understood. They just didn't get it.*

It made him angry.

All of his research had been conducted with scientific precision. He had been careful, meticulous. He had considered the variables. His conclusions were irrefutable.

This was pure *science.*

It had been knowledge for knowledge's sake and was never intended for application. He was still shaking even after they ordered. Those bureaucratic paper pushers had slandered his research, his life's work!

They wouldn't recognize genius if it jumped up and bit them!

He brought his fist down hard upon the tabletop, rattling the cups on their saucers. He couldn't remember ever feeling this exasperated. He tried to console himself with the fact that the meeting was over now, and that finally they had left the decision to him.

By the time the waitress had brought their lunches, Jim's mind had at last begun to unwind, to relax. With a resolute sigh, he bit into his juicy grilled hamburger.

Bill's lunch, however, afforded him no such peace.

"Crummy salad!" Bill thundered, chewing determinedly upon an uncooperative morsel of rubbery Chicken Romano Salad. He looked up from his plate and caught Jim's mildly curious expression. As if in explanation, he exclaimed "I'm turning into a rabbit! Damn sedentary life! The only exercise I get is wheeling my chair from one machine to another. I've got the strongest ankles in town!

"You're impossible. You really are impossible," Bill said as he clumsily discarded his salad fork onto his plate with a clunk that launched a crouton into the air. Distracted, Bill followed its trajectory until it landed on the prefabricated Roman carpet. Satisfied, he soon returned his attention to his friend and to graver matters, "Look, Jim... I have to agree with the brass on this one...but for different reasons. You must know that you can't release your findings. Think of the fallout, the repercussions. This could ruin organized religion. Are you one hundred percent sure?"

"Of course, I'm sure, Bill. Like I told those jokers in that meeting, my initial trial tested two thousand people, the second tested three thousand five hundred, and the third, four thousand five hundred. I tested atheists; I tested agnostics; I even tested priests and nuns. Hell, I'd have even tested the Pope, himself, if they'd let me. The results were always the same. The subjects who were religious always had the VMAT2 gene and the ones who weren't, never had it."

"How did you determine their level of religiosity?"

"Come on, Bill. You know that, and you heard it all again this morning!"

"Jim, look, I'm playing the devil's advocate here, okay? That is the first question that they are going to ask you. You'd better be ready for it. If you release these findings there will be a mountain of opposition, you experienced it this morning! Organized religion will battle you to the heavens, no pun intended. They will use every weapon at their disposal to discredit you. Your reputation and your career are at stake here, so you darn well better be absolutely certain."

"Of course, I am! My research group and I developed a survey of two hundred and twenty-six questions. Some of these questions were designed to gauge the degree of belief the respondents had in a higher being. You know, whether they were members of an organized religion; if so, which one, as well as how often they attend services. We were very thorough."

"Has anyone replicated your results?" asked Bill.

"You bet your life they have. Dr. Heinrich von Trop tested more than ten thousand individuals and got the same results. So did Dr. Mary Wong, Dr. Karen Conway and Dr. Marie Labeoux. By now more than one hundred thousand people have been tested. The results are the same *every* time!"

"That's all well and good, Jim, but have you given any consideration to what the consequences might be if these findings were released to the general public?"

"Consequences? *What* consequences?"

"Extremists, for one; they might exploit your results to justify a crusade against all non-believers, everywhere—atheistic cleansing."

"Extremists?"

"*Yes*, a simple…"

"I can't believe—" Bill started.

"—A *simple* genetic test could tell them everything they need to know. There are places in the world where religious cleansing have been happening for years. It's been responsible time and again for a multitude of deaths, and *your* findings may only add to the body count!"

"You *can't* be serious! *Bill*—"

"Suppose Hitler had had such a weapon? Okay, fine. If not Hitler, then what if bin Laden had it? How much blood does Al Qaida already have on its hands and all in the name of religion? Think about this, Jim, please. Consider the possible consequences of your actions. As a friend, I'm asking you, do you really want to add to the arsenal of hate?"

Feeling the fury welling up again within him, Jim looked away. He couldn't face Bill, *wouldn't* face him. Was everyone against him now? He found himself gazing at the elaborately designed patterns on the Roman carpet that spread out across the floor like its own universe. How like him it was, he mused. Meticulous. Complex. Well ordered. Then he spied the crouton that had been flung from Bill's fork—the random, chaotic event, whose ripple would alter the fabric of the universe. Suddenly a waiter juggling menus and silverware bound in white linen recklessly passed by, crushing the crouton beneath his heel into a nebulous of dust.

Chaos had entered Jim McFarland's universe and he marveled at the paradox.

MIRACLES

October 13, 2017

Religious Belief Determined by Genetic Make-up Rather than by Divine Intervention, Study Claims

Staff Reporter/agscott@suntimes.com

New York. Monday, November 15, 2004.

AFTER COMPARING MORE than ten thousand DNA samples, American geneticist, Dr. James McFarland, Director of the Gene Therapy Unit of the National Cancer Institute in America, has concluded that a person's capacity to believe in God is linked to brain chemicals, controlled by the VMAT2 gene.

The doctor's controversial findings are being criticized by clerics who challenge the existence of a "god gene." They say his research undermines the ultimate principle of faith, spiritual enlightenment can only be achieved through divine transformation and not via some chemical ooze secreted by the brain.

Dr. McFarland asked volunteers more than two hundred questions in order to determine their spirituality. The higher the score, the greater their capacity to believe in a "god". He found the subjects had one thing in common, the VMAT2 gene. A vesicular monoamine transporter it regulates the flow of mood-altering chemicals in the brain. Studies on twins separated at birth showed that those born with the gene are more likely to develop a spiritual belief even after being raised in families' miles away from each other.

Dr. McFarland also claims that growing up in a religious atmosphere has little effect on spiritual belief. According to him, the existence of the "god gene" explains why some people have more aptitude for spirituality than others.

The Reverend Dr. John Polkhope, a Canon Theologian at Canterbury Cathedral, rebutted: "Faith cannot simply be reduced to genetic survival. That exhibits the deficiency of thinking in platitudes."

Chicago Sun-Times, Page 1

More Metro and Tri-State Headlines

A driving rain had fallen all morning. The Cova da Iria had been transformed into a sea of mud. Despite the unpleasant weather, seventy thousand people had gathered to witness the miracle that had been predicted by Lucia, Jacinta and Francesco, three shepherd's children. They had been visited by "The Lady" on the thirteenth day of each month since May and today, October 13, 1917, was to be The Lady's final apparition. She promised to reveal her identity and present a miracle so that all would see and believe.

When midday arrived, there was a flash of light and a daz-zling cloud settled over the bush. The children immediately knelt. During this apparition, the children were shown visions of the Holy Family, Mother of Sorrows, and Our Lady crowned Queen of Heaven holding her Divine Son who extended the Carmelite scapular to the crowd. In a voice, heard only by the children, she requested a chapel be built upon that very spot.

Abruptly, the rain stopped. Lucia cried out "Look at the sun!" Its appearance became that of an opaque, spinning disk, signifi-cantly less bright than normal, casting multicolored lights across the clouds, landscape, and spectators who were overcome with wonder and awe.

Unexpectedly the sun careened wildly toward the earth, zig-zagging in a pattern so frightening that all who were in the crowd below cowered at the sight. Many fell to their knees in terror begging the Lord's pardon for their sins. Others, thinking it were the end of the world, turned and fled—as if any place upon the earth was safe from the impact of a hurtling sun.

Ten minutes later, the sun turned back and resumed its original position in the sky. The bewildered people stood up. They discovered to their amazement that their clothes and the ground beneath them were completely dry. Many of the suffering had been cured of their afflictions. The lame walked. The blind received sight. Those who had lost their faith regained it that day.

Such were the miracles worked through The Blessed Mother of Fatima.

"Martin, do you know what day this is?" Sylvia asked.

"Yes, it is October 13," he replied.

"Yes, but do you know the significance of this date?"

"No. Should I?"

"It's the Feast of Our Lady of Fatima. Our son has been born on one of the most important of Marian feasts."

Indeed, one hundred years after those incredible events had taken place and at the *exact time* the Miracle of the Sun had occurred, Samuel was born. He was an ordinary, unremarkable child in every way with ten fingers and ten toes, of average weight and length. He was by all accounts, *normal*. Yet as if in defiance of all of this normalcy, *this* child had a special destiny.

His parents, Martin and Sylvia, were deeply religious people—bordering on fanatical. After evening meals they recited the Rosary and on Tuesdays and Thursdays added the novena of the Saint to whom the month was dedicated. They attended daily Mass and participated weekly in the Sacrament of Reconciliation.

Sylvia and Martin regularly involved themselves in the activities of the Church, on both the parish and diocesan levels. They were catechists spending many hours passing on their *faith* to the youth through CCD (Confraternity of Catholic Doctrine) classes, and to adults in marriage and baptismal preparation classes. During the week Sylvia cleaned the rectory, changed the altar linens and did the church laundry. In addition, each day she found some time for personal prayer before the tabernacle.

Martin, a gardening wiz, personally cared for the church grounds. Outside of the Church, he held a full time job. They were so religiously busy that it was a wonder that they found time to have just *one* child, let alone the nine, that through God's grace, they had now brought into the world.

Three years later Martin was suddenly and tragically taken from his family. An accident at work left Sylvia without a husband and the children fatherless. For Martin, death was quick and merciful but for his family it left a gaping wound that would never fully heal.

As the years passed, Sylvia spent even more time in prayer, effectively cloistering herself a little more each year from the world and her family.

Samuel, the last of the brood, was closest in age to his brother Timothy. Through the years the two became inseparable. The strength of their brotherly bond was due in part to having similar dispositions and attitudes as well as the shared tragedy of their father's death when both were so young.

Sam's four older brothers valiantly tried to fill the paternal void, but despite their efforts, Sam continued to stay to himself, attaching only to Tim. He enjoyed being alone and planned to live a life of quiet solitude studying medicine and performing laboratory research at Trinity College in Dublin.

Yet, Timothy, and fate, had different ideas for the withdrawn Samuel. The news came by post.

Mr. Samuel O'Brien.

Congratulations on being accepted into the University of Pittsburgh's Medical School. The fall term begins on August...

Timothy was elated.

"Sam, what great news. What an exceptional opportunity. Just think. You'll be studying in the finest medical school in the world. Not many receive this chance. And look, you were their top choice. It says here they only accepted fifteen applicants this year, and there were over five hundred."

"I just don't know Tim. It is so far from home. I'll be there for at least seven years. You know how homesick I got when Mom sent me to bible camp. And there is the language."

"Sam, they speak English. You'll have to get used to the vernacular but you're good at languages. Heck, you studied Russian in high school."

Still Sam was reluctant to travel to a city in a distant and foreign country, but Tim finally convinced him that his acceptance was a tremendous honor not to be turned down.

Samuel was not the only child born on October 13, 2017. Across the Atlantic Ocean, at Magee Women's Hospital, in Pittsburgh, Pennsylvania another child was born at precisely the same time as Samuel; only his parents were lackadaisical about their faith—Submarine Catholics, who only surfaced when in need.

His father's name was Sidney.

He was frightfully clever.

...at least that was his opinion of himself.

His mother's name was Joan.

She too was clever.

Even though neither Sidney nor Joan attended Mass they had insisted on having a big church wedding. For six months before the grand event, they gave their envelopes to Joan's mother, to create the impression that they were regular attendees. "How clever!" they thought to themselves. Their Wedding Mass, scheduled for 2:30 p.m., went off as planned free of any unforeseen difficulties. The church provided a magnificent venue for pictures, much better than any backdrop in a studio. Although the Mass was finished by 3:30 p.m., the photographer was still tediously snapping pictures at a quarter to five. With Saturday night Mass scheduled to start at five, Father Roman politely told them the photography session was done.

"What the hell is the matter with that priest?" Joan fumed to Sidney as they left the church.

"I don't know" he replied in a huff. "There were at least four other places that I wanted a picture in…"

"Oh, my God!" Joan gasped. "They've blocked us in! I can't believe this. That jerk threw us out and now this! We should sue him and the church for ruining my big day. After all the money we gave in the past six months, I'll never, ever set foot in that building again."

It was a vow that Joan religiously kept—at least until the first of her three children, Tiffany Renee, was born.

"Joan, you must have the baby baptized!"

"Why mother?"

"For the salvation of her soul!"

"I vowed not to set foot in that building again!"

"I know dear! But think of the baby. And I'll pay for the reception."

Joan's eyes lit up. A reception. A magnificent soirée. Yes! Since marrying Sidney there wasn't enough money for parties, and Joan loved parties.

"Okay, mom. Schedule the baptism. I'll rent the hall and take care of everything else."

During the baptism, Father Roman asked of Joan: "What do you wish of the Church for you, child?"

Joan gave the customary answer, having heard it from the couple immediately before her: Baptism.

When Father posed the question to her a *second* time, Joan replied: "Baptism?"

He asked the question a *third* time, "No, child. What do *You* want of the Church?"

Now, fully realizing that the priest had called into question her commitment to the *faith*, she became livid. In her mind, Joan fumed, *How dare he judge me? Who does he think is, anyway? How dare he embarrass me in front of my relatives and friends just because we don't go to Mass! So, we haven't been here in ten months? What's it to him? We pray at home! Besides, what the hell does he know about babies and how much work it takes to raise them? Where does he get off chastising me because I don't have time to go to church? I don't even have time for Me! And this was the priest who ruined my wedding. Now he is ruining my baby's day.*

After the baptismal trauma, neither Sidney nor Joan set foot inside of the Church until their next child, Eric Hogan, required the sacrament. This time, another priest was the officiant of the ceremony, and Joan was spared a repeat of the humiliation she had endured at the hands of the Pastor.

"But Mrs. Pielaresto, the Church is adamant. The child must have at least two years of religious education before they may receive any of the Sacraments."

"That's bogus! All the church wants is *my* money!"

"Of course not! But, if you sincerely feel that way perhaps you would like to meet with Father Roman. I'll do as he says."

"No, no." Joan said remembering well this hardnosed priest. "Sign her up."

And so first grade found Tiffany Renee enrolled in CCD class.

In second grade Tiffany received her first Holy Communion and grandma funded a big, family party. There was much rejoicing, on grandma's part. Even Sidney and Joan had reason to rejoice because this sacrament thing was turning into a terrific way to supplement the college fund. They watched wide-eyed and salivated as the money rolled in from relatives and close friends. When it came time for Eric Hogan, the formula did not disappoint. With the parents' pockets full of cash, the children would not attend another CCD class until they reached the Seventh Grade. After all, it made perfect economic sense to Sidney and Joan—nothing against the Church, but there was simply no money to be made on grades three through six.

Confirmation, the sacrament of commitment, is one of the most important sacraments of the Church, a time when the individual personally chooses the *faith*. But for Sidney and Joan, it would provide them with another immaculate opportunity to throw an even bigger party, again at grandma's expense, and make even bigger bucks! After all these years, they still had experienced no conversion of the heart, no commitment to the Church. Alas, when it came to matters of faith their children were on their own and did not fare well.

This was the family environment into which Edger was to be born.

The time had come. Joan and Sidney made their way to the hospital through a gently falling snow. Even though the birth only took four hours, Joan claimed to be in agony for days afterward.

"You are fine Mrs. Pielaresto! There is nothing wrong with you! The birth was uncomplicated!"

"Nonsense! Something *has* gone horribly wrong! My back aches! My insides feel like they've been ripped out, and I have a constant headache!"

"You are a constant headache!" Dr. Jophic wanted to say but instead said "Your vital signs are normal: Blood pressure is 120/80, pulse is 75. I have examined you from head to toe three times now. You are fine!"

"I'll sue you, the nurses, this hospital and the pope! This is supposed to be a Catholic hospital. You're supposed to give me care and compassion. I've gotten neither from you nor the nurses in this hell hole. I'll never, ever have another child, because of you!"

Immediately after Joan left the hospital, the nurses and doctors threw a party.

While descending into a true psychosis, Joan's health continued to decline. She blamed all her woes on the difficult pregnancy that she endured as well as on the debilitating and backbreaking process of birthing her youngest son who was normal in every way. He had ten fingers and ten toes and was of average length and weight. Unfortunately for him, he had been the bothersome result of an unplanned pregnancy, and his mother treated him accordingly.

"I want an abortion." Joan said to Sidney when she learned of her pregnancy. "I'm thirty-five and too old to rear another child. My life is perfect now. We have a girl and a boy, we don't need another child."

"Joan, that is just the hormones talking. Having this baby won't change anything. In fact it will be even more perfect. You look radiant when you are expecting, you have that special glow. Everyone remarks about it."

So Joan allowed herself to be persuaded into having the child. But it wasn't the perfection Sidney promised. In her mind everything was going wrong, and she told her doctors every chance she got. After the birth Joan often lamented out loud and at length that she had been weak. She cursed Sidney for convincing her to have the baby instead of the abortion. It was precisely because Edger had "spoiled everything for her"—a phrase that she often used when reprimanding him for even the mildest of offenses—that she vehemently hated her youngest son.

Opening the door Sidney was greeted by a barrage of wails coming from the nursery. Quickly placing down his brief case and hanging up his suit coat, he made his way to the nursery to attend to his son, who was wet and soiled. As he was cleaning Edger, Joan called.

"Sidney. Come here! Leave the brat alone. He's been crying all day! I *need* you!"

"I'll be right there sweetheart, as soon as I finish changing Edger."

"I want you *now*!"

Understandably, Edger's mother and father became emotionally detached from each other. The immediate ramification of this marital atrophy, for Edger, was that he neither received nor felt love from his mother and the modest amount that his father was permitted to show him during his early years soon dwindled.

"Do you love me Sidney?" Joan asked out of the blue.

"Of course Joan, you know I do."

"Then why don't you like spending time with me?"

"What do you mean? I spend time with you."

"No you don't! Not like when we were first married. You spend more time with the little brat than you do with me."

Sidney didn't know what to say. Edger needed a parent.

"It's me or him Sidney. He'll grow up and leave you. I'll be here long after he leaves, unless…"

It was a veiled threat, but Sidney realized that in this high-stakes card game of emotional blackmail—Edger's hand was weak but his was weaker, and so he folded. Sidney took the coward's way out choosing to keep the bitch off his back above the welfare of his son.

Edger grew up with the basic physical necessities to which his parent's social status demanded, but with none of the love and affection of a healthy family. Joan and Sidney provided only that which would make them look good in the eyes of their social acquaintances. Truly, while he lived under their roof, no kindness was shown to him. In effect, Edger grew up without ever experiencing a legitimate sense of family.

Edger was born with a condition known as aniridia, characterized by an extremely underdeveloped iris. His eyes were dark, almost black. At first glance he seemed to lack the iris altogether, giving him a sinister appearance. His parents thought he would outgrow it, but when he did not, it only added to his mother's arsenal of complaints about her youngest.

"Freak! You little freak!" Joan yelled. Edger stared at his mother over the spilt milk.

"Stop looking at me and look at the mess you made you little freak! I should beat your behind." She threw a dish towel at the four year old.

"Clean that up, freak!"

Edger began to cry and ran to his room.

Two weeks after his fifth birthday party, given by his "Grams", Edger was playing with the remote control car she gave him. It bumped into a plant stand and knocked over Joan's prized orchid. Edger was trying to clean up the mess when Joan entered.

"What have you done freak?" She grabbed him by the shoulders, but this time, instead of crying, he bent his head down and rolled his eyes up.

"What are you doing freak. Stop that!"

But Edger continued to stare. He reminded her of the children of the corn, a movie that had given her nightmares for years after she saw it. Joan released her hold on her son and backed away. She wanted to look away but couldn't. He continued "the stare". With every step Joan took backward, Edger took one forward.

"Stop it freak! I'll spank you." she threatened. "Go to your room. Get away from me!" He took another step forward.

"Please, Edger, please, stop!" she cajoled. Reaching the kitchen Joan got out an ice cream sandwich and threw it to her son.

"Here, Edger. Mommy gave you an ice cream sandwich. Now, please stop."

Joan fled the kitchen and locked herself in her bedroom taking to her bed until Sidney came home.

Edger learned he could control his mother with the "look" and Joan eventually learned to stop calling her youngest names.

Tragically, love from his parents was not the only kind of love that Edger was denied. His older siblings, Tiffany and Eric, often taunted and teased him delighting in their malevolence. It only took one thrashing from his sister for Edger to realize that his eye trick did not work on them. Avoidance was his only escape.

Denied the comforts of family, Edger found consolation in his studies.

Subconsciously he still hoped to gain a sliver of his parent's affection through superior academic achievements. To his great disappointment, he finally realized that regardless of the number of impressive scholastic achievements he accumulated, his parents would never accept or love him. He determined to make something of himself—not for his uncaring, ungrateful parents, but for himself. The time had come for Edger to leave his past and heartache behind.

Education at every level became his new family. His professors became his new parents, and were never reluctant to praise his accomplishments. His fellow classmates became his surrogate siblings, and they generously shared their camaraderie with him. It was refreshing and positively reinforcing for the young man who had suffered so much. Upon his graduation from high school, Edger elected to study biochemistry at the University of Pittsburgh in preparation for a career in Medicine.

Like Samuel, Edger had a special destiny.

LOVE AND DEATH

2020–2042

How can I describe my emotions at this catastrophe, or how to delineate the wretch whom with such infinite pains and care I had endeavored to form? His limbs were in proportion, and I had selected his features as beautiful. Beautiful!—Great God! His yellow skin scarcely covered the work of muscles and arteries beneath; his hair was of a lustrous black, and flowing; his teeth of a pearly whiteness; but these luxuriance's only formed a more horrid contrast with his watery eyes, that seemed almost of the same color as the dun white sockets in which they were set, his shriveled complexion, and straight black lips.

Frankenstein by Mary Shelley—Chapter 5

FROM THE BEGINNING, Edger rejected by his family, and Sam neglected by a mother consumed by grief, found refuge in fantasy novels. Coincidently, in their respective fourth grade classes, the boys had chosen Frankenstein, Mary Shelley's gothic-horror tale of creature and creator as their favorite literary work. In their own ways, they had been fascinated by the incredible impact that this novel had wrought upon the scientific community, directly inspiring the research and development of such marvels as cloning, tissue engineering, and the reanimation of individuals who had been cryogenically preserved.

In fact, Shelley's classic tale had become the focus of their senior projects.

Edger concentrated on exploring the dynamics of the relationship between genetic manipulation and quality of life—in particular, he sought an answer to the question: can the quality of human life be increased through genetic manipulation? Meanwhile, Sam provided evidence of how genetic manipulation and religion were not mortal enemies, not at odds, nor polarized in a perpetual conflict.

Sam was growing into a handsome man. Slight of build, he stood a bit over six feet, weighing a scant one hundred fifty nine pounds. His strawberry blond hair, accentuated by piercing, cat-like, Irish green, almost emerald eyes, set him apart from other men, even in Ireland. Of all of the children of Martin and Sylvia, Sam most closely resembled his mother.

Edger, on the other hand, was dark in appearance and soul. Of course, who wouldn't be, growing up in that house? He was of medium build achieving an adult height of six feet one inch, and a weight of 165 pounds, which he proudly maintained throughout his life.

"How does he do it? He ate that entire box of Oreos and he won't gain an ounce!" remarked Tiffany to Eric.

"I don't understand it either, sis. He has always been able to eat anything he wants and still maintain his weight. I just look at an Oreo and gain five pounds," Eric responded.

"Hey freak! How about letting us in on your secret? How can you eat anything you want and never gain any weight?"

This was one more thing Edger took pride in, his ability to eat anything, whenever he wanted, without gaining so much as an ounce.

"Good genes I guess," Edger responded keeping his distance from his marginally obese siblings. The last time he let either get close he got beat up.

Physically, he resembled neither of his parents, but was the spitting image of his maternal grandfather.

"Joan, the baby is beautiful," Susan beamed.

"If you say so mother," Joan moaned painfully turning to look at her.

"He looks just like your father."

As he grew his resemblance to his grandfather, Howard, only increased. His walk, speech, and all of his mannerisms, was Howard's. He even had his same cockeyed half smile. From the day of his birth, Susan felt that she had her husband back and loved this youngest grandchild all the more. Joan's mistreatment of Edger hurt Susan deeply, but she suffered in silence as Joan chastised Edger for even the smallest infraction.

One day, in the mist of a Joan tirade, Susan snapped and chastised Joan in front of her friends.

"Will you leave the boy alone, Joan. He hasn't done anything that is worthy of this scolding."

"Don't tell me how to raise my son, mother."

"Well, it's about time someone does. Sidney is just too whipped to do anything for the boy. And none of your friends have the courage to tell you the truth. I should have said something years ago. You have ridden this boy since the day he was born, and you need to stop it." Joan was livid.

"How dare you speak to me that way in my own house. You have no right! Especially in front of my friends. Get out!"

After this Susan was not allowed to see Edger. She was permitted to see Tiffany and Eric but she could never see her favorite grandchild. It was like losing Howard all over again. Grief set in and Susan's health began to decline. Realizing that she would soon join her husband, she played the only card she had left. But what a card it turned out to be.

"Joan! You're spending money like it is water. You need to live within our budget!" Sidney said.

"Why? Mother isn't going to live much longer and since I am her only offspring I stand to inherit a fortune. Dad left mother very well off. Sidney, we will not only be rich, we will be very rich." Over Sidney's objections Joan continued maxing out her credit cards, spending the inheritance she had yet to receive.

"I, Susan Barbara McSorley Harris, presently residing in the County of Allegheny in the Commonwealth of Pennsylvania, being of sound mind and disposing memory, do hereby make, publish and declare this to be my Last Will and Testament, hereby expressly revoking any and all Wills and Codicils heretofore made by me."

Joan was on the edge of her seat hungrily anticipating the inheritance that would soon be hers.

The lawyer continued:

"While I love my daughter, my only child, Joan Anastasia Harris Pielaresto, I have knowingly bequeathed to her in this my Last Will and Testament the sum of $200,000 as she has been adequately provided for during my lifetime."

"WHAT!" Joan screamed standing up to lean on the lawyer's desk. "That Bitch! How dare she! I'll fight this. Who did she leave the rest of the money to?"

"I'm getting to that Mrs. Pielaresto." he continued to read.

"I direct my Executor to pay out of my residuary estate the following: after the expenses of my last illness, administration expenses, all legally enforceable creditor claims, and reasonable funeral expenses are paid, I give devise and bequeath my residual estate to my beloved grandson Edger Bartholomew Pielaresto to be paid on his eighteenth birthday or sixty days after my funeral, whichever occurs first."

"You mean the brat gets all the money?"

"Edger Bartholomew Pielaresto is to receive it, if that is to whom you refer as 'the brat.'"

"I'll fight this."

"Sorry, Mrs. Pielaresto, but your mother made sure this will is ironclad. If you contest the will you will lose the inheritance you are to receive and that too will go to your son Edger."

Joan was livid. She had already spent the meager inheritance left to her. There would be no more.

Edger received his inheritance on his eighteenth birthday, six months after the funeral, and he was at last free. His grams made sure of that.

Sam and Edger's paths inevitably crossed on the campus of the University of Pittsburgh Medical School during the Fall Term 2042. There they found themselves assigned as lab partners where, amidst their vials, chemicals, beakers and burners, they discovered common interests, including a passion for the science behind genetic manipulation. Gradually, their bond strengthened and became the bedrock of their friendship. On breaks from school, Edger often went home with Sam.

"Good to have you laddies home," Bridget exclaimed running to hug each in turn. "We've prepared a grand homecoming supper."

Bernard took Sam's luggage and Tim Edgers. Edger basked in the love he felt. He had never felt so welcome and for the first time learned what it meant to truly belong to a family

Sometime later, Edger met and fell in love with a beautiful woman named Julie. Edger anxiously anticipated the upcoming trip to see his adopted family, not only because they were the best times of his life, but because he had something exciting to tell them. He felt the way he did when he was seven and received an A+ on his spelling test. He ran home anticipating the joy his parents would have, but that was not to be. They looked at the paper and tossed it away.

The O'Brian's were different though. They always asked him about his life, what he was up to, his plans for the future, and they were truly interested. He knew this would be different.

"Sam, I've got something to tell you before I burst."

"What is it Ed?"

"I asked Julie to marry me and she accepted. Can you believe that? Julie is so beautiful. I can't believe she said yes."

"Congratulations Ed. I knew she was the one for you the first day I met her. She'll keep you in line!" Sam said as he hugged his friend.

"I can't wait to tell the family," Edger said.

"When are you going to tell them?"

"Next week, when we are home in Ireland of course!" he replied.

"Oh! I thought you meant your family."

"God no! They don't deserve to know, not yet. I don't want to expose Julie to them just now. I guess I will have to tell them though."

The O'Brian's were overjoyed at their adopted brother's news, a far cry from his own family's reception several months later.

Upon their completion of medical school, both Sam and Edger were offered residencies at UPMC, but Edger chose to follow his heart and Julie to The Big Apple where he accepted a residency at New York University Medical Center. Even though this dynamic medical duo of O'Brian and Pielaresto were going their separate ways for now, the two friends both knew in their hearts that it was for the best and that they would remain in touch.

As sometimes happens with even the best of friends, the pressures of the real world and the inherent strains of their residencies began to place an ever increasing stranglehold upon the frequency of their correspondence. Still, there were precious moments that were free enough to allow them to exchange an e-mail or two.

It was not an e-mail that would send Sam's life into a tailspin, but rather a letter that he received from his own brother, Tim.

06/05/2045
2:38 p.m.

My dearest brother, Doctor Sam,

I want to let you how very proud I am of you. You have succeeded and are making your dreams come true. You have come though some rough times, but you have become what you have always dreamed of: a doctor. You have done things that I could never have done and seen things that I will never see. I know that Dad would have been so proud of you. Your achievements are your own, Sammy, and I know you will be a success, a great physician. You have been, and always will be, my best friend. I have missed you terribly over the years that you have been in medical school across the pond. Our visits are always too long in coming and always over way too soon.

Unfortunately, I will be unable to attend your graduation. Some things have come up, and I simply can not leave home at that time. I also have something to tell you. It is something that I should tell you face to face, but in this instance, I am a coward. It is a secret that I have been keeping from everyone, even myself, my entire life. No one has ever suspected. As far back as I can remember, I have had feelings for men. At first, I didn't know what it was, but as I grew up, I realized just what I am.

I am gay and I don't want to be. Even though I have feelings for men, I have dreamed that one day I would meet a woman who would be my salvation. We would fall in love, and I would no longer be attracted to men. We would have a deep and enduring love. There would be children, and we would grow old together, content in each other's love. But, as I got older, I realized that that would never be. I could not saddle any woman with me, as I am.

I have prayed to be cured. I have begged God to take this cross, and let this cup pass from me. I have prayed novenas, said rosaries, cried my rage like Job upon Heaven and even considered making a pact with hell itself, but I fear the devil too much and love God even more. As I get older these feelings have only intensified, and now I can't let myself get close to any man, since I am afraid that these feelings will overwhelm me and lead me into even graver sins that I will only regret with the entirety of my soul.

Sam, please never think that being gay is a choice. I didn't choose this. With all the prejudice and hatred that homosexuals experience in their daily lives, how can anyone be so naïve as to think that someone would willingly choose to be openly gay?

I began to suspect something when I was about five. My only choice was to keep my secret and live a lie. I long for companionship and love, yet I know I will never have it. The stress of keeping this secret is taking its toll. I am constantly depressed. It is so difficult keeping a smiling face when you feel lower than low on the inside at the core of your soul—your very essence. I want someone to share my life, but the Church says I can't have it. Does God really give you a gift and then tell you that you can't use it? If he did, then he'd be no better than the false pagan gods who routinely placed men in impossible situations for their own amusement. My God is loving, caring and forgiving. I wish mankind could be this way, too. Unfortunately many are not.

I have been torn between heaven and hell my entire life. Thank God it will all be over soon. Please remember me with love.

Your loving brother and best friend,
Tim

Sam felt as if someone had punched him in the stomach. Tim was his closest relative, his closest friend! They were nearest in age, and Tim had been his defender. When Sam was little, it was

Tim who read to him and helped him with his studies. If it hadn't been for Tim, Sam believed he would never have gotten this far in the medical field! Tim had been Sam's confidant, and Sam had been under the impression that he had been Tim's as well. How could he have been so mistaken? After all, didn't he know his brother better than anyone else? Sam had even shared the same room with Tim until he left for university. No two bothers had ever been closer. Or had they?

How could Tim have kept such a secret from me?

It made him furious.

He felt betrayed.

Sam reflected back upon his life, and in particular all of the time that he had spent with Tim. There had been no warning. No clues. Sam had never even suspected that his brother had been anything other than heterosexual. Tim was both masculine in manner and appearance. He loved rugby and soccer and was captain of his upper school soccer team. He even coached. There had been nothing effeminate about him at all.

The ring of his cell phone abruptly brought him out of his bewildered reverie.

He flicked open the phone with a chirp.

"*What?*" Sam barked, annoyed.

"Sam?" said his eldest brother, Bernard.

"Yeah, Bern, how are you?"

"Sam, I have something to tell you. Are you sitting down?"

"No. What is it?"

"Sam, sit down. *Please.*"

"Bern, you're scaring me. What's the matter?"

"I wanted to tell you this in person, but the *distance*... It's about Tim."

"I know. I just got a letter from him today. I'm *still* numb. He sounded funny. He was rambling. He mentioned how proud he was of me and how proud Dad would have been, too. Then the tone changed and he told me he was gay. I mean, that's why you called, isn't it? To talk about Tim's homosexuality? Oh, Bern, I can't believe it, either. He was always so... *normal.*"

"Damn it Sam, will you please just *listen* to me! Tim's *dead.*"

"What? No. It can't be—I just—" Sam sank heavily onto the couch, the wind knocked out of him for a second time in the past few moments.

"He died last night. Bridget went to wake him since he was late for school. She thought he'd just overslept. When she went into his room she found him dead. Just like that; OD'd on sleeping pills. He left a note, Sam. He said he was gay and that he couldn't—*wouldn't*—live a lie anymore. He'd made his peace with God and hoped that in time, we could forgive him."

There was no response from Sam for a long time on his end; only dead air...as dead as his brother, Tim.

Finally, Bernard broke the silence, "Sam...? Sam, are you all right? God, I wish I could be there for you."

"Yeah, uh...I uh...I jus—I just—I don't know what to say."

"I know...look, Sam, there's *more.*"

"Great. Let me have it."

"Sam, there was a separate note addressed to me. Tim told me that he'd written you but couldn't bring himself to ask you something directly. He said he had no right to ask anything of you, so he asked me, as the eldest, to do it. He knew that you were researching gene silencing. While doing some work at the library, he came across a 1993 report by Dr. James McFarland, who had been the Director of the Gene Structure and Regulation Unit at the National Cancer Institute in America. According to the report, Dr. McFarland claimed to have identified a DNA sequence linked to homosexuality in males. Tim said that it was too late for him, but perhaps, if you found a way to silence this gene, you can save countless others from the pain and suffering that he endured. He begged you to forgive him and as a sign of that forgiveness, that you would consider doing what he's asking of you now, through me. It would be your final gift to him."

"My God…Does Mom know?"

"I called the convent, but Mom either couldn't or wouldn't come to the phone.

Sister Mary Phillip answered, and said that she'd give Mom the message. What nonsense! We're talking about the death of her son, for God's sake!" After a moment he calmed down and added with a sigh, "Well, I never actually told Sister Philip about Tim's death. As for mom, she made her choice. What can we do about it, right? Anyway, the arrangements aren't finalized, but we're looking at Monday for the funeral so that leaves Friday, Saturday, and Sunday…"

"for the wake," Sam finished quietly.

"That's right. Are you able to come, Sam?"

"Yeah, uh…Sure; of course…I'll uhh, I'll be there. After all, Tim and I were practically joined at the hip when we were kids, right?"

"Right. You were. Like Siamese twins…" Bernard offered a weak, humorless laugh.

"Right," Sam said for no particular reason, "How could I miss seeing him one last time?"

After a moment, Bernard pursed his lips, wanting to say something else, something comforting, something fatherly, but Sam had already terminated the call.

A CRISIS OF FAITH

I N POPE BENEDICT XVI's book, Jesus of Nazareth, he states that throughout the generations, yes even from the time of Jesus and before, mankind has fostered a view of reality that excludes the luminosity of God. The solitary issue comes down to that which can be proven experimentally. Only this is real. But Benedict elucidates that God cannot be confined to experimentation.

Yahweh made the same criticism of the Israelites' in the desert, "When your fathers tested me, they tried (experimented) me, though they had seen my work, (Psalm 95: 9 NASB)."

Using this citation Benedict clarifies that God cannot be rationalized through experimentation even though modern society wants him to be. Using this experimentalist view man has even less reason to accept the demands God places on him. To believe in God and to live accordingly would, therefore, be completely irrational. This position leads to non-grasping, non-comprehending and a "hardening of the heart."

June 9, 2045

New York City. Friday, June 9, 2045. A suicide bombing today at the corner of Broadway and Astor Place in front of New York University killed twelve people and injured thirty-two others. The AHSRUB Liberation Society claims credit…

Before Edger could finish reading the article, his doorbell rang. He got up and answered the door. There were two New York police officers standing in the hallway.

"Are you Edger Pielaresto?" The taller of the two officers asked.

"Yes. What's the matter?"

This time it was the shorter of the two who spoke, "Mr. Pielaresto, do you know a woman by the name of…" he paused briefly to glance down at his electronic note pad, "Julie Buzzbee?"

Edger felt tension enter all of the muscles in his body, "Yes, of course, she's my fiancée. Has something—*what's* happened?"

The officers exchanged glances, then looked back to Edger.

"Sir, Ms. Buzzbee was a victim of the suicide bombing at the university. She's been taken to Saint Vincent's Catholic Hospital and Medical Center in Manhattan. Your presence is required at the hospital."

Edger felt his guts drop. His voice sounded hollow as the words escaped his lips. "Wh-what's her condition? How is she?"

"Look… sir," the tall officer replied sympathetically, "I'm no doctor, but between you and me, I'd hurry."

"Yes, yes, I'll go now. Thank you."

Edger arrived at Saint Vincent's within half an hour and was shown to Julie's room. Nothing could have prepared him for what he saw. The woman he loved, the woman with whom he had planned to spend the rest of his life, lay still upon an antiseptic white hospital bed in the ICU. This once vibrant woman was now silent, unmoving and hooked up to a respirator. Tubes protruded from every part of her body, making her look like some science experiment tragically gone wrong. Frankenstein's monster came to his mind. It was a favorite movie of theirs, not the new colored versions, but the original black and white movie they made more than a hundred years ago. He remembered his love of Shelley's book and the irony sickened him. From the doorway, he saw that her head had been bandaged.

What was it the doctor had said? Coma? Yes, yes…that was it…

Edger entered the room, his heart racing as he looked at his fiancée. Gazing at her in horror, he found himself comparing the vision of the beautiful, athletic and charming woman of his memories with the broken, nightmarish vision that rested before him. His mind could not accept this was the woman he loved, and yet he *knew* it was her.

"*My God, Jules*…what have they done to you?"

Going to her bedside, he leaned over and took her hand. "Julie? It's Edger. I'm here, baby. Everything will be all right."

Hours passed as he kept vigil over her, with her hand in his, desperately searching for *any* signs of life.

None came.

Edger and Julie were so perfectly matched that they could carry on conversations with each other for hours—on any topic—with the sound of her carefree laughter punctuating the discussion. Now, the only sounds that he heard were the dull *swishing* of the respirator accompanied by the monotonous *beeping* of the heart monitor. Was this to be their final conversation—spoken only in silence and with their hearts? All night long, he waited and watched…and prayed. The next morning, Julie's parents arrived and Edger left so they could be alone with their daughter.

After leaving the hospital, Edger walked to Saint Patrick Roman Catholic Church, which was located only a few blocks away. Once inside, he knelt before the altar and poured out his emotions, exposing his heart before the Lord. Gazing upward at the statue of the Sacred Heart he humbled himself before God, and in earnest, bargained with Him for the life of his fiancée, "Please God; *please…* don't let her die. We're going to be married. *Why did this happen? Why?* If you let her live, I'll go to church every Sunday. I'll be a good Catholic. I won't ignore you any more. I'll do whatever you want… *Please…just don't let her die!*" Ultimately, emotionally spent, he rested his head on his hands.

He caught his mind wandering back to the time that he and Julie had first met. It was a pleasant memory and so he allowed his thoughts to transport him there, back to the time when he was a first year med student and Julie was a freshman at the University of Pittsburgh—back to a time that seemed less cruel and more hope-filled.

After a grueling session in the anatomy lab, Edger had decided to get a late dinner at the "New Original Hot Dog Shop"—which students and alumni had affectionately dubbed "The O" for nearly a century—since they had the best fries in town. He ordered large fries with chili and a large Coke (he needed the caffeine for the late night he was going to have studying). He looked around. There was no place to sit.

It was then that he saw her for the first time.

She was the prettiest girl he had ever seen; round face, flowing blond hair, blue eyes. To his astonishment, she caught his gaze and smiled back at him. Instantly, she had sized up his predicament and so, she motioned for him to come and sit with her. He smiled and in his eagerness, nearly spilled his Coke on himself as he walked to her table.

The words blurted out, "Hi, I'm Edger Pielaresto. Thanks for the seat. The O's more crowded than usual. I didn't know how I was going to eat these—"

"Hello, Edger. I'm Julie. Julie Buzzbee." She smiled with a hint of a giggle, "You looked like you needed some help."

"I did. Thanks again. I'm taking a break from my anatomy lab."

"Oh, really? What's your major?" She asked genuinely interested.

"I'm a first year med student."

"That's terrific. Medicine is an exciting field. I'm a freshman. Undeclared, though, I think I want to be a nurse."

"Oh, yeah?" Now it was Edger's turn to be intrigued. A beautiful woman who was also in his field? He couldn't believe his luck! "So, what makes you think that you—let me rephrase that—why do you think that you're being called to a career in nursing?"

"I don't know," she started, her face becoming flushed, "I just like helping people."

"Me, too." They had made a connection. Nothing else was said for a few moments as they sat there regarding each other.

Edger didn't return to the lab that night, instead, he took a walk with Julie. They had talked almost till morning, and he remembered, it was the night that they had fallen in love.

Edger's mind then flew to a night that they had shared a few years later when, after dinner at the LaMont on Mount Washington, they had strolled along Grandview Avenue, stopping at the overlooks to take in the magnificent view of Pittsburgh, the shining city between three rivers. From there they had taken the Monongahela Incline down to Station Square, crossed the Smithfield Street Bridge, and made their way to Point State Park, where Fort Duquesne had been completely reconstructed as it had appeared nearly three hundred years before.

The two of them sat overlooking the Allegheny River and talked about nothing in particular. Edger seemed nervous. Julie had been about to say something, when suddenly, Edger fell to his knees, "Julie, I love you. Will you marry me?"

Julie did not need to be asked twice. "Of course! I love you, too." She smiled that beguiling, playful smile of hers, "What took you so long?" Edger grinned, relieved, as he placed the ring on her finger. They embraced and kissed passionately. Soon, a policeman came by.

"Break it up," the officer said.

Julie lifted her hand and showed off her ring. The police-man grinned.

"Whoops. Carry on. By all means, carry on…and, uh, con-gratulations," he said and then walked away.

They sat enfolded in each other's arms until well after midnight.

Next, Edger's thoughts spiraled to the night that they had decided for him to do his residence at New York University Medical Center and for Julie to earn her Masters in Nursing at New York University. He remembered the excitement they felt as they left Pittsburgh to begin the next phase of their life. Since Julie was a devout Catholic, they lived in separate apartments. She had three roommates. Edger could afford his own apartment because his grandmother had left him very well off financially.

Edger came out of his reminiscences and realized that he was back in the church, in front of the Sacred Heart of Jesus. He glanced around and pleaded again with the Sacred Heart. "Please, don't do this to me, Lord. Don't do this to her. How can I live without her? Please, God, please…"

Edger hadn't realized that he had been speaking aloud. The pastor, Father Adrian, overheard Edger's outpouring of emotions from the sacristy and sought to help him. Father moved closer putting his hand on Edger's shoulder.

"Do you want to talk?" Edger looked up. "Yes."

Edger confided about everything that had caused his heart to become so heavy. He spoke about Julie, their plans to be wed, the bombing, and how she was now barely clinging to life in a hospital bed just down the street.

Father Adrian composed his thoughts for a few moments and then said, "Edger, I understand your pain, but you cannot bargain with our Lord. Things happen for a reason, and we must accept his holy will."

It was then that Julie's sister, Debra, entered the Church. "Edger" she called, "Mom and Dad asked me to find you. They need you back at the hospital, immediately."

"Is she awake?" Edger felt all his hopes raise.

"No, Edger" Debra said, "Shortly after you left, she had a seizure and she…and she…and *she died.*"

"What? *But that can't be.*" He turned to Father Adrian in his disbelief, "If God is good then *Julie can't be dead.*"

"She is Edger. She's gone," Debra said between sobs.

"I was there when she died. Mom and Dad sent me to find you. We have to get back. They won't take her from the room until you have a chance to say good-bye. They think you deserve to see her one last time."

Edger stammered, "I—I—I can't. Julie's not dead. If I don't go, then she can't be dead, right? God can't be that sadistic."

"God is not sadistic, Edger," said Father Adrian, "God is good and merciful. He doesn't put us through trials without providing us with the grace to deal with them."

Edger's logical and analytical mind screamed for a quantifiable reason, "But *why* would he do this Father? She was a good person—so young, so alive, so *giving…*"

Father Adrian sighed as he attempted to console the young man, "Edger, as we pick the loveliest flowers in our garden, so does God. It was Julie's time. She has finished her task on this Earth and is enjoying her heavenly reward. Remember, Edger, time will heal this wound. Trust in God, he will help you."

Edger's anger erupted with volcanic fury. He screamed at the priest but aimed his vitriolic words at God, a God who had done *nothing* for him his entire life. A God, who when he finally gave him something good yanked it away, as he had wrenched his grandmother from him, a God who ignored his pleas.

What little faith Edger had before today incinerated until there was nothing left of it to identify. In its place, at the core of his soul, there was left a barren agnostic wasteland. Edger cursed God with every word, "Her life was with ME! She WAS my life! We were to be married. What kind of a cruel God allows a thing like this to happen? *For what?* In the name of *religion?* In the name of *God?* That bomber was a member of the AHSRUB Liberation Society, an organization that claims that God is on their side and orders them to kill in his name. These bastards take the lives of women and children—*defenseless people!* You tell me, Father, what kind of a god would require this? What kind of twisted heartless god would command such men to kill innocent, defenseless women and children! Not any God I'd recognize! *And my Julie, my Julie.*"

Before Father or Debra could say anything else, Edger ran down the aisle toward the entrance to the church. Upon reaching the doors, he turned back to Debra and Father, raising his fists upward toward heaven drunk with fury. Wailing, he completed his apostasy, "There is no god! I renounce him! I defy him! God is dead!" and then softer, his fury spent, to no one in particular, "He died along with my Julie."

Edger barged through the doors, slamming them behind him.

After the funeral, Julie's family never saw Edger again.

Grieving, he locked himself away inside of the apartment for weeks, drowning his sorrows in booze. His life became a montage of pass-outs followed by their inevitable stupefied, brain-banging awakenings. During these weeks of self-imposed exile, Edger's pain never abated. His thoughts became deviant, polluted by an insatiable lust for vengeance against everyone, who had been responsible for Julie's death: the AHSRUB Liberation Society and other terrorist organizations like it; the Catholic Church, and especially, the most heinous offender of all, religion.

Engorged by his pain and his misery, Edger's impaired reasoning led him to the conclusion that most of the wars in history had been provoked by religious beliefs. He quickly resolved to amass as much evidence as he could to support his theory and pledged to devote the rest of his life to destroying religion and all of its fanatics for Julie's sake. Edger Pielaresto was determined to go down in history as the man who killed religion.

Two letters crossed in the mail:

July 3, 2045

Dear Edger,

What can I possibly say? What a shock? I have just heard about Julie's passing. I am so very sorry for your loss. It is a loss to all who knew her. She was a wonderful, loving woman. I know how very much you loved her and words cannot express my sympathy. I wish I could have been there for you during that time, but I have just returned from Ireland, where I attended Tim's funeral. Otherwise, you know that I would have been there with you. Julie was a wonderful woman and did not deserve that fate.

It took a lot for me to get back for graduation but now that I have two months free before I start work, I will be flying to New York to see Mary Agnes. With all that was going on at the funeral, I didn't have much time to spend with her, and she had to leave right after the wake. I am setting aside a big chunk of time to spend with you, and you have no choice in the matter, Ed, so no excuses. I'll see you in a couple of weeks, old friend. You are in my thoughts and prayers.

As ever,
Your friend and brother,
Sam

7–3–'45

Dear Sam,

I'm sorry that it's taken me this long to write you and express my heartfelt grief on the loss of your brother, Tim. The sad truth of it is that I was simply too drunk to care about anything for weeks. The stupidity of it all! Don't worry, though. I finally realized that drinking doesn't solve problems; it just numbs you while it creates new ones. You get up with a headache every single morning, oblivious as to what you did the night before. In the weeks after Julie's death, I spent more money on booze than I did on food— and I wasn't buying the good stuff. I have accepted Julie's death, but I'll never get over it. She was my life.

Sam, I can't begin to tell you how sorry I am about Tim. He was a great guy, always willing to go the extra mile. He made me feel at home whenever I'd visit. He loved you very much. Remember that. You are in my thoughts.

Yours,
Ed

TURNING POINT

June 9, 2045

W HEN SAM TURNED eighteen and left for Trinity College, Sylvia found herself alone in the house that for so long had been the nest for her children. Her husband was dead, her children gone.

Rambling around the old house, she saw reminders of the ones who had left her behind—framed portraits of Martin and the children, Sean's rugby jacket, Martin's bowling shoes, Mary Agnes' cheerleading skirt, Rebecca's blue jeans, Bernard's winter scarf, they were everywhere. From the windowsill she picked up Sam's clay kindergarten hand print and tenderly traced the faint crack that had been lovingly glued by Martin after Sam dropped it shortly before giving it to her.

Alone inside a house that seemed to grow larger and more unfriendly with each passing day, Sylvia found herself withdrawing more and more from the world. As the days passed she realized that her part-time commitment to the Church could now become full time, through the realization of her childhood dream of becoming a nun. If she had not met Martin when she did, she would have entered the convent then. Now, it was just she and God. She applied for admission, and was received into the Order of the Blessed Sacrament. Immersing herself in the semi-cloister of the order, Sylvia left the world and all that it held permanently behind.

Lost amidst her life altering choice was the realization that both she and her youngest son had, in their own ways, sought refuge from the world by cloistering themselves, she in a convent, he in a laboratory.

Sister Mary Phillip hung up the phone. Immediately, she headed for the office of Mother Hedwig Peligia. After knocking, she was admitted with customary greeting, "Ave. Enter, with the Peace of God."

"And also with you," replied Sister Mary Phillip as she entered briskly, urgently, and stood at the desk awaiting acknowledgement from her superior in the order.

"Yes, sister...?" Mother asked looking up from her papers.

Sister Mary Phillip didn't need additional incentives, "Mother, I just had another call from Bernard O'Brian, Sister Mary Sylvia's eldest son," Mother nodded her head, knowing very well the background of Sister Mary Sylvia—as she knew the backgrounds of all of her sisters. Sister Mary Phillip continued, "He asked to speak with his mother again. I told him that that would be impossible, but I could give her another message and assured him that his previous messages had been received. There was nothing further that I could do. He said it was a matter of dire importance—a *family* matter—that could only be handled by her. It was then that I told him that he would have to talk to you. He left his number for you to call him back."

She handed the phone message to Mother who took it with a reluctance suited to those who acknowledge the existence of difficult situations that offer no easy resolutions. Sister Mary Phillip furrowed her brow with the burden of this predicament. Here was a woman, now a sister, who had turned her back on her family, her children, *her flesh and blood*. Phillip's heart cried out for a loving solution. "Mother, I-I didn't know how to tell him that his mother ref—she *refuses* to have contact with *anyone* from the outside world, *including* her children. Lord forgive me, I'm trying so hard not to judge my fellow sister but—"

Mother interrupted, "*Sister...that* is not your place."

With contrition, she stood in silence as Mother addressed her, "I have given this matter a great deal of thought and have prayed for discernment about it. Sister Sylvia has created a world within this convent that was never meant to exist. Even though we have chosen the semi-cloistered life, it was *never* intended that we leave our families. We have merely extended that family. Sister Sylvia has done what few in our order have. She participated in the miracle of birth, *nine* times,"

Mother turned away from Phillip as she crossed to a stained glass window depicting St. Margaret of Scotland. There was a tremulous hint of anxiety in her voice when she spoke, "It is *hard* for me to understand her attitude in the matter, but that is in God's hands."

After an introspective pause concluding with a long exhalation, Mother turned again toward Phillip. Her tone was as reassuring as she could muster, "I will call Bernard back and see why he so desperately needs to contact his mother. That will be all Sister. Thank you."

Mary Phillip left the room, relieved after having shared her burden.

Committed to action, Mother crossed back to her desk and removed the phone from its receiver. Looking at the note she dialed the number. After several tones, the call was answered.

"Hello!" Bernard answered.

"Is this Bernard O'Brian?" asked Mother.

"Yes. Who is this?"

"Mother Hedwig Peligia. Sister Mary Phillip informed me that you had called several times wishing to speak to your mother. I regret to inform you that Sister is indisposed and can not receive calls at this time. Is there something that I can do for you?"

"Mother, this is *important*. Her son Tim died last night. The family wants… no we *need* her. It hasn't been easy on any of us since she left. Now that Tim is dead, it's even harder. Look, her children need their mother. *Please*, Mother, is there anything you can do?"

"Mr. O'Brian, I am so sorry about your loss. I will speak to Sister immediately. May I ask how he died?

"Overdose of sleeping pills."

"Suicide? Why? Was there a note?"

"Yeah…he, uh…said, he said he'd been struggling with homosexuality his entire life and that he just couldn't do it anymore. He needed peace and wanted his torment to end. He said that he made his peace with God and asked his family for their forgiveness. I can't help but think that if mom had been here, things would have been different."

"Don't blame your mother. She is doing what she thinks is right."

"How can it be right to leave your family, even if we're all grown? Death, I can understand, but this?"

"I can't say that I understand her closing herself off from her family, but she does have a true religious calling. I was her mistress of novices and was responsible for her religious formation. She is truly called by God for life as a religious. I concede that the fault is partially mine. I allowed her to make her own decision on the matter of her family. I should have intervened much sooner… Have the arrangements been made?"

"Yes. Tim's viewing will be Wednesday, Thursday and Friday at O'Leary Funeral Home from 2:00 p.m. to 4:00 p.m. and 7:00 p.m. to 9:00 p.m.. The funeral's Saturday, at 10:00 a.m. at Saint Patrick's Church. The wake is at the family home, after. Tim had so many friends. He was loved by everyone, except himself. Please, Mother, do what you can. We need her now, more than ever."

"I'll see what I can do. You and your siblings are in my prayers. God bless you."

After hanging up the phone, Mother spent a few minutes thinking about her conversation with Bernard, and she became determined that Sylvia would listen, this time. She paged Sister Mary Phillip and asked her to bring Sylvia to her office immediately.

As she waited for Sylvia to arrive, Mother thought about how they had met. She, herself had been professed seven years before she was sent to Ireland as the first Mistress of Novices of the order's burgeoning community. As she instructed the novices in the ways of the Holy Catholic Church and the rules of the order, she was inexplicably drawn to one particular novice, some fifteen years her senior. Even though Sister Sylvia was an excellent student, she had a forlorn, far away air about her, and Hedwig Peligia, having developed a fondness for the older woman, resolved to do everything that she could to protect and assist her.

Throughout the years of her postulancy and novitiate, the two women grew closer. They often spoke about God and life. Yet still, Hedwig Peligia was unable to break through Sylvia's self-installed firewall.

In April of 2042, Sister Hedwig Peligia was elected Mother Superior of the Ireland order. The novices took their final vows shortly thereafter, on May 1.

As her first official function as head of the convent, Mother Hedwig Peligia accepted each novice into the order with great joy. In Sylvia's case, she felt both pride and sorrow because despite many entreaties to the contrary, her friend did not invite her children to the ceremony. They had begun to talk about it almost a year prior, but each time Mother brought it up, Sylvia refused. The last time that they spoke of the matter was soon after Hedwig Peligia had been elected Mother Superior. She and Sylvia were out for an afternoon stroll in the lush gardens. It was a beautiful, spring day, the first of its kind after a long, cold winter.

"Sylvia," Mother inquired delicately, "Have you given any more thought to inviting your children to your profession?"

"Yes, Sister…I mean, *Mother*. I still think it is best for them not to attend."

"Have you prayed about it?"

"Yes, I have," Sylvia replied earnestly.

"No," Mother pressed, "I mean *really* prayed over it? Are you certain this is what God is truly asking of you?"

"I am."

"Sylvia, you know that by joining the convent, we *extend* our families, not *abandon* them. We don't leave our loved ones behind. My family is very important to me. Have I ever told you about my life before I entered the order?"

"No, I don't think so."

"Well, then perhaps it's time," Mother said as she gestured for Sylvia to sit with her on a nearby bench along the path next to a patch of blooming lilacs. Once Sylvia had seated herself, Mother continued, "I was born Anastasia Francine Brzozowska on May 20, 1995 in Krakow, Poland. I was the first child of Marie and Walter. My parents owned a small dairy farm. We also had a flock of chickens. As with any farm, rodents abounded. Oh, the cats tried their best to keep the populations under control, but it was inevitable that some of the rodents escaped them and survived. One of my chores was collecting eggs. Now, each morning, before school, I'd go to the chicken coop, collect the eggs, and then take them into the house. This was all fairly routine until one day I noticed a nest of yellow-necked mice next to my prized hen. Well, mice in the country weren't unusual after all, so I thought nothing of it and went on with my collection.

Two weeks later, I was stricken with what my parents thought was the flu. My temperature was103.5 degrees; I suffered from headaches, pains in my stomach, joints and lower back, and I was nauseated with a dry cough."

"Dear Lord, Mother, what a terrible affliction!"

Mother smiled mischievously at her companion, "Oh, it gets better—or should I say, *worse?* Much worse... in fact, when I began having trouble breathing, my mother and father took me to Wojewodzki Specjalistyczny Hospital for Children. Even though the doctors were giving me oxygen, I still couldn't breathe. The doctors diagnosed me with an extreme case of Hantavirus and didn't give my parents much hope for my survival. Their bleak prognosis gained even more credibility with my parents when I slipped into a coma. My labored breathing became even shallower. The doctors told my family that my death was imminent.

Our parish priest, Father Baronowski, administered the Sacrament of the Sick. My entire family was present—Poppa, Momma, Susie, Joey, Owen and even little Oscar, the baby. Together, they prayed the rosary. Shortly after midnight on May 1, 2006, I awoke from my coma and asked for something to eat. Momma was overjoyed and ran to get some food. While she was gone, I talked with my father. I vividly remember that conversation...I told him that I had had the most wonderful dream—that I'd been very sick and that I was in my bed with no one else around, when suddenly the door to my room opened and a handsome man, dressed in white robes entered. I was afraid but the man in white comforted me.

He said, "Don't be afraid."

I found myself looking into his eyes and found them full of... of *kindness*. He took the seat next to my bed and began to talk to me. He said that I was very sick, but that I would soon recover. He told me that it was not yet my time and that God had great plans for me and for my future. I was destined for great things in that I would aid in the salvation of the church and in so doing save many souls. He implored me to be strong in my faith and to have great trust in God.

He said that my faith would lead me to the convent.

It was then that I asked him his name. He stood up and gazed down upon me with a Christ-like love and said "I'm Karol. Karol Wojtyla."

Then he blessed me and I woke up. I asked my father, "Poppa, who is Karol Wojtyla?" Good thing we were in the hospital because I think I nearly gave him a heart attack. Through tears, my father told me the man who visited me in my dream was Pope John Paul II, John Paul the Great! He explained that he and my mother had made a novena to our recently departed Pope, and *they had just finished it when I awoke from my coma.* When Momma came in with a plate of food, she looked over at Poppa and me and asked what happened.

While I was eating, Poppa took Momma out into the hall and told her what I had just told him. My mother was dumbfounded. Just a few hours ago, their daughter was dying, and now she was sitting up and eating, apparently healthy. They believed that my miraculous recovery was due to the intercession of Pope John Paul II.

"Could this miracle have been from the intercession of John Paul the Great? I was only nine years old when he died, so I didn't have any memory of the athletic, handsome pope in his early papacy. My memories of him were of a frail, sickly man, after a quarter century of rule, and I never knew his baptismal name.

"Six years later, when I approached my parents to enter the Convent, they gave their blessing. On October 13, 2013, I entered the Order of the Blessed Sacrament where I took the name Hedwig Peligia in honor of my grandmother and great-grandmother. I attended Katolicki Uniwersytet Lubelski Jana Pawla II where I majored in pharmacy earning my BS degree in 2016, my masters two years later, and my PhD in 2022. But May 8, 2020 was the happiest day of my life. It was on that day that I professed my final vows. My parents and siblings were all there as

I received the habit. For me, their loving presence only enhanced the joy of that day.

"My first assignment was as a pharmacist at the very hospital where, fourteen years earlier, I had almost died. Now, here I am. I love this life, but I could never forget my family, and the love and encouragement they gave, and still do give to me."

It was now Sylvia's turn to speak, "Mother, I *haven't* forgotten them. There isn't a moment of any day that I don't think of them. They are constantly in my prayers. I pray for their health and welfare, but it is not best for them to come to my profession."

Mother was concerned about her friend's choice but put it out of her mind. She had decided to leave it all up to God, who knew the end of all stories. Furthermore, the myriad responsibilities of her new office left little time for anything else. Soon Mother and Sylvia found themselves spending less and less time together.

After her profession, Sylvia was assigned to duty in the kitchen where she prepared meals for the members of the congregation and distributed leftovers to the poor of the neighborhood. Her skill in the kitchen brought her to the attention of the priests of the local parish. They often asked her to cook for major functions, like confirmations, or holy hours or whenever Bishop McHarden chose to visit the church. The Bishop had even asked her to cook the meal when Cardinal Bernadino visited the diocese from Rome.

As her reputation grew, Sylvia withdrew into herself more and more, becoming somewhat agoraphobic. Eventually, she requested to be relieved of her responsibility of cooking outside of the convent. Mother gave this great consideration. The donations that Sylvia's cooking brought in were a big help, but priorities demanded that Sylvia's health was more important. She granted the request and informed both the pastor and the bishop that, because of her health, Sister Sylvia would no longer be able to extend her services to them. They admitted their disappointment but supported their sister's wishes.

Thus, it came to pass that Sylvia remained in the convent and rarely ventured out of it. She continued to cook for the congregation, but the groceries were brought in. Some of the younger nuns had assumed the responsibilities of taking the leftovers to the local soup kitchen.

The years swiftly passed and life continued both within and without the convent's hallowed walls.

A persistent knocking on the door catapulted Mother out of her meditation. "Ave. Enter, with the Peace of God."

Sister Sylvia entered the room, completing the greeting, "And also with you. Sister Mary Phillip said that you wished to see me."

"Yes, Sister," Mother began, "Please, have a seat. I have something to tell you. I just spoke to your son Bernard. Sister, he told me that he has left several messages for you to call him. So far, you have not. Therefore he asked me to relay the message to you." Mother turned to see Sylvia, seated on the chair with the green upholstery, gazing up at her expectantly. Mother muttered a prayer under her breath before continuing, "It is with great sorrow that I must inform you that your son, Timothy, has died."

Sylvia dropped her hands into her lap, "What?"

"Sylvia, Tim is dead."

"How? When?"

"Your daughter, Bridget, found him Tuesday morning when she went to wake him for school. He had taken an overdose of sleeping pills."

Sylvia sat there, too stunned to move.

"Sister, your family needs you at this time."

Though anguished by the news she still would not relent, "Mother, I can't leave *even* for this. After my husband died, I vowed that once the children were raised, that I would dedicate the rest of my life to prayer and solitude. I *cannot* break that vow."

"Oh, poppycock. Stuff and nonsense. *Sister,* you have used the religious life as an escape, and this convent as a fortress against living. You buried your heart with your husband, and that has not been fair to *your* children, *this* order, *or* God.

"Martin would not have wanted you to lock yourself away and stop living and I know that God does not expect that sacrifice of you, either. Our doors do not lock us in, nor do they keep the world out. Even though we are apart from the world, we remain *a part of* the world. God gave you a loving husband, and blessed you with nine beautiful children who love you. Indeed, God has blessed you abundantly but you have turned your back on nine of those blessings. You can ignore them no longer.

"You are a member of this order, and I am its Mother Superior. You have taken the vow of obedience and under that vow I am *ordering* you to attend the funeral of your son!"

Sylvia pleaded, "Please Mother, don't force me to do this. I wouldn't even know what to *say* to them. It has been *so* long since…They're constantly in my prayers but I just don't think I can ever face them again."

"Sister, it will be difficult, no doubt. Don't worry, you won't face them alone. I will come with you. We have known each other for a long time, Sylvia. I have seen you through some rough times and guided your religious journey. I'll see you through this as well. I'll call Bernard and let him know of our plans. I think it best for us to meet with your children *before* the viewing. It will give you time to get to know each of them again. Now, get packing because we leave at noon."

"Yes, Mother." Sylvia was still in shock.

"Go with the peace of God, Sister," Mother said, picking up the phone to call Bernard and to make all of the necessary arrangements.

Sister Sylvia left the office and headed for her room to prepare for the most unexpected trip of her life.

DARK MEMORIES

June 10, 2045

T HE WAKE OCCURS between the time of death and the trans-
ference of the body to the Church. Generally, it is the evening before the burial and was commonplace in Ireland until the
1970s. The departed was viewed in the parlor or living room of
the home in which they had lived or died. Family and friends
gathered at the house to show their respect for the departed by
socializing, eating, drinking and telling stories about the deceased.
This wasn't a time for tears, but a time for celebrating one's life.
More of a party than a funeral, the wake's purpose was to ensure
a good send-off for the deceased.

The trip to the funeral home took about an hour. They arrived earlier than Sylvia had anticipated, but just as Mother had planned.
They parked the car and Sylvia hesitated getting out.

"I haven't been here since Martin's wake—the memories
of those dark days. I remember sitting in this very parking lot,
thinking about the impossibility of it all. I had nine children from
three to twenty. What was I to do? Bernard tried his best to take
his father's place and really was my rock. He greeted family and
friends, answering their questions.

"I don't know what I would have done without him. The girls
took care of the house and the preparations for the wake. I was
a basket case. Tim and Sam were just too young. They played

around the flowers, running in and out of the rooms, chasing each other down the hall. They didn't sit still the whole time. Sam loved to play with Martin's mustache, touching it and rubbing his cheek against it. Martin would tickle him with it and Sam would laugh. He almost toppled the casket, trying to get his dad to tickle him again," said Sister Sylvia.

"Mother, have I ever told you how Martin died?"

"No, you never have. You only told me he was killed in an accident at work."

"Martin had just finished work for the day. He was walking across the train yard when he noticed a large rock on the tracks. An express passenger train was coming and Martin quickly ran out to retrieve the rock as the train was bearing down on him. He quickly got out of the way, by pressing against the parked train on the next track, but as the train passed, something caught his overcoat, and he was dragged several hundred meters before the train stopped."

"When I got to the hospital, he was barely alive. He knew me, but he couldn't speak. They had him on oxygen, and there were tubes coming out from all parts of his body. I lifted the blanket to see the extent of his injuries. Mother, he had been nearly cut in half. I sat with him that entire night, the next day, and that night. The doctors and nurses tried to get me to go home to get some rest, but I couldn't leave my Martin.

"My oldest boys, Bernard, Sean, and Zephan were old enough to take care of their younger siblings and the oldest girls helped out. At 9:00 a.m., on the third day, Martin took a deep breath and died. That was almost thirty years ago. It's funny how some things come back to you. I remember it as though it were yesterday."

"After the funeral, I contacted the company about the insurance. Since Martin had died at work, I applied for his death benefit. The company lawyer called me and told me that, since Martin had clocked out for the day, he was not officially at work and the death benefit didn't apply. I told him that I didn't know how many lives Martin had saved on that train.

"He said that Martin should not have removed the rock. Imagine that! He expected Martin to leave that rock on the tracks and allow the train to crash, killing heaven knows how many people!"

"Mother, Martin had worked for that company more than twenty years, and this was how they treated his memory. They didn't even send flowers to the wake. I had to go to court to get the insurance, and that took months. Eventually, I got the settlement and paid off the house. I had enough to send all the kids to college. Martin always wanted them to be educated. They all earned Bachelor degrees most have Masters and of course, Sam is in medical school. I try not to be proud of them. I struggle with the sin of pride, and that is one reason I have limited my exposure to them."

"Pride is indeed a sin, but not in this case, sister. You did a very difficult job after Martin died and with our Lord's help, you did it well. God would want you to be proud of your children. Now, are you ready to go in?"

"Yes, I think so."

They were shown into the parlor next to where Tim lay, and were greeted by Bernard, Sean, Zepahn, Mary Agnes, Kathleen Ann, Bridget Marie, Rebecca Margaret, and Samuel. Mother stayed back as Sylvia was welcomed by her children with hugs, smiles, kisses and lots of tears. If it hadn't been that Tim was dead, it would have been a most wonderful, joyous reunion.

As Sylvia was speaking to Sam, she suddenly gasped and began to swoon.

"I need to get some air."

Sam took her by the arm, and as he led her outside, Mother assured the rest of the children that their mother was all right.

"Some years back she developed a bit of agoraphobia and is sometimes overwhelmed by crowds."

Standing in the garden, Sylvia looked at Sam and said, "I saw Tim."

"Yes, Mom! That's what we are here for, Tim's wake."

"No, I saw Tim playing around the flowers at your dad's casket."

"Mom, that's Tim IN the casket."

"I don't understand. Tim was just inside peeking from behind the flowers and your dad was in the casket."

"Oh, Mom, that little boy isn't Tim. That's Michael, Bernard's son. He's six and the spitting image of Tim at that age and just as mischievous. I can see how you would have made such a mistake."

The years melted away, as Sylvia remembered her husband's wake, again.

"So many years ago, but I remember it just like yesterday—all the family and friends offering their sympathy, the girls trying to be brave and attempting to get you and Tim to sit down and stop chasing each other. You nearly knocked over several baskets of flowers. Of all of you, Tim looks most like your father. Now, with his mustache, he looks just like your father at that age."

They sat down on the bench, overlooking the fountain and eternal pool.

"This is so overwhelming. I haven't seen you in so long and don't know who you are now. I remember you as children, but I don't know you as adults. I guess, I expected you to be the way you were when I entered the convent."

Even though Sam wanted to shout at her *Whose fault is that?* He bit his tongue, knowing that this reunion was as delicate as a spider's thread.

"Well, Mom, let me reintroduce you to your children, as adults."

He filled her in on the lives of her children and grandchildren.

"Sam, you told me about all the kids except for Tim. Why? Why did he take his own life? Am I to blame?"

"Mom, you left a deep hole behind and made it deeper with your exclusion of us from your life, but that is not why Tim committed suicide. The note he left explains it all. I brought it with me, if you want to read it."

He handed the letter to Sylvia, who took and read it. When she finished, she put her head on Sam's shoulder and cried. Sam put his arms around her.

After a few minutes, Sylvia composed herself. "Sam, am I responsible? Did my leaving caused this? You were all grown, and I didn't think you would need me any more. The convent was my escape from responsibility, the world, and life."

"Mom, we will always need you in our lives even if we are ninety. We love you and always will. Tim had an inner turmoil which he never let anyone see. He struggled for so long between two worlds, between heaven and hell. I can't imagine what he went through.

"It must have been real torture. But enough of this, we must remember Tim as the person he was—kind, loving, and gentle; a man, who dedicated his life to others; a respected chemistry teacher and coach.

"Even though he may not have recognized it, Tim touched many lives, and left them better off than before. This is the Tim I will remember. Now, people are beginning to arrive. We should go back in," said Sam.

The days of the wake were long, mixed with periods of intense sadness, and an even more intense joy at being reunited. The parlor was always packed with people. Mother, true to her word, stayed with Sylvia, supporting her, but allowing her the privacy she and her children so desperately needed.

Two of the many visitors were Sister Mary Theophane and Father O'Malley. They were greeted warmly by the family, all of whom had gone to school while Sister was principal. Father was not only their pastor, but also a close personal friend of the family.

"This is such a sad day, a very sad day indeed," Sister Theophane said greeting the O'Brien girls, hugging and giving each a kiss. "Where is your mother?"

"She is in the other room with Mother Hedwig Peligia," Rebecca answered.

"Mother is here? I didn't realize she knew any of you."

"She doesn't, but she came to support Mom. From what we gathered, she and Mom are close. They became friends when Mom was a postulant and Mother was her mistress of novices. She didn't want Mom to be alone at this time."

"That is just like Mother—always thinking of others. I was in the postulant and novitiate class the year before her. She was the prettiest postulant and novice the order has ever had. In habit or out, Mother, is a flawless beauty. Her coal black hair shimmered bluish in the sun. When they cut it, at her profession, she donated it for wigs to 'Hair for Kids with Cancer', Mother is a wonderful person. Excuse me while I go say hello."

It was an exhausting time. When the last guest left the house after the wake, little time was left for the family to say their good-byes. Again, there were tears, kisses, and long hugs, before Sylvia and Mother left for the convent. Promises were made, and kept, to keep in touch. Sister Sylvia had finally realized the selfishness of her actions, and deeply regretted the years they had missed, and that she would never be able to make amends to Tim.

On the drive back to the convent, Sylvia looked at Mother and asked,

"Mother, what about Tim's soul?"

"What about his soul?"

"Mother, I fear for him?"

"Why?"

"Not only was he homosexual, he committed suicide. Isn't his soul damned?"

"Sister, in the past, those who committed suicide were often denied a Church funeral, but this was not a judgment of the deceased's eternal destiny. The Church has always offered Masses for those who have committed suicide but a Church funeral was denied in order to avoid giving scandal to the faithful and to emphasize the grave nature of suicide."

"As in the past, the Church teaches that suicide is and always will be objectively and gravely wrong, but today, she better understands the psychological disturbances that may influence a suicide; and thus, mitigate personal culpability. This being the case, those who, like Tim, take their lives are now typically provided funerals and may attain eternal salvation.

"The catechism of the Catholic Church, states 'We should not despair of the eternal salvation of persons who have taken their own lives. By ways known to him alone, God can provide the opportunity for salutary repentance," said Mother.

"As for Tim's homosexuality, I understand that Tim had never practiced the act. The Church does not condemn the individual, only the act. 'Hate the sin, but love the sinner.' Tim was a good man and I do not fear for his eternal soul, and neither should you. You must remember him with love and joy. It is God who judges."

IN JERUSALEM
A CHILD IS BORN

January 1, 2000

New York Times
Thursday,
January 25, 2001

The Y2K Fizzle

The Year 2000 problem, also known as Y2K, was the result of a practice in early computer program design that caused some date-related processing to operate incorrectly for dates and times on and after January 1, 2000, causing widespread concern that critical industries and government functions could cease operating at the stroke of midnight on December 31, 1999. Some people thought that it meant the end of the world and built bunkers stocking them with bottled water, canned goods, and toilet paper to ride out the eminent disaster they knew would come. It didn't happen. Companies and organizations worldwide checked and upgraded their computer systems, insuring that no significant computer failures occurred when the clocks struck midnight and the New Year was ushered in.

JOSHUA ABRAHAM HIEM was born in Jerusalem New Years Day 2000, the day many thought would be the end of the world, the first baby born in Jerusalem that year.

His mother and father, Sarah and Elias Hiem, grew up in the United States in very orthodox Jewish families. Sarah's grandparents Benjamin and Salomea Urbach had been married in Krakow, Poland on June 2, 1938. They went happily about building their lives together until the fall of Poland to the Germans on September 1, 1939. They managed to evade capture by staying in the woods and relying on the generosity of gentiles, particularly Catholics.

Their luck held out until December 12, 1944, when they were turned over to the Germans by Heinrich von Borne. He and his wife Margaret were farmers who had been helping to feed and hide them. Heinrich blamed Benjamin and Salomea for his wife's death. While in town, she had been accosted by a German soldier, who accused her of being a "Jew lover."

He violently attacked, raped and left her for dead. When Heinrich found her, she was too weak to say anything but "Benjamin and Salomea" while she died in his arms. She had wanted to be sure that they were safe, but Heinrich, took it as an accusation. Benjamin was sent to Plaszow concentration camp, but was lucky enough to be one of the 700 Jews transferred to an adjacent factory compound, owned by Oscar Schindler. There he was relatively safe from the depredations of the German guards, but Benjamin's every waking hour was filled with thoughts and worries about his wife. Eventually, the opportunity presented itself for him to speak with Schindler himself. He pleaded his case and begged him to find his wife and save her.

Through much work and effort, the couple was reunited on April 3, 1945. Salomea was thin, weak, and in poor health, but found strength in her Benjamin. When the war ended, the couple fled to the United States, making their home in the Lower East Side of New York, where there was a budding Orthodox Jewish population. There they raised their family. Both Benjamin, who died on September 30, 1979, and Salomea on May 8, 1980, were blessed to see their children's children.

Elias's grandparents Moses and Anna Blumenfrucht immigrated to New York in 1935, shortly after Adolf Hitler's rise to the post of Fuhrer. When Hitler took power, Jews were barred from civil service, legal professions, and universities. They were not allowed to teach in schools nor be editors of newspapers. Various laws were enacted to force Jews out of schools and professions. Moses saw the writing on the wall and fled his native country, taking his wife and children with him. Shortly after they left, the Nazis passed the Nuremberg Laws restricting citizenship to those of "German or related blood," and Jews became countryless.

Because of the sacrifices of their grandparents, Sarah Urbach and Elias Hiem were born and grew up in the Lower East Side of New York. Elias was born November 30, 1971 and Sarah on December 14, 1971. As neighbors and also childhood sweethearts, they attended the same schools, playing games with their mutual set of friends. Sarah was an honored guest at Elias's bar mitzvah as he was at her bat mitzvah. When the time came, each decided to attend New York University, she studying Jewish history, and he majoring in international law. Both had always had a religious fervor, but toward the end of their junior year, it flamed into a religious zeal.

While watching TV one evening in 1992, they came across the documentary, "Israel, A Nation Is Born" hosted by Abba Eban, an Israeli diplomat, politician and Middle East expert, whose polished presentations, grasp of history, and powerful speeches gave him authority even in the United Nations at times when it was generally skeptical and even hostile to Israel.

As they watched, Eban brought the history of the State of Israel alive examining key events of the nation's life—beginning with its inception at the close of World War II. The series showed behind the scenes and archival film footage interspersed with Eban's expert commentary on the Six Day and Yom Kippur Wars, and the historic Peace Accord between Israel and Egypt.

The series ignited the smoldering ember of their desire to know and experience their Jewish heritage.

Enthralled, the couple realized only a trip to the Holy Land could satisfy that longing. Over the next couple of weeks the feeling only became stronger, so they decided to leave NYU and spend their senior year in Jerusalem. They made a one year commitment to live and work at Barkai, an Israeli kibbutz in the Menashe Regional Council on the western side of Wadi Ara. Knowing the dangers, their parents were not happy, but in the end they gave their blessing.

Life at the Kibbutz was austere and very different from what they were accustomed to in the United States, but neither seemed to mind. Sarah and Elias were adopted by a member family who generally saw to their needs of companionship and guidance into the way of life of the kibbutz. The year went by quickly and all too soon they were on a plane back to the United States.

Elias went to law school and Sarah received her Master's in Art Appreciation. They were married on June 20, 1997, the happiest day of their lives. Even so, they could not stop thinking about their time at the kibbutz. On October 14, 1998, as the family was leaving the sukkah, Sarah's father concluded with the recitation of the traditional prayer: "May it be your will, Lord our God and God of our forefathers, that just as I have fulfilled and dwelled in this sukkah, so may I merit in the coming year to dwell in *the sukkah of the skin of Leviathan.*

Next year in Jerusalem," Sarah broke the news. She and Elias had decided to live in Jerusalem which had so totally filled the void in their lives. They knew that was where they wanted to live and raise their family.

"Is this a joke?" Sarah's father, Zachariah asked.

"No! Elias and I have given this a great deal of thought. We were never happier than when we lived at the kibbutz. I can't explain it, Daddy. I felt whole, complete in the Holy Land."

"What about suicide bombings and terrorist attacks?" Ruth, her mother, asked immediately bringing out the big guns. "They happen at the markets and don't forget about the tension between the Palestinians and the Jews. You could be killed just doing your shopping. Or worse, what if you are maimed? You would be thousands of miles away. Who'll be there for you?"

"God! Isn't that what we believe? Isn't that faith? Don't we give thanks to him for every blessing received during each day? What better place to live than in the land God gave to Abraham and our ancestors?"

"Elias, do something. She'll listen to you," Ruth implored Elias.

"There's nothing to say. We'll be safe with God's help."

Ruth and Zachariah realized that their daughter and son-in-law had made up their minds, and nothing would change it. Their parents continued to plead with them, but to no avail.

Sarah and Elias had already contacted the family who hosted them at the kibbutz. They found them a house in the Jewish Quarter of the Old City and the couple found themselves in Jerusalem for Chanukah in 1998. Sarah realized she was expecting in June of 1999, and the couple anxiously awaited the arrival of their first child.

A HOLOCAUST OF HIS OWN

The era of extreme Jewish intellectualism is now at an end. The breakthrough of the German revolution has again cleared the way on the German path…The future German man will not just be a man of books, but a man of character. It is to this end that we want to educate you. As a young person, to already have the courage to face the pitiless glare, to overcome the fear of death, and to regain respect for death—this is the task of this young generation. And thus, you do well in this midnight hour to commit to the flames the evil spirit of the past. This is a strong, great, and symbolic deed—a deed which should document the following for the world to know—here the intellectual foundation of the November (Democratic) Republic is sinking to the ground, but from this wreckage the phoenix of a new spirit will triumphantly rise.

Nazi Propaganda Minister Joseph Goebbels

JOSHUA GREW UP surrounded by the history of his ancestors. His mother took him to visit historical sites and he grew to love history. They visited the Israel Museum in West Jerusalem, the Bible Lands Museum, Mount Herzel and Herzel Museum, the Sanhedrian Tombs, the Tombs of the Prophets, Wohl Archeological Museum and Burnt House.

But his favorite site of all was Yad VaShem Memorial and Holocaust Museum. He would spend hours there, reading the text, looking at the pictures of families in happy times, interlaced with pictures of unspeakable brutality. The exhibit of the cattle car on broken tracks often brought him to tears. Even at a young age, Joshua could vividly imagine this car packed with Jews going to their slaughter. For him, the broken tracks represented the broken dreams, future and lives of more than six million Jews. He could almost hear the sobs of the people inside, see them staring in wide eyed horror from between the boards, pleading for the help that, for most, would never come. His mother would often have to pull him away.

The exhibit that hunted him the most was that of the book burning, detailing an event unseen since the Middle Ages, of German students gathering to burn books with "un-German" ideas. Books by Freud, Einstein, Mann, London, and Wells all went up in flames. Over the speaker, Joshua heard the words of the Nazi Propaganda Minister Joseph Goebbels. Under the exhibit was inscribed the words of the German-Jewish poet, Heinrich Heine. Joshua read and re-read these words taking them to heart.

"Where books are burned, human beings are destined to be burned too."

He vowed that that would never happen again.

His mother died when Joshua was twelve and in the years that followed, he kept up the tradition they began, of visiting the sites of their ancestors every Sunday. Without her vigilance, though, it was inevitable that he should venture beyond the city walls and be touched by the history of the Christian, Catholic Church as well. Even though his mother would never take him there, he began to visit sites like the Church of the Birth of Christ, the Garden Tomb, the Church of St. John, the Condemnation Chapel and Chapel of Flagellation, The Grotto of the Apostles and Mary's Tomb, and The Sanctuary of Dominus Flevit, where Jesus wept over Jerusalem. Joshua loved this place and would sit there for hours looking over the tremendous view of the Old City. Here, he found peace and contentment.

He also developed new friends, friends who were not of the Jewish faith. One of them was Wajeeh Nuseibeh, the doorkeeper of the Church of the Holy Sepulcher and keeper of the keys. During one of his visits, Joshua asked Wajeeh how he, a Muslim, came to have that job.

"Well, Joshua, the control of this church has been zealously guarded by the Greek Orthodox, Roman Catholics, Armenians, and Copts. Each oversees different parts of the Church and none trusts the others. In the twelfth century, fighting among different denominations over who should keep the key to the church, led the Arab conqueror Saladin to entrust the key to the families of Nuseibeh and Joudeh, who were Muslims and therefore had no intimate ties to the Church. Today, eight centuries later, the ten-inch metal key is still safeguarded by my family, the Nuseibeh family. Each morning at dawn, I take the key and open the massive wooden church doors. Then, every night at 8:00 p.m., I return to shut and lock them."

"Israel had tried to convince the Christian denominations to open a second exit to the Church for safety reasons. You see, Josh, in 1840 there was a devastating fire that caused a panic which led to many deaths. Israeli officials became increasingly concerned about the danger they anticipated by the crush of tourists expected to arrive for the celebrations of 2000. An agreement was finally reached in June of 1999 to open another exit, but that provoked a new dispute over who would have the key to the new door. Fortunately, it fell to the Wajeeh Nuseibeh, my father. Now I hold both keys."

A year after Sarah's death, unbeknownst to Joshua, Elias began dating again. In time, he began to see more and more of Ester

Gottlieb, a paralegal in the law firm where Elias was a partner. As they became closer, Elias decided it was time Joshua meet Ester. He sat down with his son to explain.

"Joshua, I need to talk with you. Your mom has been gone for more than a year now. First I want you to know how much I loved her and always will. She was my first love, and I thought that I could never love again, but, Josh, I have been seeing someone for several months now."

"I know, Dad!"

"How do you know?"

"I'm thirteen, Dad, not stupid. I've know you've been dating for a while now."

"I've tried to be so careful."

"That's the problem. You tried too hard. So who is she?"

"Ester Gottlieb, from the office."

"I like her. She's always been nice to me. She did so much for us at mom's funeral, but I'm not calling her mom. It would feel like I am betraying her."

"I don't expect you to. Besides, it's way too early in our relationship to be planning a wedding. I wanted to clear the air with you and promise to keep you in the loop from now on."

"Thanks. I saw how unhappy you were after Mom died. Then, about two months ago, you changed. You began to laugh again. That's when I first knew something was up. I'm glad for you. As the Torah says: 'It is not good for man to be alone.'"

"Thanks, Josh. How did you get to be so wise? It must be from your mom. I couldn't even keep dating a secret from you. I want to invite Ester to have dinner with the two of us. Do you mind?"

"I want you to be happy, Dad."

"So where do you want to eat?"

"Let's make something here."

As the relationship between Elias and Ester deepened, Joshua began contemplating a future which would include less and less of his father. After his bar mitzvah, he began spending more time walking alone through the Old City.

On June 2, 2014, Elias and Ester announced their engagement. In spite of his feelings of alienation from the intimacy he and his father had shared, he truly liked Ester and looked forward to the wedding and being best man. A week before the wedding, though, when Josh came home from school, he noticed something was different about the living room. He couldn't put his finger on it right away, but soon it came to him. The picture above the fireplace had been replaced. Sarah had painted it for Joshua just before she died. It was her last painting, a painting of the old olive grove where she and Joshua would sit eating lunch while observing visitors. In the trunk of one of the trees, Sarah had painted in the ridges of the bark, the likeness of her son, and lovingly gazing down on him from within the branches above, her own likeness. You couldn't see it, unless you were really looking for it, and the pair told no one their secret, not even Elias. Joshua loved keeping this secret with his mom and was pleased when she put it in the most prominent place in the house.

After her death, he would often sit gazing at the picture reminiscing about the times they had spent together. He believed that the painting had foreshadowed her death. Even now he felt she was looking down on him, not from the olive branches but from heaven.

Elias had left things pretty much the same when Sarah died, but now the picture was gone. Joshua searched the house for it, going through closets, in the crawl spaces, and under the beds, but could not find it. When Elias came home, Josh asked about it.

"Dad, where is mom's painting?"

"Which one, son? She painted quite a few."

"Her last one, the one of the old olive grove, the one that hung above the mantle."

"I didn't think you'd have noticed that it was gone."

"Well, I did! Where is it?"

"I gave it to Ester as a wedding present. She has always admired it, and I thought it would make the perfect gift."

"You had no right! That picture was mine! Mom painted it for ME. It was mine. Every time I looked at it, I remember her, and how much she loved me. Now it is gone! She's in the branches and I'm in the bark. It was our secret, and now it's gone."

Before Elias could ask what he meant, Joshua stormed out of the house, banging the door loudly behind him. He wandered around for a while finally founding himself in the old olive grove. He sat beneath the old gnarled tree that had been their favorite and cried.

Geoffrey Snyder had been touring the sites and was wandering around the garden when he noticed Joshua in his misery. He approached him.

"What's the matter?" he asked gently sitting near him.

"Nothing," Joshua sniffled in reply.

"My name is Geoffrey Snyder. What's yours?"

"Josh, Joshua Hiem."

"Nice to meet you Joshua. Do you come here often?"

"I used to come here with my mom, but she died."

As they talked, Joshua began to feel comfortable with the young man.

"Oh, I'm sorry. How did she die?"

"She had a major cardiac infarction."

"A heart attack."

"Yeah."

"How long ago did she die?"

"About two years ago, and I still miss her. Dad is getting married again next week."

"And you don't like her. You resent her taking the place of your mother."

"Hardly. I really like Ester and want dad to be happy. She does make him happy and I'm glad. I won't... can't call her mom though. Just Ester."

"Then, why were you crying?"

"I just found out what dad gave Ester as a wedding present. You see, it was a painting that my mom had done. It hung above the mantle. It was a painting of this spot. Mom had secretly placed a picture of me in the bark of the tree and her picture in the branches. It was my picture. Dad had no right to give it away."

"Did he know that it was your picture? Did you ever tell him about it?"

"No."

"Then how can you be angry with him? Have you sat down and talked with him about how you feel?"

"No, I was too upset and just... kind of stormed out."

"I think that you should talk with your dad before things really get out of hand. Explain it to him."

With the ice broken, they began to talk about other things. Geoffrey told him about his life. He was twenty years old and was living with his parents, who were missionaries. They had come to Israel earlier that year. Geoffrey was attending the university where he was studying to be a youth minister. He told Joshua that he really didn't like missionary work, but it was a passion for his parents. Since he was an only child, and his grandparents were gone, he had no one to stay with back home in the States.

"My parents were older when they had me. They had tried to have children earlier in their marriage but with no success. Mom had been pregnant five times before me, but could not carry the baby to term. When she learned she was expecting me, she did something she had never thought about doing her entire life. A close friend, who was Catholic, told her about Saint Ann, Mary's mother, Jesus's grandmother. She gave her a novena to Saint Ann and told mom that she was the patron saint of expectant mothers. Together, they prayed the novena for nine days.

"Mom was skeptical but was willing to try anything. They prayed the novena monthly, and believe it or not, her pregnancy went on without a hitch. The third month passed without mishap, then the fourth, fifth, and sixth. By this time, with the other pregnancies, she had already lost the child. The seventh month came and went, as did the eighth and finally the ninth. I was born on July 26, the feast of Saint Ann. That is too much of a coincidence for her to not have helped.

"Mom has believed in Saint Ann ever since. Even though we are not Catholic, Mom asked Judy, her Catholic friend, to be my godmother. Judy died last year, right before we came here. She was a wonderful woman and never forced her beliefs on us. I know she would have liked to see me convert, but she loved me just the same," said Geoffrey.

The old priest, who cared for the garden, approached the pair.

"Gentlemen, it is getting dark, and I have to lock the gates."

The two reluctantly got up and left, but before they parted company, they made plans to meet again later that week.

When Joshua got home, his dad was waiting for him. Joshua spoke first.

"I'm sorry that I ran out. I should have stayed and talked things out man to man."

"Son, I want you to go into the living room and have a seat on the couch."

"Why?"

"Just go!"

Joshua did as his dad had commanded. He sat down on the couch, and almost jumped out of it when he looked toward the mantle. There was his picture. It was back.

"How? I thought you had given it to Ester."

"When you left, I called Ester and went over there. I looked at the picture, really looked at it, and I understood what you had said when you left. I saw the bark, I saw the branches. I showed Ester and she told me that she couldn't accept this picture, that it was rightfully yours and that I should take it back. So here it is. It won't leave that spot until you get married and have a place of your own. I'm sorry son. I didn't know."

"I'm sorry too, Dad. I should have said something instead for running away. I acted like a baby, not a man. I should have told you what Mom put in the picture, but I didn't want to share it. I had a small piece of Mom that belonged to no one but me, and I liked that."

"I don't know how I could have missed it. Knowing it is there makes it so obvious now."

Joshua's friendship with Geoffrey grew and the two could often be found in the Garden of Gethsemane. There they talked about everything—from the latest songs to world politics, but always their conversations turned to religion. Geoffrey spoke to Joshua about Jesus Christ, the only begotten Son of God.

"He was born a Jew, like you. In his brief lifetime, he fulfilled hundreds of years of Jewish prophesy that predicted the coming and activities of the Messiah as recorded in the *Old Testament*, the *Torah*. I believe he is also God himself since Jesus dropped several clues to that end, one being when he said '...before the world began, I Am.' As you know, 'I Am' is one of the names of God. You also know that 'Yahweh' literally means 'I Am' in Hebrew.

'Jesus' is the Greek version of the Hebrew 'Yeshua', Joshua, your namesake, which means "Yahweh Saves."

"You see, Joshua, Christians believe that God exists as three entities: God the Father, Jesus—God the Son, and God the Holy Spirit. This is the 'Holy Trinity.' In spite of this, like you, we believe that the three entities are parts of just one God. The basic principle of Christianity is that everyone sins at one time or another. Since God hates sin, a sinner can't get into heaven. Jesus, though sinless himself, redeemed us by taking on the sins of the world. For a brief time, he 'became sin.' During that time, he was crucified and died on a cross for a crime he didn't commit. Now, those who repent their sins and accept him as their redeemer and savior can go to heaven."

Geoffrey evangelized—explaining Christianity to Joshua and he began to believe. On Christmas Eve, 2014, as a light snow gently fell into the Garden Gethsemane, Joshua told Geoffrey that he believed in Jesus, and was ready to accept him as his Lord and Savior. Geoffrey was ecstatic. It was late, and Geoffrey hugged Joshua.

"How appropriate! This is where our Lord began his passion, and it is where you have begun your journey to Christianity. I am so pleased, Joshua. It's late, and your dad will wonder where you are. Go home now. I'll see you tomorrow. We will discuss your baptism."

"Aren't you coming?" Joshua asked.

"No, I want to pray and offer my thanksgiving for your conversion. God's peace be with you, Joshua. Have a good night's sleep."

When Joshua did not hear from Geoffrey the next day or the day after, he decided to go to his home. There, his frantic parents told him they had not seen him since early afternoon on Christmas Eve. They had already contacted the police but they were now getting ready to go and file the report. Joshua went with them.

PEACE OR WAR?

January 2, 2015

A Miracle in the Middle East

November 23, 2012

"A miracle has occurred" said a leading Palestinian peace negotiator. "A peace agreement has finally been reached with Israel. The decades-old conflict is at an end."

Speaking in the West Bank on Monday, Ahmad Alsenwar, said the two sides had reached an agreement on all the major issues at the heart of their sixty-year-old conflict. The gaps had been filled to the satisfaction of both sides.

Israel and Palestine renewed peace talks at a US-hosted summit in November 2006 in Annapolis, Maryland, where they vowed to try to come to an agreement by the end of 2008. At that time little progress had been made, and there were doubts the goal could ever be reached.

US Secretary of State Condoleezza Rice remained steadfast that the US-backed peace talks offered the best chance for a meaningful settlement of the six-decade conflict. She stressed the need for the process to continue with the next president.

Nearly four years after the projected deadline, the agreement was finally hammered out.

"Everyone is pleased with the result. It has been a long and difficult road." said Alsenwar.

A WEEK AFTER GEOFFREY'S disappearance, the Snyders received a package in the mail. There was no note, just a DVD. They put it in the player and watched. The image showed several hooded men in black with automatic weapons, milling around two men, seated and tied sided by side. Agnes and John recognized both men. Geoffrey was to the left of Zaahir, one of their Muslim converts. They hadn't seen Zaahir in several weeks. He looked emaciated and thin, and he had been severely beaten. His eyes were blackened and almost swollen shut, and his jaw was broken. Agnes dropped heavily to her chair and her bottom lip began to tremble. As the DVD progressed, the leader spoke:

"Because you have violated, without provocation, the sanctity of our home with your western culture and religion, we have no recourse but to take matters into our own hands. Allah's will be done."

With that, one of the gunmen placed the barrel of his gun to the forehead of the convert and pulled the trigger.

Agnes broke into tears and was on the verge of fainting. John stood there dumbfounded. The leader went on:

"You, John and Agnes Snyder, are responsible for the death of this man because it was you who converted him away from his Muslim faith. You killed my son and so..."

Neither heard what the leader was saying next. Everything seemed to be happening in slow motion. Another gunman took his gun, aimed it at the head of Geoffrey and pulled the trigger. They saw the back of his skull explode out with a rush of blood and brains mingling with those of the convert, and Geoffrey slumped lifeless in his chair.

Two days later the bodies were found unceremoniously dropped beneath an olive tree in the garden where Geoffrey had been abducted. When the police called to ask the Snyders to identify the body of their son, John wanted to go alone. Agnes insisted on going with him. Nothing would change her mind.

John and Agnes decided to take Geoffrey home to the states and retire from missionary service. The cost was just too great to bear.

Joshua was devastated by the news of his close friend's death. He blamed himself: if only he had stayed with him a little longer that night, or walked home with him. He also blamed himself on a spiritual level, too. It was that night that Joshua had told Geoffrey that he wanted to convert to Christianity.

He looked on Geoff's death as punishment for wanting to leave the faith of his ancestors. He resolved that night to never think of converting again. Still, he would never forget Geoffrey, and the friendship he had shown him.

Two years later, Joshua graduated high school and began a year service to Israel as a soldier. The time went by quickly, and Joshua soon found himself at the university where he double majored in history and Greek, with a minor in Latin. His olive skin, high cheekbones, close set dark gray eyes, and black hair made him a striking figure, as he walked the campus in his black suit, white shirt, and thin black tie he always wore.

Because he constantly wore a black yarmulke, many non-Jews thought him to be Hasidic. He tirelessly and patiently explained the difference. Graduating Summa Cum Laude, he was swamped with offers to attend universities from around the world to study for his PhD. He chose Cambridge. His dissertation was "The History of the Interaction between the Jewish, Christian, and Muslim Faiths, from AD 1,000 to AD 2000, Concentrating on Parallels Between the Crusades and Modern Day Religious Conflicts.

THE SONS OF ABRAHAM

May 20, 2020

Now Sarai Abram's wife bore him no children: and she had a handmaid, an Egyptian, whose name was Hagar. And Sarai said unto Abram, Behold now, the *Lord* hath restrained me from bearing: I pray thee, go in unto my maid; it may be that I may obtain children by her. And Abram hearkened to the voice of Sarai. And Sarai Abram 's wife took Hagar her maid the Egyptian, after Abram had dwelt ten years in the land of Canaan, and gave her to her husband Abram to be his wife. And he went in unto Hagar, and she conceived: and when she saw that she had conceived, her mistress was despised in her eyes... Abram said unto Sarai, Behold, thy maid is in thine hand; do to her as it pleaseth thee. And when Sarai dealt hardly with her, she fled from her face.

And the angel of the *Lord* found her by a fountain of water in the wilderness, by the fountain in the way to Shur... Return to thy mistress, and submit thyself under her hands. And the angel of the Lord said unto her, I will multiply thy seed exceedingly, that it shall not be numbered for multitude. And the angel of the *Lord* said unto her, Behold, thou art with child and shalt bear a son, and shalt call his name Ishmael; because the *Lord* hath heard thy affliction. And he will be a wild man; his hand will be against every man, and every man's hand against him; and he shall dwell in the presence of all his brethren. And Hagar bore Abram a son.

Sarah conceived, and bore Abraham a son in his old age, at the set time of which God had spoken to him. And

Abraham called the name of his son that was born unto him, whom Sarah bore to him, Isaac... And the child grew, and was weaned: and Abraham made a great feast the same day that Isaac was weaned.

And Sarah saw the son of Hagar the Egyptian, which she had born unto Abraham, mocking. Wherefore she said unto Abraham, Cast out this bondwoman and her son: for the son of this bondwoman shall not be heir with my son, even with Isaac. And the thing was very grievous in Abraham's sight because of his son. And God said unto Abraham, Let it not be grievous in thy sight because of the lad, and because of thy bondwoman; in all that Sarah hath said unto thee, hearken unto her voice; for in Isaac shall thy seed be called. And also of the son of the bondwoman will I make a nation, because he is thy seed And Abraham rose up early in the morning, and took bread, and a bottle of water, and gave it unto Hagar, putting it on her shoulder, and the child, and sent her away: and she departed, and wandered in the wilderness of Beersheba.

And the water was spent in the bottle, and she cast the child under one of the shrubs. And she went, and sat her down over against him a good way off, as it were a bow shot: for she said, Let me not see the death of the child. And she sat over against him, and lift up her voice, and wept. And God heard the voice of the lad; and the angel of God called to Hagar out of heaven, and said unto her, What aileth thee, Hagar? fear not; for God hath heard the voice of the lad where he is. Arise, lift up the lad, and hold him in thine hand; for I will make him a great nation. And God opened her eyes, and she saw a well of water; and she went, and filled the bottle with water, and gave the lad drink. And God was with the lad; and he grew, and dwelt in the wilderness, and became an archer. And he dwelt in the wilderness of Paran: and his mother took him a wife out of the land of Egypt.

Genesis 16: 1–16, 21: 2 – 21 (KJV)

"AAMIR AABAN WAQQAS, why are you persecuting the seed of my brother, Isaac?"

"Who are you?"

"I am Ishmael. Why are you persecuting the seed of my brother Isaac?"

"I... I haven't! I don't know what you are talking about."

"My descendants, the Muslims, are persecuting Israel. They are killing their brothers by suicide bombings, and murder. The hatred must stop! By doing nothing, Aamir, you *Are* killing Israel, my brother's seed."

"What do you wish me to do?"

"Tell your leaders that if the madness does not stop, the Dome of the Rock will be destroyed. Not one stone will be left upon another. Tell them Aamir, tell them."

Aamir awoke in his bed at home in Turkey. He was covered in sweat. It was a dream, only a dream. Who was he that Ishmael should come to him?

He was only a simple Muslim, nothing more. He had no relationship with the powerful leaders. He was less than dung under their sandals. What could he do? He was nothing in their eyes!

Then, he remembered the prophecy from the Koran. The end-time will not be shown to the wise but to the simple. If he were anything at all, Aamir was simple. His father had always told him that he would be important some day, but Aamir never quite believed that. His name translated 'civilized angel warrior'. His father was right. Aamir was to be the angel who was to reunite Abraham's children. Indeed he was to be the civilized angel warrior.

"Who do you think you are, Waqqas coming to me with your dreams? You are nothing. Why would Ishmael choose to speak through you, a nobody? Why wouldn't he choose me, or one of the other powerful leaders? I am infinitely more qualified and deserving of that honor than you. Many an infidel has met his fate at my hands. What have you done for Allah? I'll tell you Aamir, nothing. Now, get out of here with your talk of dreams, or I will personally dispatch you to your ancestors."

And so it went. Aamir got nowhere. Rejected by the leaders Aamir began to preach in the courtyard of the Dome of the Rock, to anyone who would listen. Most thought him mad, some listened but dismissed his message. Others heard the message and took it to heart, getting as far from the Dome of the Rock as possible.

DESTRUCTION

Josephus acted as a mediator for the Romans. When negotiations failed, he witnessed the siege and aftermath. He wrote:

Now as soon as the army had no more people to slay or to plunder, because there remained none to be the objects of their fury (for they would not have spared any, had there remained any other work to be done), Titus Caesar gave orders that they should now demolish the entire city and Temple, but he should leave as many of the towers standing as they were of the greatest eminence; that is, Phasaelus, and Hippicus, and Mariamne; and so much of the wall enclosed the city on the west side. This wall was spared, in order to afford a camp for such as were to lie in garrison in the Upper City, as were the towers, the three forts, also spared, in order to demonstrate to posterity what kind of city it was, and how well fortified, which the Roman valor had subdued; but for all the rest of the wall surrounding Jerusalem, it was so thoroughly laid even with the ground by those that dug it up to the foundation, that there was left nothing to make those that came thither believe Jerusalem had ever been inhabited. This was the end which Jerusalem came to by the madness of those that were for innovations; a city otherwise of great magnificence, and of mighty fame among all mankind.

And truly, the very view itself was a melancholy thing; for those places which were adorned with trees and pleasant gardens, were now become desolate country every way, and its trees were all cut down. Nor could any foreigner

that had formerly seen Judaea and the most beautiful sub-
urbs of the city, and now saw it as a desert, but lament and
mourn sadly at so great a change. For the war had laid
all signs of beauty quite waste. Nor had anyone who had
known the place before, had come on a sudden to it now,
would he have known it again. But though he [a foreigner]
were at the city itself, yet would he have inquired for it.

Josephus claimed that 1,100,000 people were killed
during the siege, of which a majority were Jewish. About
97,000 were captured and enslaved, including Simon Bar
Giora and John of Gischala. Many fled to areas around
the Mediterranean. Titus reportedly refused to accept a
wreath of victory, as there is "no merit in vanquishing *people forsaken by their own God.*"

AND RE-GROWTH

DURING AD 7, the Muslim world was torn between two rival
Caliphs: Abdal-Malik and Abd Allah ibn Zubayr. By AD
692, Caliph Abd Allah ibn Zubayr was ruler of most of what is
now Iraq and Arabia and had taken control of the city of Mecca,
making it his capital. This forced Caliph Abdal-Malik to look
for an alternate capital for his caliphate—a place that would lure
Muslim pilgrims away from Mecca. He chose the site Haram al
Sharif in Jerusalem to build this shrine for pilgrims. Called the
Dome of the Rock, it enclosed the site where Muhammad experienced his 'Night Journey'.

Construction occurred between AD 687 and AD 691 although
the beginning date is somewhat in dispute, some placing it as early
as AD 685. Twenty meters high and ten meters in diameter, the
dome is an inspiring example of creative aptitude. The supporting
structures are made from lead and were originally covered in pure
gold. Over the years the gold has been removed and replaced by
anodized aluminum. The sacred foundation stone is encircled by

sixteen arches taken from Jerusalem churches destroyed during the Persian occupation of AD 614.

The Dome is a shrine for pilgrims, not a place for public worship. Adjacent to the Dome is the Al-Aqsa Mosque where the faithful make their prayers.

On May 20, 2020 a group of Muslim clerics began accosting Aamir, pushing and hitting him, trying to make him stop his preaching. At exactly 3:00 p.m. a violent earthquake of magnitude 8.5 hit the area, lasting several minutes. Miraculously, the only damage was the complete destruction of the Dome of the Rock. Not one stone was left upon another. Buildings to the right and to the left, in front and in back, were left completely intact. An earthquake of this magnitude should have leveled all of Jerusalem. Aamir and those who were accosting him were killed as the front wall fell upon them. That day, Aamir lived up to his name.

The Muslim leaders gathered and realized that Aamir had been treated extremely unfairly. He had indeed been contacted by Ishmael, and they decided that something must be done. Ishmael's message was one of reconciliation with Israel. The time had come for an end to the violence and hatred. The brothers must reconcile.

Negotiations began with Israel. Years later Israel agreed to help rebuild the Dome of the Rock, but in Mecca. Work began in 2035 and was completed in 2045. In return, Israel was given complete rights to the land on which the Dome of the Rock and the second Temple had once stood. Things were now in place for the rebuilding of the Temple.

The Sanhedrin hired an architect and plans for the Temple were drawn up and redrawn. Everything had to be just as it was in the second Temple. Things were progressing nicely, but two things were lacking. A kosher red heifer had to be born and the ashes of the last red heifer needed to be found.

SERENDIPITY

August 11, 2045

T HE UNITED NATIONS provides opportunities for students enrolled in a graduate program to undertake an internship at its Headquarters in New York. The objective of the Internship Program is threefold:

1. to provide a framework by which graduate and post-graduate students from diverse academic backgrounds may be assigned to United Nations Offices where their educational experience can be enhanced through practical work assignments;
2. to expose them to the work of the United Nations and,
3. to provide UN offices with the assistance of highly quali-fied students specialized in various professional fields.

Mary Agnes always had an intense interest in human rights. As a child, she defended the downtrodden, cried at the plight of the homeless, and vowed that she would make a difference. At ten, she began working in the local soup kitchen. At fifteen, she started a program providing shoes for the homeless. In sixth grade, she started the Social Awareness Club. In high school, she volunteered online for the United Nations, which contin-ued into her university days. There she majored in human rights. After graduation, she received one of the few coveted internships offered by the United Nations. She was sent to Egypt where she met and was befriended by Dante D'Andrea, the Italian Minister of Foreign Affairs overseeing the program.

Through him, her reputation reached the UN Security Council's representative Salvatore Rodolfo. He sent his personal aide, Marco Giovetti, to meet with her. Marco was bowled over by her enthusiasm, attention to detail, ability to work independently, and self motivation. Her reports were never late and were always grammatically correct. She so impressed Marco that when her year was complete he offered her a position as an aide at the UN in New York.

Arriving there on July 4, 2030, she settled into her apartment and went to work. She so thoroughly enjoyed her job that she would often forget what time it was, staying well into the evening. At these times, she would frequent the Mini Café for a late dinner. It was there that she met her future husband Joseph Seamus, a stock broker.

On Sam's last day in New York, he and Edger spent the morning shadowing his sister Mary Agnes at the UN. Returning to Ed's apartment, they spent the afternoon relaxing and changing for dinner. It had been a fun and relaxing month. Neither Sam, nor Edger had forgotten their personal tragedies, but being together again lessened the sorrow and pain. Edger had insisted Sam stay with him since his apartment was much larger than Mary Agnes's.

Returning home at 3:30 p.m., Mary Agnes took a nap before dressing for the party. As she slumbered, she dreamt about her thirteenth birthday party, and the death of her father two days after. The dream was vivid and Mary Agnes awoke with a start. Memories, long suppressed, flooded back.

Being the eldest girl, the responsibilities of the home fell to her: taking care of her five younger siblings, cooking meals, cleaning the house, doing the laundry. Her mother just could not function for weeks after her father's death. Eventually these responsibilities took their toll on her school work. She would fall asleep in the middle of class and her previously stellar work was sloppily done, if at all. Her grades dropped from an A average to just above failing.

She remembered being called to the principal's, office, arriving when Sister Theophane was attending another matter. Told by the secretary to have a seat and wait, she promptly fell asleep. Arriving a few minutes later, Sister got a blanket from the cupboard, covered her, allowing the weary child to continue her much needed rest. Sister notified the teachers that Mary Agnes would not be in class for the rest of the day. Mary Agnes slept for the better part of an hour. Awakening, she looked around and groggily asked where she was. She was horrified as it dawned on her that she was in the principal's office. She immediately sat up, straightened her blouse and ran her fingers through her hair.

"Oh, Sister. I'm so sorry. I don't know what happened. One minute I was sitting here, waiting for you, and the next…"

"That's quite all right, Mary Agnes. This is what I wanted to speak to you about. The sisters have told me that you are falling asleep in class and that your grades are suffering. You have gone from an A average to all D's. They also tell me that you have dropped out of band and for weeks, you haven't been to a meeting of the student council, of which you are president, nor of the Social Awareness Club, which you are not only president, but founded several years ago. You are also in danger of losing your National Honor Society position. In addition, I'm told you rarely see your friends socially. Please tell me what is going on, so that I may help you. Is it that you miss your father? We can arrange grief counseling for you."

"Sister, I miss Daddy terribly, and will for the rest of my life, but since he died Mommy hasn't been herself. She sits in her room and prays for most of the day. She will occasionally go out shopping, but doesn't stay out long. When I come home from school, I have to prepare supper, do the dishes and the laundry. With ten of us, there is a lot of laundry. I'm glad that Sammy is potty-trained, or there would be more. I divide it into five and do some each night. Saturday I clean the house and if Mommy hasn't gone shopping, I do that. After Mass on Sunday, I try to do my homework, but it doesn't always get done. Sister, I have no time for friends."

Sister Theophane was dumbstruck. "Mercy child, you are doing the work of five people. Don't your older brothers help out?"

"They try, Sister, but Mommy says that they are boys and shouldn't do woman's work. They cut the grass, take out the garbage, fix things around the house, and dry the dishes. When Mommy doesn't see, they do try to help with the other chores. Kate and Bridget try to help too, but sometimes it's just easier to do it myself than to explain to them how. It's hard getting Becky and Tim to put their toys away and Sam's just too little to do anything but make a mess.

"Tim and Sam have been told that Daddy's in heaven, but, Sister, Tim keeps asking me when he'll come back home, and Sam sometimes just stands at daddy's chair and says "Dada" over and over. I don't know what to tell them. Sister, I'm trying, but I don't know how much longer I can."

Sister Theophane marveled at the maturity this young girl had displayed and resolved that she would not go through this alone anymore.

"Mary Agnes, I want you to go home now. I promise you that things will get better. Get some sleep. I'll see you tomorrow."

"But Sister, my classes."

"I've taken care of that. Now go."

The ringing of the doorbell brought Mary Agnes back to the present. It was Sam and Edger. They were early, and she was not nearly ready.

"Make yourselves at home," she said as she went to finish getting ready. Joe arrived home several minutes later.

At 7:15 p.m., as they were entering the restaurant, Ed recognized an acquaintance.

"There's my friend Pete Moranny. I haven't seen him in years. Go on in and I'll be there in a couple of minutes."

A screeching of brakes and a loud thump caused Edger to turn around, in time to see a man, in his fifties, dressed in a tuxedo, lying on the street, in front of the cab that hit him. He immediately ran to him.

"I'm a doctor," he told the gathering crowd. "Call 911."

Ed assessed the man's condition and seeing that he was not breathing, began CPR After several minutes, the man revived.

"Lie still. You were hit by a cab. I am a doctor. I need to check to see if you have any broken bones. The paramedics are on their way."

They arrived within minutes replacing Edger. A policeman took Ed aside and questioned him.

"I need to know your name and what happened."

"Dr. Edger Pielaresto. I was going to dinner at the restaurant across the street when the accident happened. I immediately came to assist. He was not breathing when I arrived so I administered CPR. It was only about a minute or so before he revived. Then I checked to see if he had any broken bones. I don't think so. That's when you arrived."

"Thanks Doctor. You probably saved his life."

"If you have no further questions, my friends are waiting for me inside."

"Nothing further. Thanks again, doctor."

Edger returned to the party and found himself the hero of the night.

Sam left the next day, amid much laughter, hugs, and tears. Two weeks later, Edger received a box of gourmet chocolates with a thank you note. It was from the man whose life he had saved, Salvatore Rodolfo, the representative of the UN Security Council. He requested that Edger join him for dinner on Friday the 25th, as a way of thanking him for saving his life. Edger accepted.

A PROPOSAL AND
A BREAKTHROUGH

September 12, 2045

But from the beginning of the creation God made them
male and female. For this cause shall a man leave his father
and mother, and cleave to his wife; and the twain shall
become one flesh, so then they are no more twain, but one
flesh. What therefore God has joined together, let no man
put asunder.

Mark 10: 6–9 (KJV)

FOR SEVERAL MONTHS, Sam's life was topsy-turvy—a series
of lows and highs, sorrows and joys. After his semi-vacation
in New York with Mary Agnes, Joe, and Edger, Sam was eager
to start his career. He was to begin work at the University of
California San Francisco Medical Center in September. It was an
exciting time for him and also a way to forget his problems. Not
that he could or would ever forget Tim. He wandered around the
laboratory, equipped with the latest devices, acting like a child
at Christmas. Sam had received a very large grant to research
prostate cancer, which made him somewhat of a celebrity at the
center. The gene ATBF1 had been discovered years before to
inhibit cell growth, but sometimes, for unknown reasons, turned
off in patients who developed prostate cancer. Sam hoped to find

a way to switch the gene back on, thereby preventing the growth of the cancer.

Mildred Bovard, a twenty-five-year-old research assistant, was assigned to help in Sam's lab. Although not beautiful, Mil was pretty, and level-headed, which only added to her charms. She possessed common sense, a rare commodity in one so young. Millie proved an invaluable asset to Sam, and the two soon became a team, in more ways than one. They began to think and act in unison.

Sam had always thought that he would live and die single, but since he met Millie feelings were beginning to stir that he thought were non-existent. They had clicked immediately, on every level even religion. Mil was a devoted Catholic, willingly honoring the Church's laws. No smorgasbord Catholic was she. She did not smoke nor did she drink. Eventually the two became inseparable.

On the fifth anniversary of their working together, Sam did something uncharacteristic of him. He had a cake brought in to celebrate the occasion. During the celebration, Sam asked Mil to look into the microscope. There, written on the head of a pin was "Millie, will you marry me?" At first Mildred didn't see the message, the scope was not focused for her eyes, and then, as the message gradually focused, she gasped, looked at Sam, looked back into the scope, then back at Sam, who was now holding a piece of cake out to her.

"Do you mean it?"

Sam didn't answer. He just held out the cake to her. Sounds of music broke the silence as a barbershop quartet entered the room singing the tune of "Daisy Bell"

"Millie, Millie, give me your answer true, I'm half crazy, for I'm in love with you, you will have a stylish marriage, I can now afford a carriage, and you do look sweet upon the seat of a laboratory stool."

While the quartet sang, Mil took the cake, cut into it, and found an engagement ring just as the song ended. She placed the cake on the counter, took the ring, held it out to Sam and said,

"Sam, please place it on my finger."

Sam did, and she embraced and kissed him saying, "Yes, yes, yes.

On May 13, 2051, Mildred Cecilia Bovard became Mrs. Samuel O'Brien at Saint Patrick Church in San Francisco. It was a joyous celebration with all of Sam's siblings, his mother and Mother Hedwig Peligia attending the wedding, as did Mil's mother, father, grandparents, and siblings along with friends from the clinic.

Sam and Millie went back to Ireland with the family for their honeymoon. Sam wanted to show Millie the land of his birth. They did all the tourist activities, including kissing the Blarney Stone. He showed her the Cliffs of Moher, Dingle Peninsula, Dublin, Galway Bay, the Ring of Kerry, and other sites of Ireland not on any tourist list. Most of all he wanted her to experience the friendliness of the Irish folk, something he had not experienced since he was a student at the University of Pittsburgh where Pittsburghers were as friendly and helpful as those of home.

At O'Leary's, the local pub, his old buddies welcomed him with open arms and slaps on the back. The month went by too quickly and soon it was time again for good-byes. They returned to San Francisco with memories to last a lifetime.

Their work continued and Sam had a breakthrough six months after the wedding. He always thought marrying Millie had brought him luck. It was a simple serum, so simple that no one had ever given it a thought. Why do scientists always look for

complex answers, even to the simplest of questions? The serum worked. Thousands of lab rats were given prostate cancer, and then the serum at different stages in the development of the cancer. All were cured within hours. Now, it's time to test on human subjects. Sam received FDA approval in 2053 and organized his test groups. At the end of the ten- year study, Sam found the human results to be exact duplicates of the rats. The serum worked and without any side effects, or so Sam thought.

A NEW CAREER

August 25, 2045

O N MAY 13, 1981, the sixty-fourth anniversary of the first apparition to the children of Fatima, Pope John Paul II was rushed to Gemelli Hospital the victim of an assassin's bullet. Having received the finest of care the Pontiff was released twenty-two days later, returning to the hospital when his health required throughout the remaining twenty-three years of his papacy. Since then, Gemelli has set aside a suite of rooms for the exclusive use of the pope, thereby earning the nickname 'the pope's hospital'.

Constructed on the hill in Rome, Gemelli Hospital is a large general teaching hospital. It offers undergraduate and postgraduate education in medicine, surgery, nursing and physiotherapy. Founded by Franciscan Friar Agostino Gemelli in 1964, it provides both free and paid medical assistance. In addition to facilities for basic and clinical research, it also includes student residence halls, cafeterias, bookstores, and medical libraries. The campus incorporates four buildings dedicated to the disciplines of biology, health, infections diseases and medicine of aging.

Expanded in the year 2000, the facilities now include emergency care, operating theaters, and laboratories for genetic research.

Major renovations were undertaken in 2040 with many of the original buildings gutted and remodeled, additions put on and new buildings constructed. The latest equipment was purchased and installed, bringing the facilities into the twenty-first century.

After the dinner, Edger and Sal became fast friends, almost inseparable. Sal became Edger's mentor, coaching him in the ways of international affairs.

One day six months later, Sal asked, "Edger is such a strange name. How did you get it?"

Edger smiled. "It's an unusual story, but par for my life. Mom never really wanted me. She even wanted to abort me. My father had to talk her into having me, so when the time came for me to be named, she insisted that I would be named Edger, since she was on edge her entire pregnancy. She often took a morose pleasure in telling family and friends that being on edge did not end with my birth but continued all during my infancy and adolescence. She secretly delighted in her misery, so that made me her greatest joy. I take some consolation in that. Even Tiffany and Eric couldn't provide her that bliss. She may not have loved me, but at least I was the cause of some joy in her life."

"That is so sad—a mother, not wanting her own child."

"Remember, Sal, millions of mothers across the world abort their babies each year."

"Yes, and that is a very poignant commentary on society indeed."

Sal asked Edger about his research. He knew the gist of his work, but needed to clarify the details if his plan were to succeed.

"As you know, I have been working on retarding the aging process. It has been known in the scientific community, for many years, that the human lifespan is not as long as it should be. We shouldn't live for just seventy or eighty years. One hundred shouldn't even be the norm. You see, for some reason, almost from the time life begins, the DNA molecule does not faithfully reproduce itself, thereby causing aging. This shouldn't be. I have been trying to find out why it happens and a way to stop it from happening. Imagine it Sal, we could, conceivably live as long as the patriarchs of Genesis, nine hundred plus years, most without any sign of the aches and pains of old age."

"Impressive, Edger. Just the type of research the Church will eat up," Sal said, almost to himself. "What are your plans for the future? Where are you planning on working?"

"I was going to stay here. Julie and I really loved this hospital. But since her death, my heart is no longer here. I really haven't given it much thought, since she died. I know that I can't stay here, though—too many memories."

"Good. As you know my term at the UN is up and I have been recalled to Italy where I will assume the post of Minister of Health. I have taken the liberty of looking into some things for you. There is a post that I think will fit you perfectly. Gemelli Hospital is expanding its Department of Research and Development. They are in desperate need of young, dedicated, and enthusiastic people to help the department grow. You'll enter on the ground floor, but the opportunities for advancement are almost unlimited. You graduated top of your class, were named up and coming researcher of the year, speak several languages including Italian. You are just what Gemelli is looking for."

"Gemelli Hospital? I've never heard of it, Sal. Where is it?"

"In Rome. There is one problem though. Gemelli is a Catholic Hospital and all employees and volunteers must adhere to certain rules. Everyone must sign and abide by the Cardinal Clause. This document outlines what is expected of all employees, who may be dismissed for public immorality, public scandal, or, and this is the biggie for you Ed, rejection of the teachings, doctrines or laws of the Roman Catholic Church. Those doctrines include entering into a marriage which is not recognized as being valid by the Church, or support of activities which espouse beliefs contrary to Church teaching and laws, such as advocacy of abortion. It also mandates that all employees are active members of the Church. I know that you can handle the first part, Ed. You are a good man at heart. But what about the second?"

"I don't know Sal. I haven't been to church since I went with Sam. It's not the time. Julie and I went every week. She insisted upon it. The last time was with Sam and his sister, six months ago. You know that I feel that religion has to be changed. It has caused so much trouble in the world."

"Like a worm works from within the apple, so does change of any organization. You can only do so much from the outside. If you really want change, effective and lasting change, you must do it from within. Accept this position, Ed, and together we can effect change in the Church."

Because there is no rise to power in Italy, without being a practicing Catholic, Edger accepted the terms. More than anything, he wanted power. It would allow him to wreak the revenge he so desperately needed.

Salvatore Rodolfo was responsible for Edger's return to the Catholic Church, and his rise to power. Even though he went through the motions, Edger felt nothing.

VILLAIN OR HERO?

June 30, 2058

THE PROSTATE IS a gland is part of the male reproductive system, found below the bladder and in front of the rectum. Prostate cancer, which usually occurs in older men, happens when the cells mutate and multiply out of control. These cells may metastasize, spreading from the prostate to other parts of the body, especially the bones and lymph nodes. Prostate cancer may cause pain, difficulty in urinating, problems during sexual intercourse, erectile dysfunction and other symptoms. However those symptoms are present only in an advanced stage of the disease. In the United States, an estimated 186,320 new cases and 28,660 deaths occur per year.

Samuel was wrapping up his research on prostate cancer when he began receiving letters from the participants in the study.

You Bastard,

What have you done to me? I had the perfect life until I was treated by you. What did you give me? How could you? How dare you? I no longer can make love to my life partner. I can't get close to him and am repulsed when he wants to cuddle. He doesn't understand. Neither do I! It happened all at once. I woke on Tuesday, May 10, looked over at Jim, and it was as though I was looking at him for the first time. Even though we have been together for twelve years, it was as though I didn't know him at all. I threw up at the thought of having slept with him the night before.

We had the perfect love, and now you have destroyed that. I found the ying to my yang. Now I have lost that. We tried to work it out, really tried. I have had to move out of our home. I am now living at the Y.

My entire life I have had no stronger feelings for women than friendships. Now, I am lusting after them the way I once did only for Jim. I can't look at a woman without thinking thoughts I have never thought before.

My life has gotten bad. I have racked my brains for weeks trying to think why this happened to me. What happened in my life that could possible account for this change? I have heard of cases where some men had turned hetero— after an accident, like a hit to the head. I had no such accident. The only thing that I have done differently was taking your damn treatment for my prostate cancer. I finally realized that the change occurred the day after I took that medication.

I know I can't sue you. I signed that damn document releasing you and the clinic from all liability. I curse the day I signed up for that program. My life has been ruined because of you. I hope you rot in hell!

Michael P. Stein

There were more letters. Many more.

Dear Dr. O'Brien,
my savior,

I wanted to thank you and let you know how grateful I am to you and the University of California San Francisco Medical Center. My prostate cancer has been cured, not just in remission, but cured! I feel great. My life is beautiful. The tumor has disappeared. It is nothing short of a miracle.

And, Dr. O'Brien, there has been a second miracle. It is something that I must tell you, but it is hard to put into words. I have repressed certain feelings my entire life. For as long as I can remember, fifty-two years, I have been attracted to men. The day after I took your treatment I began to realize that I was looking at women, the way I once looked at men. I dismissed it the first day, but as the days and weeks passed, I realized that I had changed. I was no longer homosexual, but heterosexual.

And a third miracle occurred. I met a beautiful woman and we are to be married in September. We would be honored to have you attend. You have done so much for me. It is because of you that I am living the life of my dreams. God bless you.

Sincerely,
A grateful patient,
Bill Parninski

Sam received dozens of letters each day, 99 percent of them like Bill's. Men, who had been in the closet for years, who now had the life they always dreamed of. He grieved for the Michaels but realized that he may have inadvertently stumbled on what Tim asked him to find years ago, a way to silence the homosexual gene.

With the rules and regulations in the United States, and the strong gay political community in San Francisco, he could not openly test this "cure." Finding funding for prostate cancer was one thing. Few wanted to touch the hot potato of homosexuality.

Even though, according to the letters, only a small fraction of those who were gay wanted to be that way, they were a very vocal minority. It would take years to get the funding, let alone approval for this treatment.

Sam decided to contact Edger to see if he could help. He had been head of Gemelli Polyclinic in Rome for several years now. He had means that Sam lacked, and Sam hoped Edger could help.

EDGER TO THE RESCUE

December 2, 2058, Wednesday

THE SIMPLEST WAY to control something is to turn it on or off. Using synthetic peptide nucleic acid (PNA) and specifically designed RNA, genes can now be turned on or off at the chromosomal level.

Most every disease begins as a malfunctioning gene expression. Theoretically using this approach a drug for the treatment or cure of almost any disease is possible.

Edger,

I need your help. As you know, my work has been the reactivation of the ATBF1 gene, which, when switched off causes prostate cancer. You also know that I have been successful. The gene can be turned on again by the administration of a simple amino acid sequence. It works every time, even on the most aggressive and advanced cancers.

That is not why I need your help. What you don't know, what we didn't know until several weeks ago, is that it also turns off the gene Xq28, the gene that in 1993, Dr. James McFarland claimed caused homosexuality. After the trials, I received hundreds of letters from men who were homosexual claiming they no longer had these desires.

Of course, all were pleased with the cure of their cancer, and most with the cure of their homosexuality. Many of these men had been in the closet for years. Millie and

I never thought to ask about their sexual orientation. We thought it didn't matter. We were only concerned about curing the cancer. But there actually are some who were angry enough that they no longer had these tendencies, they threatened us, one even with death.

Millie and I started digging and found a connection. Just what in the serum causes Xq28 to turn off, we still do not know. Ed, I have inadvertently stumbled on what Tim asked me to find years ago, but I have a problem. It is twofold. First, I don't know if switching on the gene to prevent cancer plays a role in the switching off the gene for homosexuality. Second, I can't test the serum on homosexual men alone. Funding for cancer research is abundant, especially now, but curing homosexuality is a political hot potato. There are many men who do not wish to be cured, and the gay community has deep political roots.

Plus, I can't do anything without FDA approval. There are too many hoops to jump through, and I don't know if I will ever be allowed to test here.

That is why I am writing to you Ed. Regulations are less stringent in Europe and there have to be homosexual men willing to participate in the trial. As head of the Gemelli hospital, I was hoping you could pull a few strings and get this serum tested. Is there any way? I need to know the answer, for Tim's sake, and so that no one else will have to go through what he had to endure. If this is really a cure, I need to know, the world needs to know. I'll do what I can here. Please let me know.

Sam

Looking over the research Sam included with his letter, Edger immediately recognized another link. The Xq28 gene was very similar to the VMAT2 gene he had researched in residency. They differed by less than ten base sequences, and he began formulating a plan. Perhaps he could use Sam's work to turn off the VMAT2 gene.

In the next few weeks, Edger got things going. He set up funding, furnished a laboratory, and hired an assistant whom he trusted. When all was set, Edger wrote to Sam.

Dear Sam,

I have a wild idea that I hope you will sincerely consider. Since this is your baby, I thought that you should be the one to finish your research. Tim would have wanted it that way. I have obtained funding, and set up a lab and want you and Millie to come and head the research team.

Enclosed are your plane tickets, and I have an option on a small house. Come as soon as you are able.

Edger

Sam was dumbfounded. The offer came at a most opportune time. There were more death threats, and they were coming more frequently. Even though Sam didn't fear for himself, he did for Millie and their unborn child. After trying for seven years to have another child, the miracle finally occurred. It had begun to seem like it would never happen. Now that it had, this had to happen. He and Millie discussed the option and finally decided to take Edger up on his offer, in Tim's memory.

VATICAN ARCHIVIST

2029–2051

S INCE THE TIME of Saint Peter the popes protectively kept and
guarded a library of works important to the Church. That all
changed in the mid 1400s when Pope Nicholas V opened the
doors of the library for use by the clerics, cardinals, scholars, and
even laymen, who inhabited the Court of Rome and the surrounding area.

The library was given as much devotion as the books themselves. Popes Nicholas V and Sixtus IV set aside a suite of rooms
with large windows to illuminate the stunning decorations. Soon
they became as breathtaking a work of art as the Sistine Chapel.
The tortuously handwritten books were obtained in a variety of
ways. They were bought, borrowed, bequeathed, obtained from
military conquests or even stolen. All were chained to lavishly
carved worktops.

From the beginning the library had a special quality. First and
foremost in the collection were Bibles, works of theology and
canon law. Secular materials were also included but only the pur-
est forms of the Latin and Greek classics. Books were cherished
as the most powerful source of knowledge and counsel the world
possessed. Popes sent their agents worldwide to obtain them and
came back with Roman and Chinese manuscripts, the love letters
of Henry VIII, and the classics of history and philosophy. Because
of the vast quantity of materials obtained, the Vatican Library
formed the nucleus from which the Renaissance materialized.

In 1455 Palatina become librarian and began the immense task
of cataloguing the swiftly burgeoning collection. In just twenty-

six years the collection had grown from one thousand two hundred books to well over three thousand five hundred making it the largest collection in the Western world. Since Palatina, noted historians, scholars, and philosophers have served as the Vatican Archives' librarian.

In time, Joshua succeeded Abba Eban as the chief authority on the Middle East. Unlike Eban though, Joshua was also the expert on the three major religions of the world, Judaism, Catholicism, and Islam. His expertise was sought constantly by the United Nations, presidents, churches, and synagogues, and his renown grew. His writings were voluminous and those on Christianity soon brought him to the attention of one of the most powerful cardinals of the Catholic Church: Cardinal Giovanni Poppa had wanted to meet this remarkable man for a long time, but was never in a position to do so. In 2051, Giovanni Poppa was elected pope, taking the name Urban IX.

By this time, Joshua was beginning to think about retirement. He was fifty-one years old and had plenty of money. He wanted to get away from the arguing and mistrust of the world. He had seen too much of the secular world and knew that he could not change it. He had tried, for nearly thirty years. God knows, how he had tried. When one battle seemed to have been won, another, more fierce, would surface. He was tired and wanted something that did not require so much expenditure of energy.

It was at this time that Joshua received a letter from the Vatican. Pope Urban IX had requested the honor of his presence at an audience later that month. He willingly accepted and both men eagerly awaited the appointed time.

During their audience, Joshua and Urban spoke of many things including his role as advisor in Middle Eastern affairs. When the Pope realized that Joshua had retired, he began setting a plan in motion. The Vatican Archives had been without a curator for some time. What a coup it would be to have the famous Joshua Abraham Heim as the new curator.

Six months later the offer was made and accepted. The job helped Joshua fill the time, the hours were flexible, and he was doing something that he had always loved, working with the documents of history. He was no longer in the public eye, and he was privy to documents that hadn't seen the light of day for centuries. Joshua was like a child in a candy shop. There were days, when he got lost in reading these documents, many in the original Greek and Hebrew. It was a fascinating time for him, perhaps the best in his life.

After ten years in the curator position, Joshua's notoriety had not diminished, but his recognizability had. The years and stress had not treated him well. He could now even walk the streets of Jerusalem without being recognized. He found it a welcome change. His life was as quiet now as it had been chaotic before. He enjoyed the solitude and being able to observe people without being mobbed by reporters and the press.

Even though he had been invited to the Christmas party every year, Joshua had always found an excuse not to go, his dead friend Geoffrey was always in the back of his mind. This year, though, he decided that he needed some distraction and accepted.

At the party, Joshua did what he did best, observe people. He could practically tell what they were talking about by reading their body language. He had learned this on his outings with his mother. As they sat beneath their olive tree in the garden, eating lunch, she taught him to view the people passing by. She was an excellent observer and taught him everything she knew. During the years, he adapted and honed this skill. That is what had made him the best and most sought after mediator in the world.

As he was observing the party from the corner, he himself was being observed. Edger had arrived at the party fashionably late. He perused the crowd and his eyes fell on the gentleman in the corner. He wasn't wearing the traditional Orthodox Jewish garb, but instead an all black business suit, with a black yarmulke. Edger observed him for several minutes before approaching.

"You're Joshua Abraham Hiem."

"You have the advantage, sir. Not many people recognize me these days. And you are?"

"Dr. Edger Pielaresto. I recognized you almost immediately. I followed your career. We are neighbors as well. I am head of Gemelli hospital."

Joshua held out his hand. "Pleased to meet you, Dr. Pielaresto."

Edger shook his hand. "The pleasure is all mine. I followed your career for some time, but then you just dropped from the scene. I never understood how you could have given up all it up."

"I was beginning to burn out. If I had stayed much longer, I wouldn't have been any good to myself or anyone. I left on my own terms—at the top of my career. Actually, I am much happier now, just being a nobody."

They continued to talk for a time. Joshua had mixed thoughts about Edger. He was personable, but there was something that just didn't sit right. Joshua excused himself and went to speak with one of the workers in the archive. He needed to get away from this man. He was beginning to make his skin crawl. Joshua couldn't put his finger on it. He just knew he didn't like him.

RELICS OF ALL
SHAPES AND SIZES

2065

I N 1295, MOTHER Mary Angelica Kurzawska, foundress of the
Order of the Blessed Sacrament, was martyred for her faith.
As the one hundredth anniversary of the death of the martyred
virgin approached, a group of nuns requested permission to find
the remains of their sainted foundress and bring them back home
to Krakow. They searched and prayed for five years before their
quest succeeded. Lovingly, they placed the bones in a velvet lined
box and returned to the mother house, where they were met with
joy. Mother Mary Angelica Kurzawska had returned home. Hers
were the first relics obtained by the order.

During the previous several centuries, many relics found their
way to the motherhouse and soon they had the largest collection
of relics in the world, next to the Vatican's.

As a postulant and novice, Mother Hedwig Peligia would
spend her spare time in the reliquary museum studying the first,
second, and third class relics of the saints housed in the vast basement archives. Many were familiar to her, a piece of the true cross,
a cloth touched to the bones of St. Peter, an arrow that pierced St.
Sebastian, and of course, the bones of the foundress.

There were other, more obscure relics that she did not recognize—a canister of the ashes of the red heifer, Saint Peter the

Martyr, St. Marco, St. Gilbert, St. Jean. Who or what were these relics? she wondered. She soon found that she had a lot in common with one of them, St. Isidore of Seville, the patron saint of the Internet. She researched all these and soon became an expert on the relics in the motherhouse, as well as those around the world, well-known or obscure, but the one she never had any luck with was the canister simply marked red heifer ashes.

Mother loved speaking about relics and often dreamed of one day going in search of the Holy Grail. She knew that this was a futile dream, since the chalice used at the Last Supper was probably made of clay, and in two millennia, it would have disintegrated. There were other relics and of course, always dreams.

Approaching her seventieth birthday, Mother thought it was time that she began relinquishing her responsibilities of running the order to those younger. There were many qualified to do so. She began wondering, though, what she would do with herself as her second and last term as Mother General was coming to a close. She was a bit surprised, but pleased, to be approached by the papacy to head the Pharmaceutical unit of Gemelli Hospital. She didn't hesitate a moment, eager to get back to her roots, taking on a different type of responsibility.

For so many years, she was accountable for the workings of the order, spiritual, physical, but mostly financial. It would almost be a vacation to be doing the work she had trained for so many years before. She would still be liable for the spiritual and physical dimensions of the human person, but the financial would be in someone else's hands. That person was Edger Pielaresto, a man she had met a few times. She had formulated no opinion about him, but knew that he was somewhat of a financial wizard, taking the hospital, not only into the twenty-first century, but far beyond. Under his leadership, Gemelli had become the premiere hospital in the world. She was eager to work there, with all the latest technology and the brightest medical minds in the world.

Soon, after she assumed her position, Joshua Abraham Hiem came to have a prescription refilled. It was toward the end of the day, and there was not much to do, so the two struck up a conversation as she filled his order. Thereafter, Joshua would have his prescription filled by no one but Mother, he had enjoyed their talk so much. There was something about this nun.

At first, he could not put his finger on it. Joshua had met a number of nuns, from many different orders, but Mother was unique. Then, one day he hit upon it. Mother Hedwig Peligia reminded him of his mother. Both were courageous and strong women, but there was more. Both were friendly and outgoing, capable of speaking on any subject. Both were more than willing to share their experiences and expertise. Joshua found himself looking forward to having his prescriptions filled, even going when he didn't need to go.

They talked about everything, but there was one topic that kept creeping its way into their conversations, relics. Both Mother and Joshua loved talking about them, both knew more than any person should about them. During one conversation, Joshua invited Mother to visit the papal reliquary, parts of which not many were privileged to see. There had even been popes who for one reason or another, had never set foot into the reliquary.

During this visit, Mother mentioned the relics of her order and their usually brief discussion turned to hours, especially when Joshua found out that the ashes of the red heifer were there. It had always been rumored that they existed, but, like the Holy Grail, most thought it unlikely that they could have survived for two thousand years. Now, could they possibly be in the basement archives of the Order of the Blessed Sacrament Motherhouse?

It's only a thousand kilometers away. No wonder archeologists could never find the ashes. Everyone thought that they were hid-

den in or around Jerusalem, but they were actually twenty-four
hundred kilometers away in Krakow, Poland.

"What do you know about the ashes of the Red Heifer,
Mother?" Joshua asked.

"I don't like to admit it, Joshua, but not much. I always
intended to research them, but something always got in the way.
I know they are used in ritual purification rites."

"Technically you are correct, Mother, but there is much more.
In order to explain it, I must begin at the beginning, the time of
Moses. The ordinance of the red heifer is a chok, a divine stat-
ute which by its very nature defies human understanding. In the
Torah, the Old Testament, in the book of Numbers, chapter 19,
verses 1 through 9, Yahweh gave specific instructions to Aaron,
the first high priest, about how the temple priests were to be
purified and how the waters of purification were to be prepared.

"The Mount of Anointment, a precise location on the Mount
of Olives, opposite the eastern gate of the Temple Mount, is
the sight of this rite. There, a singular altar was erected, and the
wood for the fire was made up of cedar, pine, cypress, and fig,
because these woods are generally free from knots and holes. It
was arranged, in the shape of a small tower, wide at the bottom
and narrower toward the top. Spaces were made in the pile to let
the air circulate.

"The heifer was bound to the altar with cords made from reed-
grass, which do not become impure. It was placed with its head
on the south side, and its face westward, toward the Temple. The
priest stood on the eastern side, also facing west."

"Standing atop of the altar, the priest slaughtered the heifer
using his right hand for the act. He gathered blood in his left
hand and with his right index finger, sprinkled from it seven
times standing opposite the entrance to the Holy Temple, facing
that direction. Descending from the altar, the priest lit the fire
from the western side, the end facing the Temple and the heifer

was placed on it. As the fire consumed the carcass, cedar wood, hyssop, and wool, dyed scarlet, was placed on the fire.

"When the fire was finished and all was completely burned, everything there was ground down and pulverized, including the wood, and all parts of the animal. The entire mass was beaten with rods and sifted, and these were the ashes that were saved and used for purity.

"The ashes were mixed with the ashes from the previous ritual, and then divided into three portions; one was divided for use between the priestly shifts serving in the Temple to purify the country folk and impure. Another was kept at the burning station at the Mount of Anointment, the allotment to be used for the priest who came to burn the heifer. The last was to be preserved, until the next sacrifice, when they were to be mingled with the next ashes. These were placed in the wall in the front of the Women's Court of the Holy Temple, kept as a remembrance as the Holy One commanded: 'And it shall be for the congregation of the Children of Israel for a remembrance.'"

"The ritual hasn't been performed for a very long time. I know that Israel was not a nation for hundreds of years, but after 1947, why hasn't anyone performed the ritual, so that the temple could be rebuilt?" Mother questioned.

"Well, that is a complex question indeed. Part of it has to do with the exile. Another part is that during the time of the first and second Temple, only nine heifers have met the criteria. That is how rare an occurrence it is. The heifer must be three years old and perfect in its redness. Even the presence of as little as two hairs of any other color will render it invalid. Even the hooves must be red. It also has to be totally free from any physical blemish or defect, external or internal. It must never have been used to perform any physical labor, even if a person leans on the animal invalidates it. In the past one hundred and twenty years, no animal has been born with these stringent criteria."

"The second problem arises with the purification of the high priest who must daily be sprinkled, during the course of the week of separation, immediately before the ritual is to take place. This is done from the ashes made previously, those of earlier generations. Without the ashes from the second Temple, a mixture of the ashes of the eight heifers before, the rite cannot be preformed. It is a way of connecting us to the original heifer and Moses, who slaughtered and prepared it."

"So, Mother, as you can see, the ritual cannot be performed without them. If the canister of ashes, in your Motherhouse, is indeed the kelal, the container of original ashes, there is new hope. They would have to be verified, by the Sadducees, and a red heifer meeting all the requirements needs to be born before the third Temple could be rebuilt." Joshua said, almost to himself.

"Joshua, you seem to forget something."

"What is that Mother?"

"The ashes belong to the Order of the Blessed Sacrament."

Joshua was stunned. It never occurred to him that the ashes would not be returned to Israel. He was about to argue the point when Mother injected,

"We have a common goal, Joshua. The paths may be different, but the end results are the same. We both believe in a Messiah. The difference is that you believe he is still to come. I believe he has already come. In both cases, the Temple must be rebuilt and it appears that it is time. You will have the, what did you call it?"

"The kelal. God bless you, Mother."

THE CURE

March 15, 2066

A VERY LONG TIME ago, near a lake in Libya, a dragon terrorized an entire village. Children were sacrificed to it to appease its wrath. The king's beloved daughter was eventually chosen. He begged for her life but to no avail. Bound to a stake, Cleolinda awaited her fate. The dragon approached, and at the very moment that it was about to devour her, Saint George arrived on his horse bellowing "In the name of the Father, the Son, and the Holy Ghost."

He drew his lance, knocked the dragon down and slew it. His horse trampled the dragon's remains as Saint George rescued the princess. Looking on from afar the king, queen and townspeople were so impressed the entire village converted to Christianity.

Nice story, but not at all historical. Saint George was a Christian nobleman holding the position of Legion Commander, Rome's highest authority, during the reign of Emperor Dioclesian (AD 245–313). When Dioclesian began persecuting the Christians, George complained to the Emperor about the harshness of his decrees.

In Nicomedia he tore them down, was arrested, thrown into prison, and tortured. Unwilling to recant his faith, he was dragged through the streets and beheaded, making him one of the first Dioclesian martyrs.

In mythology, combat with a dragon or serpent is symbolic of the battle between good and evil. Therefore the moral of Saint George's battle with the dragon, the devil, is that good is always victorious over evil.

Sam and Millie arrived in Italy on March 15, 2066. Edger met them at the airport and took them to their new home, where they began to settle in. Sam was so eager to get started on his research that Edger made arrangements to have him and Millie picked up the next day, at 8:00 a.m. sharp and brought to his office. From there, he showed them to their newly remodeled laboratory. It had all the latest equipment, with everything that Sam could want or need.

"This lab was mine when I was head of Research and Development. I had it completely gutted, and all the latest equipment have been installed. If I missed anything, Sam, please let me know.

"You are very well funded. Your benefactor is extremely excited about your research. When he heard there was a possibility that you would be coming to Italy, he approached me and offered to fully fund you for the duration of the study.

"In exchange, he asks that his only son, his only child, be part of the study. I could see no harm, so he has already been included under an alias. The father picked out the name, so even I do not know his alias. His father advised him that if he did not participate in the study, or did anything to hinder or jeopardize the validity of the study, he would be disinherited and left without a penny. Needless to say, he accepted the terms.

"You see, the boy is twenty-five, and very promiscuous in the gay community. The father can't trust him. If he could provide him with legitimate grandchildren, then they could inherit his business and vast fortune. He hopes that all he has heard and read about you will prove true, and his son will have the cure for which the father has been praying.

"I have never met the son. I wouldn't know him if I tripped over him, so your results will be valid. Sam, Millie, enjoy."

As he left, Edger handed him a list of the first one hundred fifty participants. Sam and Millie immediately went to work.

Several months later Sam was working late, going through his files and documenting his results. Millie had returned home earlier that day. She was six months along and her feet and back ached. Sam told her he would see her at home. Millie knew that wouldn't be for a good number of hours. Sam lost all track of time when he was working.

Looking at his watch, Sam was surprised at the time. It had been hours since Millie had left and she would be worrying about him. As he was starting to clean up, he received an e-mail. He wanted to get home, but the e-mail address was just too intriguing. It was from a "strrmaggie." It reminded him of when he was a student at Saint Patrick's Elementary School. When a sister would ask a question, the students would wave their hands wildly in the air, calling strr, strr, to gain her attention. Sam did not recognize the name, nor the address but was intrigued enough to open it.

Dr. O'Brien,

You do not know me, but I know you. Your reputation has preceded you and I believe I can trust you. Some very important documents have crossed my path. I have no doubt you and your wife will see their importance. I was in charge of clearing out your lab, before it was remodeled.

I found some papers behind a drawer. I don't know why I kept them, since I do not understand them. When you arrived, I began to realize their importance. I must speak to you and your wife, in private. Please meet me at the Ambasciata di Capri, on Via Ennio Quirino Visconti. I will be there, tomorrow, at 10:00 p.m. I will wait for you until 10:30 p.m. Please come only with your wife. You will understand when we meet.

Sister Magdalena DeRienzo

Sam read and re-read the e-mail. He didn't know what to make of it. Could this be about his research? The Church had approved it. Pope Athanasisus was enthusiastic about the possibilities. He actually likened Sam to St. George, the dragon slayer. With the Church's approval, there was no end to the men willing to participate in the research.

What could this nun want that required so much secrecy? He was about to delete it when the phone rang.

"Sam, this is Mother Hedwig Peligia. I'm sorry to bother you so late, but I saw your lights were still on. There has been something on my mind and I must speak to you. Could you please stop by my office before you leave?"

"Of course, Mother. I was just getting ready to go. I'll be there in a few minutes."

"Good. I'll see you then."

Sam decided to print the e-mail out before deleting it. He then turned off the laptop, and the lights, locked the door, and traveled the few feet to Mother's office. He knocked.

"Enter, with the peace of God."

Sam went in.

"Thank you for coming so promptly, Sam. Please sit down."

"Thank you, Mother. Why did you need to see me?"

"Sam, something has been bothering me for some time. I can't prove anything, but I strongly suspect that something big is in the works. You see Sam, I have been working here for a long time now and have observed the behavior of many of the clergy and lay people. How well do you know Dr. Pielaresto?"

"Mother, Edger is my best friend. I have known him since we were in med school. What is this all about?"

"I met Dr. Pielaresto when he arrived in Italy. I have had numerous encounters with him and there is something...I can't put my finger on it, but I don't trust him. I think he is up to something. I don't know what, but it involves the Church in some way.

"Sam, I have known you for a long time, and I trust you. Have you noticed anything different about him?"

"He's gotten older, but nothing much else. We were not as close after med school. I stayed in Pittsburgh, and Edger went to New York, then here. He is more European now than he was, but nothing more. Although, I haven't had much time for socializing because my research keeps me pretty busy. I don't know what else I could tell you."

"I began to become suspicious by his rise to power. It has been far too quick. He advanced, it seemed, overnight. He was a physician of genetics, then head of research and development, then head of the entire hospital. Now, he is moving into the realm of the Church itself, right into the Vatican. I have observed him participating in areas that for centuries have been the domain of the religious, things that should only be handled by those properly schooled in the matter."

"I was hoping that you might be able to shed some light. You see, he has gotten pretty chummy with certain Cardinals; Cardinals that I do not trust. I have seen him in 'huddles' with these Cardinals, and when they see me, they stop talking. I know that is part of his job, that he has to 'schmooze' with the higher ups, but I believe that these men do not have the best interests of the church in mind. There are rumors. I usually do not place much stock in rumors, but these come from some very impeccable sources."

"Sam, you may not know it, but things here are recycled. The higher ups always get the brand new equipment. Those below, get their hand-me-downs. This week, I received a new computer. I was working with it today, getting it ready, deleting old files etc. and I found this. It was in a folder for correspondences. I wanted to make sure that it didn't contain anything important before I deleted the folder, so I opened it. There was only one letter in it. I printed it out." She handed him a copy.

From: Cody B.
To: Edger Pielaresto
Cc: Salvatore Rodolfo
Bcc:
Subject: Meeting

Ed and Sal,

We must meet. The plans are set and must be finalized. I have made a reservation at the Hotel Trevi, room 1323, for Thursday. Please arrive around 6.

> Cody

Sam read the e-mail. "What do you make of this Sam?

"I don't know, Mother. I wonder if it has anything to do with the e-mail I received just a few minutes ago. Mother, do you know a Sister Magdalena DeRienzo?"

"She is not of my order, but I know of her. She is head of housekeeping here at the hospital, and I don't have much contact with her. Why do you ask?"

"She sent me this e-mail." Sam handed the correspondence to Mother. "What can this mean, Mother?"

Mother read the paper, then said, "I don't know Sam, but I think you should keep the date. What do you think Millie will say?"

"Mother, Millie is an adventurer. If nothing else, curiosity will get the better of her."

"You have to think about her and your unborn baby. I don't think there is any danger from Sister Magdalena." Mother leaned heavily back in her chair. "Curiosity of curiosities."

"I wasn't going to go, Mother. I was in the process of deleting the e-mail when you called. I have to go, now. Curiosity killed the cat, but satisfaction brought it back. Now, I have to see what this is all about."

After making plans to meet on Thursday, at the Motherhouse, Sam went home. He told Millie everything. She was eager to get involved.

At 10:00 p.m. sharp, Sam and Millie entered the Ambasciata di Capri. They were looking for a nun. Someone dressed similarly to the Order of the Blessed Sacrament. They knew she was of a different order, and so the habit would be different. Seeing no one in any type of habit, they took a table in the back of the room.

Five minutes later, a spinstery-looking woman, in her fifties approached. She was dressed in a gray wool skirt, and a white blouse. A charcoal grey sweater hung unbuttoned over her slightly emaciated frame. Her hair was cut short, page boy style and she wore grey, orthopedic shoes. Taking a seat in the booth opposite the couple, she introduced herself.

"I'm Sister Magdalena DeRienzo."

"We were expecting you to be in habit, Sister."

"My order, the Sisters of Saint Martha, is small. We do not wear a habit, as such. This pin signifies who we are." She pointed to a small lapel pin, partially obscured by her sweater. "Our order is a service group. We hire ourselves out to cook and clean for a salary, usually for priests, bishops, and cardinals, but sometimes for the laity, where we act as governesses as well. The pope has also benefited from our services. Because of the funds we raise in this manner, some of our sisters are free to cook and clean for those who can not provide for themselves. We rotate in our duties, so that some are benefiting our bodily needs while others our spiritual ones."

The waiter came and took their drink orders.

"I don't have much time. The convent doors are locked at midnight. If I am not back by then, I will be missed." She handed Sam an envelope. It was thicker than Sam had anticipated. He opened it and was shocked to see the research paper he had sent to Edger. In the margin, in Edger's handwriting, were notes. One caught his eye immediately. It read "Structure of ATBF1 and VMAT2 very similar. Cure is possible."

Sam flipped through the pages. Edger had made one notation after another. Sam needed time to read and digest all this.

"Sister, may I keep this? It will take time to make some sense of it all."

"Of course, Dr. O'Brien, that is why I brought it. Please, don't tell anyone where you got it. It is getting late and I must get back."

"Can we escort you, Sister?"

"No, thank you. The convent is just a few blocks away. Good night, and God bless you."

Sam and Millie left shortly after. At home he pored over the document. Both knew it was significant, but what was Edger going to do? There was no mention of his plans.

It was well past dawn when Sam finished with the document. He needed to talk to Mother.

Edger began exploring ways in which to distribute the serum undetected. It was odorless, and colorless. The serum was also tasteless. This Edger knew since he had sampled it. He was certain that he did not possess the gene, since he had carefully evaluated his genetic make up, finding no trace of VMAT2. The only thing that he did not know, at this time, was the effect the drug would have on those who had it. He needed to test it, but on whom?

One of the wards in Gemilli was an insane asylum attached to a home for persons with Alzheimer's and dementia. Here were the perfect groups to test. Their families rarely, if ever, visited, and were unconcerned about the fate of their "loved ones." Most only came when the end was imminent, and they expected to be named in the will, not that much was ever left. Yes, he tested on the insane, and patients with Alzheimer's and dementia. That was a factor, but most of these patients were now, as the end drew near, virulently religious, their rosaries clutched between their fingers and statues of the saints adorning their tables. Edger marveled at humanities need of a god only in its time of necessity. He thought of his parents and wondered if their faith had returned on their death beds, just as these people had reached their peak of faith as death was knocking on their doors.

He tested their DNA to discover which patients had VMAT2. It was on these only he tested his serum. Edger tried various strengths of the serum finding that only two ccs. was needed for a complete transformation. Three worked no better than two and one did not do the job. After the serum was administered, and VMAT2 shut down, the patient, within days, become un-religious. Those who had faithfully received Holy Communion rejected it. Their rosaries were thrown away, and the statues broken. Even at the point of death, they refused the sacraments. Some of the families questioned this sudden change. Edger assured them that it sometimes happens with Alzheimer or dementia and often with the insane. This explanation seemed to satisfy the families, as Edger encouraged them to pray for their loved ones.

With the data collected, Edger began wondering how to administer the drug. He thought about putting it into medications. Which ones? Not everyone took the same medicines or even took medications at all. Besides, Edger wanted to "cure" as many people as possible, particularly the young, on his first try. He decided that the use of medication would not work. It was too risky, anyway.

He thought about placing it in food. Not all people ate the same things. The medium had to be global.

Water. Water was global. Every person needed it to survive. But how? Not every country had water treatment plants, and since 911, even these systems had been capped and security heightened. He knew water worked. This is how he had tested it on the patients of Gemilli's insane asylum and old folks home. Two ccs. in a glass of water was all it had taken. It was so simple.

Since the late twentieth century, water had been sold in bottles. Edger had never understood this sensation, since you could obtain water free of charge from fountains, but the phenomenon persisted and grew. Perhaps he could use this medium to transmit his serum.

Researching water bottling companies, Edger soon found more than 120 in the United Sates, 20 in Germany, 52 in France. In Italy alone there were more than 120, producing 270 brands of bottled water. He found plants in Argentina, Australia, Belgium, Brazil, Canada, Iceland, Ireland, South Africa, Sweden, Serbia and even in Siberia. In all, there were more than 500 companies worldwide. This would be a daunting task. Even if he could take control of a few of them, it would never be enough. Back to the drawing board, he thought. The idea of using water nagged at him. It was the perfect medium.

THE PREPUCE

June 1, 2066

T HE FEAST OF the Circumcision of Christ is still celebrated by many churches around the world on January 1. The first reference to survival of Christ's severed foreskin comes in the second chapter of the apocryphal Arabic Infancy Gospel which contains the following story:

1. And when the time of his circumcision was come, namely, the eighth day, on which the law commanded the child to be circumcised, they circumcised him.
2. And the old Hebrew woman took the foreskin, and preserve it in an alabaster-box of old oil of spikenard.

"This, Edger, is what will make you pope." Salvatore said pulling a bejeweled box from the safe.

"What is it?"

"It's a reliquary that contains the Holy Prepuce."

"The circumcised foreskin of Jesus? I thought that was a myth."

"Many people think so, but I have done a lot of research on the matter, and I tell you, Edger, this is the real thing. It seems that when Mary and Joseph brought Jesus to the temple to be circumcised, there was an old prophetess, named Anna, there. She was a widow who spent her days at the temple and according to Luke's

Gospel, the second person to recognize the Christ child that day. After he was circumcised, she took the prepuce as a remembrance of the day she encountered the deliverer of Jerusalem. She placed it in an alabaster box of old oil and spikenard."

"Since she was eighty four at the time, she placed the prepuce in the care of her daughter, Gomer. It was passed on to the women of the Anna's family for generations, always given the respect and adoration that Anna had given it until she died."

"It disappeared from record about AD 300, not showing up again until December 25, 800, when Charlemagne was crowned Imperator Augustus, by Pope Leo III. Charlemagne purportedly, gave it to the Pope at this time, in a bejeweled box. He claimed that it had been brought to him by an angel while he prayed at the Holy Sepulcher, but, in actuality, it had been a wedding gift from the Byzantine Empress Irene. The Pope placed it into the Sancta Sanctorum in the Lateran Basilica in Rome with the other relics. Evidently, Pope Leo didn't think much of the articles' authenticity. There were anywhere between eight to eighteen holy foreskins in various European towns during that period. If he had known that the article in his position was the real thing, he would have increased the Papal coffers thousands of times."

"Remember that at this time, the church was at the beginning stages of a corruption that would last for the next six hundred years. Relics and indulgences were central to this corruption. As you know, Edger, the popularity of relics in Medieval Europe was dependent upon the saintliness of the original owner. Third class relics are anything that has touched a first or second class relic of a saint. Second class relics are items that the saint wore or frequently used. First class relics are physical remains of a saint; bone, hair, limbs, that sort of thing and martyr's relics are more highly prized than relics of any other saints. Of course the ultimate source of relics was Jesus himself. But there was one problem. Jesus ascended body and soul to heaven. Therefore, there just wasn't any possibility of anyone acquiring an arm, leg, head, foot, or bone as has happened with so many saints. The only relics of Christ available were things like his crown of thorns, robe, sandals, pieces of the manger, the true cross, the hay on which he lay as a baby, his tunic, and the sweat and blood on Veronica's veil, and, of course, the shroud of Turin. These are the most highly prized relics in Christianity. So Leo had no idea that he was in possession of the true prepuce, a genuine, number one, grade A, first class relic.

"It remained in the Sancta Sanctorum until 1527 when a soldier in the German army, sacking Rome, looted the Sancta Sanctorum. He was captured in the village but hid the reliquary in his cell, where it remained until it was discovered in 1557.

"But, here arose a problem. There was another prepuce that had been venerated as true for centuries. It dated back to the twelfth century when the prepuce was sold to King Baldwin I of Jerusalem in the course of the first crusade. It was sent to Antwerp, Belgium, at the request of Godfrey of Bouillon, the brother of Baldwin, where it was housed on the high altar. During the celebration of Holy Mass, the bishop of Cambray saw three drops of blood that blotted on the linens of the altar, fall from this prepuce. It became an object of cult and a goal of pilgrimages. A special chapel was constructed and processions were organized. In 1426, a brotherhood was founded in the cathedral, consisting of twenty-four members, all abbots and prominent laymen, to care for the relic. The relic disappeared during the Reformation Iconoclasm in 1566, but the chapel and the brotherhood, still existed.

"The Charroux miracle was revealed as a hoax, by Abbot Bennett Louisa, a prominent member of the brotherhood. He published a report written by Abbot Maxamillian, on the miracle of three drops of blood. During this time, thanks to Martin Luther, the abbey was in desperate need of funds. The people were not making Pilgrimages to venerate the holy relics, nor were they giving alms as they did in the past. Sale of indulgences and relics were strictly forbidden by the Vatican, so the brotherhood devised a scheme to help in this crisis. The Prepuce would bleed, but not at just any time. It had to be seen by a multitude of people and by someone in authority. It was planned to have the 'miracle' occur at the Bishop's celebration of Easter Sunday Mass. The blood was actually goat's blood and the foreskin had been saturated so that some would leak out during the Mass. It worked. The Bishop was visibly shaken at the miracle, and proclaimed the prepuce's authenticity till the day of his death. Word of the miraculous bleeding foreskin spread far and wide. People poured in and the abbey's financial woes were soon over. With this report made public, the brotherhood had to disband and the Holy Prepuce of Charroux was disgraced."

"To complicate matters further, the abbey of Charroux had yet another Holy Prepuce. They claimed the Holy Foreskin was presented to the monks by Charlemagne and in the early twelfth century, it was taken in procession to Rome where it was presented before Pope Innocent III, who was asked to rule on its authenticity.

The Pope declined the opportunity. At some point the relic went missing and remained lost until 1856 when a workman, repairing the abbey claimed to have found a reliquary hidden inside a wall, containing the missing foreskin.

"The discovery led to a theological clash with the established Holy Prepuce of Calcata in Italy. By this time the Church had had enough. Holy Prepuces were springing up all over Europe and the Vatican was growing less and less supportive of relics in general. In 1900, they solved the dilemma by ruling that anyone writing or speaking of the Holy Prepuce would be ex-communicated. In 1954, the punishment was changed to the harsher degree of excommunication vitandi. Offenders would not only be excommunicated but shunned.

"Most of the Holy Prepuces were lost or destroyed during the Reformation and the French Revolution. Calcata found itself in the enviable position of possessing the last, the true prepuce, that is, until 1983. Before this time, the reliquary containing the Holy Foreskin was paraded through the streets of the Italian village on the Feast of the Circumcision, which was formerly marked by the Roman Catholic Church around the world on January 1. In 1965 the Second Vatican Council removed the day of the Holy Circumcision from the calendar.

Nevertheless, the village of Calcata continued to stage an annual procession to honor the relic. In 1983 the parish priest Dario Magnoni announced that 'this year, the holy relic will not be exposed to the devotion of the faithful. It has vanished. Sacrilegious thieves have taken it from my home. The Holy Relic had been kept in a shoebox in the back of the priest's wardrobe. Magnoni refused to discuss the event, citing the Vatican's decree of excommunication. The villagers' theories of the crime varied from theft for lucrative resale, to an effort by the Vatican to quietly put an end to the practice it had attempted to end by excommunication years ago. Some went so far as to speculate that Father Magnoni himself may have been the culprit.

"Now, Edger, here is where the story gets interesting. Dario Magnoni was my great uncle. When he died in 2046, at the ripe old age of one hundred and five, everything he owned was left to his only relative, a nephew, my father. Dad never went through any of the belongings, storing them in the attic. He just never thought that a priest could have anything interesting or useful. What did he need of another bible? Dad passed away five years ago and being an only child, I got everything. Two years ago, I finally went through Uncle Dario's belongings, and guess what I found?

"The reliquary?"

"Yes, yes indeed, my boy."

"Salvatore, how is a two thousand-year-old foreskin going to help me become pope? Does it perform miracles? Are the jewels worth enough to buy off the College of Cardinals?"

"No, my boy. You see, it's not the relic or the reliquary that are going to make you pope, but what I found in a secret compartment inside.

CONFRONTATION

August 5, 2066

CARRIED ON CHROMOSOMES, genes are the basic physical and functional units of heredity. They are base sequences that encode instructions on how to make proteins. Although genes get the majority of attention, it is the protein that performs most life functions and make up the majority of cellular structures. Genetic disorders occur when genes are altered so that the encoded proteins are unable to carry out their normal functions.

- Gene therapy is a technique for correcting defective genes. Researchers use one of several approaches to correct the faulty genes:
- The most common approach is to insert a normal gene into a nonspecific location within the genome to replace a nonworking gene.
- Homologous recombination—a normal gene is exchanged for a abnormal one.
- Returning the gene to its normal function by repairing it through selective reverse mutation.
- The regulation (the degree to which a gene is turned on or off) of a particular gene could be altered.

Sam was in an agitated state when he and Millie arrived at the lab. He had spent the past few days poring over the papers Sister

Magdalena had given him. Upon arriving at the lab he put in a call to Mother only to find out that she was not coming to the office. He called the convent and made an appointment to see her an hour and a half later. All the while, Sam paced back and forth, looking at his watch every two minutes.

"Sit down, Sam. Let's try to get some work done. It will make the time pass more quickly." Millie said.

"I can't, Mil. You know what is in those papers. What could Edger be up to? I hope Mother has some ideas." He began to pace again.

"What time is it?"

"Same as it was two minutes ago, only two minutes later. Sit down, Sam."

They went through a couple of files, but Sam's mind was not in it.

Finally, it was time to go. They crossed the courtyard, and walked the short distance to the Motherhouse. They traveled as quickly as Millie could travel in her condition. At the Motherhouse, they were admitted to a small sitting room where Mother was waiting for them.

"Sam, Millie. Good to see you. You are looking well, Millie, but I can't say the same for you Sam. Have you gotten any sleep?"

"A couple of hours a night."

"Don't believe him Mother. He's lucky if he has gotten an hour sleep since we got that envelope."

"Is it that important, Sam?"

"Yes, Mother, I believe it is." He handed her the envelope. Taking the papers out, she perused them. Surprised, she remarked, "It's your work on prostate cancer. What could possibly be so upsetting?"

"Indeed, it is my work. This is the paper I sent Edger when I requested his help in furthering my study of the homosexual gene. It is not the paper, but the notes in the margins that have me concerned. That is Edger's handwriting. He has made nota-

tions throughout the paper. If you look on page four, you will see
the notation 'ATBF1 and VMAT2 very similar.'"

"Yes, Sam, I see it."

"Mother, do you know what they are, ATBF1 and VMAT2?"

"I know they are genes, but that is as far as my expertise goes.
I am a pharmacist, not a geneticist."

"Well, ATBF1 is the gene that regulates prostate cancer. Our
study found that when this gene was on, prostate cancer did not
occur. In some men, for unknown reasons, it switches off. These
men develop the cancer. We discovered the way to switch the gene
back on. When we did this those men suffering from prostate
cancer were cured, in every case, even the most advanced cases.

"In this gene we found a sub-gene, Xq28. This is the gene we
came to Italy to study. He makes refers to it on page 8. We found
that when it is turned off, it cures male homosexuality. We have
found the way to switch it off—a simple amino acid sequence. It,
too, works every time.

"I had to do a bit of research on the VMAT2 gene, since I
wasn't familiar with it. Mother, Dr. McFarland, who found gene
Xq28, also discovered this gene. He studied it and claims that it
is responsible for religiosity."

"What nonsense. I know that genes regulate many things,
but religion?"

"There have been many studies that indicate that it does." Sam
filled her in on the work of Dr. McFarland and his colleagues.
"I researched this into the wee hours of the morning. I tried to
reach Dr. McFarland, but found that he died a few years back.
His work is legit.

"The question now, is what does Edger want with this particular gene? He was very upset and angry with the Church and
God when Julie died, but in time, he came back to the Church,
and as you know, has been very active in religious circles. He even
attends daily Mass."

"I know!" said Mother. "Maybe it is all for show. As I told you before, he has become pretty chummy with some of the Cardinals. I don't like it one bit. These men are unscrupulous. You would think that in two thousand years, the Church would be better at weeding out these kinds, so they don't scandalize the Church."

"Cardinal Lawrence DeSimone covered up for pedophiliac priests for years in his Archdiocese in the States. It was only a handful of priests, fewer than ten, but look at the scandal that created. Every priest, good or bad, is now painted with the same broad brush. Every priest has been stigmatized by what this man has done. Edger is a close associate.

"DeSimone moved to Rome to escape prosecution. He should not be living the life of a Cardinal, but be behind bars for allowing, even condoning, this to happen. When he received complaints, he would simply move the priest to a new parish, where he would find a fresh supply of youths to molest.

"There was the case of a young priest who realized that his pastor was molesting some of the children of the parish. He complained to Cardinal DeSimone. For his efforts, it was the priest who was moved, banished to a poor parish on the outskirts of the diocese. The pastor was left in his position of authority, to continue his reign of terror, not given the help he so desperately needed. In the end, it was discovered; hundreds of children were molested at the hands of this man. He died before he could come to trial.

"Rumors are abundant about the other cardinals. Edger is associating with the lowest of the low. They are known as the Fab Five in Vatican circles. One of them may be, heaven forbid, our next pope." She blessed herself. "Pope Athanasius is up in years and can not last much longer."

"What can we do? Should I confront Edger?"

"With what? His interest in a gene?" Millie interjected.

Sam and Mother had to agree.

"We will have to wait, biding our time, keeping an eye on him."

It was the only plan on which they could agree. They promised each other to keep in touch, providing any information they may acquire.

AVENGER OF THE CHURCH

June 2, 2066

A SERIOUS ACT OF disloyalty to king or country is a crime known as treason. High treason is against the king, while petit treason is against a lesser superior, for instance the murder of a husband by his wife. A traitor is a person who commits treason.

In Dante's Inferno Judas suffers the worst torments of all because of his betrayal of Jesus. His treachery is so infamous that his name has long been synonymous with traitor. It is a fate he shares with Benedict Arnold, Marcus Junius Brutus, and Vidkun Quisling. The history of the word traitor originated with Judas' "traditorem," Latin for one who delivers, of Jesus to the Roman authorities.

The evening was balmy. It had rained for the better part of the day and the humidity hung heavy over the city. Edger was the first to arrive at the hotel. Ever eager and always early, he took a seat in the lobby waiting for the arrival of the others. Shortly after Cardinal Cody Berkshire arrived, dressed in plain clothes. Without looking at Edger, he went to the elevator. Edger waited several minutes then he too headed for the elevator. He pushed the button for the thirteenth floor, got off and headed for room 1323. Cardinal Berkshire opened the door and admitted him.

"Great to see you again, Ed. Everything is going well. We have to place the final nails in the coffin, and we do that tonight. Sal called and said he would be a little late. We might as well order something from room service while we wait."

A few minutes later there was a knock at the door and Salvatore Rodolfo was admitted to the room. The three immediately got to work.

Startled by yet another knock on the door, Cody got up to answer it for the third time, expecting room service. Instead, there stood his aide, Maximillion Santiz. He was dressed in a black cassock, wearing a biretta. He calmly pushed past Cody and entered the room.

Maximillion was a handsome forty three-year-old, but looked ten years younger. At six feet two inches, a hundred and fifty pounds, Max had a swimmer's build. He was very fit, running five miles each morning at dawn and doing twenty laps in the Olympic-sized pool at the Vatican before bed, which sometimes was as late as 2:00 a.m.

Max was ordained to the priesthood when he was just twenty-four, after studying in Rome. His mother had died when he was three and his father sent him to a boarding school for Catholic boys. There, the brothers trained Maximillion in all aspects of his Catholic faith, and by the time he was eleven, he had decided to become a priest.

His coal black hair was offset by his steel blue-gray eyes. On his left shoulder was a birthmark in the shape of a large fan. 7.5 cm x 10 cm it was composed of three small fan-shaped shells with radiating fluted patterns each resembling scallops. When it got wet the interior shimmered with pastel colors. As a youngster, Max was proud of his birthmark, a pride that did not diminish as he grew older.

"Max, you have a very special mark," Brother Dominic told him when he was a Junior in high school. "The scallop is the mark of Saint James, son of Zebedee. Always pray to him, my boy. He is your special patron."

"Yes, Brother, I know, but Saint James has only one scallop. I have three!"

Maximillion was intelligent, but also had the rare commodity of common sense. He was a very religious man and an excellent priest, working his way up the Vatican ladder. He was one of the youngest priests to be raised to the level of monsignor. Maximillion was on the fast track to becoming Bishop and eventually Cardinal. He became Cardinal Berkshire's assistant almost five years previously, hooking his cart to the man who would be pope.

"How'd you know where I was, Max? What's wrong? Has something happened?" Cody asked.

"I know more about you, Cardinal, than you think. Nothing's wrong that won't be cleaned up, here, tonight."

Cody came around Max and joined Edger and Salvatore. "What do you mean?"

"I know what you are up to, Cardinal. Don't play games with me. I've worked for you for a long time and have seen and heard things. I have watched you, silently, during the past year, gone through your papers, listened in on your calls. I have followed you, and I know what you three are doing. I have stayed silent long enough. I will not allow you to ruin the Church I love. She is Jesus's spouse. I just won't allow it."

"You won't allow what, Max?"

"I know what you are planning! To make Pielaresto pope, a man without any formal religious training, someone who wouldn't even be attending Mass if Rodolfo here hadn't strong-armed him into it. There are so many qualified Cardinals, pious men who would make great popes. I once thought that you were one of them, Cody. Now, I don't think you would make a good boil on the ass of some of these holy men. I would make a better pope than he would. I just haven't figured out why you are doing it, but I will stop you tonight!"

"What do you think you are going to do about it? Things are already in place. There is nothing you can do, so just go back to the Vatican. I'll deal with you later." Cody said turning around to face Salvatore.

"I can do this!" he exclaimed as he pulled out a silenced pistol that had been hidden in the folds of his cassock. He pointed at Salvatore, pulled the trigger, hitting him in the middle of the chest. Salvatore staggered backward, blood squirting three feet from the hole in his chest, covering Cody with blood. Whether through skill, or just plain luck, Max's bullet had hit the aorta. Sal crumpled to the floor, dead, lying in an ever growing pool of blood.

Cody was shocked and spun around to see Max aiming the gun at him. Even though portly, Cody was amazingly agile. He jumped behind the sofa, just as Maximillion pulled the trigger, but was not fast enough. The bullet caught Cody in the side and he crumpled to the floor next to Sal, withering in pain.

Edger did not wait. He leapt across the room in two steps, attacking Max, attempting to wring the gun from his hand. As the two struggled, the gun went off. They stood facing each other for a moment then Edger crumpled to the floor, feigning death. The bullet caught him in the upper thigh, and with the pain, realized that he could not take Max.

Max surveyed the scene. Everything in the room was quiet. He heard stirrings in the adjacent rooms and knew he would soon be discovered. He did not have time to check each of the bodies. After looking around one last time, and not hearing anything from the three lying on the ground, Max was satisfied that each was dead, or soon would be. His work was done. He turned and fled the room, leaving the gun behind. The gun was unregistered and he had taken the precaution of dipping his finger tips in concentrated hydrochloric acid, to remove his prints. Nothing in this room would lead the police back to him. It didn't matter anyway what happened to him. His Church was now safe. The three Satans were dead. As he entered the alley from a back stair he felt exhilarated, almost euphoric. Never in his life would he have dreamed of doing something like this. It was amazing what one will do to protect something he loves. He now understood Christ's sacrifice on the cross. Undeserving as the human race is, Christ loved us enough to give his very life for our salvation. Max would do the same for his Church. He became a traitor to Cardinal Cody and had committed murder to save her.

Back in the room, Cody painfully moved from behind the couch crawling to Sal. He placed his fingers on his neck, feeling for a pulse. Finding none, he slowly got to his feet, pulling himself up using the couch. He came to Edger's side, carefully avoiding the ever growing blood pool from Sal's chest. Edger had been shot in the thigh and was just getting up. Cody realized that Max had to be stopped at any cost.

People from the surrounding rooms were beginning to tentatively peek out of their rooms to investigate. Someone had called hotel security. Soon the room would be swarming with police. The publicity would not be good. Their plans were too far along to be thwarted now.

"We must leave here now, Ed. We can't be found together tonight. I reserved the room in a fictitious name and paid for it in cash. We can leave through the back stairs. The door in the bedroom is right across from the stairs."

Helped by Edger, they took towels from the bathroom and placed one against the wound in Cody's side. Another, they used to tourniquet Ed's leg and a third was placed over his wounded thigh. The three had been shot within feet of each other and Sal's blood was spreading, covering the blood of both Edger and Cody temporarily covering the fact that there had been more than one person in the room. It is amazing how much blood a human body contains. After saying a prayer over Sal's body, they left the room.

Cody knew a physician—one who would keep his mouth shut and would ask no questions. He patched up Ed and Cody. Luckily, these bullets were not as accurate as the first. Cody's was superficial, more blood than damage. The bullet went straight through Ed's leg, missing bone, nerves and blood vessels.

Back in his Vatican suite, Cardinal Berkshire made a call.

THE AMATEUR SLEUTH

A NY PERSON CALLED to investigate particular situations by collecting facts, evidence and writing accurate reports is a detective. There are two types. Police detectives work for law enforcement and are responsible for determining the identity of the criminal. Private detectives are hired by individuals to protect or investigate the actions of another. Law firms often use them to find potential witnesses or to locate information that will help verify facts in court cases.

Though in acute pain, Edger refused to take any of the Percocet he had been given by the doctor. He needed his full faculties tonight. It was nearly 2:00 a.m. when he hobbled away from Cody. As he got into his car, he thought how fortunate it was the bullet hit his left leg, at least he was still able to drive.

Gravely distressed over the loss of his friend, Edger mulled over the unfortunate events of the evening as he drove. Approaching his destination, he put these matters aside. There would be time tomorrow for grief and pain. Tonight he had to obtain the box.

Pulling into a space in the dimness of the alley, he lifted his throbbing leg onto the asphalt, painfully pulling the rest of his body from the car. Keeping to the shadows to avoid attention, he moved as quickly and as normally as possible toward Salvatore's apartment. No need to break in—Sal had given him a key. Heading directly to the bedroom closet, he found the object in the same place Sal had hidden it the night they discussed Edger's future. Having retrieved the reliquary he scanned the apartment making certain everything was in order, then left. Driving down the street he looked in his rearview mirror to see the police arriving at the apartment.

"That was fast!" Edger thought to himself. He wondered how they had ID'd Sal so quickly. It had been close, perhaps too close. Worrying that they had seen him leave, he watched as they got out of their cars and was reassured to see no one attempting to follow him. Relieved the reliquary was now in his possession, he returned to his apartment, took several Percocet and fell into a deep sleep.

It was well past noon when Edger awoke. His leg was stiff, but he felt better. Getting out of bed, he tentatively put weight on his leg. He wouldn't be going in to work today.

"Marge, Dr. Pielaresto. Reschedule my appointments for today, and tomorrow. I'm not feeling well and won't be coming in."

"As you wish, doctor. By the way, Cardinal Berkshire called this morning."

"He did? Did he say what he wanted?"

"No, just that he would call later. Nothing important."

"Thanks Marge. I'll see you Monday."

Hanging up Edger made himself breakfast, then sat down to the task of opening the reliquary.

He tried to remember the sequence of moves Sal had performed. It took time but he finally hit upon the correct arrangement, and the secret compartment slid open. Sipping his orange juice Edger began to read. Dario's penmanship was superb. Edger soon became engrossed.

When Father Dario Magnino received his letter from the diocese appointing him pastor of the financially stressed Saint Joseph Parish in Calcata he was utterly dismayed.

"Shit!" he spat thinking himself to be alone. Dario seldom used profanity except when extremely perturbed and never in public.

"What is the matter, Father?" his housekeeper questioned. Startled, he turned around.

"This letter... the Bishop has just appointed me Pastor of Saint Joseph Parish in Calcata. How could he have done this to me? That Parish will be my end. It is as financially stable as the Titanic was unsinkable."

But being the good priest he was, Dario swallowed hard, said a silent prayer, went upstairs and packed. His mind flooded with ideas on how to get his new parish out of debt. He would need every one.

Weeks went by before Dario could unpack the last of his belongings. In the corner of the closet he found a strange little box. Opening it revealed what appeared to be a small rubber band. Further investigation showed it to be a shriveled, dry piece of what seemed to be skin. He was confused and about to throw it away when a slip of paper slid to the floor.

"The Holy Prepuce of Jesus Christ."

An indulgence of 100 years for gazing upon it.

A two hundred year indulgence gazing upon the prepuce while reciting:

> "Through the pain suffered by the Infant Jesus
> at His Holy Circumcision,
> may my sins be forgiven
> and may the souls
> of the faithfully departed
> rest in peace.
> Amen."

Could it be? Could this be real? He would find out. Going into the kitchen, where the housekeeper was fixing the evening meal, he broached the subject.

"Maria have you ever heard of the Prepuce of Jesus Christ?"

"Oh, yes Father. It used to be here, in this parish. There were big celebrations. The Holy Prepuce was processed through the streets on the feast of the Holy Circumcision. The third graders would carry huge football mums in the procession. It is one of my fondest memories. Then in the 60s the Vatican suppressed the feast and the Holy Prepuce has not been seen since."

"Is there anyone who might know what happened to it?"

Maria thought for a long while, stirring the pot of boiling spaghetti sauce.

"Giovanni Castello!" she said after a lingering pause. "He is the oldest man in the village and somewhat of an expert on the matter. He may know what has become of it."

If Dario had not been called to the priesthood, he would have become an investigator. Now, that side took over and he was eager to do some amateur detective work, but the work of the Church came first and it was days before he could seek him out. Finally getting his chance he walked to the old man's home. Expecting a housekeeper to answer the door, Dario was surprised when Giovanni himself opened it.

"Come in, Father, come in." Giovanni said, grabbing Dario's hand and shaking it vigorously. He may have been older than ninety, but he was as spry as a man in his sixties and pleased to have company, especially his priest.

Dario didn't waste any time getting right to the matter. Giovanni was a bit taken back by the frankness of this priest but answered his questions giving him the history of the Holy Prepuce, as he knew it.

"What has happened to it, Giovanni?" Dario asked.

"No one seems to know for sure Father. It hasn't been seen since the 60s, around the time the old pastor, Father DeLuca, died. Some say it was buried with him. He was very devoted to it. Others say that there is a secret society that spirited it away. You may want to go to the library. There is a whole section dedicated to it."

After thanking Giovanni, Dario quickly made his way there. To his amazement, he found several rooms filled with books and documents about the Holy Prepuce of Calcata. He began spending all his spare time there, reading, taking notes, and documenting. Within a short time, Dario was convinced he had the original item, the authentic Holy Prepuce.

Thoroughly enjoying the time he spent doing his detective work, Dario, at times, felt more like a spy, even writing in invisible ink. As the years went by, though, he found less and less time for it.

On January 1, 1980, in a simple procession through the town, Dario presented to his congregation, the Holy Prepuce. Word spread and the celebration grew. During the year more and more people came to the small church to get a glimpse of the holy item and the coffers of the parish dramatically increased, so much so that Dario was able to get the parish out of debt even setting up a trust, so there would be no financial worries for years to come. He used some of the money to construct a bejeweled box for the prepuce with a built-in secret compartment.

In 1983, Dario was ordered by the Vatican to stop the veneration of the Holy Prepuce, under threat of excommunication. Disappointed, he had no choice but to cease. Hiding the reliquary under a loose floorboard in his closet, he concocted the story of Prepuce's theft.

In 2018, on the fiftieth anniversary of his priesthood, Dario announced his retirement. He would remain in charge until a new pastor could be found. That took almost three years at which time Dario became pastor emeritus. With time now on his hands he was able to continue his research of the Holy Prepuce finally able to use the libraries across the country, including the Vatican's. His research took him way beyond its authenticity. It was here that he found a connection between the prepuce and a secret society, the Sodality of Thelema. The things he discovered chilled him to the bone. As he worked Dario sometimes couldn't shake the feeling of being watched.

In time, Dario was able to piece together a history of the Sodality and the activities of its prominent members from the time of Aleister Crowley. He was repulsed but intrigued, thinking nothing could surprise him any more, until one day he discovered a list of recently inducted members. Four names jumped from the pages. They were prominent cardinals.

Back at the rectory he would spend hours in his room, assembling all he had found. Chronologically arranging the members of the Sodality, he listed their activities. Hiding all the papers in the secret compartment of the reliquary, he kept it safely under the floor boards of the closet.

Dario celebrated his one hundred fifth birthday with a day trip to the Vatican, where he had an audience with the pope. While there he visited the library, one last time finding additional information. Back at home, he added one last name to his members list using a pen with invisible ink by mistake. Placing the papers into the reliquary, he put it in an old suitcase, instead of the hole in the floor. Going to bed he went to sleep, not to awake again.

Edger was engrossed in the papers, so much so that when the phone rang he literally jumped spilling his orange juice on them. He quickly mopped up the juice with his napkin and was amazed to see a name appearing as if by magic—a name he knew well. Cody Berkshire.

Cody was gleeful for his good fortune. Yes, Sal was dead but there was hope. Sal's reliquary would provide the ammunition Cody needed to get Edger elected pope. He was confident he held sufficient sway over him to have him dispose of Cody's rivals. Once that happened, he would use the John Paul I solution, and he, Cody Berkshire would be pope. Of that he was certain.

The morning after the shooting Cody made his way to Sal's apartment intending to find and obtain the reliquary. Approaching the apartment he saw the police cars, so he just drove by.

Back at his office he placed a call to Edger.

"Dr. Pielaresto, please."

"I'm sorry, he hasn't arrived yet. May I ask who is calling?"

"Cardinal Berkshire."

"Oh, good morning, your eminence. May I take a message?"

"No. It's not important. I'll try back later."

Cody worked for about an hour then placed the call again.

"Dr. Pielaresto's office."

"Cardinal Berkshire here, may I speak with him?"

"Good morning, Eminence. Dr. Pielaresto called to say he isn't feeling well. He won't be back in the office until Monday. May I take a message?"

"No thank you, Marge, I'll call him at home."

Edger looked at the name. There was something written next to it. Carefully dipping his napkin into his orange juice, he dabbed the paper triggering the writing to become visible. Edger couldn't believe what he saw. He never liked Cody, but Sal trusted him. With what he read it was a misplaced trust.

The phone stopped ringing, beginning again several seconds later.

"Hello."

"Edger, Cardinal Berkshire. Just calling to see how you are after last night."

"I'm fine, Cody—just a bit stiff."

"Good, good, my boy. About the issue Sal was discussing… any idea where it may be?"

"None," Edger lied. He needed time to digest what he had just read.

"I took a drive to Sal's apartment this morning."

"Oh?"

"The police were swarming all over it."

"They were?"

"Yes. I suppose they got the address from his wallet. I should have thought to take it. It would have made it look more like a robbery gone wrong."

"I wouldn't know, Cardinal."

"Well, forget about that. We must find the reliquary. May I count on you?"

"Of course, Eminence," he said, lying once more.

Hanging up, Edger pondered over what to do with the reliquary. He couldn't let Cody get his hands on it, and he needed more time to study the papers.

After dressing he took the reliquary, wrapped it in paper, put it in a bag and went to the bank. There he deposited it in his safety deposit box. For now, it was safe.

INTO HIDING

June 3, 2066

T HE CATHOLIC SACRAMENT of penance, reconciliation, or confession, has three elements: conversion, confession, and celebration. In it we find God's unconditional forgiveness, and as a result we are called to forgive others.

Max wandered the streets of Rome for hours, but it seemed like minutes, reviling in the feelings of exhilaration that the murders stirred in him. Returning to the Vatican, he went to the pool and did his customary twenty laps, and not feeling one bit tired, did twenty more. He felt alive for the first time in his life, so much so that he did not sleep that night. He reran the events of the night, the power he felt pointing the gun at his enemies, the Church's enemies. The next morning he was out before dawn running more than his customary five miles. He returned to his room to do some work there. No sense going to the office. The Cardinal wouldn't be in today, he thought laughing out loud. He had so much energy that he skipped breakfast and lunch, and feeling so good he decided to go for a run in the evening as well.

When he passed a newsstand, the headlines hit him. *Salvator Rudolfo Murdered*. Why did the headlines list Sal and not the Cardinal? Cardinals aren't murdered every day. Maybe they didn't ID him yet. He wasn't in clerical garb. He stopped and bought a paper, skimming the article for Cody or Edger's name or the mention of two unknown victims. Then he read it carefully. No mention of either. He was sure he had shot both of them. Could they have survived somehow? He had assumed that they were dead. How stupid. He had known since he was eight what assume means. He had always been more careful than that, checking and rechecking. He should have made sure. Put a bullet through the heads of those bastards. What was done was done. He needed to plan.

Max hurried to his room. Arriving there several minutes later, he began to gather all the evidence he had on Cody and placed it in a box. It wasn't very big, since most of the evidence were on DVDs or sentinel drives. He sealed the box and addressed it to the only person he still trusted in this world, Mother Hedwig Peligia Brozozowska. He had included a brief note to her, asking to keep the contents of the box safe until she heard from him, or learned of his death. He told her she would know what to do in that case. He placed the parcel in the Vatican post office and returned to his room to think and plan out his next move.

Max knew that his life was in danger, if Cody had somehow survived. He knew that Cody had "friends," the kind you don't want to meet in a dark alley or have them irritated with you. Cody was a member of an ultra-secret society, the Sodality of Thelema. Not much was known about it, and most thought that it did not exist anymore. Max gathered some information on the society when he was investigating Cody. He found out that it had started in Sicily in 1420, a society of magic. Over the years, its members became ultra-rich, founding fathers, rulers, kings and queens, many a cardinal, but never a pope. It was rumored, but never proved, that the heads of the Vatican bank were members of this society. Money was laundered through the bank, at a percentage, and funded a variety of legal to highly illicit activities drugs, alcohol, wars, and terrorism among them. Speculation had it that the money used to fund the 911 attack on the United States was laundered through the Vatican bank.

The Sodality of Thelema was the supposed home to a variety of religious artifacts, relics that had been rumored to exist, but could never be found. Max had obtained documents detailing the plans of the society. Their ultimate goal was world domination to be accomplished by acquiring significant relics from the four major religions of the world. These would be used in an elaborate ceremony, which when completed would literally bring the world to its knees. When he had first read the plans, it seemed ridiculous to him, the work of science fiction. As he got to know Cardinal Berkshire, he began to believe in demons and hellish activities. Science fiction had indeed become scientific fact.

He discovered that the Ark of the Covenant was the first of the major relics to be secured by the society. It took much time and effort to obtain it. Huge sums of money were spent, coercion tactics were used, and anyone standing in the way was eliminated. The next artifact to be obtained was the body of Buddha. After his death, his body was divided for the purpose of relics, and there was an armed conflict between factions for possession of these relics. The Sodality eventually found all the parts, leaving in their stead, body parts from their murdered victims, so none would be the wiser.

Next were the hairs from the beard of Muhammad. This was the hardest of the three to obtain, since it was housed in the Istanbul's Topkapi Palace Museum and only seen during the month of Ramadan. Through much effort and scheming, conniving and murders, the hairs were obtained. So that they would not be missed, they too were replaced with look-alikes and no one ever suspected.

The only relic that the society needed to obtain was from Christianity, the prepuce of Jesus Christ. This would give them the needed items but time was running out. There was only a bit more than three years in which to obtain the article, and no one knew where it had disappeared on that fateful day in 1983.

Before that time, the Sodality had always known where it was—thinking that it was safe enough on public display. That fool pastor actually kept it in a shoe box in his wardrobe displaying it only once a year. They could get it any time they wished. It would be the easiest to obtain, so why not leave it till last? It was safe enough where it was. They would obtain it a long time before it was need. After all, before anyone found that it was missing, the ceremony would be finished, and they would rule heaven and earth.

According to the ancient texts, the ceremony had to be performed at the start of the sacred blue moon whose numerology is 9, 20, 29, 30 and 69. This was calculated to occur on September 30, 2069. The time of the full moon would be 18:12 which adds to 30 as well. The numbers in the date add up to 29—too much of a coincidence for Max. He had been immersed in all this, when he had discovered the treachery of Cardinal Berkshire. Even though Cody was a member of the solidarity, he had not yet been baptized into it. His name appeared on the roster only as a novice, not yet permitted to take part, or even know about, the ancient ceremonies of Sodality.

Max knew, though. Thanks to his friendship with Joshua Hiem, the Vatican archivist, Max had access to rooms that no one had entered for centuries. These contained long forgotten secretes of the Papal state, and Max, being an amateur historian, was thrilled to be allowed to spend time there. It was here that he had discovered papers from the secret society, which included the levels and rituals of magic that were performed. The beginning stages were all white magic, but as a candidate achieved higher and higher levels, it became a mixture of white and black, and at the highest levels, black magic, magic of the darkest kind. Use of this magic could rip the soul from the body and the practitioner could use that soul to do his bidding.

The Sodality used relics in their rituals of magic and had obtained many for this purpose. The staff of Moses, the footprint of Muhammad, the crosses of Sts. Peter and Andrew, the blade used to behead St. Paul and the head of St. John the Baptist, were among the many others in the Sodality's immense collection.

A curious thing had happened to Max about a year earlier while reading through some of the more ancient papers. A name, a familiar name, came across his gaze. He read it, then read it again. Cardinal Cody Berkshire. The paper was evidently old, as was the ink. It was covered in dust. Could there have been another Cody Berkshire who was cardinal in the distant past? He doubted it. He looked at the paper and other names popped out at him. Max knew he had found something that was meant to remain unfound. He copied all the information from the paper on which Berkshire's name was found, realizing it was an initiation form to the Sodality. From then on, whenever Max got a chance, he came back to this room, and researched.

It was this information that Max sent to Mother Hedwig Peligia. Cody, though not officially a member, was still enveloped by the cloak of the Sodality. They could be called upon in his time of need and help would arrive. Max was among the living dead.

He left the Vatican with just his passport, and whatever money he had on hand. He went immediately to the bank machine and took out as much money as he could. His credit cards and checks would soon be useless. Cody would have them canceled. He knew, also, that he could be traced through his transactions. He had the presence of mind to change the user name and password on the computer, before wiping the memory clean. He dressed in tourist clothing, so as to blend in. Max could not be conspicuous, not if he were to survive.

From the Vatican, Max headed southeast toward Pietrelcina, the home of Saint Pio, the stigmatist. He could blend in with the tourists, who came from all over the world to visit the site where Padre Pio lived out his life. They were Italian, English, French, German, Russian, Polish, Japanese, and American among others. Being from America he blended in well with the tourists. Besides speaking English, Max also fluently spoke Italian, French and German. He took the train whenever possible but wanting to not be exposed to too many people, Max walked a lot of the way. He slept wherever he could find an empty spot. On rare occasions he would get a room, to shower and try to relax. Max was always looking over his shoulder. While there, Max took the opportunity to participate in the Sacrament of Reconciliation with one of the many priests of Padre Pio's Capuchin order.

"Bless me father for I have sinned. It has been two weeks since my last confession. I have committed the following sins. I killed a man and wounded two others."

The priest had thought he heard wrong. "I'm sorry my son, could you repeat that. The noise in the church must have done something to my hearing."

"I said, father, I killed a man and wounded two others. He was a very bad man, father, and I had intended on killing the other two, but was not successful. Father, they were the enemies of Holy Mother Church. I had no other options. They intended on bringing the Church down and I could not let that happen. Even so, I am so very sorry for my sins, these and those of my past life."

"When did this happen, my son? You said that your last confession was only two weeks ago."

"Father, it was the evening of my last confession."

"My son, are you truly sorry for your sins?"

"Yes, father, I am. I wish with my whole heart that it had never happened."

"Have you talked to the police, my son?"

"I can't do that father. I am a wanted man. I am not afraid of dying, or going to jail, but there is further work that I must do, before I can turn myself in. The Church is still in danger."

"My son, I must insist that you turn yourself into the authorities."

"I will, father, but I can't, not just yet."

"What else do you need to do?"

"Father, I can't tell you that, I have involved you in this matter far too much already."

"My son, you know that anything you reveal to me is under the silence of the confessional. I cannot reveal to anyone what you tell me. Remember, when you leave this confessional, it is as if the act and the knowledge of the act are gone."

"I know that father, but I have involved you too much already."

"As a man, and a priest, I don't understand taking a life, but you seem truly sorry. I wish that you could confide in me further. Please make your Act of Contrition."

"Oh, my God, I am heartily sorry for having offended Thee. I detest all my sins because of Thy just punishments. Most of all, because they offend Thee my God, Who art all good and deserving of all my love. I firmly resolve, with the help of Thy grace, to sin no more and to avoid the near occasion of sin. Amen."

"For your penance, reflect on the act you have committed, say the twenty decades of the rosary, and seriously consider turning yourself into the police. I am sure that they can help you. 'God, the Father of mercies, through the death and resurrection of his Son has reconciled the world to himself and sent the Holy Spirit among us for the forgiveness of sins; through the ministry of the Church may God give you pardon and peace, and I absolve you from your sins in the name of the Father, and of the Son, and of the Holy Spirit.'"

"Amen."

"Give thanks to the Lord, for he is good."

"His mercy endures forever."

"My son, my name is Padre Maximillion. I want you to know that if you ever need me, in any way, I will do what is in my power to help you. I am stationed here at the monastery. Go, in the peace of Christ."

"Thank you, Father. I'll remember."

Max left the confessional leaving quickly via the side door, so as to become lost in the crowd. He saw the priests name as a sign that God had indeed forgiven his sins and was with him now.

That evening, Max left Pietrelcina and headed north toward a second tourist attraction in Italy: Assisi. All the time he was hoping to lose anyone who might be following him, by walking, hitching, and finally taking the train. In Assisi, Max mingled with the crowds, hoping for a sign from Saint Francis. While praying at the crucifix, in the Porziuncola, the small church in the parish of Santa Maria degli Angeli, situated about four kilometers from Assisi, the place from where the Franciscan movement started, three white doves flew in and perched, one on the left arm of the cross, one on the right arm and the third on the head of the dying Christ. This was his sign. Father, Son and Holy Ghost.

He needed to get back to Rome. Time was running out. Next week was the first Sunday in Advent. The Sodality must be stopped!

A DECISION OF SAFETY

September 19, 2066

THELEMA IS A philosophy of life based on the rule "Do whatever you want." This principle was fully developed by Aleister Crowley, who founded Thelema a religion based upon it.

Aleister Crowley (Edward Alexander Crowley) was born October 12, 1875, in Leamington Spa, at 11:30 p.m. He was a Libran with Pisces moon and Leo rising. He died on December 1, 1947.

Before leaving Assisi, Max had formulated a plan. It involved his returning to Rome and to Mother Hedwig Peligia. He had now been on the run for more than three and a half months, returning during the warmest part of the year. He believed it safest to meet her in her office at the hospital.

Mother had met Maximillion Santiz when he came to study at Pontificia University where she had been teaching a required course on Church ethics. Max proved to be a worthy student, brightest in the class. He was motivated and charismatic. People took an immediate liking to him, and Mother was no exception. Max would remain after class, and he and Mother would have long discussions on ethical issues of the day facing the church.

"Max!" Mother said. "I am so glad you are alive! I have prayed for you daily since I received your package."

"Mother, I need your help. I need sanctuary. I am being hunted by some unscrupulous men. Please, Mother. If you don't grant me sanctuary, and hide me, I am a dead man."

"Max, what is this all about? I received your package and note and then I had heard you were missing. Where have you been?"

"Mother, I can't tell you much. I don't want to endanger you more than I have already. Perhaps, I shouldn't have come here at all. You are the only person in the world whom I trust."

"Max. I told you when you finished my class, that if you ever needed me, I would do all in my power to help you. We have been friends for some twenty years now. I hope you realize that you can come to me with any problem."

"Thanks, Mother, but my problem is bigger than any ethical problem we have ever discussed."

"We discussed some pretty deep ethical issues Max."

"I know, Mother, but this is different. The issues we discussed were about other people. This involves me."

"Well, Max, you better tell me about it then."

"I told you, I can't tell you much. The less you know the better. I can tell you this. It involves a secret organization called the Sodality of Thelema. Mother, these are debauched, ruthless people, who will stop at nothing to bring down the Church and take over the world. If they have their way, life, as we know it, will cease to exist.

"What do you mean? I studied the Sodality. They provided me with many ethical issues for my class. I thought that they were defunct. No one has heard of them in more than a hundred years. Not since the death of Aleister Crowley."

"That's just it. No one realizes that they still exist. That is the problem. Since no one believes that they still exist, they can work undetected."

"How do you know about them?"

"Mother, have you looked at the material that I sent to you?"

"No. Since I had not heard that you had died, I respected your wishes."

"Good. It will come better from me. Since I have been working for Cardinal Berkshire, I began to see some irregularities. I began looking into some matters. What I found shocked me. Mother, I found out that Berkshire is to be indoctrinated into the Sodality. I also found out that several other Cardinals are already members—high ranking members. Mother, they plan on making Edger Pielaresto pope."

"What... how?" Mother sat heavily back in her chair, her expression one of shock and dismay.

"Mother, that is not the worst of it. When Dad died last year, I went through Mom's stuff. I found out that I was illegitimate. My father was not my biological father. When he married my mother, she was already pregnant with me. I found a letter that Mom wrote to me before she died. In it, she revealed the identity of my biological father. It was Paul Crowley, the grandson of Alister. She also revealed that I have a half-brother, Ahren Arachne. Guess what? Ahren is now the head of the Sodality. It is he who needs to be stopped. Ahren will preside over a ceremony that will bring the Sodality back into power, big time. I have learned the date of that ceremony, September 30, 2069. That doesn't give us much time, a little less than three years to stop them. That is why I need your help. I need a safe place to plan on how to stop this."

"Max. I need time to think about and pray over this. I don't know where I could possibly hide you. If you were a woman, I could pass you off as one of the sisters. Can't you go to the authorities?"

"Berkshire has the authorities in his back pocket, mother. I would be just as dead with them as I will be wandering the streets of Rome."

"Let me think. Where can I send you to be safe?" Mother sat back in her chair. "For tonight you can stay in the guesthouse on the convent grounds. No one will be there until later this week. By then, I am sure I can find you something."

With Max securely in the guesthouse, Mother called Joshua Hiem. She requested to meet with him that evening. When he arrived she told him the story and asked for his help.

"I don't know what to do, Joshua. Max needs a safe place to stay until I can think things through. Can you think of any place?"

"Mother, may I tell you something, in confidence?"

"Of course, Joshua."

"Mother, Max and I know each other. We met several years ago when I came to the Vatican. I have been allowing him to work in areas of the Vatican Archive that don't get much attention. In fact, they get no attention at all. Max has been the only visitor there since I began as archivist. He seemed really excited one day a couple of months ago. I was going to ask him what he found, but thought better of it. Max was always excited to have access to the archives. He just couldn't get enough history. I figured that he had seen something of historical significance for him. I wonder now just what it was."

"I wouldn't know, Joshua. He sent me a package about three months ago. In the letter attached, he asked me to keep it safe until he returned or I learned of his death. I don't know what to do. My faith tells me that I must help. I can't sit idly by and watch him die. He seems certain that he will."

"I have an idea, Mother. There is a small room, with a bath in the Sancta Sanctorum. Not many people go to the Sanctorum, and I am always notified well in advance if someone requests access. He will be safe there until he decides what he must do."

"Then it is settled. He will stay here tonight and go with you tomorrow."

"I think it best for all that we get Max to the safety of the Sancta Sanctorum tonight. There is no need to endanger the convent any further. I have tinted windows in the car and have access to the underground parking lot with a private entry to the archives. There is no one there at night, so I can get him in without being seen."

"Please be careful, and God be with you and bless you, Joshua." Mother said as they went to retrieve Max.

TRANSGENDERED

December 20, 2066

IN THE YOUNG pubescent male the hormone testosterone is produced in copious amounts. Most of the tissues within his body contain testosterone receptors and as the hormone surges it has a penetrating affect throughout his body causing facial and body hair to develop and grow, fiber size to increase, muscle cells to strengthen and external genitalia to mature. Aggression, risk taking and territoriality are among the behaviors testosterone enhances.

"Please, father, please don't."

"It's for your own good."

"But they hurt and I am sick for hours after the shot."

"Don't whine son, it's not manly."

"But I'm a girl, father!"

Slapping her hard across the face Paul said *"You are not!* Don't ever say that again! You are a BOY! I will not have my legitimate child be a girl. What good are girls anyway? You are my son, and these shots will insure that! Your mother always did what I commanded her. I don't know why she betrayed me in a matter of such importance. She knew that in my entire line, going back to the 1500s, there has been only one legitimate child per pairing, and that has always been a boy. There have been numerous illegitimate children, but they don't count. I need an heir, a son, to take my place in the Sodality. Only my SON can bring lifetimes of work to fruition."

He gave her the shot.

Ahren awoke with a start. He was in his room, fifty years later.

Ahren had been born on December 25, 2000, the first and only child of Paul and Margaret Crowley. The birth had been very easy, only two hours of labor, and not much pain. An ugly baby, Ahren closely resembled man's nearest relative, the chimpanzee.

Paul wanted—no he needed—his first born to be a boy. This would be the only legitimate child allowed by the Sodality. They ordained that each member have only one. So this child could not be a girl. If the child were a girl, he would be thrown out of the Sodality, his memory erased. He and Margaret had discussed the matter before and during her pregnancy. Paul mandated it to be a boy and had already named the child, Ahren. Something had gone wrong, terribly wrong. All his potions and spells had been for naught. Somehow Margaret had defied him, giving him a girl instead of the boy he was desperate to have. This was unacceptable, and Margaret would be punished.

Margaret was to defy him twice more though. Margaret's ultimate betrayal was her death just hours after Ahren's birth. Paul was so angry; he left her body at the hospital.

"Mr. Crowley. What arrangements have you made for your wife?" inquired the nurse as he was preparing to leave with his "son."

"None."

"What do you mean? She has to be buried. You can't leave her here!"

"I don't care what you do with her. Incinerate her or throw her on the garbage heap. Treat her like the trash she was," he said as he left with the baby. The hospital gave Margaret a pauper's burial.

Margaret's second betrayal, her last, was the birth certificate. There, in black and white, Paul saw the name of his child, Ahren

Ariana Agatha Arachne, two girls' names and Margaret's maiden name. How dare she? What a bitch he had married. It was a good thing that she was dead. What pain he would have inflicted on her for her deceit. The anger burned inside him, eating away at him. Sometimes it was great enough to cause him to conjure a maleficium on some unsuspecting Margaret look-alike, he saw on the streets. He should have married Susan. At least, just hours before Ahren was born, Susan had given him a true son.

Ahren lived up to her name. As she grew, she became more spider-like, devouring anyone who got in her way, especially men.

Throughout her life, she was treated like a boy and eventually began to think and act as such. The hormone mixture had the desired effects. Not only did Ahren not develop, she developed male secondary sex characteristics, including facial and chest hair and a deep voice. Whether from the shots or just genetics, Ahren grew to a bit more than six feet.

When Ahren was eighteen, Paul had her indoctrinated into the Sodality. Paul never dreamed Ahren would rise to the level to which she was destined. In his prime, Paul was considered a gifted sorcerer, but even so, he had only attained the tenth level. Something seemed to have left him after Ahren's birth, and as she grew stronger in the occult, Paul grew weaker. Jealousy set in as Paul saw his influence and prestige within the Sodality slipping away from him and going to his "son."

Ahren was much more like his mother than his father. Paul began to remember Margaret's betrayal. Would Ahren do the same? With all that he sacrificed, for the good of the order, for Ahren's good, betrayal was in his eyes. Every time Paul looked at Ahren, he saw Margaret's eyes, and he knew something had to be done.

Ahren was intuitive and saw her father's attitude change toward her. The only people in the world who knew her secret were he and Paul. During the first three years in the Sodality, Ahren realized what a fantastic thing Paul had done for her. The

Sodality was everything she expected and more. As a male he was gaining a power he never could have dreamed of as a woman. Paul had made him the man he was, but with the jealousy he was now exhibiting and Ahren's realization that he could bring him down, by exposing him for who, and what, he really was, her father became excess baggage.

A plan formulated in her mind, and Paul was eliminated by the strategic placing of a pillow over his face as he slept. It was easy. Ahren didn't feel anything. The old man didn't struggle, much. Ahren had developed thick, strong muscles.

"Thanks, Dad," he thought as he lifted the pillow from his father's lifeless face. The pain had all been worth it. Years of agony as the serum took hold. Now, the injections were no more than a bee sting.

Looking down on the flaccid face of his father, Ahren contemptuously spat, "Well, old man, you should have married that bitch Susan, who bore your true first born son. Maybe you would still be alive. I would wager that you didn't know I knew about him. Now, there is nothing you can do to save him."

As Ahren turned to leave the room, he heard his father. He said only one word, "Max." Ahren went back into the room. No, he was dead. Imagination. What a useless thing. He had doubted himself, he had doubted his kill, something that would never happen again.

Paul had been weak, physically and magically, but not Ahren. Even though Paul hadn't spoken much about Margaret, Ahren found out that she had been an extraordinary sorceress, much stronger than her husband. Ahren inherited his skills from her, not from Paul. As the years went on, Ahren developed a reputation in the Sodality and it was one of fear. No one dared cross him.

Soon Ahren was the undisputed leader having achieved the highest level in the Sodality, performing the most powerful magic. Ahren's authority was unquestioned. Either through skill or intimidation, he climbed higher and higher. Many rivals were found dead under mysterious circumstances.

Cardinal DeSimone came to the Arachne's lair. He had just returned from Calcata, where Ahren had sent him to retrieve the last relic needed for the ritual which would make Ahren ruler of the world.

"What do you mean it is not there? Where is it? You said that it would remain safe at that parish in Calcata," Arachne said as he fumed. No one had ever remembered his being so mad.

"It did, but in 1983, it supposedly disappeared," Cardinal DeSimone tried to explain.

"The order had inside information that the parish priest had stolen it. He was under the threat of excommunication if he so much as mentioned it in public, so he conjured up the theft. Since it would not be needed for eighty years, your predecessors decided it would be safe left with the priest. The Sodality kept an eye on him. He died in 2046, and the Sodality thought that it remained safe under the floor boards of the priest's cupboard, still secure in the old shoe box. Before returning here, I found evidence that in 1983, the Vatican had secretly spirited it away and that it is now in the Sancta Sanctorum in the Vatican. They left the priest to play the ruse. With our access, it should prove little effort to obtain it."

"Well, do so immediately. I want that last piece of the puzzle in my hands within a fortnight, or your spirit will be doing my bidding." Arachne stormed out. Alone in the room, with the drapes tightly shut, Ahren lay down and fell back into the semi-coma of sleep.

SANCTUARY

September 19, 2066

POPE PAUL V established the modern archives of the Holy See in 1610. He was not the first Pope to carefully preserve the manuscripts of faith as Popes from the time of Peter had also done so. Kept in the Scrinium Sanctae Romanae Ecclesiae, these works followed the Popes wherever they moved. With political upheavals and the fragility of papyrus the entire collection was nearly lost by the time of Innocent III, late in the twelfth century. By the fifteenth century these precious documents were safeguarded at the Castel Santé Angelo and along with papal bulls and briefs, and the collections of documents up to the papacy of Pius V, were retained in three halls establishing a new archive— the Vatican Secret Archives.

Urban VIII and Alexander VII considerably increased the archives during their reigns in the 1600s.

The first half of the eighteenth century saw the library supervised by three archivists who organized the documents and books and through acquisitions, deposits, and transfers, greatly increasing the size of the collection.

In 1783 the archive was finally moved to the Vatican from Avignon. Great losses were incurred in 1810 when Napoleon ordered the Holy See to return the archives to France and their subsequent return to the Vatican between 1815 and 1817.

With the birth of the Italian State in 1870, the archives had a new adversary. The documents found outside the Vatican walls were seized and formed the core of the new state's archive.

In 1881, free access to the Vatican Secret Archives was granted to scholars by Leo XIII. Because of his generosity the library became one of the most important historical research centers in the world. Access was further liberalized in the 1970s by Paul VI.

Joshua transported Max safely to the Sancta Santorum, settling him into the secret room. It was small, comfortable, and very private. From the outside, it looked like a small closet, but inside, it contained a bed, a plush chair, a TV, a small refrigerator, and a bath. Unless you knew it was there, you would be hard pressed to find it. It was tucked in the back corner and to the unobservant eye, the room just was not there. The door was sunk into the wall blending well with its surroundings, and unless you were specifically looking for it, you just did not see it. Most staff had to be initiated into the fact of the room's existence. Even after all these years, Joshua sometimes lost sight of the room himself. It was as though the room disappeared and then reappeared. There was something mystifying, almost magical about it.

From all outward appearances, the room was a small closet. Only the curator knew its secret. The wall at the back of the closet contained a secret panel, which opened into a bed room. To open the door required a key that resembled a jimmy. There was only one and that was kept by the curator. The key was inserted between the paneling on the left side and pushed up, like a large light switch. When the panel slid to the right you entered the bedroom. The bath was through a door in the back.

It had been used by various curators as a kind of retreat where they could relax from their duties, but also keep an eye on things. A two way mirror had been placed on the left wall for this purpose.

Joshua brought meals to Max, and the two would talk about their lives, where they grew up, and why they chose their careers, but any discussion always turned to how to stop the Sodality.

Mother came whenever she could, and Max was always happy to see her. When he did not have visitors, Max welcomed the time, in safety, to relax and pray. He did miss receiving Holy Communion, though, and sometimes thought about sneaking out for that purpose. He always thought better of it. After all, Joshua had the only key to get back in. Max knew that in order to save the Church, the Sodality must be stopped. Josh and Mother agreed. If the three of them succeeded in stopping those who were determined to hurt the Church, Edger would not be Pope, now or ever.

On Hallows Eve, Halloween in the United States, Joshua brought Max a bag of candy.

"Trick or Treat," Josh said as he entered presenting Max with the bag.

"I think you got it wrong, Josh. I'm suppose to give you candy when you come to my house on Halloween."

"Maybe I did, but it's more fun this way. We can share."

Many an evening was spent with the two or three talking and planning, but noting solid was forming. How? How could things be stopped? The Sodality was powerful and they were only three. The days turned into weeks and the weeks into months and still no plan. Then, on the evening of December 19, as they were talking they heard a noise. Josh looked at Max indicating that no one was to be in the archive. As a precaution, he turned off the lights and made sure that the door was securely closed. Going to the two way mirror he gestured for Max to join him.

Entering the room were five figures holding flashlights. They stopped in the middle of the vast room. Josh flicked the switch below the mirror, a speaker, to hear what was being said.

"I don't like this. What if someone comes in? What if Hiem comes back?"

Don't worry about Hiem. We're cardinals, remember? What can that Jew do to us? We have every right to be here, any time we want. Besides, it's not Hiem you need to worry about. It's Arachne. We can't go back without the item. It must be here. Start looking, but keep everything neat. We can't afford any unnecessary publicity as to what we are doing."

As he said this, he turned to the mirror to adjust his zucchetto. Josh gasped as he recognized the figure. It was Cardinal Cody Berkshire, whom he had always thought of as a friend. Leaning closer to Josh, Max said,

"It's the Fab Five, Josh. Cody Berkshire, Alfrado Bennadetto, Domingo Saferino, Lawrence DeSimone, and Brendan Callahan. Each wants to be the next pope, and I told you that they are all members of the Sodality. Arachne is my half brother."

"What do you think that they could possibly be looking for?"

"I don't know. Just listen. Maybe they'll give us a clue."

DeSimone headed for the door to Max's room. Cody stopped him.

"Larry, that's just a closet. There's nothing in there except cleaning supplies. Make yourself useful and go search the next room."

The group searched for almost two hours, at which point they gathered in front of the mirror.

"It's not here!" Bennadetto said.

"I know that Al. Stop stating the obvious!"

"I was sure it would be here" Larry said. "I told Arachne it was here. What are we going to do?" He sounded scared and was beginning to lose his composure.

"Calm down Larry!" Brendan said.

"How? It's not your soul that will be doing Arachne's bidding."

"We'll find it," Dom said. "It's getting late and we are due at a meeting at 9:00 a.m. We'll do a fresh search tomorrow. We still have time. I promise Larry, we'll find the prepuce."

The five left the room. After a minute, to be sure that they would not return, Joshua turned on the light.

"What is the prepuce and why would it be here?" Max asked.

"I don't know, but something in the back of my mind rings a bell. I just can't put my finger on it."

Joshua's phone began to vibrate.

"Who could be calling me at this hour?"

He answered. It was Mother. She was waiting outside and wanted to come in. Josh went to get her. A few minutes later they were all together.

"I was coming to see Max, but as I was coming up the walk, I saw the five cardinals entering the building. It struck me as odd that they would be coming to the archives at night with flashlights, so I waited until I saw them leave. What were they doing here at this hour, Joshua?"

"They were looking for something, Mother."

"What?"

"Something called the prepuce. I have heard of it, but can't come up with what it is."

"Josh, it's the foreskin of Jesus. It was stolen from Calcata almost a hundred years ago, in 1983. What do you suppose they want with it?"

"Mother," Max injected. "Remember the ceremony. I told you both about it. It is the last piece of their puzzle. When they obtain it, they will have everything they need to rule the universe to be gods. The ceremony must take place on September 30, 2069, at exactly 18:12, or all is lost for them. We have less than three years to infiltrate the Sodality and put a stop to this madness. If the Fab Five are looking for the prepuce, we must stop them."

"What can we do? Do you have any idea where their headquarters is?" Josh asked.

"No! I have got to think." Max sat on the bed, deep in thought. Suddenly he sprang to his feet. "Mother, do you still have the items I sent to you?"

"Of course, Max. They're safe, in the convent."

"Mother, I need to have access to them. I think there may be a clue in the contents of one of the sentinel drives. I must look."

"You can't use the computers here Max. They are monitored, and I couldn't explain why one was on this late at night. There would be an investigation."

"There are computers at the convent," Mother said.

The three set off for the convent.

"Max sat at the computer, opening one flash drive after another. Eventually he found what he was looking for.

"Look at this."

Mother and Joshua came and leaned over his shoulder.

"There is a book, an ancient history of the Sodality. Joshua, is it in the archives?"

"What is its name?"

"I don't know. The documents don't say."

"If you had a title, I could tell you if it is there, even in the darkest recesses of the archives. Without a title, there is little I can do."

"I can search, was Max's reply.

Back in the archives, Max did just that. After closing time, he would come out and search. Days went by, then weeks. Max started to believe he would never find it. Maybe it didn't exist anymore. Maybe it had never been written.

PRE-CONCLAVE DISCUSSIONS

December 23, 2066

Pope Clement IV died on November 29, 1268, leaving the Papal Throne empty for almost three years. From the beginning of the conclave, held in the province of Viterbo, about fifty miles from Rome, the cardinals divided into two factions, French and Italian. To be elected, a two thirds plus one majority is required, but neither group had the resources for their contender to be elected. And neither was willing to give in. The city officials, during the summer of 1270, were tiring of the stalemate and resolved to compel a vote. Confined to the Bishop's palace the cardinals had their daily food allowance brutally reduced but to no avail. At this point, the French and Sicilian kings got involved. They hammered out a compromise in which the fifteen Cardinals selected a group of six from their ranks to ruminate the selection. On September 1, 1271 they agreed upon Teobaldo Visconti, archdeacon of Liege. He was neither a cardinal nor a priest. At the time of his election, he was on a pilgrimage in the Holy Land with Prince Edward of England. Beginning his return trip on November 19, 1271, he arrived at Viterbo on February 12, 1272. Declaring his acceptance of the Papacy he chose the name Gregory X, but did not arrive in Rome until March 12, 1272. There he was ordained on the nineteenth and officially consecrated Pope on March 2. Gregory X died on January 10, 1276.

Cody waited a day after the pope's death to contact the other cardinals, Alfrado Bennadetto, Domingo Saferino, Lawrence DeSimone, and Brendan Callahan. He requested an urgent meeting with them. All replied in the affirmative and the meeting was set for two days hence. Even though the conclave was not starting for seventeen days, time was running out and Cody was getting antsy. Once in the conclave, there was no way to contact the outside world. All must be in place before the cardinals were sequestered.

Cody opened the meeting. "Fellow Cardinals, as you know, the pope is dead. Technically, we are not allowed to politic, but since St. Peter's ascension to the papal throne, politicking has been a major part of pre-conclave. We were all part of the conclave which elected Athanasius. We all did our share to have him elected. We were all screwed."

"Now, the church is at a crossroads. Athanasius did not follow through on the principals that got him elected, our principals, but chose to go his own way. Fortunately, he died before any real damage could be done."

"We were a gnat's whisker from being exposed. We must act now, ensure that a pope is elected who will do as we wish. None of us has the ability to be elected on our own, and not one of us trusts any of the others. So, we are at a standstill. We can go into the conclave and pray for a solution, or we can go into conclave with the solution."

"What I am proposing, gentleman, will seem controversial and unnatural to you, but I assure you that when you think the matter through, you will see that it is our only way out."

"I propose the election of Edger Pielaresto as pope."

Stunned silence hit the room. The Cardinals looked from one to the other, none knowing what to say. Then Saferino said, "Cody, this can't be. You must be a cardinal to be elected pope."

"Man's rules, Dom. Remember Peter? The College of Cardinals didn't even exist until almost AD 1100. The first 160 popes weren't cardinals. Pope Celestine V wasn't even a priest. Rules can be bent or broken if necessary."

"But why Edger?" DeSimone asked. "Why not some obscure bishop or priest? Why a layman?"

"First, he speaks seven languages, including English, Italian, Spanish, Arabic, German, Russian and Mandarin. As you know, China has the fastest growing Catholic population in the world. The uprising in 2032 caused the fall of Communism and the rise of semi-democracy in China. The people, having had enough of the one child rule, challenged the government, who by this time didn't have enough young men to fill the ranks of the military. The people won and allowed to worship freely, chose Catholicism which allows a couple to have as many children as God will give them. Edger, speaking Mandarin, will endear himself to a quarter of the world's population."

"Second, he was the chief administrator of the Gemelli hospital for years, and has an intimate knowledge of the running of a large cooperation."

"But, Cody," Bennadetto interrupted, "how does any of that help us? There are many bishops and priests who can do as much or more. What makes Edger so special?"

"Because he can be controlled. Knowing little of the inner workings of the Vatican, he will need advisors. We will be there... to advise. Besides, there is no time to find anyone else and Edger is already in place, eager to serve."

After talking well into the night, the Cardinals came to no consensus. Cody began to wonder if Edger Pielaresto would ever be pope.

THE ASHES OF THE RED HEIFER

February, 2067

This is the ordinance of the law which the LORD hath commanded, saying: Speak unto the children of Israel, that they bring thee a red heifer without spot, wherein is no blemish, and upon which never came yoke.

Number 19: 2 (KJV)

S HORTLY AFTER THE conclave began, Edger received a brief e-mail from his sister Tiffany. It surprised him, since he had not heard from any of them since moving to Italy. He had almost deleted it. How did she get his address anyway? Oh, well. He opened it.

Edger,

Mom died Thursday, cremated Friday. Buried next to dad's ashes in Mount Royal Cemetery. Thought you should know. She didn't want you to come. I've attached the obituary, which she wrote herself a few days before she died.

Tiffs

Pielaresto,
Joan V.

84 of Ross Township, formerly of West View, died
Thursday, February 3 2067.

Daughter of the late Howard and Susan (McSorley)
Harris. Wife of the late Sidney Pielaresto. Mother of
Tiffany (Christopher) McNeil, Eric (Cecelia) and Edger
Pilaresto.

Grandmother of Renee (Giles) Rafferty, Crystal
(Odell) Odysseus, Emily (Francis) Ballard, Matthew
(Fanymore) and Tom (Barbara) Pielaresto.

Great-grandmother of Monica Rafferty, Denise, Paul,
and Bertha Odysseus, Edward, Peter, Thomas, and Brooke
Pielaresto. Joan valiantly suffered for many years from
various ailments stemming from the birth of her youngest
son Edger. She was always patient during her excruciating
pains, never complaining, although she had every reason
to. Memorial service will be Saturday, at 10 a.m. Interment
in Mount Royal Cemetery.

Edger read the e-mail again. Well, they were both dead. He
wondered when his father had died. No one had contacted him.
His Dad was still alive when Edger left the states, back in the
'40s. Could it have been that long? He wondered why he felt
nothing for either of his parents. Once, in a philosophy class, he
was told, the opposite of love was not hatred, but indifference. He
certainly didn't love his parents, but he didn't hate them either.
He felt nothing, nothing at all:

Edger began to think about his life, about Julie, how he had
been robbed, what could have been. Feelings of envy and hatred
crept back in. His life, since Julie had died, was miserable and
lonely. Her birthday was February 9. She would have been forty
six next week. He felt himself becoming depressed. He had to
stop. He needed to work, put his mind to something else. He
went to the lab.

During this time, Sam, Millie, Mother, and Joshua would meet, whenever possible. Mother and Joshua had decided not to tell Sam and Millie about Max or the Sodality. It was not that they didn't trust them. They had so much on their plates. Taking care of four growing children was a full time job as it was. Then, there was VMAT2. Since receiving the information from Sister Magdalena, Sam had devoted every spare hour trying to find an antidote, just in case Edger somehow succeeded in turning it off. He didn't know how Edger could do this monumental task. There were more than a billion Catholics in the world.

But Sam knew Edger well enough to know that when he wanted something badly enough, he got it. He would move heaven and hell to get what he wanted. Sam also knew that religion was an integral part of people's lives. Those who were truly happy were those who had a deep religious awareness, a sense that, no matter what, they were not alone and that this life was not all there was. Those who had no religious feelings, often were not happy, longing for something more, something that eluded them. So Sam worked. During the day, he tested and refined the serum for the Xq28 gene, and at night, he worked on the reactivation of VMAT2.

Mother and Joshua were tired. So much had happened lately. Things that no one should see, and there was more on the way. Sam recognized this, and he and Millie invited them for a nice quite evening, as quiet as it could with the kids around. After dinner, coffee was served in the parlor, and the discussion soon turned to the Ashes of the Red Heifer. It was a bright spot among the darkness they had found themselves.

"About a year and a half ago, Mother and I were discussing relics, one of our favorite topics. She told me that the Order of the Blessed Sacrament had the largest collection of relics in the world, outside of the Vatican. As we were talking, I asked if she had ever heard of the Ashes of the Red Heifer. She thought for a moment and then said not only had she heard of them, that they were part of the order's collection. I didn't think I heard her correctly, and she said that she distinctly remembers seeing a container marked as such. She didn't know much about them, so I explained their significance for the Jewish people and the rebuilding of the temple."

"How do you know they are real, Joshua?" Millie asked.

"We traveled to the Motherhouse in Poland several months ago. While there, Mother and I were permitted to examine the ashes. Sister Anastasia, the curator of the collection was at our disposal. She, herself, is a wealth of information."

"Sister has held that position, it seems, since I was a novice." injected Mother.

"She has documentation on each piece and knows exactly where everything is. Within minutes Sister had not only located the vessel, but the document as well."

"Sister has a photographic memory. That makes her perfect for the job. She told us exactly what was in the document, even though she hadn't seen it in years."

"'In the fourteenth century,' Sister Anastasia told us, 'an old Jewish man came to the door of the convent. He introduced himself as Rabbi Goldstein. He told the sisters that he had journeyed far, to escape the persecution in his homeland, and asked to stay the night. The sisters granted his request, gave him a much-needed meal and a bed for the night. During dinner, he wove his tale of the red heifer ashes.

"'When Jerusalem was destroyed, the ashes from the women's section were saved from extinction, by a former servant to the temple. The wall had collapsed but by some miracle, the jar with the ashes remained intact. The servant spirited them away and soon a secret society formed for their protection. They were passed from one trusted member to another, revered, but could not be used since the temple had been destroyed. This went on for centuries, and fifteen years ago, I was entrusted with the grave task of keeping safe the Ashes of the Red Heifer. When the Mameluke rulers of Egypt conquered Palestine, becoming the new masters of Jerusalem (AD 1260), I knew that the ashes would no longer be safe there. I stole away one night and have been on the move ever since, always with one eye looking back. I have searched for someone worthy, to keep them safe. Now, I fear death is near, and my mission will fail.'"

"'Death was nearer than he thought, for when sister came to awake him the next morning, she found him at the bosom of Abraham. The sisters didn't know what to do. The rabbi had told them that he had no family, that he was alone in the world. Since he was Jewish, they buried him outside the convent walls, in unconsecrated ground, after which Mother Superior went through the bag which, the old Jew said, contained all his worldly possessions. All they found were some old clothing wrapped around a sealed stone vessel, which contained the ashes. The sisters decided to keep the vessel until a worthy recipient should present himself. In death the old Rabbi found what he could not in life, worthy recipients of his treasure. The container was placed in the reliquary and eventually forgotten, until recently," said Mother.

"When I saw the vessel, I immediately knew that it was what we had been looking for all these years." Joshua said. "The shape, the designs etched into the stone, all matched the description of the lost vessel."

"During the Second Temple period," Joshua explained "vessels were made from easily worked, soft local limestone, abundant in Jerusalem, and obtained from Mount Scopus and the Mount of Olives. In general, they were sixty to eighty centimeters high with thick straight or rounded walls, goblet shaped set upon a pedestal. The stone industry flourished in Jerusalem during AD 1, but not after."

"Jewish laws, governing ritual purity, allowed the use of stone vessel, because stone does not absorb impurity. The ashes would have to have been in such vessels. The coup de grace was the etchings on the vessel, a seven-branched menorah, 20 cm high and 12.5 cm wide. It has seven high branches, with a flame on top of each branch, standing on a tripod base and decorated with circles separated by pairs of lines."

"This decoration corresponds to the biblical description of the menorah:

Exodus 25:33 states: On one branch there shall be three cups shaped like almond blossoms, each with a calyx and petals and on the next branch there shall be three cups shaped like almond blossoms, each with calyx and petals. They are the real deal. I contacted Rabbi Eidel Ehud Raanan, the head of the Sanhedrin to inform him of our discovery via live-com."

"Noted Rabbi, I have great news. The ashes of the red heifer have been found, and returned to Israel. The only details that need to be worked out are when and where."

"Are you sure of this, Rabbi Hiem? We have been disappointed before."

"I am 100 percent sure that these are the ashes we have been looking for for centuries."

"Two thousand years, Rabbi," corrected Rabbi Raanan. "We need proof, Rabbi, that these are the ashes."

Rabbi Raanan insisted on sending a team of noted Jewish scientists, handpicked by the Sanhedrin to run tests on the vessel to ascertain its authenticity.

To keep the ashes safe, it was decided that they would be kept in the Motherhouse, until the ashes return. The media would not be informed of their possible existence, until they were sure. The scientists would do the necessary research on the premises, after which they would return and report to the Sanhedrin.

A week later, a group of thirty scientists, along with three truckloads of equipment, descended upon the Motherhouse. Dr. Jeremiah Schultz presented himself to the Mother Superior, giving her a synopsis of what they intended to do.

A temporary laboratory was set up in the basement of the convent. The sisters wouldn't see anyone from the group again, until they left a month later. They had even brought their own cook and food. Before they left, a large contribution was presented to the sisters for the use of their facilities.

Upon their return, Dr. Jeremiah Schultz presented the findings of the committee to the Sanhedrin.

"Rabbis, this committee was charged with the monumental task of studying the relic housed at the Convent of Our Lady, Order of the Blessed Sacrament, in Krakow Poland, which some believed to be the ashes of the red heifer. Our examination began with no such preconceived notions. I was the only member of the team to know what we were studying.

The thirty scientists were divided into three groups. Each concentrated on one particular aspect of the relic. The first examined the exterior of the vessel, looking for items like soil, pollen grains, and such. Group two examined the container itself—its size, shape, and physical and chemical characteristics. The last group examined the ashes.

This presentation is divided into those three parts, and will be given in layman's terms, in as succinct a manner as possible. The members of the Sanhedrin have written copies of the report containing the finding of the committee.

Part one, analysis of the pollen grains. Micro-examination of the exterior of the vessel revealed numerous pollen grains, which were removed, examined and identified. Most were of no significance, since the plants that produce them grew in numerous areas throughout Palestinian and Eastern Europe. These gave us no clue as to where the vessel found itself at any particular time, although, several were found that have importance in the movement of the vessel. They grew in one particular area only, during the time before the receptacle took residence with the sisters.

We found pollen grains from the Jerusalem cherry, artichokes, olive, and fig trees from Jerusalem. All these were expected, since the vessel was housed for many years in Jerusalem.

But others give us insight into the path Rabbi Goldstein took to Poland. The chart shows the probable route he took. At the time he was traveling, the plants listed were native only to their country of origin.

Table 1

Country	Native plants	Other plants
Jerusalem		
Syria	jasmine,	carnation,
Lebanon	cedar, hyacinth,	Hibiscus Syriacus, tulip
	Cedrus libani, Damask rose	cabbage flower
Turkey	Tamarisk (salt cedar) red pine,	oak, maple
oriental spruce	alder, Scots pine,	cherries, plum
Bulgaria	Kazaniaska Roza, (Kazankuk rose of Bulgaria), Gentianella bulgarica	chrysanthemum, delphinium, larkspur
	Hungarian snowbell, Lilum Jankae	Lesser Twayblade, Macedonia pine
Romania	Rosa canian (dog rose), Acanthus Hungaricus, fuchsia	crocus banaticus

| Ukraine | Vinctoxicum rossicum | (dog strangling vine) |
| Poland | Papaver Rhoeas, (corn or red poppy), popies, iris Sibirica, crocuses, pink amaryllis | geranium, (Siberian iris), Trollius Europaeus (globe flower), freesia |

Part two—Analysis of the vessel. This group was commissioned with discovering the makeup of the vessel and its age. The group used chemical and physical methods of analysis. The container is made from limestone of the area in and around Jerusalem.

Electron Spin Resonance dating, also known as Radiometric Dating was used to calculate the age of the vessel. It is a method that uses radiation exposure to date materials, mostly minerals, such as sedimentary quartz, fossilized teeth, flint, egg shells, coral and calcium carbonate (limestone), found in archaeological sites.

Using radiation, electrons are separated form the atoms and become trapped in the crystal lattice of minerals; thus, changing the magnetic field of the materials at a predicted rate, allowing the item to be dated.

This method is important, since it is the only one that detects the paramagnetic center and does not destroy them when the measurements are made. Therefore, the same sample may be used repeatedly, without using it up.

Electron Spin Resonance was performed on the vessel a dozen times. Without a doubt it dates from 100 BC to AD 100.

Part three—Analysis of the ashes. This proved to be the most difficult part of the analysis because only the high priest may open the vessel. We needed to devise a way of examining the ashes without actually opening it.

X-ray was our first choice and revealed particles throughout, sized 2 cm and less in diameter. Some were denser than others. Upon closer examination of the X-rays, it was determined that the less dense were bone and the others, wood. Even though X-ray did give us some valuable information, more was needed.

We had to analyze the actual ashes. Could this be done without compromising the integrity of the jar and the ashes?

Examining the vessel, Dr. Simon Cohen noticed that embedded under the clay cap overlapping the vessel were what seemed to be ash, which, most probably spilled when the vessel was being filled. We removed some of the overlapping clay to examine the ash fixed within.

In order to insure what was found under the clay was indeed from the material inside, we needed a way to sample the ashes inside the container. This proved to be the most difficult part of our examination process. Much thought was given as to how best to do this, and at times, we were on the verge of opening the vessel, just a little.

Dr. Benjamin Alpine suggested the use of a relatively new piece of equipment he had read about in Scientific America, a microscopic drill, used in areas where only the smallest of samples could be taken, areas that could not be disturbed. The as yet unnamed equipment is a high speed pulsating needle which penetrates solid structures, such as limestone, without leaving a hole. As it moves the needle excites the molecules, speeding them up, causing them to move away from each other, creating the hole. A micro-scalpel is inserted to extract some of the sample. When the needle is removed, the molecules return to their original position and speed, closing the hole, leaving nothing to show that a compromise had occurred. The equipment is experimental and there are only a few around the world.

We were lucky. Dr. Alpine found one being tested just one hundred sixty kilometers away in Rzeszow, Poland. A day later we had the equipment and our sample.

The two samples were individually tested. First, each was carefully separated into similar structures, wood, bone, and ash, and analyzed for composition. The larger pieces of bone and wood were examined for DNA, which was then analyzed to discover what it had been.

It was soon realized that the two samples were one and the same, but we continued to test each separately.

Genetic examination of the fragments and ash proved to be cedar, hyssop, reed grass, and wool. Carbon dating showed some of the wood had been burned between 100 BC and AD 100, others between 600 BC to 400 BC, still others from 4500 BC to 4300 BC, indicating a mixture of several burnings from the time of 4500 BC to AD 100.

The bone was more difficult to analyze, since we needed to find some intact DNA to tell what the animal had been. After searching the pieces, we discovered two samples, one from the vessel's lid, and the other from inside. Carbon dating of lid bone places it between 100 BC and AD 100. The piece from inside was determined to be between 3500 BC and 3300 BC.

It is necessary to give some background about coat color, which, for domesticated animals, has always been a marker for breed identity. For the past one hundred years, breeders have distinguished the differences at the DNA level. In inherited traits, differences have always been attributed to specific alleles.

The major phenotypic variations in coat color is dependent upon a few genes. The Extension (E)-locus is very important. Genetic variants at this locus are responsible for either Eumelanin (black) or Pheomelanin (red) pigmentation. In both of our samples, a frame shift mutation was found at position 309 of the MC1-R sequence, which is know to cause a nonfunctional receptor responsible for red hair color.

To summarize, we found pollen grains indicating the vessel not only traveled through, but remained for some time, in Jerusalem, Syria, Turkey, Bulgaria, Romania, Ukraine, and Poland.

Second, the vessel is made from limestone dating to the period before the destruction of the temple. The etchings on the vessel are characteristic of the type that would have been on the vessel.

Third, the wood ash is consistent with the woods that would have been used for the sacrifice.

Fourth, analysis of the bone fragments indicate they are from, not one, but two, three year old heifers, whose deaths occurred some time apart.

Fifth, genetic analysis indicates that these heifers had red hair.

All this has led this committee to conclude that the vessel has ashes from several sacrificed red heifers.

It is the opinion of my colleagues and me, that the vessel and ashes housed at the Convent of Our Lady, Order of the Blessed Sacrament, in Krakow, Poland, are authentic. Rabbis, we have back, what we thought was lost."

IS AGING PREVENTABLE?

February 2067

Dᴵᴰ ᴅᴇᴀᴛʜ ᴇxɪsᴛ prior to the fall of Adam and Eve, or did it come into the world with their sin? Evolutionists claim death decay and extinctions have always been a part of the world since the beginning of time. The record of creation given in Genesis chapters 1 to 3 begs to differ.

"And God saw everything that He had made and behold, it was very good," (Genesis 1:31 ᴋᴊᴠ).

"And the Lord God planted a garden east of Eden; and there he put the man whom he had formed," (Genesis 2:8 ᴋᴊᴠ).

"But of the tree of the knowledge of good and evil, thou shalt not eat of it: for in the day that thou eatest thereof thou shalt surely die," (Genesis 2:17 ᴋᴊᴠ)

There is no mention of death until Adam is warned not to eat of the tree. Also, death is not mentioned again until Cain killed Abel in Genesis 4:8.

It was already late when Edger made his way to his laboratory. Deep in thought he absentmindedly turned on the TV, not that he intended to watch anything. It provided background noise while he worked. He examined the data from the past week. Nothing new!

Maybe, I'm just not meant to find the cure for aging. Maybe, there just isn't one. Maybe, I'm just no damn good at this. Sam is, though.

Perhaps I should ask for his help. No! Sam is already famous world-wide for his prostate cancer cure. Now he is closing in on the cure for homosexuality. A tinge of jealousy touched him. *Sam has everything. It isn't fair. He always has. Yeah, his Dad died when he was three, but he had a mother and siblings who cared deeply about him. I never had that. Now, not only does he have the love and support of his siblings but also of his wife and kids. He is the perfect Catholic, too. Bishops, Cardinals, even the Pope often seek his advice.*

To top it off, he has some sort of knack working with genes and genetics. These are the only loves I have left, but Sam is better at it than I am. I can't let him take these away from me. I want to be known throughout history as the scientist who cured aging. I was never one to share.

Sam is my best friend. In college, he shared his family with me. He still does. Sam and his families have been there when I needed them the most. Jealousy was dissipating as quickly as it had begun. As these thoughts were going through his mind, something from the TV caught Edger's ear.

"Why does man die? Why do all living creatures suffer the same fate? With the passage of time, is the body's slow process of decline unavoidable? Can the secrets of longevity be revealed? During the past several decades, scientists studying the workings of genes and cells have uncovered some of the clues necessary to solve this mystery."

He walked to the TV.

"Tonight, we will look at the problem of aging, beginning with the Tibetan monks, whose life expectancy is nearly double that of the average person. Do they know something the average person does not? Do they eat better, live healthier, have better genes? Or could it be something else?"

"As we shall see, these monks can perform fantastic feats. They can drastically reduce their respiratory and heart rates, lower their body temperatures, dry chill, wet towels with only their body heat

in rooms cold enough to make an average person uncontrolla-
bly shiver.

"Why do these monks live so long? No one has yet to figure it
out, even though many have tried."

Immediately Edger thought, genetics. This is what he was
working on. He became engrossed in the program.

"The worldwide life expectancy averages sixty five, with a low
of thirty-two in Swaziland to a high of eighty four in Macau.
This is, of course, much lower than in Biblical times, when man
lived hundreds of years. The following chart is a list of the ages of
the fathers of the Bible."

Table 2

Person	Age
Adam	930
Seth	912
Enosh	905
Kenan	910
Mahalalel	895
Jared	962
Enoch	365
Methuselah	930
Lamech	777
Noah	950
Seth	500
Arphaxad	403
Shelah	403
Eber	430
Peles	209
Reu	207
Serug	200
Mahor	119

| Terah | 205 |
| Abraham | 175 |

"As you see, the ages generally decreased from generation to generation. Why? There are several theories—from the absurd to the ridiculous. One such theory is that the Sons of God were aliens from outer space who came and mated with the sons of man. A second theory is that Adam's sons mated with animals that looked like humans, creating a genetic mutation. The Sons of God mated with sons of man thereby giving rise to the aging process."

"Thanks to modern science we know that, as aging occurs, the body's immune system begins to attack itself, and the code for genetic sequencing shuts down. Also, the genes themselves are programmed to replicate only so many times. The number of replications is somehow kept track of against a set point, and when this set point is reached, the code for sequencing shuts down. All this leads to aging."

"From the time of Adam to the present, each and every organism is always only one mutation from death. Our bodies are constantly in the process of trying to kill themselves. Can this be stopped? If so, how?"

Yes! Edger thought. *Can this be stopped?* He became lost in thought. He had been looking for an on/off switch on the genetic level. Maybe it wasn't that simple. Had the monks found a way to add to the number of replications allowed? Or could they turn off the count? What if the answer was to reset the clock? You could live forever in good health. With this in mind, Edger began again, from a new angle. This time, his focus would be on the hypothalamus gland.

In med school, he had studied the hypothalamus, but that was twenty years ago. Since you lose what you do not use, Edger needed to do some research. Accessing the Internet, he began researching the gland.

"The hypothalamus (4g), located at the base of the brain (1400 g), performs a wide range of vital functions necessary for survival. It acts to regulate and coordinate functions such as electrolyte balance, feeding, energy metabolism, wake/sleep cycles, thermoregulation, stress response, sexual behavior and reproduction. It is located in the middle of the base of the brain encapsulating the ventral portion of the third ventricle (*ventriculus tertius*)."

"The hypothalamus protects the vital capacity of an organism through homeostasis, which regulates electrolyte and glucose concentrations, osmolality, and body temperature."

The intracellular biochemical system of the human body is such that even a small alteration in it cannot be tolerated. For example, raising or lowering the body temperature by just four degrees to five degrees Celsius, can substantially degrade brain function. The body maintains a temperature which is held within a few tenths of a degree of optimum. This tight control of body temperature is required for the proper functioning of cellular biochemical reactions. During an infection, white blood cell activity increases, with a modest two degree Celsius rise. At this temperature, most bacteria are less able to reproduce. This benefit, though small, gives the host an advantage that could mean the difference between survival and death."

"The hypothalamus accomplishes this via neurons that either receive inputs from sensory systems, or are themselves sensitive to them. These neurons attempt to regulate the parameters against a set point, just as a thermostat in a home is adjusted to a set point."

Set point. This term was familiar. He had just heard about it in the documentary. It was the term used in gene reproduction. "The number of replications is somehow kept track of against a set point, and when this set point is reached, the code for sequencing shuts down." He continued to read.

"The hypothalamus helps anticipate daily events triggered by the external day/night cycle. Whether an organism is diurnal or nocturnal, they have predictable times of feeding, drinking, sleeping and sexual behavior. These are regulated by the circadian timing system in the brain, so that the body anticipates its various demands and opportunities. Wakefulness and cortical levels peak at the time of day necessary for an animal to forage for food, while the set point for body temperature falls a full degree during the time of day when the animal sleeps."

"Neurons in the posterior half of the lateral hypothalamus promote wakefulness. These are under the influence of the ventrolateral preoptic nucleus, a sort of master switch, which inhibits the components of the arousal system during sleep, and is necessary for normal sleep states to occur. The wake/sleep system is under the control of the circadian system, and interacts with feeding, drinking, sexual behavior, and defensiveness, all of which require a waking state. There is also a strong interaction between sleep and thermoregulation."

"When an animal is attacked, it must quickly reach full arousal, mobilizing energy stores, ready for fight or flight. All other activities, reproductive behavior, food foraging, and non-essential tasks must be inhibited. It is the function of the paraventricular nucleus to control the stress response. Contained within this nucleus are neurons that produce corticotropin releasing hormone. This causes the release of ACTH which enables the release of adrenal steroids. Many of the autonomic control neurons necessary for adrenaline release are located here as well. Sexual behavior is inhibited by stress, and in some cases, may even lead to interruption of pregnancy. Stress is inherently non-specific, and so can interact with any of the hypothalamic regulatory systems."

This is one hell of a gland, Edger thought. He didn't remember being impressed when he studied it twenty years ago, but what he had just read. WOW! An organ, just three tenth of the mass of the brain, and what it controls: all life functions! He knew he was on the right track. If only Julie...

Edger continued to research and work. The hypothalamus was where the solution to the mystery of aging would be found, and he, Edger Bartholomew Pielaresto, would be the one to solve it. Even as he was getting closer to his answer, events were in the works that unfortunately, or fortunately, would stop him from achieving this final goal.

THE PAPAL CONCLAVE

September 30, 2067, Wednesday

Viterbo, Italy
Papal Conclave
May 13, 2067

"THE CHURCH HAS been without its leader now for over four months, Monsignor. This is turning out to be one of the longest conclaves ever. How much longer do you think it will take?"

"I don't know Pete, but this is far from the longest in the history of the Papacy. That occurred in the thirteenth century when Pope Clement IV died. The plague was running rampant in cities across Europe and the Popes had been living in the country to avoid it. The cardinals decided to convene the conclave in the country as well.

As the conclave dragged on, the people of Viterbo began to be annoyed and decided to lock the cardinals in. The term conclave, you know, literally means with a key. It was their hope that making the cardinals uncomfortable would hurry up their decision. When they still could not decide, someone tore off the roof. The joke around town was the hole would let in the Holy Ghost to help with a decision.

Two years, eight months after the conclave began, it finally ended with the election of Gregory X making it the longest conclave in history. Still there were problems. Gregory was not a cardinal nor even a priest; he was a crusader fighting in the Holy Land. It took him eight months to return. One of his first acts as pope was to establish strict rules to ensure faster conclaves in the future.

Pope John Paul II changed the rules in 1996 allowing the cardinals to leave the Sistine chapel during the conclave, and eat and sleep in relative comfort. There are some who worry that that could lengthen future conclaves. He also changed the two third plus one majority to a simple majority in 1978, but Benedict XVI changed it back in 2007. He joked that he would not have been elected with a two third plus one margin."

"So, do you think this will last much longer, Monsignor?"

"One never knows Pete. Remember, when Gregory X was elected there were only fifteen cardinals and they couldn't get eleven to agree. At this moment, inside the Sistine Chapel there are one hundred fifty cardinals. They need a hundred and one to agree on a candidate. It really takes time. The Holy Spirit does indeed work in mysterious ways, but so does the devil. One never knows."

Cody had done his job efficiently, coercing, cajoling, and politicking. Even so, the other cardinals would not concede. Each believed he could be elected pope. The conclave began on January 8, twenty days after Pope Athanasius's death. It dragged on. The days became weeks, and the weeks became months. Still, the Fab Five would not agree with Cody's plan. This was turning into one of the longest conclaves in history.

Nine months later, on September 30, 2067, Cody, frantically fumbled through the pockets of his robes and found what he thought was his pen. He pulled it out, looked at it and was somewhat surprised by the object. Instead of the pen he expected to find, he was holding a sentinel drive. He studied the object and for a moment did not recognize it. Then it dawned on him. It was the sentinel drive that Salvatore had given him the night he died.

Sal was about to explain what was on the drive when that idiot Santiz burst into the room. The drive brought back all the memories of that terrible evening which Cody had tried to suppress. Even though he had used all the resources of the Sodality at his disposal, including hiring their top assassins to find and kill Santiz, they soon came to a dead end, coming back empty-handed. It was as though Max had disappeared off the face of the earth.

Cody turned the sentinel drive over in his fingers.

What is on this? he wondered. His curiosity would have to be left unsatisfied, at least for the moment. There had been yet another call for a vote.

The conclave had been in session for nine months, and there had been at least one vote per day since it began. They had used a forest of paper for balloting, all going up in smoke, black smoke. Still no pope had been elected.

This balloting would prove no different than the hundreds that came before it. A call was now made for a recess. The cardinals were growing frustrated. Too long had they been cooped up without the luxuries of their homes—their rooms were purposely kept sparse to insure that the cardinals were not too comfortable so that the conclave would not extend too long. They had spent too many hours in close contact with the same men. Even their friends were now grating on the nerves.

None of the Fab Five could get the two thirds plus one majority. Damn Benedict XVI for reinstating this policy. Saint John Paul II had instituted a simple majority plus one, under which Benedict had been elected. If this policy had still been in effect, someone would have been elected months ago. When one of the five was proposed, the others made sure that he was not elected. The cardinals were wondering what could possibly be done to break this stalemate. Prayer definitely seemed to not be working.

Back in his sparsely furnished room, Cody had time to see what was on the sentinel drive. Laptops were allowed, but there was no Internet access, assuring that the cardinals could not communicate with the outside world.

After booting up the laptop, Cody inserted the drive and opened the only file. He almost fell off his chair. Here was the solution. Cody knew the stalemate could now be ended. He also felt very strongly that he would be the next pope. First, he had to meet with the others.

OCTOBER 5 2067

That time came a couple of weeks later. Once the five were assembled in Cody's quarters, he passed out a page to each of the cardinals each with their name emblazoned on the top. Cardinal Alfrado Bennadetto's copy listed all the illegal transactions he had allowed between the Vatican Bank and the Italian mob.

Cardinal Domingo Saferino's copy documented his activities with the drug czars, having provided the funding to buy properties in Turkey, Mexico, and the Middle East, on which were grown the majority of the world's supply of marijuana and white poppies for cocaine. Cardinal Lawrence DeSimone's paper included his activities in prostitution rings around the world. There were hints the funding included child pornography and slavery. Cardinal Brendan Callahan's copy included his activities in funding known terrorists. All four had used the Vatican Bank as their source of funding. All four had become rich.

The most damning was the page which Cody handed out after the initial shock had worn off, somewhat. Here was a list of the members of the Sodality of Thelema, outlining the activities of the Sodality as well as their most prominent members. The top four were sitting in this room.

Cody played it cool. This was the last ammo in his arsenal, but never tell that to your enemy, or your friends. He told them he had detailed papers of the Vatican Bank's spotted history, and their involvement in it. Because of their intimate involvement in the Vatican Bank, each cardinal now realized that he faced the possibility of excommunication, and worse, criminal charges. What were they to do, at their age?

As they read the documents, each cardinal sat in silence. Cardinal Bennadetto shattered it by bellowing, "What is the meaning of this Berkshire?"

With the silence broken Cardinal DeSimone said, "Where did you get these?"

"All in good time, gentlemen. You have read the papers. I hope their full meaning has not been lost on you. Imagine, my good cardinals, if these papers were to slip out, get into the wrong hands. What damage could they cause!"

None of these men were stupid. Each immediately understood the meaning and cost of having these documents in the wrong hand—excommunication and jail.

"What do you want Berkshire, as if I couldn't guess?"

"Just this. I want your support. If you back me for pope, these documents will never see the light of day. If not, they go public. You will be the most famous jailbird cardinals ever. What would the faithful think when they find out that four of the top cardinals were in the Sodality?"

"You overstep yourself, Berkshire. Remember you are a novice in the Sodality," Callahan said.

"Maybe, but my name is not on this list," holding up a copy of the list.

"You forget Cody," Cardinal Bennadetto injected coolly. "We too have documentation." Cody hadn't thought of this possibility. As far as he knew, the Sodality never kept written records, that is why he was so surprised when he found his list.

"Yes, things that could send YOU to jail, or worse. Didn't you forget about Max?"

It was Cody's turn to go pale. "What about him?"

"You are trying to have him killed."

"How could you possibly know that?"

"Attempted murder is punishable by life in jail. Two can play this little game of yours, Berkshire."

"How?" Cody stammered.

"We have ways. Nothing goes on in the Sodality that one of us does not know about."

"Well, Gentlemen. It seems we continue the stalemate," Cardinal Saferino said.

Silence ensued again.

Then, Cardinal DeSimone injected. "Gentlemen, I know I am not the only one who is tired of this standoff. I want to go home, back to my bed and my cook. Who knows how much money we have lost being locked up in this place. Nothing good is coming from it. The solution seems clear to me. I propose we resolve the stalemate using the solution Berkshire proposed before the conclave began."

"You mean the Edger Pielaresto solution?" Saferino questioned.

"Yes. We all know Edger well. He can be controlled. We will make sure that each of us is placed in the key positions. He will be able to do nothing without our knowledge and approval. And, if that fails, and he gets too high for his britches, there is always the Pope John Paul I solution. I believe this will work."

Silence again. After several minutes Cody said, "Well, gentlemen. Are we in agreement?"

THE LOST CHILDREN OF ATLANTIS

October 5 2067

THE ANCIENT PHILOSOPHER Plato, told the tale of Atlantis, a highly advanced civilization. Through a character named Kritias, the tale unfolds. Kritias reveals the account had been told to him by his ancestor Solon who claimed to have acquired the story from an Egyptian priest.

West of the "Pillars of Hercules", on an island in the Atlantic Ocean, existed a powerful empire founded by Poseidon, god of the sea. Here he brought forth five sets of twins. This island and the surrounding ocean, was named after his first born, Atlas. Poseidon subdivided the island into ten sections appointing one of his sons as ruler of each.

The capital city was a spectacular feat of engineering. It had concentric circular walls with canals leading to a hill upon which sat the temple of Poseidon. The pivotal point of the temple was a gold statue of the god piloting his chariot propelled by six winged stallions.

The people lived in peace until about nine thousand years before Plato. At that time they grew corrupt and greedy. Eventually their abominations escalated to a point where the gods decided to destroy them. The land shook violently tearing it apart as titanic waves washed over its shores causing the island to sink into the sea. Atlantis has yet to return.

At 3:00 a.m., Max was startled from a sound sleep. He had heard his name clearly and distinctly called. Wiping the sleep from his eyes, he looked around expecting Joshua to be standing beside his bed. He was alone. As he lay back down, he heard it again.

"Maxwell! Here is the answer for which you have been searching."

It wasn't a dream. He was wide awake now. He didn't recognize the voice. It was no one he knew. Getting up, Max went to the two way mirror and looked out into the darkened room, lit only by the exit sign above the door. Max saw no one. Nothing moved. Thinking it was just his overactive imagination, he was about to give up and go back to bed, when the voice called again.

"Maxwell, I need you. Come!"

It was a male voice. Of this much, Max was certain. Quickly dressing, he grabbed a flashlight. Not only would it provide the light he needed, without turning on the overheads, but could be used as a weapon. Slowly and as quietly as he could, Max opened the door.

He used a chair to prop it open. Slowly, he exited the closet into the darkness of the archives. He stopped, looking, and listening. Hearing nothing, he turned on the flashlight, sweeping the darkness. At the far end of the room, lying on the table was an open book. Someone had been here. Maybe, he was still here. Approaching the table, Max used the light to pierce deep into the darkness of the stacks of books, searching for the man who had called his name. Not finding anyone lurking in the darkness, Max drew near the book. He knew he did not leave it out, and Joshua, as far as the archives were concerned, was a neat freak. Every book had a place, and a place for every book. That was his motto.

Slowly, he crept forward, ever nearer the table. Apprehensively, he searched the darkened stacks, again and again. Finally reaching it Max saw a note lying on the left hand page of the open book. He picked it up and shown the light on it.

"The BITCH must be stopped!" was all it read.

He read the note again. There was something familiar about the cursive. Max had seen it before. He knew it wasn't Joshua's or Mother's, not that Mother would use such language. Where had he seen it? It hit him like a bolt of lightning. He almost dropped the flashlight. It was his father's penmanship.

How? He was dead. His mother had never mentioned him, but when she died, beside the letter she left him, he found other letters—letters from him. Some were to her, but others were addressed to Max. Max never realized he was fatherless. His stepfather more than adequately filled that role of Daddy. After reading the letters, Max shredded them. What good were words on paper? Even if he had wanted, Max could never have a relationship with his biological father. One of the items was the newspaper obituary of Paul Crowley.

What could this be, then? How could this be? Evidently, someone had a warped sense of humor. Only Mother and Joshua knew he was even here. Could one of them be responsible for this? He thought better of it. They had been so great to him. He trusted his life to them, literally. Had one of them let it slip? He didn't think so. Then who?

Max picked up the book. Under his father's note was a translation of the page, also written by his father. What had the voice said? Something about the answer for which he was looking. Could this be the book? As Max read it, he knew it was and that the voice was right. Max had always known what he had to do, but now he knew where. He went quickly to the exit, entering into the night, to meet his destiny.

Joshua and Mother had made plans to meet with Max on Wednesday. Both had the day off, and the archives were closed. Joshua picked up Mother at 2:00 p.m. and together they took a lunch to have with Max. They made their way to the secret room. Joshua entered the closet first, having the only key.

"What the...?"

Mother, concerned, pushed in beside him. The door had been propped open by a chair. Josh pushed it aside. Entering the room, followed by Mother, they did an exploratory survey. Mother called "Max?" There was no answer. They searched the room. It didn't take long. Max was not there.

Leaving they began to search the archives. Soon Mother came across the open book.

"Joshua. Look at this." He left the room next door where he had been searching and came over.

"What is it Mother?"

"This book. Did you leave it here?"

"No, Mother. It is one of my pet peeves, putting everything back in its place. When I left here yesterday nothing was out." As he was speaking, he noted a crumpled piece of paper on the floor. Picking it up, he unwrinkled it and read it. He handed it to Mother.

"What could this possibly mean?" she asked, almost to herself.

"Let me see the book." Joshua requested. She pushed it to him. Looking at the cover he translated the title for Mother— *The Unauthorized History of the Lost City of Atlantis.* Joshua looked through the pages, sitting down to do so. The book was massive and very old. It was written in ancient Hebrew. Besides being a history of Atlantis, it documented the history of the Sodality of Thelema. Joshua turned the book over in his hands.

"This book is not in the archives collection. I have heard of its existence, but no one has ever been able to find it," he said.

"Are you sure?" Mother asked.

"Yes. I know each and every book in the archives. This one is not part of it."

"Where did it come from?"

"I don't know, but I don't like this. Someone has been here. I fear that our friend has met with no good."

"There isn't any sign of a struggle, Joshua. Max wouldn't willing go with anyone but you or me."

Joshua looked at the pages of the open book, and began to read. What he read amazed him.

The ten kings began to modify their stance toward the outside world. In one of the penta-annual parliaments, the kings decided that it was time for those who benefited from Atlantean technocracy to become subjects and pay tribute to their bravura potentates. So, they embarked upon the subjugation of the world. Their ships went to Central and South America, where they vanquished the Incas, Aztecs, and Mayas sending rich plunder back to Atlantis. Other forces conquered North Africa, invaded Greece and sweep eastward through the realms of Asia.

Before long a great invasion fleet sailed into Athens. Even though enormously outnumbered, the Athenians courageously anticipated the attack. The armies collided, the arrows soared in such numbers as to blacken the sky, and the hooves of the chariot horses were like thunder. The vivid armor of the Atlanteans blinded the eye and their spearheads appeared as numerous as wheat in a field. The Athenians fought pugnaciously in defense of their country. Ultimately the mammoth regiments of Atlantis faltered, fell back, and turned in headlong retreat toward their ships. When the defeat was communicated to Atlantis, several noted scientists, including Polycarp, recognized it would not rest well with Poseidon. Conjecturing an extraordinary disaster was imminent they gathered a select group and swiftly left their home.

Page after page detailed the travels of this remnant.

The group was small. As a result they kept close to each other, distrustful of outsiders, not knowing whom they could trust. They were in *their* world now. Atlantis, as predicted, had been destroyed.

Joshua wanted to continue to read, so enthralled had he become with the story, but Mother, her normally generous supply of patience giving out, had tapped him on the shoulder.

"What is so interesting to have you so engrossed?"

"I'm sorry Mother. I wish you could read these pages. They are very interesting indeed." He gave her a summary of what he had read so far.

"I am just getting to the pages where the book was open. It details where the remnant finally settled. I don't know where this is."

He read it to Mother.

"The group finally settled in a lush valley lying between the junction of two rivers, Arno and Auser, in the Liguria Sea forming a Laguna area. I know where the Arno River is, but I have never heard of the Auser River."

Mother thought for a moment. "I recall some ancient Italian history. I don't know where I heard it, but I believe the Auser River disappeared in ancient times. The junction of the rivers is now where the city of Pisa lies."

"Of course! I should have remembered that, but there is more. He began to translate out loud so Mother could hear.

Skeptical of outsiders the remnant formed an exclusive society called the Sodality of Thelema for protection. Because of what the ten kings had done, they kept to themselves, fearful for their lives and those of their children. Reaching the valley, they saw that it was deserted and by human criteria very attractive, but only slightly more than bearable to them. It did not possess the beauty of their home, a home they would never again see, so this valley would have to do.

There they established a community, farming the fertile soils. The scientists, who in Atlantis candidly and freely gave of their knowledge and technology to anyone who asked, now became secretive and close mouthed about their discoveries, which became more and more supernatural and less and less scientific.

Magic grew within the Sodality, as generation followed generation. All too soon, science was lost to the Sodality and magic, first white then black, took its place.

Over time, a new problem arose. As their numbers burgeoned, and a city sprung up around the farms, the remnant could no longer keep out of the world's eye. Trade commenced with the outsiders to the north and south, and people began to move to their city. Try as they might they could not keep it pure. The outsiders were now living side by side with the Atlantian descendants.

The Sodality, too, was growing and the hierarchy saw the need for a temple to act as a secret place to meet with people of one's own kind. From the beginning the Sodality kept the line pure, allowing only descendents from the original group to join. Atlantis had gleamed in the sunlight. The hierarchy decided that the Sodality temple should never see the light of day, so dark had the souls of the members become. Instead of building up, toward the sun, the Sodality built down, into the ground, into darkness itself.

The entrance was jealously guarded. Only the right people knew its location. A full blooded Atlantian, though, always instinctively knew.

Over the years, many Atlantian descendents married outsiders, and the number of the pure dwindled. As the world entered this once peaceful valley, strife and war followed, dispersing Atlantians to all parts of the world. The temple location was lost. Atlantians were left on their own to make it in a hostile world.

"Joshua! Could this be the book Max was looking for?"

"I think so. If it is, Mother, I think Max may have gone to Pisa. Remember, he had talked about the Sodality, and how they must be stopped. Perhaps he knows where the temple is."

"Then, it is off to Pisa," Mother declared.

Mother picked up the book and placed it under her scapular.

"Why take the book?"

"Two reasons. I don't trust leaving the book here. Whoever left it might come back for it. Secondly, it might come in handy, especially since we don't know where in Pisa we are headed. We can continue our search of the contents on the train."

Boarding the bullet train, they left Rome, arriving in Pisa several hours later. Departing from the train, the pair quickly made their way to the Campo del Miracoli, Field of Miracles. Mother reasoned that it would take a miracle to find Max.

BROTHERS?

October 6, 2067

T HE THIRD OLDEST structure in Pisa's Cathedral Square, and located behind the church, the Leaning Tower of Pisa is a freestanding bell tower.

Due to a poorly laid underpinning and loose substrate the foundation began to shift direction almost immediately after the start of construction in 1173. Originally intended to stand vertically, the tower currently leans to the southwest.

The height of the tower is 183.27 feet from the ground on the lowest side and 186.02 feet on the highest side. The width of the walls at the base is 13.42 feet and at the top 8.14 feet. It has an estimated weight of 16,000 short tons. The tower has 296 or 294 steps because the seventh floor has two fewer steps on the north-facing staircase. The tower leans at an angle of 3.97 degrees causing its top to be 12 feet 10 inches lower than if the tower were perfectly vertical.

Leaving the train station, Max made his way to the souvenir shop. He didn't know why he had come here, but he intuitively knew that it was right. Etched in the glass of the shop door was a strange cipher, three scalloped shapes in the form of a large fan. Max intently looked at it. Seeing his reflection in the glass it seemed as though the symbol was emblazoned on his left cheek.

As he gazed a slight recognition set upon him, then, the full impact. It was the same as his birthmark.

"Scusami signore!" came a voice behind him. He turned to see an elderly woman donned in a long black pleated dress with a multi-gray colored vest. Covering her snow white hair was a black cap. She walked with the aid of a crude stick like cane. With her was a girl about twelve.

Her wrinkled face was contorted in a smile.

"We wish to enter the store signore."

Max realized he had been blocking the entrance. He moved aside and held the door open for the two ladies to enter. Following them inside, he began to browse. Feeling as though he were being watched, Max stopped to look at the tourist brochures, one which immediately caught his eye. It was for this shop.

He picked it up to read, and as he did, he looked around. Seeing the cashier glaring intently at him, Max placed the brochure in his outer pocket, turned quickly and ducked into a nearby aisle. Making his way to the end, he looked up into the round security mirror mounted in the corner, and was gratified to find the clerk waiting on the old lady. Staying at the far end of the aisles, he made his way to the back of the store, toward which he was drawn. There he found a door. Looking around, to be certain he wasn't being watched, Max tried to open it but it was locked. He tried again, with the same results.

He was about to give up, when his right hand was inexplicably drawn to a spot about three meters above the floor. He tried to resist, but his hand continued slowly to rise. As it did his fingers spread far apart, and came to rest on the wall. Max found it warm and getting warmer. The wall continued to heat up until, he felt as though the skin on the palm of his hand was being incinerated. When he thought he could stand the pain no longer and was about to call for help, the wall suddenly cooled releasing his hand and the door swung open.

Max looked at his palm expecting to see it severely blistered with third degree burns. There were not even first degree burns. In fact it wasn't even red. He flexed his fingers. How? Why? Realizing the door had opened he did a quick scan of the surroundings and entered. The door closed behind him.

Following the hallway to its end, Max found a set of descending stairs. Proceeding down, it seemed they went on forever. Deeper and deeper he went seemingly into the bowels of the earth. Finally and abruptly, the stairs ended at the entrance to yet another long hallway. Max had counted the steps as he descended. There were 905.

A quick calculation told him that he had descended about .16 kilometer. About halfway down the corridor, he noticed a light coming from an open door on the left side. He approached, cautiously. Inside was a desk, with a high-backed swivel chair. On the wall behind the desk were three large structures that looked like enormous fish scales. Not from any fish that Max was aware. They were fan shaped and measured, Max guessed, about three to four feet each. The largest hung at the top of the wall, the others to the right and left forming somewhat of a large fan. There was something otherworldly about them. They glistened, shined, and glimmered with colors of aquamarine, cobalt, magenta, emerald, fuchsia, gold, lavender, rose, ruby, salmon, vermillion, and butter yellow. The colors changed as you moved from one side to the other. They were the most beautiful things that Max had ever seen.

"Beautiful, aren't they?" said a voice from the chair which slowly turned to face Max. There sat a man about Max's age, a strange familiarity about him. As he studied the face awareness slowly crept upon him. Max had seen this face and knew it intimately. He saw it daily, when he shaved. It was him! This man looked so much like Max that they could have been twins, but Max knew this was not possible, since he was an only child. The man looked up.

"They are beautiful. They have been here for centuries—the scales of Neptune. The scallops and their arrangement are the mark of true Atlantians. Legend has it that all of Neptune's scales were scallop-shaped; and thus, arranged. He gave us this set many years ago, long before Atlantis was destroyed as a reminder of whom we serve.

They are a prized possession of our people, one of the treasures the scientists took with them when they left, immediately before Atlantis was destroyed. They had magical powers but these were lost, or taken from them, when they were taken from Atlantis. Now, they are just beautiful, but soon, oh so soon, they will regain their power."

He had a far off look, seeing something that Max did not or could not see. Suddenly his gaze came back, and he looked directly into Max's eyes.

"Now, down to business, Max. I was wondering when you would show up."

"We've never met, Ahren. How did you know my name? I didn't know you existed until last year, when my mother died," Max said.

"I've kept pretty close tabs on all my illegitimate brothers Max. If our father hadn't married my mother first, he would have chosen yours, and you would be here, instead of me. So, Max, you are second in line, but you know what they say about being second. You're the first loser. Even so, you have a gift, given to you by our father, a great gift. I can help you develop it, if you join me."

"Join you? I've come to destroy you, Ahren. I won't let you destroy the things I love. You have already corrupted five servants of God. I won't allow you to destroy the Church I love."

"I'm not after your precious Church, Max. You should know that! I want the world and soon, very soon, I will be its undisputed ruler. Join me, Max. Together we can rule this world and I can make you pope of that church you love so much."

"How are you going to rule the world when your ceremony is still lacking a key ingredient?"

"What ingredient?" Ahren asked coolly.

"The prepuce of Jesus Christ."

Ahren was taken aback. "How could you know that?"

"It's not important how I know. You need the prepuce to complete the ceremony, and I know where it is."

"What?" Max had completely unnerved Ahren. "You know where it is? Tell me, Max. Join me, Max. You have a power that is lacking in all our father's children, except you and me. We can be gods, Max. Think of it. Anything you want, anyone you want, go where you want, do what you want. Max, think of the power. Give me the prepuce!"

"You're worse than our great, great, great, grandfather, Aleister Crowley, that self proclaimed most evil man alive."

"Why, thank you, Max. That IS a compliment."

"It wasn't meant to be."

"Join me, Max."

"I'd rather die!"

"That can be arranged, but first you will give me the information I need."

"I'll never tell you!"

"Your cooperation would make it easier, but with or without your help, I *will* rule this world! Your soul will soon be doing my bidding, and I will have the information you refuse to give me in life."

Ahren threw an execration at him. Max contorted his body, and the execration, looking somewhat like ball lightning, whizzed by, close to his ear with a demonic droning. Ahren threw another, and then another, his face contorting in rage mixed with confusion. Max easily evaded all that Ahren could throw at him. He hurled several more execrations, Max dodging each without difficulty.

Was it his many years of athletic training that provided him with the agility or, could it be the room, the scales? He didn't know. There was a power here that Max had never felt before. His mind was becoming cloudy. He was becoming confused, disoriented. He tried to pray but no prayer came. Something was after his very soul. He felt alone, abandoned, a darkness overtaking him.

God, where are you in my darkest hour? He reached to his chest and felt the Benedictine crucifix he always wore. The moment he touched it, his despair vanished and he knew what he had to do. He needed to get out of this room.

Ahren was growing ever more frustrated and angry. No one had ever needed a second attempt. Being a perfectionist he had always killed with deadly accuracy, the first time. Max should be dead. For some reason the execrations were not working. What could incinerate a man at a hundred meters, for some reason had no effect on Max at all. They simply hit harmlessly into the wall or floor. In the past, anger had increased his powers. Now, it seemed to be having the opposite effect. Could Max be this powerful? Could Ahren have underestimated this half brother? Could it be that Max was a... man?

With growing horror, Ahren began to realize that her father's power had been transferred to his true heir. That was why Paul had seemed so weak and his death so easy to accomplish.

Never had he run up against anyone so powerful. Without training, Max was nearly Ahren's equal. Too bad he wouldn't join the Sodality. What a team they would have made. But there could only be one, and that would be Ahren. He knew this when he killed his father. With training Max would soon be superior, and he, not Ahren, would be the undisputed leader of the Sodality. Max had to die. No rivalry could be tolerated.

It was futile for Ahren to waste any more energy launching execration after execration at Max, who so easily evaded their terrible effects. Growing tired, Ahren decided on a physical attack and suddenly lunged at Max, jumping, with the stealth of cat, over the desk. Max was just as nimble and quickly moved to the right, leaving Ahren to sail past him into the wall. He ran past the slightly dazed Ahren into the corridor running its full length passing one door after the other. He didn't have time to see if the doors were unlocked or where they led. Ahren was on his heels.

Max sped up and was beginning to outdistance Ahren when the corridor abruptly ended. There, was one last door. It was his only chance. Max pushed at it, and it swung open revealing a set of steps. The door swung shut and Max could not see where the door had been. It was as though it disappeared. He could hear Ahren coming and saw light edging from a crack in the wall. He knew Ahren was coming fast. He understood that when pursued, you never go up, but there was no other choice. There was just no place else to go. Max made the only decision he could. He ascended, spiraling up farther and farther, finally finding himself at the top of the Leaning Tower of Pisa. Ahren came through soon after. Max was ready. The two locked in mortal combat, using every fight tactic there was.

The sun was dropping below the horizon, as the two punched and clawed and scratched at each other, but Ahren had a secret weapon. He knew Max's one weakness, a weakness possessed by all men, except him. Using this knowledge, Ahren placed a knee squarely, abruptly and forcefully, between Max's legs. Instead of crumpling in pain, as Ahren had expected, he grabbed Ahren around the waist, pushing with all his remaining strength. The two flipped over the rail falling one hundred fifty feet to the ground below. Max landed on top of Ahren, who's back was broken in the fall, dying on impact. Max rolled off the body, living just long enough to say a pray for the soul of his brother. "I'm sorry, Jesus," were his last words.

Mother and Joshua arrived on the scene just as the two came over the rail, but there was nothing either could do. The two hit the ground with a decisive thud. The crowd parted as Mother ran to Max's side, and knelt beside his body, silently praying for his soul, as well as that of Ahren. Joshua followed pushing his way through the crowd that had gathered to witness the fight and which was growing larger by the minute.

"I saw the whole thing." said an old lady approaching Mother and Joshua. "We came when we saw the light show begin. It was beautiful with lights flashing from every side, in every color. Then, my granddaughter asked about the two men at the top of the tower. That is when I first saw them. They were fighting. I thought they were filming a movie, but couldn't see any equipment. All of sudden they fell over the rail."

As her gaze alighted upon the two deceased, she gasped.

"What is it?" Mother asked.

"That mark! I have seen it before."

"What mark?" Joshua inquired.

"Why… that one!" Joshua and Mother followed her pointing finger to an area on Ahrens left shoulder. His shirt had been ripped in the fight and a birthmark, the exact replica of Max's was evident.

"Where did you see it?" Mother inquired.

"I don't remember. It was this week though. It wasn't Monday. Mondays I do my laundry, so I didn't go anywhere that day. Tuesday morning is ironing and grocery shopping in the afternoon. Wednesday, I visited a sick friend and my granddaughter, Gina, came for a visit that afternoon. We got an early start this morning and have been to many shops." Even Mother was exasperated.

As she was speaking, the police arrived. After taking pictures of the scene, the examination continued with Max's body being turned over. The old lady again gasped. "Were they twins?" she asked. It was then that Mother and Joshua saw the resemblance.

"No, they were brothers." Joshua said.

"I saw him today at the souvenir shop. He was blocking the door."

As she was speaking, one of the policemen pulled the brochure from Max's pocket. Mother walked over.

"May I look at the brochure?" she questioned.

Officer Rossi was filling out the information required for the proper handling of evidence. He had already filled in the name of his agency, case number, item number, date, and his identifier.

"I can't Mother. You know the importance of physical evidence cannot be underestimated. The credibility and integrity of the evidence is directly predicated upon the proper handling of the evidence from its initial observance through presentation in court." He continued writing: date and time found, where and by whom, a description of the item.

"I understand." Mother replied, but as he was sealing the evidence packet and writing his initials across the seal she caught the heading: The True Atlantian.

The old lady had come to Mother's side. "I have that brochure, Mother, right here in my handbag." She pulled it out and handed it to her.

The True Atlantian Shop. We specialize in replicas of the lost city, books and fine jewelry. In addition we carry materials from the Mediterranean Sea and the Atlantic Ocean. 1123 Piazza del Duomo, is all she read.

Mother and Joshua went with the police to answer their questions and help with the investigation. They told them about, Max's suspicions, the Lost City of Atlantis, the Sodality of Thelema, and the sentinel drives.

Mother insisted on being permitted to come along when the police searched the shop. As the chief of police had been a student of Mother's, he permitted it. What they found, Mother could not have prepared herself.

FINALLY, A POPE

October 13, 2067

THE PROPHECY OF THE POPES

ONE OF THE most recognized traditions of the papal succession is the release of white smoke from the chimney of the conclave room. Its message: A pope has been elected. This happens but once in a conclave, that of black smoke many times each indicating an unsuccessful vote. During these times the ballots are mixed with straw and burned, creating the black smoke. In recent times chemicals have been substituted for the straw. When the vote has been successful the ballots are burned without chemicals or straw and white smoke bellows forth accompanied by the ringing of the Vatican bells. It is the solitary way the cardinals, who have been kept in seclusion, have to notify the public of the result.

"Sic transit gloria mundi",

"Thus passes the glory of the world."

Popes have come and popes have gone, but the papacy endures providing spiritual guidance to over a billion Catholics.

Saint Malachy is recognized for having comprised a list of 112 short Latin phrases describing the popes and a few anti-popes. Beginning with Clestine II (elected in 1143) it concludes with "Peter the Roman", whose pontificate will end in Rome's destruction. The longest and final motto reads:

"In persecutione extrema S.R.E. sedebit Petrus Romanus,
qui pascet oves in multis tribulationibus:
quibus transactis civitas septicollis diruetur,

et Iudex tremendus iudicabit populum suum.
Finis.

"During the final persecution of the Holy Roman
Church, the seat will be occupied by Peter the Roman,
who will feed his sheep in many tribulations;
and when these things are finished, the seven-hilled city
will be destroyed, and the formidable Judge will judge his
people. The End."

At long last, the white smoke, indicating that a new pope had been elected, streamed from a chimney above Saint Peter's Square. The crowds cheered. The media speculated on who had been elected. None of their theories would prove correct.

He wasn't a cardinal, nor was he a bishop. In fact, he wasn't even a priest when he was elected to the office of Pope. He was brought secretly to the Sistine Chapel where the Cardinal Dean asked, "Do you accept your canonical election as Supreme Pontiff?"

"Absolutely!" he replied without hesitation.

Within the hour, the Cardinal Dean ordained him deacon, priest, and then bishop. He was then rushed to the Papal apartments where he dressed himself, choosing a set of pontifical choir robes, including a white cassock, a rochet, and a mozzetta, from the three sizes, small, medium, and large, set out before him.

Once he was properly attired, he was escorted to the "Room of Tears," a small red room next to the Sistine Chapel. The name holds its origins from the intermingling of the joy and sorrow felt by each newly chosen leader of the Catholic Church, a most monumental task. There, thinking over the responsibilities that had been thrust upon them, many a pontiff had shed countless tears. But once the new pope was alone, he chuckled, almost laughed out loud. Everything was going according to plan. After several minutes he emerged.

"Eminence?" the papal advisor questioned. "What name have you selected?"

"Peter" he replied.

"But Eminence, tradition holds that since the first pope was named Peter, the last shall also be named Peter. Don't you wish to reconsider?"

"It is God who has chosen," was his answer.

The date, October 13, 2067, fifty years to the hour after his birth, Edger Bartholomew Pielaresto, was proclaimed one of the youngest popes in history, and the first pope from the United States of America.

SECRETS REVEALED

POLYCARP THE LEARNED was responsible for discovering the link between magic and science. He spent his life researching and experimenting with various powerful spells. Wise enough to heed the warning of Leviathan, he was the first to leave Atlantis before its destruction. Abandoning the majority of his life's work, he and his wife Zenobia packed only those notes and documents which they could carry into the boat.

The most important among these was the document that told the story of and included, the exact location of The Book Thoth written by the Egyptian god of wisdom, time, writing, magic and the moon. This book permitted the reader to connect with animals, cast great spells, and bewitch even the earth and sky. It told about Prince Neferkaptah who stole the book from Thoth. Upon touching it, he felt a supernatural force surge through his body. This caused him great unease, but he was unwavering in his quest to find the spell which would allow him to resurrect his beloved wife. The first page cut him to the quick, but nothing could be worse than the heaviness of his heart:

"Cursed be you who read these words. Those you hold most dear will one by one be removed."

The prince spent months interpreting the spells and incantations, but before he could find the correct one, the curse began to take hold: his mother, the heir to his throne, and a favored daughter, died within days of each other. The pain of his losses was now intolerable. He had suffered too much! He concealed the book within six boxes each secured with a key. The book was placed in a golden box which was contained in a silver box inside a box of ivory and ebony, encased in a sycamore box, inside a bronze box enclosed in an iron box.

These were buried in the city of the dead. The prince placed enchantments and curses upon the keys which he committed to secret locations throughout the world. Each key was guarded by several beasts. He intended the book never to see the light of day again.

This was the research Polycarp carried from the island. He knew the legend to be factual and had successfully calculated where each key lay hidden. Quickly packing the boat he and his wife left the island.

At a safe distance Polycarp turned off the boat's propulsion, and embraced Zenobia looking one last time at their beloved Atlantis. As they watched, Poseidon reared up from the waters in a mighty pose above the island. As he thrust his trident toward it, lightning bolts shot from the three points hitting the island, which exploded and sank beneath the waters of the sea.

Polycarp and Zenobia dashed to the lower deck. Once below, Polycarp turned a lever causing a clear plastic-like covering to roll over the top from the starboard to the port side, effectively sealing the boat. They sat secured to their seats as wave upon wave lifted and tossed the craft. What seemed like hours passed before the sea became calm enough to emerge. Only then did he set out to find not only the keys, but the book itself. Polycarp was determined to see Atlantis returned to its former glory.

The Book of Thoth by *Aleister Crowley*, describing the philosophy and use of his *Thoth Tarot* deck.

During the days that followed, Mother made arrangements with the Pisa police for the bodies of Max and Ahren to be sent to the Motherhouse where they would be buried in the convent cemetery. It wasn't until the autopsy that Ahren's secret was finally revealed. On her tombstone, Mother had inscribed, "Judge not, lest ye be judged."

Continuing their investigation the police of Pisa sent a select group, including Mother and Joshua to thoroughly search the souvenir shop. The door at the back of the shop was securely locked. The police rammed it open, splintering it with some difficulty. The wood was much stronger than oak and later proved to be of an unknown species. Its genetic makeup baffled arborists.

The descent took a bit out of Mother and Joshua and by the time they reached the bottom, the police had already searched the first rooms of the large underground maze. They were filled with grotesque statuary depicting men in vulgar sexual positions with all sorts of animal life, real, and mythical. As they attempted to enter Ahren's office, the door swung shut. None of the police officers was successful in opening it. Just as they were going to use the ramrod, Mother arrived.

"May I give it a try?" she asked.

"Be my guest, Mother," Sergeant Gattuso replied. Standing aside he waved to the door with a gesture of mock chivalry. Turning to the officer on his left, he whispered with a snicker,

"What does she think she can do that none of us could?"

Mother went to the door, turned the handle, and it swung open. The police were befuddled.

"Uh…um…How?" Gattuso stammered, but Mother simply entered the room. In the corner was another, smaller room, which seemed to have been used as a bedroom.

"Sergeant, you start here. Joshua and I will begin in the other room," Mother said, making it sound more like a command than a request.

"Not yet, Mother, please. Before any search can be undertaken the rooms need to be photographed."

A half hour later, every inch of the rooms had been documented and the search began.

"Sergeant! Can you come here for a minute?" Mother exclaimed.

"Yes, Mother," he said entering.

Mother was on her knees near the corner of the eastern wall.

"I don't know sergeant, but I have a strong feeling that there is something here."

After what had happened with the door, Gattuso wasn't taking any chances. Helping Mother to her feet, he called in the officer with a circular saw who cut through the boards of the floor. They found nothing unusual. Mother pointed, looking at Gattuso, her eyes nearly vacant.

"Above… the lower part of the wall," she said, clenching her teeth. Her voice was strange, raspy. Cutting through the boards they found a vault. Pushing Gattuso aside, Mother reached in and pulled out the only occupant…a book. She opened it while Gattuso and Joshua looked over her shoulders. The book was handwritten and contained not only a list of the Sodality's members but very accurate and detailed accountings of each; their levels and dates achieved, deeds, activities both legal and illegal. Ahren had left nothing to chance.

"This will make our job much easier," Gattuso said, reaching for the book. For a moment it didn't seem as though Mother would relinquish her hold. Baffled by this behavior, and questioning how she knew what she did, Gattuso checked the pictures of the area, looking for what had led Mother to this vicinity.

He just couldn't get his mind around it. How was she doing these things? It appeared that the wall was whole, intact. Even when the pictures were enlarged no seam was apparent.

"Joshua, may I see you for a moment in the hall?" Gattuso was still checking the photos. It was the opportune time.

"Indeed, Mother."

Making sure they were alone, Mother pulled the book she had taken from the library from under her scapular and handed it to Joshua.

"I want you to give this to Sergeant Gattuso."

"Why Mother?"

"I can't put my finger on it but there is something not quite right about it, and this place. As we were searching the room, I felt as though something or someone was pushing me to certain areas. There was a power here that allowed me to open that door, and it seems to be getting stronger. Just now, when Sergeant Gattuso mistakenly cut open the floor, I wanted to call him things I have never... It was as though I was not myself.

That I was looking on, from inside me but did not have complete control. It took all I had not to call him such words. I wanted to run from the room with the diary, keep it, do not allow anyone else to even touch it. I feel as though my very soul is at stake if I keep this book any longer. Sergeant Gattuso can have the book taken to the station for safekeeping. I fear there will be no good to come from keeping it here."

Joshua took the book, and, for the first time since they had found it in the library, he too felt the power.

"You are right, Mother. We must get it out of here immediately."

Giving the book to Gattuso, Mother and Joshua insisted that it be removed from the premises straight away. Even though puzzled, he acquiesced. He wasn't about to doubt Mother again. He had already sent the diary to the station for analysis.

"Take this to headquarters, Officer Russo. Be sure it is safely secured."

"Yes, sir." he said ascending the stairs.

Coming through the shattered door at the top of the steps, Russo was suddenly spun around as though someone had grabbed his right arm and was trying to wrench the book from his hands. His training as an elite member of the police force kicked in. Curling over the book, clasping both arms tightly around it, he hurled himself ever forward while being grappled by the unseen force. The book was his responsibility. The distance to the door was only a matter of a few meters, but to Russo it seemed hundreds of kilometers away. Summoning all his remaining strength, he lunged through the door bursting into the midst of a group of tourists. He landed on his face, the book still held tightly to his chest.

"Are you all right mate?" asked one of the group, who came to his aid and was helping him up.

"Yes, thank you," said Russo, who was soaked with perspiration, between gasps as he steadied himself. Once outside, Giuseppe was released from the force that was trying to seize him. It was only then he realized the initial wrench had broken his right arm. Thanking the sightseer again, he made his way to the station and secured the book before seeking medical attention.

A PROPHECY THWARTED

THE MOST PROMINENT of the fallen angles are Beelzebub, Lucifer, and Leviathan. Of the three, Leviathan is the least known. He is king over the proud and is described as a sea monster, perverse, and convoluted. His name has become synonymous with any large sea creature.

The Torah says Leviathan was fashioned on the fifth day of creation. It was made male and female but God killed the female so they could not reproduce, for if they did the world would be destroyed.

The Jewish festival of Shavuot celebrates the giving of the Torah. During the observance a hymn is sung:

'...the sport with the Leviathan and the Behemoth... when they will interlock with one another and engage in combat, with his horns the Behemoth will gore with strength, the fish will leap to meet him with his fins, with power. Their creator will approach them with his mighty sword and slay them both and from the beautiful skin of the Leviathan, God will construct canopies to shelter the righteous, who will eat the meat of the Behemoth and the Leviathan with great joy and merriment, as a huge banquet that will be given for them.'

Leviathan lives in the Mediterranean Sea drinking water from the Jordan River. His breath is so hot that it boils the waters of the deep. No living creature can endure his odor. He eats one whale per day and legend says that he narrowly missed eating the whale, which swallowed Jonah.

The temple was not easily discovered. The entrance, an inconspicuous, narrow door, barely four feet high and only two feet wide, was flush with the wall and made from the same paneling that covered the hall. Even knowing its location one could not see it. It was serendipitously discovered when an officer tripped over the hidden switch in the floor. The door slowly swung open with a loud hiss, sounding almost like a possessed laugh.

Entering the room, the task force was overwhelmed by the enormity of the scallop shell-shaped amphitheater before them. They entered at the center of the curve. Directly across, at the far end was a black granite slab.

"This place must be at least a hundred meters across and a hundred meters long," Joshua exclaimed. "Who could have done this? Even today we don't possess the technology to do something of this grandeur."

The rows of the amphitheater sloped at an angle of thirty degrees. Alcoves, cat-stepped every eighteen meters along the side walls, contained a variety of artifacts. Several held the relics. Others, toward the rear of the room, were dedicated to Atlantis and contained artifacts from the mythical city, machines that resembled modern computers, light bulbs, a laser, a holographic projector, along with other technological devices whose function were not at the time identifiable, knowledge far beyond anything archeological discoveries suggested. Lining the walls between the alcoves were aerial maps of the world pinpointing the Atlantian continent. Scientists would study these for years to come.

At the bottom of the amphitheater was a pit, approximately 2 meters deep, 14 meters wide and 29 meters long. The height from the floor of the pit to the ceiling was approximately 30 meters. At the far wall, a statue of Leviathan rose menacingly from a shallow pool. The body snaked and coiled to within centimeters of the ceiling. His tail looped and twisted around his body. From his gaping mouth a long red, snake-like tongue protruded from between the glistening yellowish teeth. The eyes possessed great illuminating power. The statue was beautifully carved from an unknown wood. The skin, reddish, almost maroon, in color, seemed to shimmer. Just looking at the statue was mesmerizing.

In front of the statue was an altar, the hub of a large pentalpha, an inverted crucifix hanging above. The pentalpha was made from black granite and set in the stone floor. The top point was oriented toward Leviathan, coming within two meters of the tip of his tail. At each point of the star was a chair, with names inscribed in what looked like blood, on the back. North was Ahren Arachne, then counterclockwise, Alfrado Bennadetto, Domingo Saferino, Brendan Callahan and Lawrence DeSimone. At the foot of each chair, except for Arachne, was a chest. Encircling the pentalpha were new black candles.

The northern wall behind Leviathan was a slab of polished, absolute black, granite approximately 10 meters wide rising into the ceiling. Water cascaded over the face of the edifice tumbling into the pool below with a loud thundering reverberation. The red Leviathan contrasted with the black granite making it eerily beautiful.

"Will someone turn off that water? The sound is deafening." Gattuso shouted.

There was a flurry of activity as the officers went in search of the shut off valve.

When the water had stopped, all became strangely silent. Staring at the drying black granite Joshua's voice suddenly broke the stillness.

"Gut Shabbes."

"What is it Joshua?" Mother asked concern in her voice.

"Look at this! It looks like Aramaic."

"What does?"

"What is written on the granite!"

As the granite continued to dry, other symbols appeared, as if by magic.

"Can you read it Joshua?" Mother asked the question that was on everyone's mind.

"Yes, yes, I think I can. Aramaic is the mother language of ancient Hebrew. Give me a few moments."

Everyone went about the business of searching and documenting the items of the temple.

Thirty minutes later, Joshua called Mother and Sergeant Gattuso.

"I'm a bit rusty, but I have a translation. As I said, it is Aramaic. It reads:

> Leviathan urgently came upon the island of Atlantis,
> found the learned of the learned
> and spoke thus to them:
> "All is gloom and doom.
> Soon Atlantis will be no more
> Poseidon's wrath is rapidly felt.
> Abscond without lapse of time.
> Search the land of the obsequious
> Always aiming to the East
> Turn your eyes toward the valley
> between forks of running water
> Make that thy home
> Avoid the servile
> Keep only to thyselves
> Wait for the time
> When the magnificence of Atlantis be restored
> When Selene twice flies the night
> 9, 20, 29, 30, 69
> Explore the east
> Uncover the content of Bezalel's moving sanctuary,
> The one who awakens,
> The one who is praised,
> The one and only son
> Collect the whole or the parts

All of that which is left
Bring these together
Place them before the birds of religion
When the shehe rules
All will come to past
Atlantis will be restored
And acumen will rule the world
Avoid the woman in black
Power and spirit unite in her
Beware the man twin
Only he can bring to an end"

"That is all there is. What do you think it means?"

"Well, we know the birds of religion. That has to refer to the four cardinals. Their names are on the back of the chairs."

"I agree, Mother, but what does the fifth verse mean?" Sergeant Gattuso asked.

"I don't think we will know that until we open the boxes."

Each chest measured 2.75 meters long, 1 meter wide and 1 meter high. They were made of a maroon wood, similar to that of the statue. The top was frosted glass in which was etched the symbol that was on the door of the shop. Brass handles were affixed to the sides. Each had a hinge lock from which hung an ornate pad lock.

Not knowing what could possibly be in them, the bomb squad was called in. The building was temporarily evacuated until they finished their job. Mother was on pins and needles. She had wanted to open them. After several hours the all clear was given and Mother, Joshua, and Sergeant Gattuso, followed by the other officers, again descended the stairs. At the entrance to the temple, the group was met by the head of the bomb squad.

"What did you find, Ottavio?" Gattuso asked.

"Nothing, Luigi, that is nothing bomb oriented. We X-rayed each box trying to see what was inside. There didn't seem to be any explosives or wires. It took some effort to remove the padlocks. They broke one of my best saws. We finally got the things off and opened the boxes. We found some strange stuff. Prepare yourself for what you'll see. It's all pretty strange."

"We've seen some pretty strange things already Ottavio."

"Yeah, but nothing like this. The first box was empty. The second had a hair, a single brownish strand, in a silver and crystal bottle wrapped inside three cloth bags. The third was the strangest. There were mummified body parts, two arms, two legs, a torso, and a head. At first we thought we might have a murder to hand over to you, but on removing the parts we found that they were extremely old. The last box contained another which looked gold. We opened this box and found two pieces of stone. It's all laid out in front of the boxes. There are some really strange and bizarre things in that room. That statue scares the bajeebers out of me."

As the bomb squad left, the group squeezed back through the temple door. Surveying the room they found things the way Ottavio said. Mother was immediately drawn to the golden box in front of Bennadetto's chair.

"Joshua, could this be..."

"I was thinking the same thing." Joshua said picking up one of the pieces of stone. He ran his fingers lightly, almost lovingly, over its face. "Mother, it is Aramaic. I think these are the Ten Commandments. Do you think this is real?"

"I don't know Joshua. Anything is possible. We've seen some fantastic things this day. What is written on the wall?"

Joshua went back to the northern wall and read. "'... the content of Bezalel's moveable sanctuary.' Bezalel was the chief architect of the Tabernacle, which contained the Ark of the Covenant."

Excitement was growing in them as they turned to the next chair, Saferino's. Picking up the glass vile they examined it carefully. They were stumped.

"What could this be? It's a single strand of hair." Mother said.

"I know. Let's go over this again. What do we know? The chair was to be occupied by Saferino. No help there. We also know that

DeSimone was looking for the prepuce of Jesus. That must be the one and only son—Judaism and Christianity, world religions. There are two chairs left. That leaves two other religions. What two? The last two clues, the one who awakens, and the one who is praised. What are the last two great world religions?"

"Well, Islam has to be one. The great prophet was Muhammad," Mother chimed in.

Joshua pulled out his phone. Accessing the Internet he researched Islam. To his surprise he found the following:

The name Muhammad means "praiseworthy" and occurs four times in the Qur'an.

"Then, this must be a hair from the beard of Muhammad," Mother said. "But how did Ahren obtain it?"

"Here is an article on Muhammad's hair. It says:

'The single brownish strand is kept in a silver and crystal bottle inside three cloth bags, three wooden boxes, and a locked cabinet. The cabinet, protected by four guards, resides in the innermost of four cells at the mosque of Hazratbal in Srinagar, Kashmir. Only on Muslim holy days is Muhammad's hair presented to the faithful, who crowd into the mosque's great quadrangle. On such days one of the hereditary keepers of the relic removes it from its resting place and attaches it to a chain worn around the waist.'

"But that doesn't answer my question. How could it have gotten here? The security surrounding this vial seems to have been impenetrable."

"Well, the article continues:

'Despite the enormous security provided for Muhammad's hair, the relic was stolen in 1964; to the great relief of thousands of Muslims, it was recovered within a few days and returned to its sanctuary.'"

"So it seems the Sodality did obtain it more than a hundred years ago."

"I wonder whose hair has been venerated for these last hundred years." Mother quipped.

"I don't know Mother. Well, that is three pieces of the puzzles solved, now for the most repugnant."

Making their way to the chair with Callahan's name on it, they looked at the unpleasant sight before them.

"The last clue is the one who awakens. Judaism, Catholicism, Islam... what is another major religion?"

"Look to the East. Isn't that what Leviathan said?"

"Yes."

"Well, Judaism, Catholicism, Islam...where did they all have their beginnings? In the East! What other religion had its beginnings in the East?"

Quickly accessing the Internet again, Joshua soon found the answer.

"Buddhism! It's about as far east as you can go. It says here:

'In Buddhism, relics of the Buddha and various saints are venerated. Originally, after Buddha's death, his remains were divided into eight portions. Afterward, these relics were enshrined in stupas wherever Buddhism was spread, despite his instructions that relics were not to be collected or venerated.'"

"So, all Ahren needed was the prepuce."

"So it seems Mother."

"Thank God he didn't get it."

"Amen."

With the information gathered in the temple, the maze of rooms, and the papers Max had left, prosecutions would be swift. The members of the Sodality were already being rounded up including many high ranking officials of Pisa. But the highest ranking of all were the five cardinals. They would be the last to feel the wrath of the government, since they were still in conclave, being allowed no contact with the outside world.

Because of the aid that Mother had given in the investigation, and her reputation for fairness, the officials of Pisa decided that it would be in the best interest of all involved to have the relics transferred to the Order of the Blessed Sacrament for safekeeping. After much consultation, the order and the government eventually decided to return the relics to their rightful owners. The Atlantian artifacts were sent to the IMA, the Italian Ministry of Archeology, to be studied by the brightest scientific minds of the twenty-first century.

A FATHER'S REVENGE

He tasks me! He tasks me! And I shall have him. I'll chase him round the moons of Nibia and round the Antares maelstrom and round perdition's flames before I give him up!

Captain Ahab, Moby Dick

I T HAD ALL been too surreal but things were coming together. For the next several days, Mother and Joshua were busy. There was work to do, and not much time to do it. Yes, Max was dead, as was Ahren, but the danger of the Sodality did not die with him. It must be wiped out to the last member, as a nest of vipers has to be eliminated to the very last one. The evidence found in and under the shop was a great start, but other things were needed.

It was essential the Vatican be informed about the situation. Mother contacted the head of the Swiss Guard, Vladimir Vitus Emrey.

"Colonel Emrey, please."

"Who's calling?"

"Mother Hedwig Peligia."

"Yes, Mother, please hold."

"Emrey here, Mother. Are you all right? The sisters have been worried about you."

"Yes, Colonel. Please let the sisters know I am fine and will explain all upon my return, but there is a matter that demands your immediate attention. Rabbi Heim and I are in Pisa. We followed Monsignor Santiz here several days ago. He had info..."

"Mother," interrupted Emery, "we have been looking for the monsignor. We thought he was dead."

"He is, now, God rest his soul. Max was under my protection for some months. We arrived in Pisa just in time," Mothers voice began to shake, "to see he and his half-brother... plunge... from the top of the Leaning Tower." Her voice was stressed, tears began filling her eyes. She composed herself. It wouldn't help if she broke down at this time.

Mother continued her story telling him all the dark details. At first Emery didn't know whether to believe her, but he knew Mother well enough to know she would not have contacted him unless it were of extreme importance. If Mother said that the sky was green, then, by God, it was green.

"In the temple, center stage, is an enormous statue of Leviathan overlooking an altar in the middle of a pentalpha, above which hangs an inverted crucifix. At each point is a chair. On the back of each chair, written in blood, are names. Names I am sure will be familiar—Alfrado Bennadetto, Domingo Saferino, Brendan Callahan, Lawrence DeSimone, and Ahren Arachne."

"Saints preserve us," Emery drew in a deep breath. "Four of the most influential cardinals. How could this be in this day and age? Magic, black magic, Satanism... all occurring right under our noses!? It can't be."

"But it is! There's more, and it gets worse. Max had researched this for many months. He left documentation incriminating these men in a long list of illegal, unethical dealings. Cardinal Berkshire is implicated as well. All were members of a secret society, the Sodality of Thelema. The Pisa police have these records. These men must be stopped Colonel. I will send Max's documents to you today with Sister Maria. It is important that the five cardinals be taken into custody as soon as possible. Has the conclave ended yet?"

"Not yet, Mother."

"The saints be praised. At least none of the five have been elected...yet. Holy Mother of God, let us pray none does. Sergeant Gattuso, from the Pisa police, will be contacting you about this matter. I must go now. I have to speak to Sister Maria."

"Thank you Mother. I'll see you upon your return."

Almost immediately after hanging up, the phone rang again. It was Sergeant Gattuso requesting his assistance in apprehending the Fab Five.

Mother called her convent and asked for Sister Maria, a trusted friend.

"Sister Maria, how may I help you?"

"Sister Maria, I need you to do me a favor."

"Mother, where are you? We have all been so worried."

"I'm in Pisa and am fine. I'll tell you all about it when I get back. Now..."

"Yes, Mother."

"I need you to go to my cell. There, under the nightstand, you will find a box. In the box are a dozen sentinel drives. Would you be so kind as to deliver these to Colonel Emrey of the Swiss Guard. He is expecting them."

"Yes, of course, Mother."

"I forgot to ask Colonel Emrey to make a copy of these drives and send them to Sergeant Gattuso with the police in Pisa. Would you do this for me?"

"Yes, Mother."

"Thank you, Maria. It will aid the police in their investigation."

"What investigation, Mother?"

"Later, Maria."

"As you wish, Mother."

"One last thing. These need to be in Colonel Emrey's hands today, as soon as possible. Speak to no one, and stop for nothing until you reach the guard. Thank you and God bless."

"God bless you, too, Mother." Immediately upon hanging up the phone, Sister Maria hurried to carry out her instructions.

It was chaotic in Pisa. With the affiliate list discovered in Ahren's office, the police were quickly rounding up the members of the Sodality. As with any dragnet, though, it was inevitable that some would slip through the cracks. One such person was Simon Grody, the owner/operator of the Souvenir Shop. After having seen, who he thought was Ahren in the shop, Simon had a premonition of impending doom. He closed the shop, took the receipts from the cash register, and went home, where he packed his meager belongings, gathering all the money he had lying around.

Who could help him? Having seen his patron, Ahren, plunge to his death, he knew there would be no help from him. The Sodality couldn't help him this time either. By now, he had heard that many were already in custody. What about the Fab Five? They were in conclave. No help here, either. He couldn't face jail again, and so he ran. He had no idea how long he would be on the run this time.

Simon registered at a nearby hostel under the name of Lee Krieger. A few days later, as he had just fallen asleep, he heard his name. It was Ahren.

"Simon! You have been chosen. You must perform the rite. Only then can you resurrect me. THE ceremony must take place as planned. Sister Maria is taking evidence to the Swiss Guard. She has to be stopped and the sentinel drive retrieved. An alternative ceremony is detailed on it. Recover that drive! Kill her if you must! I have given you the power of execration. You will take my place until I return."

With that, Simon awoke. As he reached for the lamp, a pow-erful surge left his fingertips just missing the lamp and leaving a black scorch mark on the wall to its left.

"What the Hell!" he exclaimed. Then he remembered Ahren's command from his dream.

Dressing quickly he left the hostel heading for the park. He found a secluded spot to practice and trained for several hours.

I'm getting pretty good at this, he thought.

"Simon! Get to the Vatican courtyard. Do as I have commanded!"

Simon looked around and saw no one. Christ, Ahren was just as bossy in death.

Coming into the courtyard of the Motherhouse, Sister Maria was surprised to see that it had snowed. Taking in the view, she marveled at the works of God. Everything looked crisp, so clean. It wasn't often the Vatican experienced a snow, and never this early. Closing the massive Iron Gate behind her, she made her way across the Vatican mall.

With each step she felt a growing apprehension, as though a pair of sinister eyes were watching her every move. Several times, she looked around, but saw nothing.

Stopping yet again and surveying her surroundings, she remarked out loud, "My imagination! The mall is empty. It is dusk and there is not a sound. My mind's playing tricks on me. "

Approaching the door to the Swiss Guard, her peripheral vision caught a man sliding behind one of the pillars, but when she looked, out from the other side came a mangy dog.

"The devil!" She blessed herself. "Saints preserve us from all evil. Angels of God come to my aid."

Simon's chances were quickly slipping away. As he moved behind the pillar he knew he had almost been spotted. Sister Maria was almost there. It was now or never. Stepping out from behind the pillar, he took careful aim, summoned all his might, and threw a most powerful execration toward the nun, just as she climbed to the final steps to the office.

It left his fingertips as though in slow motion, seconds seeming like hours. The execration was just inches from its target, when Maria seemed to be shoved up the last step and into the lobby of the Swiss Guard. It hit harmlessly to the right side of the glass doors. From the top of the steps came a blinding flash like lightning hitting close by. Ahren would not be coming back after all. Paul had made sure of that.

Sister Maria stumbled into the lobby and was caught by Manfred, a brawny Swiss Guard who was just leaving after his shift.

"Sister, are you all right?"

"Yes, I think so. Someone pushed me."

Going to the door, they looked out at the dusting of snow covering the ground. There were only one set of footprints in the snow—only those of Sister Maria.

"Stay here Sister." Summoning his fellow guard, Lorie, they went outside to investigate. One hundred feet away they found a body. Where his chest should have been was a gaping red hole, showing through to the ground beneath, the smell of burnt flesh lingering in the air. Manfred turned and threw up. This was no ordinary weapon.

Inside, after giving sister a cup of tea, and allowing her to gather herself, she was escorted to the office of Colonel Emrey. Handing the sentinel drives to him, she said, "Mother asked me to give this to you. She also asked that you make a copy and send them to the Pisa Police, a Sergeant Gattuso."

"All right, Sister, I will. I have been waiting for these. Please, sit down. I am glad you are all right. Did you see who tried to kill you?"

"No, colonel. I thought I saw someone as I was entering the building, but it turned out to be a dog."

"A dog? How odd. What kind of dog?"

"I don't know. It was black and mangy, about the size of an Irish Setter."

"Was there anything else that you noticed?"

"Well, as I walked through the mall I felt as though I was being watched."

"When did that begin?"

"Immediately upon entering." There was a knock at the door. It was Manfred.

"Sir, the body has been searched. We found his drivers license. He's Simon Grody. Our records indicate that he was a notorious henchman, wanted in France and Germany. They have been searching for him for years. Now that he is dead, dozens of crimes finally will have closure."

"Sister, do you know this man?"

"I have never heard of him."

"Thank you, Sister. Please call us if you think of anything. I will have my men escort you home, for your safety."

"That is not necessary, Colonel. The man who tried to kill me is dead isn't he?"

"Yes, but there may be others."

"I don't think there will be. I believe you have what he was after. Good night, Colonel." Colonel Emery insisted on an escort and Sister Maria finally agreed.

"Sergeant DeGroot, please come in here," Colonel Emrey said over the intercom.

"Immediately, sir."

"Take these drives, have them copied, then send them to Sergeant Gattuso in Pisa, under guard.

AN ARRESTING CONCLAVE

THE SISTINE CHAPEL is located in the Vatican Cities' Apostolic Palace, the official residence of the Pope. Architecturally, it is of no interest having the shape of a rectangle. Its dimensions are similar to that of Solomon's Temple as given in the Old Testament: 163 ft 8 and 9/16 in by 40 ft 8 and 3/16 in. The chapel is 67 ft 10, 61/64 in high. It has a flattened barrel vault ceiling. Set into the walls of both sides are six tall windows which form a sloping triangle. Originally the chapel was divided into two equal parts, one for the laity and the second for the clergy, by a marble screen and mosaics on the floor. Later, the screen was moved to make the presbytery larger. Visitors, focused on the ceiling, often miss the murals on the walls, which are the work of Renaissance masters. The left wall depicts scenes from the Old Testament while the right has corresponding scenes from the New Testament. The artistic beauty is as impressive as the ceiling and well worth a look.

Ahren was dead, the world was safe, for now, but Mother and Joshua's problems were far from over. They still needed to help Sam. There was nothing more they could do in Pisa, so exhausted, they began the trip back to the Vatican. Mother tried to sleep on the train, but her mind just would not let her. She looked over at Joshua who was having the same difficulty.

"I can't sleep. I keep going over the events of the past few days. It seems so surreal. I keep thinking that I will awake at any moment from a bad dream."

"I know, Joshua. I feel the same way. I keep thinking about Max and that brother. How could two siblings be so different?"

"Remember Cain and Abel? They had the identical parents. And look what happened to them. Max and Ahren had different mothers. I have always believed that children are shaped more by their mothers than their fathers. It was so in my life."

"Max's life wasn't easy. I had a hard time, at first, believing what he told us, even when he showed us the information of the sentinel drives. I have always known, Joshua, that the devil and demons exist, but when I saw that temple, with its grotesque statuary and the inverted crucifix hanging in the middle above the altar with the statue of Leviathan behind, I felt almost overwhelmed by that dark power."

"I wish I could have protected you from it, Mother, but you were through that door before I could stop you."

"Fools rush in where angels fear to tread. I have always been impulsive. What I don't understand are the cardinals—five of the most powerful men in the Church. They had everything."

"They wanted more and thought this was the way to obtain it. They wanted the Church to be a world power, again, a return to the glory days of the Middle Ages, where the Church ruled the world and the Pope ruled the Church. He who sat on the Seat of Rome had almost absolute power. Power has always corrupted, and absolute power always corrupts absolutely.

Disembarking from the train, Mother and Joshua walked the short distance to Vatican City. Entering St. Peter's Square, Joshua pointed to the chimney which was billowing white smoke. A new pope had been elected. It was noon, October 13, 2067.

"Who could it be?" Mother asked.

"I don't know. What if it is one of the Fab Five?"

"I pray not, Joshua! I don't think the Church could survive the scandal. These cardinals are going to spend a long time in jail. It is bad enough to have five top cardinals caught up in that web of lies, deceit and black, satanic magic, but if one of them has been elected...It is too much to fathom."

They wouldn't have long to wait. Soon the doors of the central balcony to St. Peter's Basilica opened and the Senior Cardinal Dean, the Cardinal Protodeacon, Anthony Rodgers appeared and announced:

"Annuntio vobis gaudium magnum:

Habemus Papam!

Eminentissimum ac Reverendissimum Dominum,

Dominum Edger Bartholomew,

Sanctae Romanae Ecclesiae Cardinalem Pielaresto,

Qui sibi nomen imposuit Peter II."

"I announce to you a great joy:

We have a pope!

The Most Eminent and Most reverend Lord,

Lord Edger Bartholomew,

Cardinal of the Holy Roman Church, Pielaresto,

who takes to himself the name Peter II."

Stunned Mother asked, "How could this have happened, Joshua? Edger isn't even a priest! I thought Max was wrong about him. I never liked the man, but I didn't think even he was capable of this. And, the cardinals? How could they have allowed this violation of tradition? What could they hope to accomplish?" Mother didn't ever remember being so angry.

Even as Mother and Joshua wended their way through the excited crowd of worshipers, Emery and trusted members of the

Swiss Guard and the Italian police were waiting. When the doors of the Sistine Chapel opened to release the cardinals, Emery entered, closed and locked them again, his men coming in from the rear of the chapel.

"What is the meaning of this Vladimir? The conclave is over. These men are free to go. They are eager to return to their diocese and the everyday work of the Church," Cardinal Rodgers, the Cardinal Cameralgo said.

"I am sorry, your Eminence, but there have been certain... developments on the outside that will take a bit more of the cardinals' time. I assure you, and them, that it will all be over soon. I beg your indulgence for just a few more minutes. May I speak to you, privately?"

Walking to the opposite side of the Chapel, Emery explained all to Cardinal Rodgers.

"I can't believe this. How can this have happened? No one had a clue."

"You know how I feel. As head of the Swiss Guard, I should have seen something, or heard something. I have let my Church down, but I can, in a miniscule way, make up for it now. I must do the right thing. These men must be stopped! The Italian police are waiting behind that door," he said pointing to the old entrance to the Chapel. "I don't want the public to know about this until we can meet with the new pope and get his input on the matter."

As they were speaking, the cardinals were discussing matters amongst themselves.

"What do you think is the meaning of this sacrilege?"

"How dare he do this! The conclave is over."

"We are needed to meet with the new pope."

"When this is over, I am going to speak to the new pope and have Emery replaced."

Cardinals Berkshire, Bennadetto, Saferino, DeSimone and Callahan withdrew slightly from the rest of the group. In whispered tones, they discussed the matter at hand.

"What do you think Emery wants?" DeSimone asked, the most timid and suspicious of the group. "Do you suppose Arachne has something to do with this? Maybe he sent them."

"Not at all!" Berkshire answered. "We know all of Emery's men. None of them are remotely involved with the Sodality. Besides, why would Arachne use the police, especially the Swiss Guard? They are mostly ornamental, show pieces."

"Maybe it has to do with the prepuce," Bennadetto injected.

"Get real, Al," Cody said. "Arachne doesn't need the help of the police. He has powers not of this world."

"Yes, but look at them over there. All huddled together. What could be so important?" Saferino supposed.

"It looks like we will soon see," Callahan said. "Rodgers is coming back."

Following Rodgers were several of Emery's men. As Rodgers approached the small group of cardinals, the others went to the larger group.

"Gentlemen, would you please follow me?" Rogers requested of the Fab Five.

"Why? Where are you taking us?" Cody questioned.

"Just to the back of the Chapel, Your Excellency."

"What is this all about?" Bennadetto demanded. "We demand to know NOW why this sacrilege!" His voice was beginning to rise.

"Eminence, please, remember where you are. Please keep your voice down! All will be revealed in just a few moments. Please, just follow me and don't make a scene."

Several Swiss Guards surrounded the five who immediately began to cooperate.

As they made their way to the back, Cardinal Rodgers went to the larger group of the cardinals.

"Most sincere apologies, Your Eminencies. It was unavoidable. I must have your solemn promise not to disclose what you are about to hear. The fate of the Church rests upon it." After obtaining this promise from each of the cardinals, he gave them a brief synopsis of what had transpired. Unbelief and shock was the order of the day.

"When you leave these doors gentlemen, please act normally. Remember, you have just elected a new pope. Joy must be what the press sees, joy at the election of a new shepherd for the Church. I have your solemn promise. You are now dismissed. Thank you for your service," Rodgers said, opening the doors.

The cardinals were met by various members of the press, but most refused to be interviewed continuing on to their waiting cars. The press was so pre-occupied running from cardinal to cardinal trying to obtain an interview they had not the slightest knowledge of what was transpiring just a couple hundred feet away behind the Chapel.

"What do you suppose is the matter?" one member of the press asked her photographer.

"What do you mean?"

"I haven't met a cardinal yet who refused to be interviewed."

"You forget, Sue, these men have been cooped up for almost a year. I'm sure they just want to get back to their dioceses and have a good rest."

"I guess you're right, Jer. But something just doesn't sit right with me."

She was so right. Cardinal Rodgers returned to the back of the chapel just as Vladimir was placing the Fab Five under arrest.

"Victor, do something. These charges are preposterous. They can't do this. We are cardinals of the Church," Safriano pleaded.

"There is nothing I can do eminence," said Victor Rodgers, who had endured years of maltreatment at the hands of these men. In the past few minutes, things began to gel in his mind as he put things together, making sense of matters that had not been clear.

"You are the Cardinal Cameralgo! You must grant us sanctuary."

"You are wrong, Your Excellency. When I dismissed the cardinals, my position as Cardinal Cameralgo ceased. We have a new pope and it is to him you must appeal," Rodgers said as he walked away.

"Yes, we can appeal to Edger," Berkshire said. "This is a mere inconvenience gentlemen. We will be home by evening. Edger will see to that."

The Swiss Guard escorted them to waiting, unmarked police cars just outside the old entrance to the chapel. As they drove, the cardinals realized they were leaving Vatican City.

"Where are we going? The Vatican Swiss Guard is that way!" Callahan told the driver. Vladimir riding shotgun was understandably pissed off. He would have liked nothing better than to do away with these men himself. He couldn't believe this could have happened under his watch. But it had, and it could have been worse. Max could have failed in his mission, and the Sodalities threat could have become reality. The Church had been so close to extinction that Emery shuddered. He had known nothing of the antics of these cardinals and said a silent pray for Mother, Joshua, and Max, secretly wishing that they could be part of his team.

"We are taking you to Pisa," he told them after calming himself. "The police there are in charge of this investigation."

Shocked, the five rode in silence for some time.

After a while, Berkshire said one word to himself. "Arachne."

Vladimir heard him. "Can't help you either." he said, a joy in his voice. "Dead!"

The cardinals were flabbergasted. There would be no help from God or Satan. The Fab Five were on their own.

AN UNLIKELY SPY

IN THE ANCIENT Christian church, an encyclical was a letter sent by any bishop. In the modern Roman Catholic Church the term is used exclusively for Papal letters. In its strictest sense, a Papal encyclical is used to treat some aspect of Catholic doctrine. The arrangement of the address varies widely. A Papal brief is a letter of a more personal nature while a Papal bull is an official document covering a wide range of situations from excommunications to canonization of a saint. The Vatican Archives contains many historical papal bulls.

It didn't take long for Pope Peter to surround himself with people he trusted. Even if the Fab Five had not been arrested, and would soon be on trial, Peter had decided to keep them at arms length until the time was right. Then he would have picked them off, one by one, starting with Cody. Cody was the antithesis of what a good priest should be. How he rose to power, Peter didn't know, but he had a good guess. After being together with Cody, Edger always felt dirty.

He had used Cody, and Cody didn't even realize it. Cody had always been too anxious to take control, tell anyone he came in contact with what to do. Peter wondered how Cody would feel in jail, not being in charge, being told what to do twenty-four hours a day, seven days a week. It gave him a silent chuckle. How fate had worked in his favor. Peter didn't need Cody, always at his side, telling him what to do, how to do it, if his plan were to work. It was the only real lesson his parents had taught him. It was an accidental lesson he was sure. His parents never willingly gave him anything. Edger learned this lesson well—never, never be controlled.

When he was informed about the arrests, Edger saw it as a sign. He was on the right path. He wouldn't have to deal with these men on his own. The government would do his dirty work for him. His first papal encyclical addressed this issue:

> Beloved in Christ Jesus,
>
> It is with a saddened heart that I must write to you. The joyous celebration of the election of a successor to Saint Peter has been tainted by the arrest and prosecutions of five prominent cardinals. The crimes they have committed were horrendous and cry to heaven for justice. I have spoken to each, each admitting to their crimes, but none has demonstrated repentance. Satanic worship requires the full weight of the Catholic Church. This is a crime that cannot be overlooked, or forgiven. Therefore, Cardinals Bennadetto, Berkshire, Callahan, DeSimone, and Saferino, according to Canon law, have not only been stripped of their offices, and defrocked, but have been excommunicated from the Holy Roman Catholic Church, the most severe punishment the Church may administer. The faithful are urged to have nothing to do with these men, or risk excommunication themselves. The loss of one soul is cause for mourning. Five causes us to grievously weep. Continue to pray for their souls, that the Lord may touch them before the sting of death removes them forever from the love of Christ Jesus.
>
> Sincerely in Christ
> Pope Peter II

Peter chose Sr. Magdalena DeRienzo as his housekeeper. He had worked with her at Gemelli Hospital and was always pleased by the quality of work she provided. He also liked her mouse-like qualities—quiet and efficient, keeping to herself, and never questioning. She was a good nun, respecting—no, revering—authority. There had been times at Gemelli that Edger hadn't even realized she was in the room until she was leaving. Magdalena had a wonderful way of blending into the furniture. He knew he could trust her.

Sister Magdalena accepted the position of papal housekeeper, beginning her duties the day after the election. The apartment needed a thorough cleaning since the last occupant had left it ten months before. The rooms had been shut off, sealed, until the new pope was to begin occupancy. Peter II would stay in the guest apartment until his rooms were ready. Sister Magdalena did her job efficiently, cleaning and scrubbing, waxing and polishing, until everything shined. God had given Magdalena a gift, the gift of cleaning.

When Mother heard that Sister Magdalena had been appointed papal housekeeper, she offered a silent prayer of thanksgiving. A month after Peter's election, Mother Hedwig Peligia phoned Sister Magdalena, requesting a meeting. She set it up for the next day. They were to meet at Mother's convent along with Sam, Millie and Joshua.

Arriving an hour before Sister was expected, the group discussed the matter.

"Why would Sister Magdalena accept the position?" Millie asked. "She doesn't trust Edger. That was apparent when she gave Sam the notes she found in his office."

"No, Millie. Magdalena does not trust Edger, but it isn't the man she serves. She serves the office. Faith is a peculiar thing. As religious, we are taught to respect the office, regardless of who occupies it. We believe that God himself has appointed and his ways are not ours. Besides, we hold a card that is in our favor. Edger doesn't know that Magdalena doesn't trust him."

A knock on the door brought the conversation to a halt.

"Enter, with the peace of God."

"Mother, Sister Magdalena is here to see you."

"Thank you, Sister. Please send her in."

No sooner had the door closed than there was another knock.

"Enter, with the peace of God."

Sister Magdalena entered the room.

"Welcome, Sister. Please sit down. I believe you know everyone here."

"Yes, Mother. Thank you." Sister shook hands with all in the room before sitting down.

"Sister, we wanted to meet with you, to discuss a very delicate matter. I think, and I believe you feel the same way, that Edger Pielaresto has no business being pope. The cardinals broke with long standing tradition, and I don't know why, perhaps never will. Now, he is the pope."

"I don't much like it either, Mother. I worked for Dr. Pielaresto since he came to Italy. He has always been nice to me and my staff, but I have seen things, heard things that I just do not like. There wasn't anything big, just small things, things that one may overlook in others. That is why I approached Dr. O'Brien with the papers I had found. They just felt wrong. There is something not quite right here."

"Exactly! We know he is up to something, something big. We know it has to do with the VMAT2 gene, because of the papers you brought to Sam. After intensive study of the papers, Sam discovered that Edger has found a way to turn the gene off. Sister, can you imagine a world where people have no kind of religion? There would be chaos. In doing so, he would remove the very conscience of humanity."

"I agree Mother, but what can we do? What can I do?

"Keep your eyes and ears open, your mouth shut. You have access to the papal quarters. No one else has the clearance you have. You can enter when he is there and when he is not. We need you, sister, to discover how he intends to implement his plans. Will you help us?"

"I'll do what I can, Mother." With that, Sister left.

"Well, that is all we can do, I'm afraid. I don't know if Sister is up to the task."

Joshua responded to Mother's comments. "She may seem mousy and mild-mannered, Mother, but I have made a career of reading people. Sister Magdalena is still waters that run deep, very deep indeed. She possesses an inner strength that few have. I believe she will prove very useful."

Sister Magdalena went about her daily chores with the efficiency she had always exhibited. She made sure she kept out of the pope's way, when he was there, but listened closely to what he would say. When she was alone in the apartments, she would search, looking for a clue as to what he was up to. One day, as she was cleaning the bathroom, the pope entered and sat at his desk. His personal phone rang. She knew that only a handful of people had this number, so as she cleaned, she listened.

"Hello."

"Hi, Mark. Have you found what I need?"

"I see. What is the address?" He wrote it on the pad.

"Thanks." As Peter hung up, there was a knock at the door. Magdalena heard something about being needed and the door was shut. She looked around to be sure the pope had left and went to the table. Picking up a pencil, she did a rub on the tablet.

La Florentina Beverage Company
Franciacorta, south of Lake Iseo

Calvina, Michelina., Ezzelin La Florentina elderly owners
Gagliano–local bishop
Water is the key!

Tearing the sheet from the tablet, she folded it, placed it in her pocket, finished the bathroom and left.

LA FAMIGLIA LA FLORENTINA

December 2067

ALL CHRISTIAN DENOMINATIONS recognize the importance of the Eucharist but they differ about its meaning. For Roman Catholics, the bread and wine is transformed, beyond human comprehension, into the body, blood, soul and divinity of Jesus, while physically remaining in the shape of bread and wine. This is called Transubstantiation.

Protestants believe that Jesus made his sacrifice once, on the cross. In memory of that event, they celebrate the symbolism of the Last Supper's importance in his life.

Churches also differ on how often they receive the Eucharist. Those placing more importance on the sacraments encourage their members to receive the Eucharist more often. For Roman Catholics, the Eucharist is the most important act of worship and members are encouraged to receive the Eucharist at least once a week.

Other denominations receive Holy Communion less frequently, usually once every few weeks.

At the same time as these events unfolded, soon after his election, the solution to his problem made itself clear. It would never have occurred to him had he not been elected pope.

While looking through some papers in the papal library, Edger found the recipe for making hosts.

The finest white, wheat flour, salt, and pure water.

That was all. Pure water jumped off the page. This was it! It could be done. Checking into the assets of the Vatican, he found they owned five water bottling plants. Looking through their prospectuses, he immediately rejected all.

Frustrated, Edger contacted a trusted associate he met while at Gemelli Hospital. The call Sister Magdalena had overheard was from him. He found Edger a small family company owned by three elderly siblings, two sisters and a brother; The La Florentina Beverage Company in Franciacorta is located at the southern part of Lake Iseo. The sisters, each older than eighty, and the brother, quickly approaching eighty, had started the company at the turn of the century when water bottling was just beginning to take off. At that time the area was renowned for its sparkling wines. The key to their notoriety, water from the glacial lake, was discovered by the siblings who risked their minuscule family fortune to start the business. It was successful and the three earned a generous income which they used to fund various charities, including support of their parish church and diocese. None had ever married and there were no relatives waiting in the wings to take over the company.

Edger decided to pay them a visit.

Cradled deep in a glacial valley northwest of Brescia, life at Lake Iseo was simple and continued as it had for centuries without much interference from the outside world.

Even with its close proximity to Rome, no pope had ever come there which is why Bishop Gagliano was so shocked to receive a letter from the Vatican announcing the Papal visit.

> Your Excellency Bishop Gagliano,
>
> Pope Peter II requests permission to visit your diocese, between the feast of the birth of Our Lord, Jesus Christ and the Solemnity of Mary, His Immaculate Mother. He has heard about the area of Lake Iseo and the gracious simplicity of the people, living their quiet lifestyle. It

sounds ideal for His Holiness' purposes as he is searching for a quiet, out of the way area, where he may relax and do some fishing, away from the public eye. He is considering the purchase of some property as a permanent Papal retreat.

Pope Peter II requests that his visit be kept as quiet and confidential as possible, fearing disruption of the life of your parishioners.

Sincerely in Christ,
Monsignor Christopher Scott
Secretary to His Holiness
Pope Peter II

Bishop Gagliano was more than apprehensive. Was that the only reason? There were other areas more suited. Did he do something that had aggravated the new pontiff? Did his flock? Senora Castelnuovo was always writing letters about the activities of her parish priest or of this parishioner or that. She would attend Mass at neighboring parishes and find fault with them as well. Most of her letters went to him, but occasionally, some reached the Archbishop. Then, there was hell to pay. Bishop Gagliano tried to pray for this poor soul, but sometimes she was just too aggravating. Now! Could she have written to the new pontiff? What could she be complaining about? No! The letter distinctly said that his holiness was looking for a quiet place to rest and relax. What better place than here? The fishing, some of the best in the world, was a well-kept secret. The pontiff could not have chosen a better place.

A list of sites the pontiff wished to see on his visit was forwarded to the bishop. Among them were the winery and La Florentina Beverage Company.

The elderly siblings were beside themselves with joy that their lowly company had been selected by the pope. The "girls" went out and bought new dresses for the occasion and brother bought a new suit, tie and hat. Nothing would keep them from this historic occasion.

"Oh, to meet the pope, Calvina, and not have to travel to Rome. I can't believe he is coming here."

"Neither can I, Michelina. God has been good to us, and now this blessing."

Ezzelin entered the room, strutting like a peacock in his new attire, his shoes highly polished.

"Looking good, eh, ladies?" he said as he checked himself out in the mirror.

"You old gum bat. The girls didn't want you when you were young and somewhat good-looking." said Michelina.

"Ah, but then I didn't have the pope coming to see me."

They all laughed.

Two days later the pope arrived dressed only in black, looking rather like their parish priest. The village was dismayed. Where was all the Papal regalia? To say they were disappointed was an understatement.

On the first afternoon, Pope Peter was warmly welcomed to La Florentina Beverage Company by the three siblings. After the tour, they invited him to their home where he was treated to a buffet of antipasti, minestrone, agnolotti, ravioli, cannelloni, seppie ripiene, followed by a variety of desserts including cannoli, frittelle, and zeppole, all personally prepared by the sisters.

By the time dessert and coffee were served in the parlor Edger knew he had found the perfect facility in which to work his plan. He wanted to spend as much time with the La Florentina's as possible, worming his way into their good grace. Somehow, he would have that plant.

"So how long has the bottling company been here?"

"We will celebrate our sixty-fifth anniversary next year, Your Holiness, God willing," Ezzelin replied.

"That is a long time. How is business?"

"Not so good, Eminence. When we began the company, water in a bottle was new and business was good. Now, people aren't buying as much bottled water. There were the scandals of the early 60s, dealing with companies using tainted water from mines, and it didn't help that several deaths were linked to the leaching of Bisphenol-A from the plastic bottles. Changing to glass helped, but sales are still down and costs are way up."

"I am sorry," Edger said with a gleam in his eye. He could pick up the plant cheaply too. "This is just the kind of property I had in mind, a quiet place for retreat, close to the lake, secluded. If you ever think of selling, please allow me the first bid." Then, before anyone could answer, Edger looking at the sisters remarked "My, what handsome women you two are. I can't imagine why no one has ever snatched you up."

The girls giggled, and Michelina replied, "You should have seen us sixty years ago."

"Your Eminence, Michelina was pretty, but Calvina was striking. Oh, what a face with a figure to match. Let me show you."

Ezzelin went to the bookcase, and from the shelf taking an old photo album handed it to the pope.

Edger opened it and began to thumb through the old photos which contained all the standard family portraits. There was a picture of the family, with the mother and father seated, a man in his early twenties standing on his mother's right and a girl about six on her father's left. On the lap of the mother was an infant and the father held a girl of four or five. Turning the page, Edger's eyes fell upon a picture. As he stared at it for several minutes, his eyes dimmed with tears.

"Julie."

Calvina who was seated next to the pontiff, was explaining who the people were.

"Oh no, Your Eminence. My name is Calvina, not Julie. That's me, when I was twenty-one. It had been taken right here in this very room, next to that fireplace."

"Didn't I tell you she was a beauty?"

Edger looked up, gazing deeply into Calvina's eyes realizing for the first time since they met, her resemblance to Julie. Then reaching into his pocket and pulling out his wallet he took out a picture and handed it to Calvina. Michelina and Ezzelin came and stood behind the pontiff, looking over his shoulder.

"It seems to be a picture of me. But how? I don't remember taking this. This picture isn't old enough to be me."

"Calvina, it isn't you. This picture was taken in '42. Her name was Julie. She was my fiancée. She died many years ago."

Edger now realized why he felt completely at ease with the family from the time he had met them. It also explained the reason he felt especially drawn to Calvina. He began Julie's story.

When he had finished, Michelina said, "I wonder. You see, Your Eminence, our eldest brother Nino was fifteen years older than me. By the time we were born, our parents thought that he would be an only child. Try as they might, mother just couldn't conceive again. When they stopped trying, I came along, then, shortly after, Calvina. Ezzelin was unexpected, and has always acted that way. By that time, Nino was off to college. He received a scholarship to study for the priesthood at Duquesne University in the states, in Pittsburgh."

Edger looked up, startled by the revelation. "I know Duquesne. I grew up north of Pittsburgh and attended the University of Pittsburgh."

"What a small world this is, indeed. When Nino was a senior, he met Marge, and from his letters, we knew he would never be a priest, although it took him five years to finally marry the girl.

They had only one child, a daughter named Jill. Nino received his doctorate in Theology from Duquesne and became a professor there.

We were so happy for him and just as happy when he married Marge. We couldn't attend the wedding. Poppa wasn't working steady, and we couldn't afford the plane fare for the five of us. Poppa wanted Mother to go, but she refused saying 'If God wants me to go, then he will arrange for all of us to go.'"

"When Nino died, we lost touch with Marge. Jill eventually married. We received an invitation to the wedding in Pittsburgh. Business here kept us from attending. Then there was Mother and Poppa who needed round the clock care. We just couldn't leave them. Calvina, do you remember who Jill married?"

"I can't remember Michelina. Isn't the invitation in the album?"

"Yes, yes it is. Let me see the album, Eminence." Fumbling through the pages, Michelina found it.

"Here it is. She married a John Buzzbee."

"May I see that?" Edger asked, almost in a whisper. Could this be? Could this be happening? Was it a sign, a sign that he was doing the right thing?

"Julie's last name was Buzzbee."

"How ironically coincidental? You don't think... "

"Yes. Julie is the spitting image of you Calvina. You've seen her picture. Julie must have been your grandniece."

Ezzelin stood up to get another cup of coffee, walked several steps, clutched his arm, stumbled and fell to the floor. Edger was by his side in an instant, examining him, taking his pulse, looking at his pupils.

"I wish I had my bag," he said as he explained to the sisters that he was a physician in his previous life.

Ezzelin was beginning to gain consciousness.

"Lay still, Ezzelin. How are you feeling?" he asked.

He had some trouble speaking, his words slurred as he told Edger of a sudden numbness to his face, arm and leg, on the right side.

"I am having trouble seeing from my right eye. Everything is blurred. When I got up, my head began to ache. I became dizzy, and I lost my balance."

After Ezzelin was stabilized, Edger called for the papal helicopter to prepare for immediate departure.

"Ezzelin has had a stroke. We must get him to the hospital quickly. Gemelli is the best."

"How can we get him there? It is a four-hour drive and neither Calvina nor I drive."

"I have arranged for him and you to be flown there in the papal helicopter."

"We don't have the means to pay, Your Holiness. The business hasn't been doing well for a long time."

"Don't worry. It will not cost you anything. Now get ready. The helicopter will be here in a few minutes."

Within the hour, Ezzelin and his sisters were at Gemelli Hospital. The prognosis was not good and several days later, Ezzelin went home to his mother and father.

The sisters were devastated by their loss. Edger requested that they honor him by allowing him to concelebrate Ezzelin's funeral Mass. The entire village turned out, some just to see the pope, but the majority because of the high esteem they held for the LaFlorentinas.

Edger attended the wake, and when the last guest had gone he was left alone with the sisters.

"Your Eminence, Calvina and I are so happy that you would take the time to concelebrate Ezzelin's funeral. It was a wonderful gesture. We are grateful, too, that you could stay for the wake.

We wanted to present you with a small token of our gratitude for your kindness in our time of loss."

She handed him an envelope. Inside, Edger found the deed for the plant and the house. Edger had wanted this, but not this way. He couldn't let the sisters, Julie's great aunts, be destitute.

"I can't accept this. It is too generous a gift. I can't accept your home," he said trying to hand back the envelope. It would be like throwing Julie out of her home. He couldn't do it.

"Yes, yes you can. It is all we have to give. You have been so kind to us."

"If you give me your home, where will you go? How will you live?"

"We'll survive. God has been good to us over the years. There have been ups and downs, and in all we have seen God's hand. There is a small boarding house in the village. Calvina and I will take a room there. Our needs are simple."

"You will stay here, for the rest of your lives. This is your home and will remain so. I insist. It is only right, and the only way I will accept your generous gift."

In the months that passed, he made sure the sisters had no money worries and the best of care.

During that time, he set his plan in motion. Having researched companies that made hosts, Edger found that only one was a religious order, the Passionist Sisters in Pittsburgh, on Churchview Avenue. All the rest were secular. Anonymously, Edger donated a sum of money, to the sisters, sufficient to build and staff a facility for making hosts.

Shortly after it was complete and operational, Pope Pete issued a decree. All Catholic Churches, across the world, would obtain their hosts from the Passionist Sisters of Pittsburgh.

Protests flooded in from the secular companies, but Peter held his ground. Within the space of several months, these groups gave up and concentrated on other items, both religious and non religious. The Passionist Nuns held exclusive rights to make hosts for the Catholic Church.

The nuns made hosts for the Orthodox Catholic Church as well, adding yeast to the mixture. Without competition the Passionists were kept busy making communion wafers for all Christian sects. They became the largest employer in the City of Pittsburgh. The Passionist Bread of Life Company even began making Matzah and Kekel.

A PAPAL AUDIENCE

March 22, 2068

IN 537 BC, using stone blocks that weighed nearly a hundred tons each, a substantial platform was built in preparation for the construction of the second temple. Quarried from beneath the Old City, the stone was white and of fine texture. Legend asserts Solomon used this very same quarry to erect the first temple.

The temple was supported by fifteen columns nearly three hundred feet high in some places. Architecturally remarkable, it was not festooned as extravagantly as the first.

The Temple was finally completed in 514 BC, more than twenty–three years after it was started and dedicated during the reign of Darius I, Emperor of Persia. The time elapsed from the dedication of Solomon's Temple to the dedication of the Second Temple was 420 years.

King Herod the Great (37 BC–4 BC), in an unsuccessful attempt to gain popularity, appreciably expanded the temple. He constructed an immense piazza, consisting of a series of porticoes and buildings for housing of staff and animals. It was safeguarded by a sizeable fort and tower. Notwithstanding a series of attacks by the Syrians, Greeks, and Romans, and periods of neglect, the temple remained functional for nearly six hundred years.

After the deaths of Max and Ahren, Mother and Joshua began planning the transfer of the ashes of the red heifer. It had been an ordeal that had taken much out of them. Mother, now almost seventy three, and Joshua, nearly sixty eight, had gone through what no one should ever have to, let alone people of their age. They had lost a friend, but other work needed to be done. It was time. In May of '67, a red heifer, meeting all the requirements had been born in Jerusalem, a sign the Sanhedrin had taken to mean the construction of the temple should begin. Mother and Joshua had also taken it as a sign, which meant that they had less than three years to return the ashes. They agreed on a simple ceremony to be celebrated at the spot where Jesus wept over Jerusalem.

By New Year's 2068, plans were already underway for the reconstruction of the temple. Now, with the ashes to be returned, momentum would build. Jews from around the world would unite once more and be brought back from their two thousand year exile.

"But, why?" Joshua wanted to know. "The ashes belong to your order. They have been in your possession for centuries. I doubt Edger even knows what the ashes are or the meaning they hold for my people."

"Perhaps not," Mother replied. "But though we are a self sufficient, self governing body, we belong to a larger group, that of the Holy Roman Catholic Church, to which we have pledged our obedience. As head, like it or not, Edger must be informed!"

Obtaining an audience with the pope was more easily said than done. It seemed he was perpetually on vacation, leaving the running of the Vatican in the hands of Cardinal Libator Rozzini. In essence, Rozzini was pope, without the title or the election, making decisions, paying the bills, saying Mass in the Pope's stead. He had gotten pretty good with the pope's signature. One of his major tasks was making excuses for the pope's absences.

Finally, on March 22, Mother, and Joshua obtained their audience. Peter and Mother had known each other when both worked at Gemelli. Peter also knew Joshua, who he was and had been, having met him at the Christmas party several years prior. Since then, their paths hadn't crossed and Peter often wondered if Joshua was avoiding him.

"Eminence. May I present Mother Hedwig Peligia Brzozowska and Rabbi Joshua Abraham Heim," said Monsignor Christopher Scott, his secretary.

"It is a pleasure to see you again, Mother," he said extending his hand. Mother dutifully kissed his ring. Peter really liked this, everyone groveling to him. In the short time he had been pope, Edger had grown quite used to it.

"I wish I could say the same," Mother wanted to reply, but instead said

"The pleasure is mine, Eminence."

"Rabbi Heim. It is nice to see you again." Again he extended his hand but Joshua took it and shook hands. He knew the protocol but Joshua wasn't about to kiss this man's ring, or anything else.

"Your Eminence!" was all he replied. If it disturbed Peter, he didn't let it show.

"I understand you have an urgent matter to discuss with me."

"Yes, your Eminence—one of great importance. Eminence, have you ever heard of the ashes of the red heifer?" Mother inquired.

Peter thought for a moment.

"No! I can't say I have. What are they?"

Joshua gave a cliff notes version, after which Peter asked

"What does that have to do with me?"

Could this man possibly be this dense? Mother wondered to herself.

"Eminence, as you know, the Sanhedrin is re-building the temple and a red heifer having all the required characteristics has already been born. All that is needed now is for the ashes currently housed at my motherhouse in Poland, to be returned. The order has had them for several hundred years, and Mother Gwendolyn Eleninska has decided to allow their return. We have come for your blessing on the venture."

"I need time to look into the matter." This was Edger's pat answer when he was confronted by a matter on which he didn't want to decide.

"Give me a few days to think it over," Peter said and dismissed them with a wave of his hand.

Monsignor Scott took down the e-mail addresses for both Mother and Joshua and escorted them out of the office.

Alone, Peter thought about the ashes. Why would they have thought he would have the slightest interest in them?

"I could care less what happens to a bunch of centuries-old ashes," he said aloud.

Monsignor Scott came back.

"So Chris, what do you think?"

"Eminence?"

"What do you think about the ashes?"

"They are important to Jews around the world. They are also important for all Christians."

"How?"

"As you know Eminence," Chris said stroking Peter's ego. "The ashes are used to purify the priests of the temple. Even though the temple is currently being built, it cannot be consecrated without the ashes.

"The Jews believe that once the ashes are in their possession, and the temple dedicated and consecrated, the Messiah will come."

"Hogwash! The Messiah has already come and the Jews did not recognize him."

"Remember, Eminence, Christian tradition also holds that the temple must be rebuilt for Jesus to return."

'Watch therefore, for ye know neither the day nor the hour in which the Son of man cometh,' (Matthew 25:13)."

"Indeed, Eminence. But, tradition is a powerful tool. What harm could come from returning the ashes in a simple ceremony. It would, for a time, reunite Jew and Christian."

This struck a cord with Peter. The ashes were important, not only to the Jews, but to all Christians as well. The seed of a plan had been planted, and this seed would not be denied. The idea crept into his subconscious and lingered there. Edger couldn't stop thinking about those damn ashes.

Try as he might, the thought returned time and again. He read about them, studied them. In a short while Edger knew more about the history of the ashes than almost any other man, Christian or Jew. Yes, they needed to be returned to Israel, but how? Mother and Joshua could simply hand them over. No! That certainly wouldn't do. There had to be some gain for him. Another idea had laid its seed in his subconscious. Perhaps there was a way to incorporate the return with his dark dream of the past four decades.

As the days went by, Edger thought more and more about the matter, becoming obsessed with it. Could it be done? Could the two be united; the return of the ashes and the distribution of the serum all in one fell swoop? An intricate plan began to develop in Edger's mind and grew larger with each passing day.

The transfer would take place on Easter Sunday, March 30, 2070. From what Edger had read, this date represented the two thousandth anniversary of the beginning of the siege that destroyed Jerusalem and the second temple—a fitting date for the return of the ashes and a more fitting date for the destruction of religion. Edger's serum would take hold, and religion would be as dead as the temple in AD 70.

It would be an ecumenical ceremony with Peter himself celebrating that Mass at the very site where the temple was being built. After Mass there would be a grandiose procession with members of the Sanhedrin and the College of Cardinals, processing side by side up the central aisle. Mother and Joshua would bring up the rear carrying the ashes. As they made their way to the altar, an arch of rainbow colored fireworks would be set off every six paces, reminiscent of David's triumphant return of the Arc of the Covenant, from the house of Obed-edom to the City of David (Jerusalem).

(And it was so, that when they that bare the Arc of the Lord had gone six paces, he sacrificed oxen and fatlings, [2 Samuel 6: 12–13].) All the while the orchestra would play Edger's favorite symphony, Saint-Saens Symphony No. 3 in C minor.

In addition to an array of cardinals and bishops, assemblies from the major world religions, including Archbishop Edwin James, Archbishop of Canterbury; Dr. Matthew Tooney, from the Judicial Council of Methodists; Archbishop William Ghibbelin, Patriarch of Jerusalem; Archbishop Chirstocandulous, Patriarch of Constantinople; Patriarchy Alexander Poskow, Patriarch of Moscow; would be in attendance along with their envoys. The entire Sanhedrin would also be there, and along with them, all of Jerusalem. All the networks would carry the ceremony, making it a worldwide event. Jews from around the world were making plans to be there.

The first sacrifice in more than two thousand years would take place on Tisha B'Av, July 30, the date when the second temple was destroyed. Everything was now in place.

Things were also going well for Pope Peter II. His plans were finally coming to fruition.

THE PUZZLE,
PARTIALLY SOLVED

January 1, 2070

NOT EVERYTHING SAID by the Holy Father is infallible. Just how many times in the two thousand year history of the Church has the pope spoken infallibly? No one really knows, but we do know he has spoken infallibly at least three times. These were concerning the Immaculate Conception, the Assumption of Mary into heaven, and the doctrine of the infallibility of the pope.

When the pope does speak infallibly, the statement made is without error. He can never introduce a new dogma but can only clarify a position already held by the Church. During these times, the pope is expected to demonstrate the teaching has been held by the Church throughout the centuries. Once made, it cannot be contradicted or denied. Few popes have been willing to invoke infallibility. He must be absolutely sure the conclusion reached is free from error. When it becomes necessary to speak infallibly, the pope must make his intent clear. The Church cannot grant this power, Infallibility is a gift from Christ.

The matter of faith being defined must be consistent with Scriptural principles, even if it's not explicitly stated in the Bible. Luke 1:28 is an example:

"And the angel came unto her, and said, Hail, thou that art highly favored, the Lord is with thee: blessed art thou among women."

The concept of the Immaculate Conception is loosely implied by this scripture and is not contradicted by ancient tradition.

It has been infallibly defined that the Pope's authority is not above Holy Scripture.

An encyclical lacks the force of infallibility. It is a letter, from the pope, to clarify the Church's stance on such issues as birth control, contraception, midwives, war and peace. Between 1878 and 2013, the ten men who had sat on the Throne of Saint Peter have written over one hundred and fifty encyclicals averaging one every six months.

Pope Pius XII issued ten encyclicals, many protesting the Soviet Union's invasion of Hungary. Paul VI used the spoken word to educate the Catholics about the Vietnam War and John Paul II did the same for the war in Iraq.

In his New Year's Day message, Pope Peter had decreed that across the world, there would be only one Mass on Easter Sunday. This Mass was to coincide with the Mass said in Jerusalem, which was scheduled for sunrise. The bishop of the diocese was to be the main celebrant and the Mass held in the largest arena or amphitheatre available, to accommodate as many of the faithful as possible. The Papal Mass would be televised for shut-ins, who would receive the Holy Communion from the Ministers of the Eucharist of each parish.

The Papal Mass would begin at 6 a.m., sunrise, March 30, in Jerusalem. All Masses around the world would begin at exactly this time. That would mean Mass would begin at 11:00 p.m. on the twenty-ninth in New York, 8:00 p.m. in Los Angeles and Seattle, 7:00 p.m. in Anchorage, and on March 30, 5:00 a.m. in Rome, 7:00 a.m. in Moscow, 2:00 p.m. in Sydney, and so on. The exact times would be sent to each diocese in the next several weeks.

All the bishops of the world would celebrate the Lord's resurrection at the same moment with all the faithful of the world participating.

Even the cloistered Passionists were given a day dispensation from their vow of seclusion to participate.

Peter had left little to chance. All was going well, very well indeed.

It was time. The papal apartments needed a thorough cleaning, again. Lying prostrate, Magdalena wedged beneath the pope's bed and began dusting the slats from the foot to the head. Under the first slat, she noticing a manila folder securely wedged. Pulling it out, she squeezed from under the bed. Taking the folder to the desk, she opened it and read the papers inside. At first, she didn't understand them, but it began to dawn on her that these had to be important to the group. Taking her cell phone, she took a picture of each page. Placing the packet back into the folder, she carefully replaced it exactly as she had found it. Magdalena finished her work, and then returned to the convent. Placing a call to Mother, she requested an appointment.

Six that evening, Magdalena met with Mother, Sam and Joshua. Millie was unable to make it, remaining at home with the kids, who had the flu.

Magdalena handed the phone to Mother, who looked at the pictures, but was unable to read the tiny print. She downloaded them and made copies for Sam and Joshua. Handing the phone back to Magdalena, they perused the papers.

"I found these wedged under one of the bed slats and I thought they may be important."

"They are indeed, Sister," replied Sam, looking up from the papers. "These appear to be research Edger did when he was at Gemelli. It is the results of tests he did on the senile and

Alzheimer patients there. It says he placed the serum into the patients' water. This has to be the reason he bought La Florentina Beverage Company. And, look! In every instance, the patient lost any religious feeling. In every case, it didn't matter whether the patient was Catholic, Protestant, Jew or Muslim."

"How unethical. Those patients had placed their trust in him. Their families trusted him. How could he do this? How could he be so cruel? Religion was all some of those poor souls had left." Mother was furious. She had never disliked a person as much as she now disliked Edger Pielaresto.

"That is over now, Mother. All we can do is pray for them, many of whom are probably in God's hands by now. Our present task—how to stop him from doing this again," Sam replied.

"Yes, of course. I am letting my emotions carry me away. Magdalena, when you brought in the rub you made, I was wondering what he wanted with such an obscure company. It isn't a moneymaker that much is for sure. Even if he does place the "cure" in the bottled water, they are just too small to reach everybody. He couldn't 'cure' the number of people he has in mind."

"There is one more thing, Mother. A few months back, I overheard the pope on his private line. He was angry, yelling at poor Cardinal Bentz. 'It's the way it will be, Bentz,' he said. 'I don't care how much it costs! The water for the transfer ceremony will be from there and nowhere else. Do you understand?' At the time, I couldn't imagine what he was talking about. It seems that somehow he is going to use water at the transfer ceremony on Easter. Is it possible?"

"Yes, sister, it is," replied Sam. "But the ceremony doesn't use water, except for the washing of the hands. Only Edger does that."

"Doesn't the wine have water mixed with it?" Joshua questioned.

"Yes, but not much. Certainly not the amount needed for such a crowd," Mother said. "Let's not forget, too, he has proclaimed that Easter Mass would be celebrated across the world at the exact same time. Edger's plans are much bigger than just for the crowd in Jerusalem, I fear. He wants the world! How can he get the cure to the most people at the same time?"

"Communion," Sam said, almost to himself.

"What?" Joshua asked.

"Of course! I should have thought of it sooner. All communion wafers are now manufactured by the Passionist Sisters of Pittsburgh. No one else makes them any more. They stopped production when Edger decreed that all Catholic Churches buy only from the Passionists. Even non-Catholics have to buy from them. No one else makes them."

"Easter is a major Holy Day for all Christian faiths. Every one will be distributing communion that day, all from the Bread of Life Company. That is also the day the Poinsettia and Lily Christians, the marginal Christians, show up."

"Passover coincides with Easter this year," Joshua said. "The Matzah and Kekel are even made by the Passionists. Think about it. There are seven billion people on the earth. Three billion are Catholic. Another two billion are Christians. There are a billion Jews, and three quarter billion Muslims. That is almost the entire population of the world."

"But how is he going to get the serum to the Muslims?" Magdalena asked.

"Well," Sam said. "Recently, the La Florentina Beverage Company has been making water for Muslim ceremonial purification. It must be absorbed by the skin, as well."

"Sam, how much of the serum is needed?" Mother asked.

"It says here, a couple of cc's."

"Hosts are flour and water, in almost equal proportions. More than enough would be in each host to affect the results Edger desires. At the least, half of the world would have their religious gene turned off. How do we stop him?" Mother asked.

SAIF AL HAKIM

2068–2070

TERRORISM IS THE organized use of violence and damaging acts committed by individuals or groups, not for financial gain, but to further a philosophical goal. They include deeds such as suicide bombings. These acts are meant to cause fear and are done without regard to who gets hurt. Often non-militants are targeted. A terrorist is one who participates in acts of terrorism.

The United Nations Security Council Resolution 1373 defines terrorism as criminal acts under the jurisdiction of the nation in which they occur.

Their hatred was vibrant, growing with every breath they took. They hated every aspect of the Muslim/Jew reconciliation of the late 20s. They hated the Muslim leaders. How could they have done this, made peace with Israel, their enemy since its inception in 1948. They hated the Jews. The Koran couldn't be clearer. It was their mandate to destroy Israel and the infidels of the world. Muhammad himself had so decreed.

A small group, they were like-minded men, calling themselves Saif al Hakim—Sword of the Wise One. Having only five members, they were too small to effectively accomplish anything meaningful, not that they lacked the funds. Oil had made each man's family wealthy in his own right. Their only option was to lay low, bide their time, build their fortunes, and hope an opportunity would present itself for something big.

The hatred was passed from father to sons, through two generations, thereby increasing their numbers. Finally, in late 68, a solution was dropped into their laps. One that could, with proper planning, potentially bring the world to its knees.

The Vatican had announced an ecumenical service for the return of the red heifer ashes to Israel, on Easter Sunday 2070. Among the guests would be large contingencies from all the religions of the world. The most powerful leaders of each major religion, including Jews from around the world, as well as the heretical Muslim leaders, would be there. In addition, world leaders from the United States, England, France, Germany, Russia, China, Canada, Australia, Poland, Spain, from every country of the world were expected.

All these high dignitaries are in one place, at the same time. Strategically placed nuclear devices could do the trick, dirty bombs placed in just the right areas could make 911 look like child's play. If only they could get beyond security. Religions of the world would be shepherd-less. Governments would be left in turmoil—easy pickings for Saif al Hakim which would immediately take credit, then control. Muslims from across the world would flock to them for guidance, returning to the roots of their faith. The idolatrous relationship with Israel would cease, and Israel would be no more. Saif al Hakim would become the most powerful force in the world.

The transfer ceremony would take place where the new temple was being erected. The platform would hold the altar and all the dignitaries. It had been decided that the stage would be in the shape of the Star of David. The altar would be erected on the point facing east, the pope seated directly behind it on an elevated throne. The cardinals and bishops, their attendants seated on either side, would be on risers behind the pope.

The Sanhedrin and Jewish authorities would be seated upon the southeast point of the star, while the northeast point was reserved for the Muslim dignitaries. The workers had dubbed these Isaac and Ishmael. Seated on the northwest point would be the high ranking members of the Anglican and Lutheran faiths, while the southwest point was assigned to the high ranking members from the Baptist, Methodists, Protestant and Mormon faiths. The king of England, the president and vice president of the United States, the heads of state from China, France, Germany, Spain, nearly all the countries of the world, including many from the continent of Africa, would be seated on the western point, just behind the cardinals and bishops.

In June 2069, the plans for the stage were revealed to the general public. Even though Saif al Hakim had only a handful of trusted members their plans were taking shape.

"What if we don't plant bombs under the stage? There is an inherent danger in this, the danger of discovery. If this occurs, all will have been lost. We are too few, yet. We must get it right the first time," Ahmad said.

"What do you suggest?" Zakaria asked.

"Have you seen the plans for the stage?"

None of the members had. He opened his brief case and pulled out the morning paper. Laying it on the table, he turned the pages until he got to the one for which he was looking.

"See? The stage is in the shape of the Star of David," he said, tapping on the picture for effect. "Jewish idolatry that can serve our purposes well."

"How?" asked Khaled.

"Remember 2001? September 11 to be exact? What method of transport was used by al-Qaida?"

"Airplanes. But how? They were huge passenger planes that crashed into buildings. We don't have access to these anymore," Ebrahim exclaimed.

"We are not going to be blowing up buildings, only people. That star makes an ideal target from the air. They may as well be building a bull's eye. We don't need Boeing 707s, only small Piper Cubs. One man per plane, three coming in from the north, south and east, loaded with explosives, and fuel, all hitting the stage at the same time. Can you imagine it? So much chaos, so much confusion, so much death. Even if only one gets through, there will be more than enough devastation. Allah will be pleased," Ahmad exclaimed.

"Who will fly these planes?" asked Ebrahim.

"I have chosen Mawsil, Rusdi, and Idris. They will begin flight training tomorrow, one in Syria, one in Iraq, and one in Saudi Arabia."

"What about your son Natair, Ahmad? He already knows how to fly. Why is he not on the list?"

"He is too important to the cause, Khaled. He will coordinate the efforts on the ground and when all is done, it is he who will gather the faithful and be the catalyst for the new regime."

"My son, Mawsil, can do that and yours can offer the sacrifice."

"I have chosen, Khaled. *Do not oppose me!* I still have my doubts about you."

Khaled knew better than push his point. Mawsil was his only son, and Khaled had a secret that he never revealed to Mawsil, a secret that was never revealed to anyone.

The platform was begun in January 2070. It would require weeks to build. Laborers from across the world came just to be part of this monumental event. They would be able to tell their grand-children about the time they spent building the pope's altar.

Security was tight. The Israeli Security Forces had been in-charge of every aspect of the planning. Metal detectors, Geiger counters, bomb sniffing dogs, and frequent sweeps and searches were conducted. Many a person came back to his room, after an exhausting day's labor, to find that the police had been there, searching through their things. The searches grew less frequent as they became known to the police. There would be no inci-dent in the Holy Land, not while the Israeli Security Forces were in control.

The plans for the attack were going very well. The explosive Cyclotrimethylenetrinitramine (RDX) was chosen because a small amount packed a big wallop. It was purchased and stored in Ahmad's warehouse.

The boys had been sent to flight school the day after the June meeting, and now each possessed his pilot license. With fund-ing from Saif al Hakim, three older model planes were bought. New ones, with all the updated gadgetry, could more easily be detected. The boys flew as often as they could, honing their skills. The flight had to go as smoothly as possible. The time schedule was tight, so no mistake could be afforded if the plan was to work. Everything had to be done at the exact same time.

In 2015 the United States Infantry had almost perfected cloak-ing technology. They understood that if you can see the enemy, but the enemy could not see you, it is much easier to kill him, and much harder for him to kill you. Aircraft and ships are expensive.

So are infantry war fighters, the soldiers and Marines. They realized that the American people were much softer and more sensitive to casualties than they used to be. Every additional death
reported caused public relations damage. Ninety five percent of
all military casualties occurred in the infantry, since they are the
most exposed, even with adaptive camouflage. With cloaking
technology they would no longer be easy targets as they moved
through battle space. Simultaneously, their lethality and surviv-
ability, would be greatly enhanced.

Panels had been developed measuring one meter square. Held
in front of an object, like a person, that portion of him seemed to
disappeared. The only way to spot someone completely covered
was by a very slight visual anomaly, or shimmer, against a stationary background when he is standing still, and a moving visual
anomaly when moving against a stationary background.

Unfortunately, with the collapse of the stock market worldwide and the US federal bailout of the major banks and loan
companies, little money was left for research and development
for the military. Only several hundred panels were manufactured
before the research was discontinued. These panels were packed
up in trunks, left out of sight and out of mind, until they were
discovered by the commander of the base in the 60s. There was no
documentation with them. The boxes were simply labeled roofing tiles. No one had ever looked inside. The obviously old boxes
were ordered thrown out to make way for other materials. There
was no need for old roofing tiles anyway. A pack rat soldier took
the panels for future use, figuring that at least some of the tiles
could still be usable. Leaving them in his garage, his wife soon
tired of parking her car in the cold and ordered her husband to
get rid of them or risk divorce. It was against the soldier's nature
to throw anything away, so when he heard about a collection of
building materials for Habitat for Humanity being sent to Israel,
he stingily donated his boxes of roofing tiles.

Once in Israel, the boxes remained in storage until Mawsil picked them up to redo an elderly neighbor's roof. Once he got them home, he opened the first box. It was covered with cloth. He peeled it aside and peered into the box. It was empty, but it was too heavy to be empty. He knew because he had just carried them. He opened the second box. The same thing happened. Plunging his hand deep into the box, he was shocked by a sudden pain he felt as his hand hit into something solid. Quickly pulling it back, he hugged it to his chest with his left arm, stamping in pain. Slowly, he drew his right hand from under his arm, and looked at it. It was red and the knuckles bruised. What could have happened? He flexed his fingers and tried to shake out the pain. He peered into the box, this time slowly reaching in. He felt something hard and cold. Sliding his fingers along the top, he continued toward the left side of the box. Once he reached the edge, he slipped them between the cloth and the solid structure. He was surprised to find what appeared to be thin sheets. Lifting one out, he held it up. It was like he was looking through a pane of glass. When his neighbor unexpectedly came through the door, he dropped the panel. It didn't shatter, which perplexed him all the more.

"What have you got there, Mawsil? I thought you were coming over to redo my roof. Are those the roofing tiles?"

Maswil thought for a second, then replied, "Nothing, Sami. I'll be there in a short while." He instinctively knew he had something special, something he wasn't willing to share, quite yet. Something that was definitely NOT roofing tiles!

Khaled, too, had been busy. A week after the meeting, he contacted a childhood friend, Saul Kandelcukier.

"Khaled, it's good to see you old friend. I must say, I was surprised to hear from you after so many years. Sit down, please. Can I offer you something to drink?"

"No Saul, thank you."

"I haven't heard from you since I bar mitzvahed. It was an unexpected pleasure when I received your message. We had some good times together, Khaled, but I don't really think that is why you came to see me."

"You're right, Saul. I have a son, Mawsil, my only child. Since he was born, he has given me trouble. Last year, he joined a group calling themselves Saif al Hakim. I don't know how he met them, but he became too involved, too quickly. He began to change, slowly, at first, then more quickly. I tried to talk to him, but he wouldn't listen. He never does. There are times when he rants about the reconciliation. He has an intense hatred of the Jews, blaming them for all his and the world's problems. His hatred extends to anyone who is not Muslim."

"He opposes me at every at turn. I am worried about him. He is far too trusting of everyone but me. About six months ago, I went with him to one of his meetings. I thought that might help our relationship. Once inside, I believed I could change Mawsil, get him out. I was having some effect, but then..." he trailed off.

"Then, what, Khaled?" Saul asked.

"I have learned what they intend to do. Saif al Hakim is planning murder, no, many murders. And my son is to be one of their victims. Their plan is to re-establish Sharia Law with Allah as the only god worshiped throughout the world. They not only hate the Jews for all the atrocities, real and imagined, but also the Muslim leaders whom they feel have rejected the true Muslim faith."

"Khaled!" interrupted Sal. "What DO they intend to do?"

"They have trained Mawsil, along with two other youths to fly small airplanes. These will be filled with compact explosives and crashed into the Star of David."

Saul didn't need further explanation. He knew that he meant the papal platform even now being constructed in Jerusalem. He didn't need Khaled to tell him that this was going down on Easter Sunday.

"Khaled, there isn't much time."

"I know, Saul, but what can we do?"

"Thousands of people are expected. It is already too late to call off the ceremony. Where did you say the planes would be launched?"

"I didn't, and I don't know. Ahmad and his son Natair are the only ones who do. The planes are presently housed at Amman civil-Marka Airport. The boys will leave that morning for secret locations where they will refuel. The flight to Jerusalem can't be too far. Ahmad wants as much fuel remaining as possible, to enhance the explosion when they crash into the Star. It will only be when they are in the air that they will receive instructions disclosing the refueling station."

Do you have access to the planes?"

"As of right now, yes. Why?"

"I have an idea."

Their meeting was about to begin. Plans needed to be finalized.

"Where is Mawsil?" Ahmad questioned.

"I don't know. He left well before I did. I thought he would be here by now," Khaled answered.

"Well, he better get here soon," Ahmad said, taking his seat which, as he sat, was pulled out from under him. He hit the floor, hard. A few in the group were aghast but most broke out into laughter.

"What the hell do you think you are doing?" Ahmad screamed quickly getting to his feet, and turning to face his assailant. But no one was there. The snickering continued, as Ahmad began to accuse each in turn.

"No one has been out of their seat," Fareed ventured to say, through a snicker. Ahmad had to admit to that. Getting no satisfaction, he tried taking his seat again, this time holding onto the arms so as to have no repeat of the previous few moments.

"Now, let's get down to business. Mawsil has disappointed me, Khaled."

"He has never missed a meeting before. I don't know where he is."

"I am here, Ahmad," the voice seemed to be coming from Mawsil's empty chair.

"Who said that?" Ahmed questioned.

"I did!"

"And who are you?"

"Ask my father."

"And just who is your father?" Ahmed began, but Khaled interrupted.

"It sounds like Mawsil."

"You're right, father. I am here." Mawsil removed one of the plates.

The group gasped as his disembodied head appeared, floating in the air. It rose about three feet before it began to speak again.

The members were horrified. What hellish thing was this? The head moved to the center of the circle. Some members tried moving away to avoid any contact and fell off their chairs. Others gazed on the apparition in disbelief.

"Who are you and what have you done with my son?"

"It is I, father, Mawsil. I have discovered the perfect solution to our problem, gentlemen." He removed two more cylinders. To the amazement of the group, the apparition now had arms. It was just too much—two arms and a head, just floating in mid air. No one knew what to do or say. As they were looking from one to the other, the apparition suddenly had feet and legs. "How?" was on the minds of all in the group, but they were too shocked to ask.

Mawsil began to explain. "When I went to Habitat for Humanity, to obtain building supplies, to fix Sami's roof, I was given eight boxes, each simply labeled roofing tiles. The boxes were obviously old and heavy. I brought them home. When I opened them, guess what I discovered? These. It took a while for me to find out exactly what I had."

As he spoke, Mawsil handed a cylinder to his father. Khaled couldn't see anything as he took it, but he felt a sudden weight in his hands, which had disappeared.

"There's...there's a hole in your stomach, Khaled!" Ebrahim exclaimed.

Khaled looked down, and where he should have seen his stomach, he saw the back of his chair. He dropped the cylinder which fell to the floor with a klunk. His hands and stomach reappeared as if by magic.

"Obviously, the tiles are not for roofing," Mawsil continued, taking off the rest. The group was relieved to see him whole again.

"I think the United States has screwed up. I did some research and discovered that the US.. military had worked on cloaking devices at the turn of the century, but didn't perfect them. These are the prototypes that were scrapped when the US economy went belly up in '08. Their loss, gentleman, is our good fortune. Allah be praised. Our planes can now be cloaked. No one will see them coming. Nothing can foil our plans.

TO MAKE A DIFFERENCE

January 19, 2070

A MAN WAS WALKING along a beach one beautiful day. The sun shone brightly in the sky. In the distance he saw a man going back and forth between the surf's edge and the beach. As he approached, he saw hundreds of starfish stranded on the sand, the effect of the tide.

The man picked up one starfish, walked to the ocean's edge and returned it to the sea. Stuck by the apparent futility of the task, he approached the man as he continued his undertaking.

"There are far too many, most of them are sure to perish!" he exclaimed. "You must be daft. There are thousands of miles of beach all covered with starfish. You can't possibly make a difference."

The person looked at the man, then bent down, picked up one more starfish and returned it to the sea. Turning to the man he said, "It sure made a difference to that one!"

PALMING

The art of palming is one of elusive misdirection. The magician deliberately twists the audience's attention by use of his hand or a beautiful assistant. Unless the spectator trusts you this misdirection will not work.

Your attention must be on the audience. Your eyes, conversation, and body language must lead them away from your manipulation. This can be done by getting the spectator to talk about themselves as this will keep them from watching you. In addition, it puts them at ease. They begin to trust you and think of you not as a magician, but as a friend.

On May 23, 2070, Palm Sunday, Mother, Sam, Millie, and Joshua met at Sam's home to discuss what possibly could be done. Sam was trying to entertain his two youngest, Bertram, 8, and Wade, 7, who had just made his first Holy Communion. The older children were staying the night with friends but the two youngest couldn't yet be left alone. Sam was performing some slight of hand to keep the kids amused.

"What we know is that Edger has perfected his 'cure', he is capable of shutting off VMAT2." Mill was saying. "He can transmit the 'cure' through water. We also know that he owns La Florentina Water Company, and that he decreed the only papal sanctioned hosts were to be produced by the Passionist Sisters of Pittsburgh."

"I can't imagine these women could be willing participants. They are a cloistered order devoted to prayer for the world. I don't think they know what Edger is doing. There is still a blind obedience to the papacy here," Mother injected.

"According to the papers Sister Magdalena brought to us, it appears we are too late. The hosts are made, ready for the Easter celebration. Making things worse is the ecumenical factor that the ashes of the red heifer have created. There is not a denomination that will not be represented. Even the Matzah and Kekule have been shipped for the occasion," Joshua said looking over the papers yet once again.

"There is something I can do," Sam said. "Edger will be distributing Holy Communion to a select few. Ten of the most trusted cardinals, Mother, Millie, me and the kids. He also has Matzah for Joshua, and the leaders of the Sanhedrin. In all, slightly more than 20 people will receive from his hands. I can't save everyone, it is too late, but I can save these."

Sam outlined his plan. He knew that Edger was just paranoid enough to keep these hosts safe with him. Sam would gain access soon after they arrived in Jerusalem, and using slight of hand, exchange the ciborium for another, with hosts not made for the occasion.

"How are you going to do this?" Joshua asked.

"Haven't you been watching?" Sam replied.

"Not really."

"The papal ciborium is small needing only to hold a dozen or so hosts. My brother Tim taught me slight of hand, palming things. I began using it again after the kids were born. Tim who was a natural at it taught me everything he knew. As long as I can obtain a twin ciborium I can switch them."

"No problem. Sister Magdalena should be able to accomplish that task."

"Then it is settled. I must work on getting in to see Edger."

Mother, Joshua, Sam, Millie, and the kids, traveled together to Jerusalem on the bullet train, arriving at 10:00 a.m., on Wednesday, March 26. Mother had arranged for the group to stay in the guest house of the Sisters of Saint Joseph. Imitating their patron, the ultimate host, the Sisters primary ministry was hospitality. The group was welcomed as returning family. Meals were shared, and even though sparsely decorated, the rooms were charming and comfortable. The group immediately felt at home and soon settled in.

Joshua was anxious to show everyone around Jerusalem, the place of his birth.

He hadn't been back since taking the position as curator of the Vatican Archives. That afternoon they ventured out, going to the old city. As they walked along the narrow streets, Joshua stopped and pointed to a house across the street.

"That is the house where I was born and grew up." He stared at it with a faraway look.

"It is exactly the same, as when I left it last. Only the curtains are different. It is even the same color."

Their next stop was the Pater Noster convent.

"The convent was built over the site where Jesus taught his disciples the Lord's Prayer," Joshua explained.

Entering the iron gate, the group came across richly decorated plaques lining the white stone walls.

"These contain the entire Lord's Prayer, from Matthew 6: 9–13. There are 140 colorful ceramic tiles. I know because I counted them. Each is inscribed with the Lord's Prayer written in a different language. It is one of the most popular sightseeing stops in Jerusalem. My mother would never take me here. I guess she didn't want me to get any notions. She never took me to any place that was not Jewish.

"After she died, though, I found it and would spend a lot of time here. I learned to read these translations. You see, I was blessed with the gift of languages. I found it therapeutic try- ing to translate the various tiles. Two of the plaques, near the cloister, are in Hebrew and Aramaic, both of which I knew. The first panel I cracked was in Chaldean, whose letters are curiously like Hebrew. Other tiles are written in Guarani, Maltese, and Icelandic. A metal French version in Braille was vandalized, but a copy is still on view in the gift shop. Several of the plaques are written in truly unusual languages including Tagalog, Pampango, and Ojibway."

They made their way to the Pater Noster chapel just off the cloistered walkway. It was a rather stark, high-ceilinged sanctuary with wrought iron lamps and large painted statues of Mary with baby Jesus, which added charm and beauty to the austere chapel.

Joshua led the group down to the end of the walkway.

"This is the sepulture of the French Princess de la Tour d'Auvergne, Bossi Aurelia, who purchased the land for the Carmelite convent in 1872. For nearly a decade, until the convent was well established, the princess lived nearby in a wooden cabin she had brought from France. She loved the site so much that she requested to be buried within the confines of the cloister, even preparing her own coffin, the magnificent marble sarcophagus you see before you. Dying in 1889 the princess's request was granted. Above the coffin, a life-size effigy is a beautiful memorial to her. Her favorite and most comforting prayer was the Lord's Prayer."

After dinner, they returned to their rooms and got ready for bed. It was a day well spent. The tour had taken their minds off of the task at hand. Tomorrow would come all too soon. With only four days left until Easter, Peter's plans seemed to be coming to realization. There was still time. An answer would present itself. It had to.

CONFRONTATION

March 20, 2070

And Adam knew Eve his wife; and she conceived, and bare Cain, and said, I have gotten a man from the LORD. And she again bare his brother Abel. And Abel was a keeper of sheep, but Cain was a tiller of the ground. And in process of time it came to pass, that Cain brought of the fruit of the ground an offering unto the LORD. And Abel, he also brought of the firstlings of his flock and of the fat thereof. And the LORD had respect unto Abel and to his offering: But unto Cain and to his offering he had not respect. And Cain was very wroth, and his countenance fell. And the LORD said unto Cain, Why art thou wroth? and why is thy countenance fallen? If thou doest well, shalt thou not be accepted? and if thou doest not well, sin lieth at the door. And unto thee shall be his desire, and thou shalt rule over him. And Cain talked with Abel his brother: and it came to pass, when they were in the field, that Cain rose up against Abel his brother, and slew him. And the LORD said unto Cain, Where is Abel thy brother? And he said, I know not: Am I my brother's keeper? And he said, What hast thou done? the voice of thy brother's blood crieth unto me from the ground. And now art thou cursed from the earth, which hath opened her mouth to receive thy brother's blood from thy hand; When thou tillest the ground, it shall not henceforth yield unto thee her strength; a fugitive and a vagabond shalt thou be in the earth. And Cain said unto the LORD, My punishment is greater than I can bear. Behold, thou hast driven me out this day from the face of the earth; and from thy face shall

I be hid; and I shall be a fugitive and a vagabond in the earth; and it shall come to pass, that every one that findeth me shall slay me. And the LORD said unto him, Therefore whosoever slayeth Cain, vengeance shall be taken on him sevenfold. And the LORD set a mark upon Cain, lest any finding him should kill him. And Cain went out from the presence of the LORD, and dwelt in the land of Nod, on the east of Eden.

Genesis 4: 1–16 (KJV)

AT THE INSISTENCE of Pope Peter II, Sam, Millie and their four children were to be honored guests at the celebration. Edger wanted, no, needed, Sam there. He was the closest thing to family he had ever had, and he wanted Sam to share in his triumph. Pope Peter's monster would purify the world, bringing it back to its pre-fall condition. He was convinced that without religion, the world would find peace, the peace of Eden.

On Holy Saturday, Sam was finally able to speak to Edger alone.

"Sam, I'm so glad you could make it. I hope your accommodations are adequate. How are Millie and the kids? Are they enjoying their stay in Jerusalem and all the festivities?"

"Knock it off, Edger. I didn't come to speak to you about pleasantries. I know what you are up to, and I intend to stop it."

"Stop what Sam?"

"VMAT2."

Edger was caught off guard. He had been so careful! How could Sam know about VMAT2?

"I don't know what you're talking about."

"Don't play dumb, Edger. It doesn't suit the office. I know you have been working with this gene and have found a way to turn it off. The only thing I don't know is why you would want to suppress religion. Look at all the good it has done for the human race."

Edger was beginning to lose his cool. "Why would I want to suppress religion Sam? I'll tell you why. Religion is Frankenstein's monster. Man created it, changed it, rearranged it, and thought he could control it. Repeatedly, man has found that he cannot, never could, and never will. It must be destroyed for the world to be safe."

Edger stood. Sam could see his countenance begin to change, as his passion changed to rage. "Sam, how can I make you understand? Since Cain killed Abel, wars have been fought in the name of religion. Cain was jealous because God loved Abel more, or so he thought. Since that time, it has not only continued, but intensified."

Edger began to pace back and forth. Since the first day they had met, Sam had never seen Edger so emotional. Sam began to feel intimidated by his ranting, but quickly regained composure. He had a job to do, if Millie, the kids, Mother and Joshua were to be spared. Sam looked around the room and spied the ciborium on the table next to Edger's desk. It was small and round, not much bigger than a music box. In order to make the switch, he had to get Edger to the other side of the room.

"Edger, you can't make this personal. Even though Joan loved Tiffany and Eric more than you, God doesn't. He plays no favorites."

"How dare you, Sam. You of all people know what religion has taken from me. If it weren't for religion, Julie would be alive. *I* would have the wife and children."

Sam slowly began to edge between Edger and the table.

"Sam, this is NOT just about me. From ethnic cleansing to just plain intolerance of anyone different, once started, religious strife has a tendency to go on and on, becoming permanent feuds, and no one can remember why the feud began in the first place.

"There have been religious wars in Northern Ireland, between Protestant and Catholic, in Palestine between Jew, Muslim, and Christian, in South Asia between Hindu and Muslim, in Rwanda between the Hutu and Tutsi, in Bosnia-Herzegovina between Muslim, Roman Catholic, and Serbian Orthodox.

"Attempts to bring peace to these regions are met with dismal failure. Extremist elements always invoke past injustices, imagined or real, and succeeded in torpedoing peace efforts bringing about another bout of hostility. War changes everything. Thousands are forced to leave their country. Intolerance breeds injustice, which leads to escalation on the part of both, making reconciliation almost impossible. Stress, despair and frustration cause people to become increasingly irrational; doing things they never thought themselves capable. Hideous brutality perpetrates from the most gentle of people.

"Wars change lives in moments. The total number of deaths due to the crusades was around nine million, at least half of whom were Christians. Many were simply innocent civilians caught in the carnage.

"In a thirty year period, there were more than three thousand six hundred killings and assassinations in Northern Ireland. You, of all people Sam, should know about that.

"About 20 percent of the population of East Timor, a Roman Catholic country, died by murder, starvation or disease after they were forcibly annexed by Indonesia, a mainly Muslim country. After voting for independence, the Christians were exterminated or exiled by the Indonesian army and army-funded militias, in a carefully planned program of genocide and religious cleansing.

"911 saw 2,998 victims, most of whom were civilians, killed, evaporated, burned alive or smashed on the ground, after jumping from eighty stories up.

"March 11, 2004, 191 people were killed while another 1,755 were wounded in an attack directed by al-Qaeda in Madrid, Spain.

"The 2045 New York attack by the AHSRUB Liberation Society killed 12 people and injured 32 others.

"The number of dead is astounding, but far outnumbered by the grieving families left behind. Children lose parents, parents lose children. Grandparents, aunts, uncles, cousins, friends, all left to grieve for lives so abruptly and needlessly taken. That's not to mention those who have been mutilated, losing every conceivable body part, left less than whole.

"It goes on and on, in every country of the world. There is safety nowhere. An attacker could be the person next to you in the grocery line. One moment you're here, the next you're in pieces.

"What do all these incidents have in common, Sam? They were all done in the name of religion! Religious hatred and intolerance. The people follow like sheep to the slaughter.

"All this madness can be stopped, Sam. I have discovered the secret. I am doing this for the good of mankind. I am doing it for you and your children, and their children. I am doing it, so that all may live in peace. Imagine it Sam, a world without war, where people are free to go where they will."

"That's the problem, Edger. The world was born in strife and will probably go out the same way. There is strife in just plain living. Border disputes start at the lowest levels—neighbor against neighbor. 'You are on my lawn!' or 'Your tree overshadows my backyard.' There will always be corrupt government officials and governments. Everyone is out for number one. There will always be war and strife, Edger. You can't stop it by getting rid of religion. Sometimes, it is religion that stops war."

"It is a good start, Sam. The other things will take care of themselves."

"I'll stop you, Edger. The gene can be reactivated."

"Not so Sam. Once it is turned off, it is permanent. I have made sure of that. Everything is in place. Tomorrow, at this time, the world will need religion no more. Even your God can't save his Church now."

Sam stormed out, leaving Pope Peter II to bask in his coming glory.

Walking from the building, Sam pulled a small, round, golden container from his coat. Looking at it, he smiled and returned it to his pocket. Maybe he couldn't save everyone, but he certainly had saved those who would have received the hosts from this ciborium tomorrow.

THE CEREMONY

March 21, 2070

With the fastest growing Catholic population in the world, China made Catholicism its number one religion. The Pin Yang uprising of 2032 caused the fall of Communism and the rise of a semi-democracy in China. People had had enough. Not only were they frustrated by government intervention into their financial lives, but into their bedrooms as well. There was a growing dissatisfaction with the "one child" law. Many a baby girl had been left to die in some back alley, or wander the streets.

The lucky ones had been adopted, usually to American couples who were themselves childless. Many a mother had psychological problems, later in life, after "disposing" of their daughters. Suicides increased as more women found that, after ridding themselves of the girl, they could not conceive again.

Some went crazy; others searched for, but could not find, the daughter they had so willingly cleared out. The lucky found their child, but that presented other problems. She was often wild and aggressive. For some, no amount of patience and love could counter the effects of years on the street.

Having lived so long on the streets, the girls had become wild. They would travel in groups, more like packs, which had been dubbed "The Unwanted". The older girls were always on the lookout for the newly abandoned, who they would take under their care and control. As they grew into womanhood, they were inaugurated into the gang, which was involved in every aspect of the life of the underworld, including sex, robbery (often violent home invasions), and prostitution. The government tried to rid

the country of these gangs, but by the time they involved themselves, it was too late. The public began to take action, arming
themselves, even though possession of a gun was against the law,
except for the military.

The citizenry gathered, secretly at first, in vigilante groups,
whose power steadily increased. The problem began to subside as
hundreds of gang members found themselves unceremoniously
dumped into a landfill, rivers or the ocean, dead.

Even so, the problem of marriageable young women increased.
By 2020 China's population had begun to decline, drastically.
With the male to female ratio a bit over 8 to 1, the government
feared a total collapse. When it came time for the young men to
marry, there were few eligible women from which to choose. Men
had to begin paying dowries, the size of which caused the family
financial hardships, often putting the parents into bankruptcy.

The girls adopted to the United States, were no longer safe.
They were contacted by the government, asked, and then ordered
to return.

Yeah, right! was the thought of these completely Americanized
women. And so began the kidnappings. Many found themselves,
against their will, back in a China that had disposed of them
years before. Now, though, they had power, a power that women
born and raised in China lacked. They would stay, marry, and bear
children, but on their terms. They would rule the roost.

Laws were changed, including the ones allowing only one
child and those of religion. Many of these women were raised
Catholic, and would die rather than abandon their faith. By the
time the government realized what it had done in bringing these
women back it was too late. Democracy began to take hold.

Finally, in 2032, the communist Chinese government was
replaced by a semi-democracy. The people, now allowed to worship, overwhelmingly chose Catholicism, which allowed a couple
to have as many children as God would give them. China, for the
first time in centuries, was free.

"Welcome back. I'm Chet Johnson with KDKA TV in Pittsburgh Pennsylvania, reporting, live, from Jerusalem. I am here with Monsignor Giuseppe Finocchio, papal secretary for worship. We are covering a ceremony so unique, that it has never taken place before. In a few minutes, in an elaborate ecumenical, Easter ceremony, Pope Peter II will have the ashes of the red heifer transferred to Rabbi Eidel Ehud Raanan, high priest of the Sanhedrin. Rabbi Joshua Abraham Hiem and Mother Hedwig Peligia Brzozowska will have the honor of making that presentation. Monsignor, what is the significance of these ashes?"

"Well, Chet, the ashes of the red heifer were used by the Jewish community in rituals of purification for anyone entering the temple. Sort of like holy water for Catholics. It remains one of the least understood of God's commandments. In fact it is more than a commandment. It is a chukah."

"God bless you, Monsignor."

"No, Chet, a chukah."

"A what?"

"A chukah."

"What does that mean, Monsignor?"

"A chukah is an ordinance that is to be followed without question or understanding."

"What does that have to do with the red heifer?"

"It is believed that the red heifer is linked with the sin of the Golden Calf, which Moses pulverized, poured into water, and forced the Israelites to drink. Moses was also the first person commanded to perform the chukah, slaughtering an unblemished red heifer, pulverizing, and mixing the ashes with water to bless the Israelites. Since that time there have been only nine heifers that fit the chukah. Also, red is the color of sin. Isaiah chapter one verse 18, 'though your sins be like scarlet, they shall be white as snow.'"

"That explains, Monsignor, the red heifer, but what is the significance of these ashes being transferred today?"

"They are of utmost importance, Chet. The ashes of subsequent red heifers had to be mingled with those of the previous sacrifice. These ashes being transferred today, therefore, have the ashes of the previous nine sacrifices, forming a link back to Moses himself. When a red heifer is sacrificed, the pulverized ashes are divided into three sections. The first were used by the Levites guarding the entrance to the temple for the purification of those entering. The second were stored in the Mount of Olives, and used to purify the priests. The remaining third was placed in the wall known as the chail, which faced the woman's gallery of the temple to remain undisturbed, 'as a keepsake for Israel,' until another red heifer was sacrificed.

"They were then mixed with the ashes of the new sacrifice and these were separated into three portions, again. It is this portion that was thought to have been lost in the destruction of the second temple in AD 70, two thousand years ago today. Mother Hedwig Peligia is responsible for discovering them."

"I see that the ceremony is about to begin, Monsignor. Would you please explain to our audience what is taking place?"

"Yes, yes, Chet. The procession is starting. The crucifix leads the route, accompanied by the acolytes, to light the way. Behind is the censor, purifying the area. It will be used to purify the altar, in preparation for the great sacrifice of the Mass. Next are the members of the Sanhedrin, followed by the leaders of the Muslim faith. Then will come the heads of the Anglican, Lutheran, Methodist, and Baptist churches. The bishops and cardinals follow, and finally Mother Hedwig Peligia Brzozowska and Rabbi Joshua Heim carrying the ashes. Pope Peter II is last."

"What an historic occasion, Monsignor. Christians, Jews, and Muslims together, without hostility—this is probably the first time in history. Think about the significance of this moment."

"I know, Chet. As far back as Isaac and Ishmael these groups have not gotten along. We are making history here and now. The pope has now reached the altar, bowing he kisses it. Taking the censor, the pope consecrates the altar. Handing the censor back to the Master of Ceremony, he obtains the asperigillum.

"Dear Friends, this water is used to remind us of our baptism. Let us ask God to bless it and to keep us faithful to the Spirit he has given us... We ask this through Christ Our Lord."

"Amen"

"The priests are being given the Holy Water from Pope Peter to bless the congregation. The readings are next, Chet. When they are finished, Pope Peter will give his homily. I am told it will be given in English, Italian, and Mandarin."

"Mandarin? No pope has ever given a homily or even a speech, in Mandarin. Why has he chosen this language?"

"Mandarin is the most frequently spoken language in China, and China has the fastest growing Catholic population in the world. He is taking this opportunity to reach out to them and welcome them."

"The homily is beginning. Let's listen."

"My dear friends in Christ,

Esteemed Rabbis, and members of our mother faith, the descendants of Israel, notable descendants of Ishmael, colleagues, and family: Today we celebrate the resurrection of Our Lord Jesus Christ and the two thousandth anniversary of the destruction of the second temple, which had stood on this very spot.

Today, with joy, Holy Mother Church returns to the Sanhedrin, and the people of Israel, the Ashes of the Red Heifer.

On this spot, the patriarchs, Abraham, Isaac and Jacob, walked, lived and worshiped.

On this spot, Muhammad and his horse ascended into heaven.

On this spot, Jesus worshiped and prayed.

On this spot, Jesus suffered and died.

On this spot, Jesus was raised victoriously and gloriously.

On this spot, Jesus ascended again to the heaven he obediently left.

The days are coming, they are already knocking at the door, when religion will no longer be needed, and peace will reign supreme on this earth."

He was good. Returning to his throne, Pope Peter couldn't help but smile. In just a few days, the work of a lifetime, or so it seemed, would come to completion. The age of religion would be at an end. People would no longer have a need for it. Edger had put his mind to killing it, not God, and in moments, the death knell would begin, growing louder and louder, as his serum took effect.

The rest of the ceremony seemed a blur to Edger, so engrossed in his thoughts had he become. The time for distribution of the Eucharist arrived.

Sam was the last to receive from the hands of Pope Peter. Gazing into his eyes, Edger saw something he never expected to see there. They were not Sam's eyes, but his mother's, looking on him with the same look of fury and hatred she had always had for her youngest son. Edger was taken aback for a moment. Sam would grow to understand. He was certain of that. He had to. Sam was the closest friend he had.

CLOAKED

March 29, 2070, Midnight

Science Disciplines Today
(The non-scientists, science magazine)
July 15, 2015

SCIENCE HAS NEVER been closer to making the invisibility cloak of Harry Potter a reality than it is today. Scientists from Xenon Trent Inc. funded by a large grant from the United States Infantry have successfully completed a six month trial on an invisibility archetype. Their work was based upon a 2006 study done at Duke University where the first prototype was constructed. A variety of cloaking shapes and patterns have been made including panels of various sizes. Though cloth is still in the realm of science fiction some small pieces have been developed having the feel and texture of highly starched linen.

Cloaking devices work by bending light waves in such a way as to make the object invisible to the eye, as though it is not there. The effect is similar to that of a road mirage on a hot summer day. Looking into the distance we often see what appears to be water but when we get to the area the road is perfectly dry. The spot has essentially been "cloaked". Mirages appear not only on roads and pavement, but also in deserts or any open area subject to heating by sunlight.

Experiments aiming microwaves at the cloaking device have shown they bounce off the surface at exactly the same angle as they hit it.

Made from fiberglass and etched with copper the cloaking devices of Xenon Trent measure 104 cm by 104 cm and are .25 cm thick. Each board is made from 20,956 individual pieces arranged in parallel rows.

The hope is that within the next twelve years functional devices will be on the market.

Midnight, March 29, 2070 saw Khaled at the hangar of Amman civil-Marka Airport. He had already place tracking devices, the size of a pen point, on two of the planes when he heard a noise. He turned, only to be confronted by his son Mawsil.

"What the hell are you doing here, Father?"

"I was sent to check the planes," Khaled lied.

"Ahmad said nothing about having the planes checked. I must call him." he said reaching for his cell phone.

"No. Mawsil, you can't do this! This is not right. Are you prepared to die for this cause?"

"Yes, I am. The world must be taught a lesson. The Jews and the infidels must be exterminated. The angel prophesied it to Hagar when he said that Ishmael would 'live in hostility toward all his brothers.' The Qur'an instructs that the Jews be treated as brothers, unless they refuse to convert to Islam.

"For centuries, they have refused to convert. Because of this, they are to be attacked and exterminated. Remember, father, the Qur'an has told us that Ishmael was Abraham's intended sacrifice, not Isaac. Allah's promise to Abraham was fulfilled through Ishmael, not Isaac. During Muhammad's life, he was taunted and mocked by the Jews who charged him with ignorance. They began to connive with his enemies in Mecca to overthrow him despite having signed a peace treaty. Accusing the Jewish tribes of treachery, he attacked each in turn, expelling them from the Arabian Peninsula."

"Muhammad is also known to have had Jewish friends," Khalid said. "His wife, Safiyya, was a Jewess. The degree of respect he showed for the religions of Judaism and Christianity was remarkable."

"At first, yes. According to the Hadith (recordings of deeds and sayings attributed to Muhammad), Jews are men whose malice and enmity is aimed at the Apostle of God, and a Jew will not be found alone with a Muslim without plotting to kill him. Muhammad said, "The hour will not be established until you fight with the Jews, and the stone behind which a Jew will be hiding will say, 'O Muslim! There is a Jew hiding behind me, so kill him.'"

"The Jews are debased, cursed, anathematized forever by god, and so can never repent and be forgiven; they are cheats and traitors; defiant and stubborn. They killed the prophets; they are liars who falsify scripture and take bribes. As infidels they are ritually unclean, a foul odor emanating from them, degraded and malevolent."

"The Jews take what is not theirs, claiming inheritance through Isaac. They have always taken what is not theirs. The United Nations had no right to give any of the land of the Palestinians to the Jews in 1948. We will take it back. We will have the inheritance promised us through Ishmael."

"And what of you, Mawsil? What gives you the right to be so sanctimonious? You, yourself are of the bastard spawn."

"What do you mean, old man? Make sense."

"You have always been slow, Mawsil, but I have loved you anyway. Do you really want to know what I mean? Can you handle it?"

"I can take anything you throw out."

"Can you take the fact that you are a Jew?"

"What?" Mawsil was taken aback. What possibly could he mean?

"You are half Jew, son. Your mother was a Jewess."

"You liar. I am no Jew. Why are you doing this? What do you hope to gain?"

"I vowed to your mother, on her death bed, to never tell you about her heritage, but you need to see what you are doing to your relatives."

"No Jew is my relative." Mawsil screamed as he rushed his father, shoving him hard. Khaled, stumbled backward, tripping over a broom. Falling to the floor, his head hit the steel wheel stop. He fell silent as blood began to seep from the back of his head. Mawsil rushed to his father's side. He felt for a pulse but found none. He paced through the hangar. What to do? A plan began to formulate in his head. He took a blanket from the locker and wrapped Khaled's head in it. Picking up his father's body, he carried it to the plane and placed it as far back as it would go. Going back he cleaned up the blood, and put the bloody rags over the body. Covering them with explosives he mused that he and his father would finally do something together. Together they would meet their maker. He sat in the cockpit chair and went to sleep.

Mawsil's phone vibrated.

"Hello."

"Mawsil, where are you?" Ahmad questioned.

"I am with my plane. I just returned from checking the cloaking panels on the other two and am about to do the same with mine," he lied.

There was no use letting Ahmad in on his sin, Mawsil thought. Of course it wasn't a sin, to kill the enemy, and his father was that. Didn't he try to stop him from doing Allah's will? Well, in a few hours it would be finished. The job would be done and Allah would be very well pleased.

"I have the refueling location for you." He gave him the coordinates. "You will take off at precisely 9:34 a.m.." They ran through the itinerary. There could be no deviation. Everything had to go precisely as planned, down to the second.

After refueling, the planes took off at the exact same time. Khaled had put trackers on two of the planes, but had dropped the third when he was confronted by Mawsil. It had not been activated. Now, the planes were only 500 km from Jerusalem and their target.

On the ground, Saul and his crew, with the Israeli military, tracked the two planes, perfectly. Their guns were locked on each target. They were not to fire until the last minute or the third plane was located. The commander was anxious. Why hadn't Khaled put the third tracker in place? It made no sense. All three planes had been together. The first two came on line immediately, but the third still hadn't. Could it be a faulty transmitter? It would have made things so much easier if they could have destroyed all three planes at a safe distance; thereby insuring that no one at the festivities would have the slightest idea that anything had gone wrong. Not only had it gone wrong, it had gone terribly wrong. Time was running out.

Mawsil had been flying for a short while, when he noticed a decrease in air speed, as if there were a sudden drag. He placed the plane in auto pilot, unbuckled his seatbelt, and went to examine the plane. This drag was costing seconds that could become minutes, and that meant miles. The planes needed to hit the platform at exactly 1:11:11, Allah be praised. Everything in the interior was in place. He checked the right side of the plane, looking out each of the windows. Nothing was amiss. Moving to the left windows he looked out and was unnerved to see the propeller suddenly appear. It had stopped, and was breaking apart, as if something had violently struck it.

Those idiots, he thought. *I told them to double rivet the panels.*

The engine burst into flames causing the plane to lurch violently to the left. Mawsil was thrown against the wall and knocked unconscious. The plane, now out of control, veered to the left, losing altitude.

On the ground, no one saw it coming. All they heard was a rushing sound as though a strong wind had picked up, but they felt nothing. Many in the audience looked up, but most were intent on the service. Pope Peter II was making the presentation. The time was 1:11:11 p.m.

Mawsil regained consciousness. Getting to his feet, he headed toward the cockpit. It was slow going the plane was lurching so badly. Finally, he made it to his seat and tried to regain control. Looking out of the window he saw the Mediterranean Sea coming up fast. Valiantly, he made a last ditch effort but the plane violently hit the water, skipped several times, and as the front end hit into the wave created by the plane's crash, the rear was raised straight up, perpendicular to the sea. It remained in this position for several seconds then collapsed.

Mawsil had only seconds, no nanoseconds. What could he do? He tried getting up, but was forcibly hit by an object that pinned him to the windshield. As the tail began to fall Mawsil recognized the object that was pinning him down as his father's body. He attempted to scream, but the explosives ignited just as the sound rose in his throat. The plane, Mawsil and Khaled were completely consumed by the fireball that ensued. The water that had cascaded a hundred feet into the air began settling back around the demolished plane, putting out the fire and refilling the hole in the sea the explosion had caused.

"We can't wait any longer, sir," the young corporal manning the radar station said. "The planes are within 60 km of the stage, well within the no fly zone. If we don't take them out now, there will be casualties." The time: 1:07:52 p.m.

"Do we have any sighting of the third plane? There should be three. Damn it, where is he?"

"No, sir. There are only two unauthorized planes. We must act now, sir."

"Make it so!" 1:08:52 p.m.

"Fire, fire, fire." The missiles were launched. With them ended the hopes and dreams of Saif Al Hakim.

It only took seconds for both planes, north and south, to be completely destroyed in a brilliant light display, occurring just as the fireworks, signifying the ashes had been received, ended. Most in the audience thought it was part of the display.

"What an exhibition, monsignor," said Chet. "The fireworks were magnificent. And that ending! Who would have thought to end with twin mini-explosions of brilliant white in the north and south? I guess that is why the Zambelli group, from Pittsburgh Pennsylvania, is truly the best in the world."

"Yes, they are Chet. Wow," Monsignor said, as the smoke from the fireworks settled. "The colors... brilliant. This is indeed a fitting ending to a magnificent Easter Sunday service—a fitting ending to a new beginning."

A LEGEND FULFILLED

March 30, 2070

AN IRISH LEGEND

A LONG TIME AGO, there lived a young man who fell in love with a beautiful young lass, but he could never speak his love for her. As a lad, the young man had made an arrogant mistake, one that he much regretted. The lad and his father were walking along the road when a troop of soldiers came riding by. It was Easter, and they had been visiting the boy's grandmother who had given him a brand new set of Sunday clothes, which she had made for him. He was very proud of these and insisted on wearing them home.

As the soldiers passed one splashed mud on the lad's new clothes. To the horror of the father, the lad yelled at the soldiers. Too late, the father clasped his hand over his son's mouth, hoping the soldiers had not heard, but they had. As they returned to slay the lad, the father pleaded for the life of his only son, his only child. The mud splashing soldier showed leniency. Instead, while two soldiers held the father, he cut out the offending boy's tongue. Horrified the father picked up his unconscious son and took him home as the laughing soldiers rode away.

The years went by and the lad became a man, tall and handsome of appearance, with blue eyes and wavy, coal black hair. On Saturdays, he would go to the village market to buy food for his aging parents. One day he saw the most beautiful maiden he had ever seen. For months he admired her from afar. Unbeknownst to him, she was admiring him as well. Eventually their paths crossed and even though he could not speak, they fell in love. Love, after all is a language unto itself.

As the months passed, the lad began to yearn for a voice so that he could vocalize his love for the maiden and tell the world of his devotion to her. The maiden's father found out about his daughter's affair and knew that this was the boy whose tongue he had cut out of years before. He forbade his daughter to ever see the young man again.

But the maiden was in love. The two planned to run away the first opportunity that presented itself. That day came, and the couple fled into the forest, pursued by the maiden's father, knowing that if they were caught, he would be killed and she sent to the convent. After fleeing as far as their strength would take them, the exhausted couple took refuge behind a fallen tree.

As they rested in the forest the hush of the crisp winter's day enfolded them. Hearing a gentle, tinkling sound they looked around, and saw a snowflake falling to the ground. At that moment, the lad regained his tongue and the couple was transported to a village where they lived out their lives in love and peace.

So, me darlins, when ye hear a snowflake fall, expect a miracle.

Easter Sunday came and went.

With the hosts consumed, Pope Peter awaited the scattering of the faithful and the emptying of the pews. Sunday after Sunday, he went through the motions of celebrating the Mass fully expecting the numbers of the attending parishioners to gradually dwindle. After all, lifetime habits were hard to break and he had convinced himself that Mass attendance for these people had been merely a habit.

Yet attendance did not dwindle.

In fact, attendance actually seemed on the rise. Pope Peter had kept accurate records of church attendance numbers since he had executed his plan. Leaving nothing to chance, he repeatedly verified and re-verified his data. Each time, his mathematical conclusions had been the same. The numbers had increased.

How could this be?

Not only was Mass attendance up in Rome, but reports had come in of attendance increases from churches in every hemisphere of the world. It could be truly said that Pope Peter was dumbfounded. Still in denial of the veracity of his findings, he shut himself away inside the papal apartments meticulously sifting through his work. Countless times, he ran the numbers, and countless times they all checked out. The irrefutable data had clearly confirmed that the religious gene had been silenced…and yet people were attending Mass in record numbers! The evidence to the contrary was staggering.

The silencing technique had not worked, and it *should* have!

He reviewed his research on religious wars (a project that he had begun shortly after Julie's death) and began to formulate a theory. Initially, he had disregarded this theory due to his blinding hatred for God—a fact that had colored his objectivity. He came to the realization that the wars in question had not been fought over the issue of religiosity. Rather, these wars had been fought over the issue of power and control. The group that has power must fight to maintain it while the group, who does not have power, must fight to obtain it.

THE HAVES AND THE HAVE NOTS

It was a conflict as old as the planet itself. It had been no different, he now realized, during The Middle Ages when the man who controlled the Papal Throne also controlled the world. The kind of power that the popes of the Middle Ages wielded had been Power in God's Name. At the heart of every so-called religious war that had ever been fought upon the stages of history, had been the political motivations of selfish humans who coveted power.

In the end, it had all come down to power.

Even terrorists' attacks were about power; the power to control large groups of people through fear, thereby forcing them to do what you want them to do, while making God the convenient scapegoat for myriad atrocities. Excuses ran aplenty: *"If it were up to me, I wouldn't have bombed the elementary school, but it was God's Will."*

The litany of rationalizations for violating Christ's Commandment to "love your neighbor as yourself" was endless *"My god is better than your god"* or *"My god loves me more than yours loves you. I will prove it by blowing myself up and taking you infidels with me!"* What hubris! For mere mortals to presume to know the mind of God!

Unconsciously, Pope Peter began pacing across the sandstone tiled floor. Next, deep in thought, he traveled along the corridors of the papal apartments, and eventually found himself in the Vatican's courtyard. It was here amidst the thriving vegetation, like a new Garden of Eden, that he heard the first of the ringing bells. They had begun softly and humbly as a small and persistent tinkling sound—like wind chimes hanging from a front porch wrapped up in a cool but gentle breeze on a summer's eve. Gradually, these ringing sounds increased in duration and stature until they became a thundering cacophony. He gazed about him hoping that the source of the ringing bells might reveal itself but to his great wonder and awe, he noticed something that he never could have anticipated—a variable that had for him existed far outside of the realm of credibility, thereby negating even its very consideration as plausible.

It was snowing.

Snowflakes of the most brilliant and elaborate design were falling all around him. His mind became immersed in the revelation that man has continually and arrogantly disregarded the principles of God. God was not the root of the world's conflicts and sufferings—man was! It had been man all along! Indeed, was it not man's refusal to obey God's commandment to live the beatitudes and to "love one another as I have loved you" that had been the root of both Edger's and the world's sufferings?

Suddenly, he found himself inside the Sistine Chapel standing before the door to the Room of Tears. He wasn't sure how he had gotten there. Had he been so consumed by his thoughts that he hadn't realized where his walk had taken him? Undaunted, he entered the room...and for the first time since he pleaded for Julie's life, he wept.

He had shed no tears when he had been informed of Julie's death; nor at her funeral, nor at any moment since...until now. Now his tears flowed as freely as waters that breached the restraining walls of a crumbling dam. He wept for all that *could* have been and wasn't. He wept for what *had* been and shouldn't. He wept for Julie and her family. He wept for himself. Finally, he wept because he had now begun to understand the monumental and significant responsibility that he had taken upon his shoulders as the latest in a long and mostly distinguished line of popes. The promulgation of the faith was his burden now.

At long last his heart had awakened; the metanoia had taken place. From this day onward, he consecrated himself to God and devoted the remainder of his papacy to the creation of peace between brother and sister among the struggling children of God and through each one of them, peace upon the Earth.

So, me darlins, when ye hear a snowflake fall, expect a miracle.

TIME TO REST?

Then God said, "Let us make man in our image, in our likeness, and let them rule over the fish of the sea and the birds of the air, over the livestock, over all the earth, and over all the creatures that move along the ground." So God created man in his own image, in the image of God He created him; male and female He created them.

God blessed them and said to them, "Be fruitful and increase in number; fill the earth and subdue it. Rule over the fish of the sea and the birds of the air and over every seed-bearing plant on the face of the whole earth and every tree that has fruit with seed in it. They will be yours for food. And to all the beasts of the earth and all the birds of the air and all the creatures that move on the ground—everything that has the breath of life in it—I give every green plant for food." And it was so.

Genesis 2: 18–20

MOTHER DID NOT need to run the numbers. Church attendance was increasing. She saw it at daily Mass. She did not question why the serum apparently had not worked. She knew with her entire being it was the saving power of God. Over the weeks and months following the Easter celebration, she, Joshua, Sam and Millie had many discussions about the matter.

As Pope Peter II's pontificate continued the group saw a dramatic change in the man. Heart and soul he had been transformed. He and Sam's friendship blossomed once again and Sam became the friend and ally he had once been to Edger.

As things began to resolve, Mother and Joshua expected to settle back into lives of quiet contemplation and ease, but life has a way of throwing a monkey wrench into to best laid of plans. Along with Sam and Millie they soon found themselves intertwined in yet another set of difficulties as the hearing of the Fab-Five began. Anticipated to be the trial of the millennium it would far exceed the most bizarre of expectations as the Atlantian artifacts began to reveal their secrets: gamma ray weapons capable of vaporizing a person; apparatuses for the control of animals, and people; teleportation devices; detailed charts sequencing the DNA molecule; guides for the manipulation of atoms, molecules and genes; records on the precise make-up of atoms down to the most miniscule levels; and extensive volumes on magic, both white and black, of the highest degree. Life would not be the same for any of them.

EPILOGUE

ADAM GAINED CONTROL over the beasts of the earth and the birds of the air when God allowed him to name them giving him complete understanding of them, and so they served him. The fall broke this understanding, and man has been seeking it since.

When Moses meets God, he asks his name. "I Am Who I Am" was his reply. The unadulterated translation is "I Am Who I will be." God's Name is not permitted to be uttered either via the spoken or written word. Whenever the authors of the Old Testament wrote his name, they left out the vowels. This has led to the confusion between the two names used for God today, Yahweh and Jehovah. It is not known if either is correct, nor is it known if his name has ever been pronounced. So powerful is his name that the second commandment strictly forbids it. "Thou shalt not take the name of the Lord thy God in vain: for the Lord will not hold him guiltless that shall take the name of the Lord his God in vain."

Working at Mount Kosciuszko Astrophysics Laboratory in Tasmania, a young scientist named Bennett Andrew was working on sub-dimensional electron flow. Framed upon the wall above his desk was a banner emblazoned with the slogan "Shut Up and Calculate". On his desk was an article by Doctor Matthew P.

Brookenstein which describes the dangers Neils Bohr's interpretation faced by science classrooms in the United States.

The problem? Bohr's interpretation of quantum mechanics as it related to subatomic particles. The paradox: sometimes electrons act as particles while at other times like a wave. To further augment the inconsistency, the two are mutually exclusive. According to Heisenberg's Uncertainty Principle, electrons should be able to be confined when acting as particles but not when they are acting as a wave. Experimentation had yet to prove the electron is anything other than a particle.

The article went on to say the answer to this contradiction may have been proposed in the 1920s by Louis de Broglie. His theory stated the electron has two properties, that of a particle and wave, which are NOT mutually exclusive.

As he read the article, for the thousandth time, Bennett mused over something he had not seen before. A connection between the two natures of the electron and the three natures of the triune God: Father, Son and Holy Spirit. In proving the dual nature of the electron he could also prove the triploid nature of God. Knowing the nature of a substance gives you power over it. He knew this and believed it with all his heart. Many a disease had been cured only after science had figured out the make-up of the pathogen. Recognize your enemy before he recognizes you.

As he was pondering this point, he remembered a Bible passage he had heard when a boy. Quickly looking it up he read:

> And he said, Go forth, and stand upon the mount before the LORD. And, behold, the LORD passed by, and a great and strong wind rent the mountains, and brake in pieces the rocks before the LORD; but the LORD was not in the wind: and after the wind an earthquake; but the LORD was not in the earthquake: And after the earthquake a fire; but the LORD was not in the fire: and after the fire a still small voice. And it was so, when Elijah heard it, that he

wrapped his face in his mantle, and went out, and stood in the entrance of the cave.

1 Kings 19: 12–13 (kjv)

God was not found in the ostentatious, but in the tranquil. Instead of looking to the heavens for God, Bennett would look down, down into the sub-atomic world below the quarks, lepons, gluons, bosons, and gravitons, where he was convinced he would find, define, and control God.